TRUTH'S EVIL LIGHT

TRUTH'S EVIL LIGHT

Cheveyo Series Book 1

MICHAELA MCGREGOR

McGregor Publishing, L.L.C.

ISBN-13: 978-0-9839482-0-9

ISBN-10: 0983948208

My thanks to everyone that provided input and support on the long road. This would not have been possible without you. And especially for my husband, Derek; I love you.

GLOSSARY

anoigo: (AH-nee-goh) Greek (v) Open. The spell word used to open the portal to Tweentown.

the Antechamber: (n) The sole exit from Tweentown. A building housing all the doors created by using the spell word *anoigo*.

the Council Chambers: (n) The mansion used by the Zephyri Council in Tweentown and home of the Tsái.

the *Damastís*: (dah-MAH-stees) Greek (n) An amulet that negates Zephyri magic.

doolally: (DOO-lah-lee) English (adj) Insane.

the Empusae: (ehm-PEW-see) (n) The six original vampires, the makers, the progenitors.

fanós: (FAH-nohs) Greek (n) lantern. The magical light globes used in Tweentown.

the Farm: Officially named the US Psychic Research and Training Facility, it is where Chevy spent her remaining childhood years after her parent's death. John Murphy headed the program to harness Chevy's talent for the government. The facility is a horse farm in an undisclosed location in the state of Virginia.

the Gate: (n) The entrance to Tweentown.

koutsoúvelo: (KOOT-soo-veh-loh) Greek (n) brat.

lýsi: (LEE-see) Greek (n) solution, key.

mikroula: (MIH-kroo-lah) Greek (n) little one. Eryx's pet name for Chevy.

the Pixie Colony: (n) (also known as the Colony) Home of the pixies in Tweentown.

the Praetorian: (PREE-tohr-ee-an) (n) The Tsái's personal guard. Consisting of 24 warriors, the 6 strongest soldiers from each kingdom are assigned to the Praetorian. During times of peace, the Tsái uses 2 of the available guards as his personal escort.

the *Rígma*: (REEG-mah) Greek (n) Rift. The rift between dimensions that surrounds Tweentown.

signet piece: (n) It can take the form of a ring, pendant or stamp but is usually a ring. The signet is used as a magical debit card. The owner stamps the receipt of whatever purchase he wishes to make and the payment is transferred to the merchant's account.

skatá: (SKAH-tah) Greek (n) Shit.

sou gia pánta: (SOO yah PAHN-tah) Greek Forever thine.

the Tsái: (Sahee) Greek (n) Maker. The supreme ruler of the Zephyri. Eryx heads the Zephyri Council, bringing all Zephyri kingdoms under a unified rule.

Tweentown: (n) The magical city of the Zephyri that exist between dimensions and follows the night.

the Zephyri: (zeh-FEER-ee) A race of magical creatures, consisting of many species. The Zephyri nation includes four kingdoms; Fairy, Elf, Shifter and Vampire, which represent every creature known in legend.

the Zephyri Council: (n) The ruling council, representing all the kingdoms of the Zephyri. It's members include, Eryx-the Tsái, Ellarian-the Fairy Queen, Fenion-the Elf King, Aadí Khanna-the Shifter Rajah and Baldr-the Vampire Regent.

CHARACTER REFERENCE

PRIMARY CHARACTERS

Alida- (AH-lee-dah)
> Species: pixie

Anthony Vincent Romano-
> Species: human
> Title: NCS Collection Management Officer
> Alias: Tony
> Chevy's best friend

Aspen- (ASS-pehn)
> Species: gold fairy

Cheveyo Onida Singer- (Sheh-vay-oh)
> Species: human
> Title: NCS Operations Officer
> Alias: Chevy (Sheh-vee)
> Protagonist

Kegan MacIntyre- (KEE-gan)
> Species: vampire
> Title: Praetorian Guard
> Alias: The Celt

Leukosia- (LOO-koh-see-ah)

Species: unknown

Michael Faraday-
Species: human
Title: Dr. Faraday
Alias: The Butcher

Sophia Ulfer- (OOL-fehr)
Species: wolf shifter
Title: Trainee Praetorian Guard

THE ZEPHYRI COUNCIL

Aadí Khanna- (AH-dee KAH-nah)
Species: tiger shifter
Title: Shifter Rajah

Baldr- (BAHL-der)
Species: vampire
Title: Vampire Regent

Ellarian- (EH-lair-ee-uhn)
Species: gold fairy
Title: Fairy Queen

Eryx- (EH-rihx)
Species: unknown
Title: Tsái

Fenion- (FEHN-yuhn)
Species: light elf
Title: Elf King

SECONDARY CHARACTERS

Aerandir- (EHR-an-deer)
> Species: light elf
> Alias: The Seer

Andrew Greshner-
> Species: human
> Title: President of the USA
> Alias: Andy

Anne Thomas-
> Species: human
> Title: British Prime Minister

Bangle-
> Species: pixie
> Alida's sister

Bob-
> Species: ogre

Bram Ulfer- (BRAHM OOL-fer) *deceased*
> Species: wolf shifter

Bubba Dawson-
> Species: human
> Title: SWAT Lieutenant

Cain Vanderpoole-
> Species: tiger shifter
> Title: Aadí's nephew
> Faraday victim

Chaytan Singer- (SHAY-tahn) *deceased*
> Species: human

Alias: Joseph Singer
Chevy's father

Cinny- (SIH-nee)

Species: pixie
Alida's brother

Dante- *deceased*

Species: vampire
Faraday victim

Dave-

Species: human
Assassin

Doyle-

Species: gargoyle
Title: The Antechamber Greeter

Francis Harlin-

Species: human
Title: Doorman for Chevy's building
Alias: Frank

Gary Swanson-

Species: human
Title: Solicitor for the 9th Judicial Circuit Court

Gene Carver-

Species: human
Title: Charleston Sherriff

Gus-

Species: goblin
Faraday victim

Hanlin- (HAN-lihn)

Species: gnome
Title: Tweentown Shopkeeper

Jan-

Species: pixie
Alida's father

John Murphy-

Species: human

Kleítus- (CLEE-tohs)

Species: Empusae
Title: Empusae
Kegan's maker

Layla Romano- *deceased*

Species: human
Tony Romano's wife

Magnus Blackthorne- (MAG-nuhs)

Species: unknown shifter
Title: Rajah's Chief Personal Guard

Malachai Romanus- (MAL-ahk-eye)

Species: vampire
Title: Personal aide to Baldr
Faraday victim

Mercedes-

Species: vampire

Mitch-

Species: human
Assassin

Nissa- (NIH-sah)

Species: dark elf

Title: King's Chief Personal Guard

Ritgir Blackfist- (RIHT-guhr)
Species: dwarf
Title: Tweentown Banker

Sawyer-
Species: human
SWAT team member

Shayle- (SHAYL)
Species: pixie
Alida's mother

Staton- (STAY-tuhn)
Species: unknown

Steve Johnson-
Species: human
Title: Mayor of Charleston, SC

Tagokk- (TAG-ahk)
Species: troll
Faraday victim

Tokori Singer- (Toh-KOH-ree) *deceased*
Species: human
Alias: Nada Honanie
Chevy's mother

William Green-
Species: human
Title: Director of the FBI
Alias: Bill

TRUTH'S EVIL LIGHT

PROLOGUE

JULY 18, 2001 - THE FARM

Daddy's words echoed in my head as my knees shuffled along the carpet. "Make sure you crawl on the floor, sweetie. Most people die of smoke inhalation, not the flames. Meet us by the big pine tree. Do not go looking for us, if there's a fire; just get out. Okay?"

"Okay, daddy. I'll remember."

"Good girl."

I was a good girl. I felt the door before I opened it and the clean, cool air soothed my burning lungs. It was difficult to see through the tears but I managed to make it down the steps and stumble toward the tree. In my rush, I tripped over my nightgown and landed hard on the packed dirt, scraping my hands. Daddy would be ashamed; you must always be aware of your situation and surroundings. Hiking up my skirt, I ran the rest of the way and turned to look for mommy and daddy.

Wiping my eyes, I saw flames engulfed the entire house. Where were they? Their bedroom window exploded and I jumped. I couldn't see them anywhere. I should go look but daddy said no.

As loud as my lungs would allow, I yelled, "Mommy? Daddy? Where are you?"

A long blood-chilling chorus of screams answered me. Holding my hands over my ears, I tried to shut out the sound. It wouldn't stop. I wanted it to stop. Please, someone make it stop.

***

It hurt so bad. I shrieked and wailed but they wouldn't stop. Why wouldn't they stop? They hated me; I could feel it. I was strapped to the bed; arms, legs and head held immobile by thick leather. Four men in white surrounded me and a man straddled my chest. I couldn't move, as he pushed a giant needle into my temple. What did they want? They wouldn't tell me. I was helpless against them and the pain. Screaming myself hoarse, I screeched, until nothing escaped but air.

"Wake up child. You are dreaming. Wake up. It's all right now. I have you. You're safe."

Pity overwhelmed me, as I opened my eyes. "John?"

"Yes, it's me child. You're home. You're safe."

My nightgown was soaked in sweat and I sat in his lap. Trembling, I told myself everything was all right and tried to forget. John said I didn't have to worry about those people hurting me anymore. He saved me. He would take care of me and teach me how to defend myself. I would never be helpless again. Laying my head on his chest, I inhaled the familiar scent of arthritis ointment and cologne.

"Does this happen often?"

The stranger's voice jerked my head around and I

glared at him. He was the biggest man I had seen since my father died. A little on the scruffy side, his hair was wavy black and he hadn't shaved in a few days. His eyes were brown and he looked mad.

Nodding, John answered. "Yes, every night. She barely sleeps at all."

Snapping at John, I said, "Who is he? Why is he here?"

"This is Tony, child. He's going to be staying with us for a while."

"I don't like him. Send him away."

Lifting an eyebrow at me, Tony said, "I'll grow on you."

"That's what I'm afraid of."

"You have a smart mouth for a runt."

Scowling at him, I said, "I'm not a runt. I'm tall for my age."

"Is that right?"

"Yeah. I'm only ten. You look old though."

"You need your eyes checked kid. I'm twenty-four."

"Like I said, ancient. Practically on your deathbed."

Folding his arms across his chest he said, "I don't know, John. I don't think this will work."

Waving away the objection, John said, "Don't worry, she'll warm up to you after a while."

"I will not! He's an asshole. Get him out of here."

"Young lady, I have told you about that language."

Pouting, I mumbled, "Sorry."

"Apologize to Tony."

"For what?"

"You know why."

"I'm sorry you're an asshole, Tony."

Setting me back on the bed, John said, "I think you

have recovered from your nightmare. You are restricted to your room for a week."

"You're grounding me?"

"Don't sound so surprised. That is what happens when you don't behave as a lady should."

Tony asked, "Does she ever get out?"

***

Grumbling, I asked, "Where are you taking me?"

Tony said, "We're going to play a game."

"It's the middle of the night. How are we going to play anything in the dark?"

"You'll see."

"What game?"

"Hide-and-Seek."

Rolling my eyes, I said, "Jeez, what a dumbass. You can't play that in the dark."

"Watch your mouth, runt or I'll tell John."

"I told you, I'm not a runt. Quit calling me that."

"I'll stop calling you runt, when you stop calling me names."

"If that's the deal, runt is fine."

"On second thought, I think brat suits you better."

Mumbling under my breath, I said, "Whatever, geezer."

"You must like staying in your room."

"Where's John, anyway? I haven't seen him since last night."

"He's gone."

Freezing in my tracks, I asked, "For how long?"

Puzzled by my reaction, Tony said, "I'm not sure. Probably about a month."

"He left me alone?"

"The Farm has plenty of people, you won't be by yourself."

"They don't like me. He didn't even say goodbye."

"Aww, come on. A sweet kid like you? What's not to love?"

Tears ran down my cheeks before I could stop them. Humiliated, I ran into the forest. Weaving through the trees as my father taught me, I found a log leaning against a large oak and crawled into the shelter. Pulling my knees to my chest, I covered myself with my hair and tried to disappear.

I would run away. No one would miss me. They didn't care. I was alone. John was the one person that liked me and now he was gone too. I would find a cave in the mountains and live there alone. It would be better than being surrounded by people that hated me. I knew how to hunt and fish; I could make my own clothes and be— happy. Sobs wracked my chest and I couldn't hold them back.

A twig snapped. Scuttling through the leaves, I tried to escape. A large hand held my leg tight. Kicking and thrashing, they reeled me in and I lashed out. My fist connected with a hard jaw and a deep voice cried out in pain but he didn't let go.

"Damn it! Cut it out. I'm not going to hurt you, brat."

"Tony?"

"Yeah. Who were you expecting?"

Caught, all the fight left me and he pulled me into his lap. Tucking me under his chin, he stroked my hair and back. "I'm sorry. What I said was mean. You didn't deserve that."

Sniffling into his chest, I said, "Yes I did. I'm bad."

"No you're not. You're just angry."

"No. You don't know. I am bad. That's why everyone hates me. They know what I did, what I am."

"What are you?"

"Evil."

"Where the heck did you get an idea like that?"

"They told me at the lab. They said it was my fault that my parents were dead. I set the house on fire because I'm a demon from hell. I killed them."

Fury swamped me and he pulled me away from his chest. Shaking me by the shoulders, he said, "Don't you EVER say that again! You were not responsible for your parents' death. I read the file; it was faulty wiring. It was an accident. You are not a monster; you're a special girl and your parents loved you."

"How do you know they did?"

Pulling me into his arms, he said, "Because, if I had a daughter like you, I would cherish her for the rest of my life."

"Really?"

"Yes. You're cute, in a Chucky sort of way."

"Who's Chucky?"

"Never mind. My face is killing me. What did you crack me with?"

"My fist."

Working his jaw, he said, "Fuckin' A. You pack one hell of a punch."

Dropping my eyes, I said, "I'm sorry." I was a freak; too big, too strong, gawky and hideous.

Lifting my chin, Tony said, "Hey. You should be proud of yourself. You kicked my ass and I was a SEAL."

"You're a selkie?"

"What's a selkie?"

"A person that can change into a seal."

Laughing, he said, "No, that's a myth. Things like that don't exist."

"My daddy said they did."

"He was pulling your leg. Kids like those kinds of stories."

Disappointed, I said, "Oh." I would have liked to meet one.

Tony asked, "Do you forgive me for being mean to you?"

"I guess so. I wasn't very nice to you either."

"Do you feel like playing our game now?"

"How are we going to play in the dark?"

"I'll hide and you use your other senses to find me."

"You really want me to?"

"Yes. You don't have to hide what you are from me, brat."

CHAPTER 1

JULY 19, 2012 - CHARLESTON, SC

"Ready or not, here I come."

Tony had been quiet but not silent. It was his age showing. At thirty-five, he was no spring chicken. Following his audible cues, I searched for signs of his passing. After a few minutes of fumbling around in the dark, I found his trail. The codger had knocked a piece of bark off a pine tree. *Sloppy, sloppy, sloppy.* Deeper into the dark forest, I found more of his trail. I checked the time. I had an hour and thirty-three minutes left. The toe of his boot gave me a new direction but I lost him for a while after that. At least I didn't have to worry about the trees. They were too small. Hurricane Hugo had taken out much of the larger growth in the area, which limited the places he could hide. The brush was a damn nuisance though. "Come out; come out, wherever you are."

Finding a shifted stone, I glanced at my watch again. I had an hour left. No sweat, he was mine. My phone vibrated. Knowing it was Tony, I debated whether to answer or not. We were on strict silent mode, so he may be testing me or he might have fallen and couldn't get up. Either way he wouldn't cheat. Adjusting my earbud, I answered the call and shoved the cell back in my pocket. "Yeah, what's up?"

"I heard something. I'm going to check it out."

"What was it?"

"I don't know. I've never heard anything like it before. It was as if the ground groaned. I can't explain it any better than that."

"Okay, the game's on hold. Want me to come to your position?"

"Nah, it's probably nothing and I'm beating you. You aren't anywhere near me."

Smirking at his false bravado, I said, "You have no idea where I am."

"No, I don't but you obviously didn't hear what I did, so you can't be close. It was pretty loud."

He was posturing, trying to psych me out. "This could be classified as cheating, you know. The rules state that you can't move once your time is up."

"I know, I know, I'll just have a look and go back to my spot. You can monitor on the two-way until I'm finished."

"You're going to muck up the prints. How am I supposed to read your tracks, if you stomp all over them?"

"Bad guys don't always leave a pristine trail for you to follow. What's the matter? Can't you beat me in a real world scenario? I thought your daddy taught you all the injun ways."

Jerk. "Oh, right. Dream on old man. Make it quick. The sun will be up in two hours and I have an hour left."

"Actually, it's more like fifty-seven minutes."

"Just hurry up."

"Yeah, yeah. You stay put. I'll let you know when I'm back in position."

"Roger."

I couldn't hear anything over the crickets, so I turned up the volume on my earpiece. Listening to Tony's breathing and the forest sounds, I waited five minutes, then ten. Impatient, I asked, "Are you there yet?"

Whispering, Tony answered, "Almost. I hear people talking. Shh."

"Well, that's stupid. They can't hear me."

"No, but I can't hear them with you yammering in my ear and they can hear me talking to you."

"Then don't talk to me. Duh."

"Brat."

"Geezer."

Another five minutes passed before Tony's voice sounded over the two-way, "Oh my God. What the hell is that?"

"What? What is it?" To hell with the game, I ran, using every trick at my disposal. Dropping the shield that I used to block my talent, I thrust my mind into the earth and felt my way through the labyrinth of trees and brush toward Tony. I sensed every blade of grass, leaf and animal in the area. More importantly, I could feel how Tony had affected them.

As I ran, Tony yelled, "Don't move!" He almost blew out my eardrum and I stumbled over a downed tree. Was he talking to me? As if I cared, he needed me. Making a quick adjustment to the volume, I was up and sprinting through the maze again.

A feminine voice purred, "Well, what have we here?"

Tony's response stunned me. He whispered in awe, "Jesus, Mary and Joseph."

Damn it, I needed to get there now. "Tony, what's wrong? What's going on?"

No answer.

The woman said, "Search him."

Cloth brushed over the loop around Tony's neck, sounding loud in my ear. A man's voice said, "He's wearing a transmitter loop. There's someone else out here."

"It does not matter. They cannot find us—or him." I heard a girlish giggle, as the call ended.

Shit! Not good. Not good at all. I still wasn't close enough to hear or feel them. My empathic power had a range of about fifty feet outdoors and using the earth amplified it to about a hundred and fifty feet. I had to be close. He couldn't be that far ahead of me. Tony and I had been playing Hide-and-Seek since I was ten and he had never beaten me. I could find him; I would find him. I trained eleven years for this. Now the game was real.

Crashing through the undergrowth, I pushed my talent to the limit. An old fear crept into my thoughts, breaking my concentration. Losing Tony was unacceptable; he was all I had left. *You are not losing him! Come on; focus.*

A few minutes later, I burst into a clearing. Nature held its breath while I gasped for mine. This was the place. Scanning the area in the bright moonlight, I searched for some evidence of whom I was dealing with. Discarded like garbage, in the center of the glade were Tony's smashed phone, transmitter loop and earbud. Snatching them off the ground, I took a closer look at the footprints left behind.

Four sets of prints tromped through the sandy soil. Tony's were immediately recognizable and another man's size ten sneakers. Dainty soft cloth soles, like moccasins led north. Was she out in her pajamas? As odd as that was the last set of tracks stopped me cold. Did South Carolina have a Sasquatch? Over eighteen inches, the footprints sank deep into the soft dirt. Whoever made these tracks wasn't wearing shoes and it was no wonder. Where would you shop for feet that size? He must be over eight feet tall and weigh a ton.

Reading the sign, I determined the four people got into an off-road vehicle and drove away. Tony hadn't struggled or fought. Why? Were they armed? They had to be. He would never have given up and left willingly. The giant probably helped make up his mind though. Following the trail left by the all-terrain tires, I was able to move much faster.

Half of a mile later, I slid to a stop. They had turned onto a paved road and my path ended. *Now what?* I hoped this was a deserted area, at least at four in the morning. If not, I might be making a serious mistake and it may cost Tony his life.

Bowing my head, I stretched my mental tentacles through the earth in both directions. Nature's tension faded after fifty feet to the left but to the right it remained constant to the end of my range. *Right it is then.* The thought that this was ridiculous flitted through my mind for an instant. They could be driving to Columbia or even Virginia for all I knew. Cross-country running came naturally to me but even I couldn't make it that far. Maybe I should go back for the bike. It was close to three miles back through the woods and I had no idea how far along the highway. Panic threatened, every second wasted might be life or death. Deep breath. Another. Logic dictated that I go back to where we stashed the cycles. No matter how far I had to go, transportation would help. My decision made, I spun to the left. My feet wouldn't move. I couldn't do it. Backtracking, even if it helped in the end was beyond me. Therefore, like an idiot, I ran down the pavement in the dark.

Minutes seemed like hours, as I raced to save Tony. What were they doing to him? Nothing. If they wanted to kill him, they would have left him in the clearing or I would have heard a shot. He was alive, I still had time. I should have gone back for the bike. Tony would have; he was always telling me I was too impulsive, too hotheaded. Distracted by my own thoughts and slapping footfalls, I almost missed it. Cheerful chirping surrounded me. They hadn't come this far. Alert now, I retraced my steps slower, scanning the roadsides. I was close, I had to be but there was nothing. Where had they gone? A quarter of a mile back, the insects were quiet. Pacing along the blacktop, I walked fifty feet more and stopped. This was the location but I couldn't find it. Closing my eyes, I searched. Catching a slight disturbance, I turned my head to follow it and opened my eyes. To my right, an inky black hole parted the tree line, almost invisible in the dark. *Come out; come out, wherever you are.*

Standing at the mouth of the entrance, I let my

eyes adjust. Blanketed in a thick carpet of pine needles, two wheel ruts stretched into the darkness. An eerie hush made my skin crawl. The creatures of the night weren't quiet; they were gone. Nothing lived here but the moss covered trees. Grateful that I would not be running to the state capital, I jogged ahead cautiously. The smell of mulch and decay hung stagnant in the air, clogging my nostrils. Tree roots snagged my feet, sending me headlong into a marshy wallow beside the trail. *Moron.* My clothes were soaked and I shook off as much of the putrid debris as possible. Feeling like an ass, I decided that maybe a nice stroll through the creepy forest wasn't a bad idea.

Soft ambient light penetrated the gloom and I had hope. Unable to contain myself, I hurried ahead. A solid wooden gate blocked my path, flanked by an eight-foot brick wall. Locked and too high to climb, I didn't think anything but explosives was going to work. Walking the perimeter didn't offer another way inside but I did find the remains of a fallen tree near the wall. With the boost, I was able to make it to the top and sat there for a moment to survey the grounds.

At the front of the property stood a large plantation home, with several outbuildings dotting the premises. Parked in the circular drive was a topless four-door, white Jeep and a black SUV, which was all the confirmation I needed. *Hang on Tony; I'm coming.*

Sliding off the wall without a sound, I worked my way closer to the house. At times like this, I wished I were a telepath. Empathy is useful but situations such as these would be much easier if I knew what the bad guys were planning. Three people were inside on the first floor and none of them was Tony. The two men were anxious and trying to persuade the female of something. They weren't making much headway, if her bored, icy attitude meant anything. Engrossed in their conversation, I was sure they weren't going anywhere for a while. Time to find Tony.

Five structures were strewn across the back yard and didn't seem to be in any particular order. The first two I searched appeared to be old slave quarters and empty of all but their ghosts. A converted barn served as the garage and I couldn't make up my mind what the fourth building was in a former life. They all had one thing in common—age. Tucked back against the rear wall of the property was a new, red, corrugated steel, pole shed that did not belong. Over fifty feet in length with no windows and a single door, I didn't think the owner kept the lawn mower and volleyball equipment inside it.

Sending out my feelers, I found six people in residence and Tony was one of them. *Yay me!* It was strange though, he was there and I couldn't sense any physical damage or pain but he wasn't all right. He felt dead inside, no emotions whatsoever. If they drugged him that would explain a lot, but not how he felt or—didn't feel. His normal persona was missing or muted somehow, he was a shell. Almost all the other occupants were in the same condition, except for a girl near Tony's location. From what I could tell, she was younger than the others and her emotions were intact. Heart-rending sadness and terror poured off her in waves. Confused, I put that aside for the moment and went for the door, praying that it was not locked.

CHAPTER 2

Rushing through the door, I closed it, as quick as I could and leaned against it. Black as pitch, I sensed no one else in the room but couldn't help drawing my Beretta. Single-handed, I groped for the light switch and blinked to clear my vision. As expected, I was alone. It was just an empty office, a desk, chair and couch. On the desk, stood a cheerful vase of yellow Jonquils. Breathing a sigh of relief, I didn't waste any more time and went to the next door. Reaching around the doorframe, I turned on the light before entering. Thankfully, I didn't have to do it in the dark this time.

As the door banged against the wall, the pungent scent of antiseptic assaulted my nose, making my stomach knot. *Ugh, I hate that smell.* Nothing good ever came with it. The anticipated echo from the door fell flat. The building was sound proofed. Why did they need sound proofing? Scanning the room began to answer my question.

Opposite the entrance, stood a floor to ceiling shelf filled with specimen jars. Hearts, kidneys, livers, eyes and one even had the mutated head of some poor soul. An

autopsy table, measuring about ten feet long, dominated
the room and I began to understand the terror the girl felt.
What the hell was this? Drawers, microscopes, machines
and equipment that I didn't recognize lined the cabinets.
In the corner stood a commercial size freezer door and I
didn't want to know what they kept inside it. A phone
and a large ring of keys hung from the wall. My vision
blurred for a moment.

*"No! No more needles." Arms and legs strapped to
the metal table, I couldn't move, couldn't escape.*
"Hold still. This won't hurt—much."
*Defending myself in the only way left, I projected my
fear into the three doctors holding me. A smug smile
quirked my lips at the sight of them running for the door.
There, that would make them leave me alone—until next
time. Angry tears scalded my skin, as I stared unseeing at
the ceiling.*

Overcome with a sense of urgency, I grabbed the
keys and opened the next door. Bright and sterile, it was a
long white hall with four numbered doors on either side.
Each one had a small window at eye level and a steel
handle. Flipping through the keys, I found eight
numbered keys corresponding to the doors. Wonderful,
organized psychos.
Looking through the window of cell number one, I
had to stare for a moment to make sense of what I saw.
Standing frozen in the center of the small room was a
bipedal creature about three feet tall, muscular, with
blackish-green skin. Large pointy ears protruded up from
the sides of its bald head. Surgical staples circled it's
skull like a silver crown and sharp claws tipped each of

its four fingers and toes. The word that sprang to mind was *demon*. A stitched Y-incision extended from collarbones to groin. Were they genetically engineering monsters or sewing them together like rag dolls? Reaching out with my mind, I discovered he had no reaction to my presence. The demon's emotions were like Tony's but I didn't think letting it out was a smart move.

I did not want to see what else they were cooking up. Steeling myself, I looked through the porthole. I must have been in shock because when I peered through the pane, I thought, *so that's a Sasquatch*. Repulsive beyond imagining, he was at least nine feet tall and massive. Small nostrils rested between tiny, deep-set eyes, shadowed by a thick brow ridge. Corded muscles fastened his head to his shoulders. Contrary to the reported sightings, this Big Foot was not as hairy. Wearing only bracers and a loin cloth, patches of sleek red fur covered his shoulders, back and chest but fish-belly white skin showed on his legs and arms. The size of the creature made me notice that the ceilings were ten feet tall but the walls six by eight feet. He wouldn't be able to lie down, which wouldn't matter because they didn't have beds or even a pallet. The only fixture added to the rooms was a toilet in the corner. Pitying the brute, I thought about opening the door. A great sigh heaved his massive chest, scaring the shit out of me and I took two steps back. Was he awake? Double-checking, I found he was still unresponsive. I was not unlocking that door.

Number three and four were empty, which was good—I think. Had there been people in them before? Possibilities bombarded my mind and I fought them off, trying to concentrate on my task.

Horrified by the contents of cell number five, I

gagged, slapping a hand over my mouth. Large square patches of skin were cut from his chest, arms and legs. One eye was missing and he stared through the open socket into space. Charred black burns covered half of his body and the rest was gray from blood loss. He was emaciated to the point that he resembled a walking corpse. His ability to continue stand was mystifying. How could anyone do something like this to a human being or any creature for that matter? Unlatching the door, I hurried inside. The smell was gut wrenching. Touching his cold skin, I checked for a pulse. A dead man wouldn't be standing but... Thump. I breathed again. He was alive—for now.

Another man, at least I thought it was a man, stood mute like the others but he appeared to be merged with a cat. Rounded tiger ears peaked out of brown human hair, long razor sharp claws grew from human fingers and tufts of striped fur sprang sporadically from his tan skin. If he woke up, I did not want him sneaking up on me, so I left this one locked as well.

As I approached the end of the row of doors, overwhelming fear and despair thickened the air. I didn't look before opening the door. Charging across the threshold, I froze mid-step. Where was the girl? The room was empty but there had to be someone here. I had never been wrong before. Something flew at my face and I ducked. Spinning and drawing my weapon, I tried to get a bead on it. Zipping through the air like a hummingbird was the biggest bug I had ever seen. It was hard to see any detail with it zooming around the room but it was red and had six, stick-like legs hanging below, similar to a giant wasp. Diving at my head again, it growled. *What the hell? Bugs don't growl.* With nothing to lose, I threw reason out the window. "Hey, hey! I'm here to help. Knock it off!"

Abruptly, it stopped mid-air and tilted its little head. Light dawned, as I realized this was my girl. Could she understand me? The double set of wings blurred while she hovered, studying me. Getting a better look at her, I found that two of the legs were arms with little four fingered hands. Her torso resembled a human's; with ribs, collarbones and neck but that was where the likeness ended. Two glossy black beads stared, while an almost invisible slit turned down in a frown. Subtle at first, her red coloring faded to gray and a tiny voice said, "Who are you?"

Many times, I have read the word *poleaxed* but never had a true understanding of what it meant until that moment. Jaw slack, I stared dumbfounded at the insect suspended in front of my face.

Speaking in exaggerated, slow speech she repeated, "I said, who are you?"

"I don't get it. How can a bug speak?"

Flushing red again she said, "I am NOT a bug. I'm a pixie. Now, I asked you a question, human. Please do me the courtesy of answering it."

Unbelievable. I wet my dry lips and tried to gather my wits. "Sorry, uh, my name is Cheveyo."

"That's better. My name is Alida. Why are you here, Cheveyo?"

Alida's pigment changed to purple and blue. "I thought pixies looked more um—human."

"You're thinking of fairies."

"What's the difference?"

"Didn't we cover this? Fairies look like small humans with wings. Pixies look like me. Now, why are you here?"

"Oh!" Jolted out of my stupor, I hurried over to the last cell and unlocked the door. Heart pounding, I shook him saying, "Tony! Tony, look at me!" Nothing. He couldn't hear me. Examining him showed no obvious injuries or, God forbid, surgeries. Relieved, I grabbed his arm and led him toward the door. Responding to the force of my pull, his body moved automatically. When I crossed the threshold, he froze in place and refused to move another step. *Okay, there's more than one way to skin a cat.* Bending at the waist, I pulled him over my shoulders in a firefighter's carry and straightened. *Damn. It's time to lay off the burgers, buddy.* Adjusting his weight, so that it was more comfortable, I took the last step out the door. Panic flooded my mind, as he came alive. Thrashing until I dropped him, he scuttled back into the cell, calm and dead as before. What had they done to him? How was I going to get him out if he fought me? I could try to knock him unconscious but what about going over the wall and the hike back to our cycles? For that matter, how would I keep him on the bike? What was I going to do? I couldn't leave all these creatures here to suffer. All of them needed medical attention, including Tony. If he wasn't out of it, he could call our bosses. We worked for the National Clandestine Service, a branch of the CIA, but Tony was the Collection Management Officer and I had no way of contacting anyone. It might seem strange but with my power, they were afraid that without a buffer between us I could discover classified information. It might be dangerous for everyone. In this situation though... What I needed was help. Alida wouldn't be able to do much. I didn't have any other choice.

My mind made up, I went out into the corridor. Alida was banging her little fist on the door where the demon was being held. "Gus! Gus, can you hear me?"

Seriously? His name was Gus?

Noticing me, she turned and asked, "Why didn't you unlock this one too?"

Stammering, I said, "I, well, I um—didn't think it was a good idea at the time. I take it he's a friend of yours."

"Of course he is. They're all my friends."

"How can you be friends with a demon?"

"Demon? He isn't a demon, you idiot! He's a goblin and before you ask, he does not live or work in hell. Ugh, humans. Just open the doors. All of them!"

She had turned fire engine red again. I think I might have made her mad. Not wanting to argue, I did as she said before going into the lab.

Hoping with all my heart that the people at the house stayed put, I dialed 911 from the landline.

"911, what is your emergency?"

"A hostage situation."

"Are you one of the hostages?"

"No ma'am. I discovered five of them, when my friend was abducted and I went after him."

"Your name?"

"Cheveyo Singer, ma'am."

"Okay, Ms. Singer can you give me the address?"

"No, I'm sorry, I can't. It's a big plantation house at the end of a long drive off highway 41. We're in one of the outbuildings at the back of the property. It's surrounded by a big brick wall with a gate at the front."

"That's all right. We have your location on GPS. Do you know how many assailants are involved or their identities?"

"I don't know who they are but there are three people in the main house; two men and a woman. I think this line is connected to the one in the house, so if we get cut off, please don't call back."

"No problem. We'll just hope we aren't disconnected. I have alerted SWAT and the Sheriff is on the way. Are the suspects armed?"

"I don't know. Probably."

Are there any injuries?"

"Yes ma'am. All five victims are catatonic and have been tortured. I have no idea what was done to them but it's horrible."

"Deputies and EMT's should be there in a few minutes."

"The people in the house don't know I'm here and I'd like to keep it that way."

"That won't be a problem, Ms. Singer. They are coming in silent with lights off."

"Good, that's good. I'll be glad to see them. Uh, I'm armed and not real keen on laying down my weapon until its safe. Could you tell them not to shoot me when they get here?"

Snickering, the dispatcher said, "Sure. What do you look like?"

"Native American, six feet tall, long black hair and green eyes. I'm wearing black jeans, a black tank and boots." A gasp made me turn. Alida hovered in place shaking her head and turning yellow. Frowning, I mouthed, "What?"

She didn't answer but zipped over to the phone and pressed the receiver button. "Why did you hang up? That was the police, they're on their way."

"I know who it was. You shouldn't have done that. Oh, no. This is bad."

"Why, what's wrong?"

"We can't be found by humans."

Making a wry face, I said, "Well, I'd say it's a little late for that, don't you think? Besides, I told them there were five of you. I didn't think you would want to go to the hospital and get poked and prodded, since you're fine. You're okay, right?"

Trembling, she said, "Oh, no, no, no. This is a disaster. They'll kill you."

"What? Who's going to kill me?"

"The Praetorian. Oh, what are we going to do?"

"Simmer down, Alida. Nobody is going to kill me. I can take care of myself. Why would these Praetorian want me dead, anyway?"

"For exposing us to humans."

"Well, what was I supposed to do? We can't move them and there is still the small matter of your captors. We needed help; now, we have it."

"I can get help. You shouldn't have called the police."

Frustrated, I said, "Where? We're in the middle of nowhere and this is somewhat time sensitive."

"I could have had half the Zephyri nation here within fifteen minutes. It doesn't matter now." She wrung her tiny hands.

"You neglected to mention that before."

"I know."

Struggling with the unfamiliar word, I said, "Who are the Zeh-feer-ee?"

Motioning toward the prisoner's cells, she ignored my pronunciation, "We all are. Pixies, goblins, vampires, shifters, elves and many more."

"Wait. I thought that the people here created you. You mean..."

"Zephyri are all the creatures of legend. We were captured by these humans. I was locked in that cell for two days."

"How did they catch you? It can't be easy to trap a pixie."

"It's not. I was hitching a ride on my friend Gus. For some reason he fell over on top of me. I must have been knocked out and when I woke up, here I was."

"Why haven't they done anything to you yet?"

Shaking her head, she said, "I don't know. No one even came to check on me. I never saw anyone and it is hard to hear anything in here. Once I heard Malachai scream but that was all."

"Let me guess, Malachai is the guy with the burns."

"Yes. What they did to him is dreadful."

"I know. I'm sorry, Alida. At least you're out now. No more worries, right?"

"Not for me but yours are just beginning, I think."

"Look, not to brag but I'm no slouch when it comes to self-preservation. Everything will be fine, you'll see."

Unconvinced, Alida said, "I hope you're right."

"Sure I am. The doctors will fix up Tony and your friends. These Praetorian will see I was trying to help. They can't hold that against me."

Still not persuaded, she gave me a sad look and nodded.

"I should take a look outside to see if the cavalry is here yet. I don't know how long it will take them to show up but you might want to leave before they do."

"You're right. What a mess. I had better tell

somebody at home. Maybe the Tsái can fix this."

"Who's that?"

"He's our leader and the most powerful being in the world. He'll know what to do."

Yeah, sure. "Okay, sounds like a plan."

Alida asked, "Will you open the door for me?"

"No problem. Listen, Alida—be careful, okay?"

Nodding, she said, "You too. The Praetorian are scary, Cheveyo. I'm afraid for you."

"Don't be. I'll be fine."

We moved through the office and I peeked out the door to see what was happening. Apparently, the soundproofing was exceptional because a lot had changed and we didn't hear a thing. The front gate stood open and armed men in black were advancing on the house. Coast clear, I waved Alida out and she disappeared over the edge of the roof.

Another group of SWAT team members worked their way toward the lab, securing each building they passed. Not wanting to startle the big men with big guns, I swung the door open wide and clasped my hands over my head. Taking a single step out the door, I stood and waited for them to finish their search. A loud crash and men yelling made me jump; then my shoulders dropped an inch in relief. They had taken the house. Those bastards were going to jail for a long, long time.

Approaching from every direction, six SWAT officers converged, weapons held steady and ready. One stepped forward and asked, "Name?"

"Singer, sir."

The leader jerked his head in my direction; one of the six came forward cautiously, patting me down. Finding my Beretta, he circled around to my back. Never thrilled with anyone standing behind me, I was nervous but couldn't do a thing about it.

Drawing my attention away from the guy behind me, the first officer said, "Are you the one that invited us to this little shindig?"

I didn't appreciate his cavalier attitude. "Yes sir. I hope I didn't interrupt your beauty sleep, sir."

Smirking, he said, "The name's Bubba. What's a pretty girl like you doing carrying around hardware like that?"

He was yanking my chain. "Your mother actually named you Bubba? Didn't she like you?"

Breaking into a shit-eating grin, Bubba said, "Naw, these guys did but you shouldn't pick fights with the police—Cheveyo."

"Thanks for the tip."

"Any time. I'd like an answer to my question though. What are you doing out here in the middle of the night, running around with a 9mm?"

Reciting my cover story, I said, "I'm FBI." Eyebrows rose at my statement. "My partner, Tony Romano and I were out in the forest, uh running scenarios. He called me and said he heard something. When he got to the scene, they abducted him. I heard the whole thing and went after him."

"Do you have any ID on you?"

Fishing out my wallet, I flipped it open to reveal my bogus FBI identification.

"Okay. Any hostiles inside?"

"No but the victims won't leave their cells."

"Cells?"

"You'll see. I tried to carry Tony out and he freaked. He scrambled back in as fast as he could. Other than that, none of them reacts to anything. They're catatonic."

"Okay, thanks Singer. We'll take it from here."

"One more thing, Bubba."

"Yeah, what's that?"

"When you see them—remember they're people; living, breathing people."

Brow furrowed, Bubba said, "What aren't you telling me, Singer?"

Pulling my hands down, I shook my head. "Just remember what I said. Can I have my weapon back?"

"Not yet. Stay put, while we secure the building. Sawyer, stay with Agent Singer."

Sawyer remained at my back and I watched as they entered the little shop of horrors. It took ten minutes for Bubba to come out. Revulsion clear on his face, he was stark white.

"Sawyer, get the EMT's in here."

Something in his voice or maybe his expression must have spooked Sawyer. "You okay, Bubba?"

"Yeah, go on."

"Yessir."

Once he was gone, Bubba said, "What the hell are they, Singer?"

"People."

Silent for a long minute, he said, "How are we gonna get the big one in an ambulance? Hell, how are we even gonna get him out the door?"

"No clue. Why do you think I called you guys? I didn't know what to do either. Did you bring a doc?"

"Yeah."

"Good. I think they'll have to tranquilize them for transport, especially the big one."

"Here they come."

Carrying two stretchers over the soft ground, four paramedics and a doctor rushed toward us. Picturing Sasquatch, I didn't think they brought enough people. Bubba escorted them inside, leaving me alone for a few minutes.

What had they done to Tony in such a short amount of time? It couldn't have been more than an hour before I arrived. If it was a drug, would it wear off? Had I found him, only to lose him again? Familiar boots followed a uniform out the door. They had managed to get Tony onto a gurney. As his face rolled into view, I saw he was sleeping. Smiling, I closed my eyes and relaxed a fraction more. He would be all right; he had to be.

"Oh, watch him Mike!"

Eyes snapping open, I watched the second pair of paramedics wrestling another litter through the door.

"Shit! He's gonna push it over."

Poor Malachai thrashed uselessly against the straps holding him to the stretcher. Unable to speak, his whole body screamed for him and fear filled his mind. *I'm sorry.*

"Hey doc, you wanna give him another shot? Maybe two?"

Grim faced, the doctor came forward. "I want to get my hands on the son-of-a-bitch that did this." Injecting a sedative into Malachai, he calmed almost immediately. "We have to get him to the hospital, stat. If I give him any more, it might kill him."

Concerned, I asked, "Are they going to be okay?"

"Are you a friend or relative?"

"Tony," I said pointing to him, "is a friend. I found them."

"You're friend should be all right. This man, I don't

know. I don't even know how his heart keeps beating. There's hardly any blood left in him and the wounds he has... Everything in my experience says he should be dead. And then there's this." Pulling back Malachai's upper lip, the doctor revealed a pair of inch long fangs where his incisors should have been.

Had Alida said vampires were included in the Zephyri? She said they were all her friends; she had named him. Why had I continued to assume he was human? Maybe because I still didn't believe any of this was real. My father claimed that all the monsters in stories existed but grown-ups didn't believe in fairy tales. He was just teasing a child. Wasn't he? If that was true, why did he name me after one?

The doctor continued, "Now, I'm not a fanciful man but this will make anyone wonder." Shaking his head, he said, "We have to hurry. Are you riding along?"

"Uh, no. I have to retrieve my bike but I'll be at the hospital as soon as I can."

A quick nod and they pushed past me toward the gate.

"Ahem."

Swinging my head around, I noticed Bubba had come out of the lab. "You okay, Singer?"

"Yeah, why?"

"I dunno; you look a little lost."

"I'm fine. Can somebody give me a ride to my cycle?"

Studying my face for a moment he said, "You'll have to go down to the station to make a statement later today but we can live without Sawyer for a few minutes. I assume it's nearby?"

"About three miles south."

"How did you get here?"

Shrugging, I said, "I ran."

"Through the woods? In the dark?"

Kicking a stone across the ground was my answer.

"Damn, girl. No wonder you're such a mess."

Self-conscious, I glanced at my hands and saw they were filthy. Now that I was aware of my appearance, another question occurred to me. What was that stench?

"Yeah, it's you."

Embarrassed, my eyes flicked to Bubba and I said, "What's me?"

"The smell. What did you get into?"

Mumbling, I said, "I fell in a puddle or something in the driveway."

"Or something is right." His chuckling was drowned out by a loud shriek and we both turned to see the pole shed shudder.

Sprinting for the rear of the building, we were in time to see a huge arm punch through the steel shell. The arm darted back inside for a moment and the wall split open in a ragged line. Sasquatch stepped through, stopping for a few seconds to examine the wall surrounding the property. Turning sideways, he braced his arm and rammed the bricks with his shoulder. Masonry exploded, as he broke through with a grunt. From the other side, I could hear the sound Tony had described. A low rumbling vibration that sounded as if the earth groaned. Trotting over to the rubble, Bubba and I stood gawking as the giant strode into the forest.

Radio in hand, Bubba said, "I need a team outside the wall, southeast side. The big guy just flew the coop."

Glaring at him, I folded my arms across my chest.

Bubba said, "Hey, we can't let that thing run around

loose."

Unmoved, I didn't say a word. He had forgotten what I told him. They were people; living, breathing people. I understood what he thought but it wasn't right. To him, this was Frankenstein's lab and Sasquatch was the monster he created. Unable to correct them without revealing what else I knew, I was stuck. Maybe Alida got the help that she mentioned.

Black clad men shot into the forest and I couldn't watch. Besides, Tony was on his way to the hospital.

Bone tired, I walked to the main house, collecting Sawyer on the way. He said, "It's gonna be fun trying to get out of here."

"Why, what's going on?"

"The press is crawling all over the place. They had the road blocked for a while. We got them moved but they're going nuts. The evacuation of your friend and the other guy is probably all over the news by now. The doc is riding with them and coming back for the other two. I guess they're stable enough to wait."

Great, my bosses were going to love this. Some Operations Officer I was turning out to be. Two weeks out of training and this is what happens. Rounding the side of the house, it looked like a circus; three rings and I didn't know where to look first.

A deputy escorted a man in handcuffs to the back of his cruiser, which stood in front of the white Jeep. The black SUV was gone. Reporters yelled unintelligible questions at the pair, while the cop opened the door and sat the prisoner down. He looked normal. Isn't that what everyone says, when they find out their neighbor is a serial killer? It's true. Forty-five, five feet ten, brown hair, clean cut, he looked like someone's dad. Evil hides in the dark recesses of the heart. "Who's the psycho?"

"Dr. Michael Faraday. He's the only one we found and won't say a word about anybody else. His attorney is meeting him at the station."

"Figures. Get me out of here, will ya?"

Pointing to a pickup parked on the other side of the yard, Sawyer said, "That's us."

The crowd parted, allowing the Sheriff's Deputy through with his charge. Surging back like the tide, they turned their ravenous eyes on us.

Amid the shouting, one voice sang out clear. "Chevy, is this a CIA operation?"

My head on a swivel, I tried to locate the source of the question. It was an impossible task, in the sea of faces. *Shit!* How could anyone have found out who I was? And the nickname? *Fuck, fuck, fuck. This was bad.* The initials CIA rode through the rest of the journalists like a wave. I needed to get out of here, now. Ignoring the speculation and accusations hurled at me, I jumped in the truck and slumped in the seat. Could this day get any worse?

My chauffeur made it through the press line and onto the highway. "Where to?"

"I'm not sure. Try the next left."

Sulking and angry, I bit my lip staring out at the dawning day. Sawyer rolled down his window for some air. A minute later, he powered mine down as well. Turning in the seat to face him, I dared him to say a word.

SWAT didn't hire wusses. "Sorry Chevy. It's really bad."

As Sawyer turned down the first available road, I recognized the area. "It's up here on the left. Pull over next to those bushes."

Cutting the engine, Sawyer walked me across the highway. Rounding the shrubs, I found our bikes safe.

"What are you gonna do with the other one?"

"I don't know. We'll come back when Tony is better, I guess."

Sawyer said, "I'll have impound pick it up."

"Thanks, Tony would be wicked pissed if something happened to it."

Straddling my bike, I pulled on my jacket and sat, dropping the helmet into my lap.

"Hey, can I have my Beretta back?"

"Yeah, got it right here."

The familiar weight was soothing on the best of days. With all that had happened in the last few hours, I needed all the reassurance I could get.

"Is that a Triumph Thunderbird?"

Smiling with pride, I said, "It sure is. Her name's Delilah."

"Nice."

"I know." Pulling on my helmet, I turned the key. "Thanks for the ride Sawyer. See ya."

"No offence but I hope not. At least, not on the job."

CHAPTER 3

Reactions from Bubba and Sawyer convinced me that I needed a shower in the worst way. The hospital and Tony could wait a few more minutes. Pulling into my complex's parking lot, I almost turned around and went without the bath. Media vans, newscasters and gawkers crowded the entrance to my building. It just kept getting better. All I wanted was to crawl under the covers and hide. Putting on a blank face, I braved the big scary reporters.

Two steps and they were on me. "Chevy, what happened out there?"

"Chevy, what were those creatures?"

"Chevy, what is the CIA's involvement with Faraday? Do they routinely use monsters as operatives?"

Ugh, Chevy, Chevy, Chevy. I made it through the door and no one followed me. Why? I have no idea.

Behind the sign-in desk, Frank jumped to his feet. "Ms. Singer, you're home. I'm glad you're okay."

Nodding toward the door, I said, "How long have they been outside?"

Frank said, "I came in early when I saw the news.

They were there when I got here at six. Wow, you never said you were a CIA agent. That is so cool."

"Not today."

Looking down at his shoes, he said, "No, I guess not. Listen, about last week, I hope I wasn't being too forward. I wanted to apologize if I made you uncomfortable."

"It's okay, Frank. I don't date anybody. It's not you."

Beaming, he said, "Thanks, Ms. Singer. Oh hey, your brother came in this morning. He was worried about you and with all the media outside; I thought it would be all right to let him into your apartment."

"My brother, huh?"

"Yeah, Mitch. I found him up on the second floor. His key wasn't working. I know what a private person you are but he's family and he had a key, so I figured it was okay."

Glancing toward the elevator, I asked, "Is he still here?"

"I think so. I didn't see him leave. He said he would wait until you got back from the hospital."

"How did he know that I was going to the hospital?"

"Well, I expected that you would want to go see Mr. Romano."

"You told him I was going?"

"Yeah, he asked when you would be back. I said that you were probably gonna be gone most of the morning with Mr. Romano laid up and all."

"I see. Thank you Frank. If any more of my relatives come calling, make sure they stay in the lobby. Okay?"

Finally getting the idea that I wasn't happy, Frank said, "Oh, okay. You ain't mad are ya? Did I screw up?"

"It's all right Frank. I'm going to talk to my brother now. I'll see you later."

"Yes, ma'am. I'll be here. If you need anything, let me know."

"I'll do that."

Taking the elevator, I got out on three and walked down to my floor. Whoever was in my apartment wasn't my brother. I'm an only child and both my parents are dead. It could just be an overzealous reporter but it was best to be sure.

Moving as quiet as possible, I sidled up to my apartment. This was a nice building, so sound didn't carry well but I might get lucky. With my ear to the door, I listened, while reaching out with my mind. Two men were inside and I didn't know either of them. Their minds were serious and business-like. Glass shattered and I wondered what they had broken. What were they doing and why were they here?

"Just curious, but what did she do, Dave?"

"She saw or heard something she shouldn't have. Same ole, same ole."

"What'd she see?"

"I don't know. They don't tell me stuff like that. If they did I'd be dead too."

"Oh, right. She's cute though. It's a shame. Do you think maybe we could play a little before we kill her?"

"Not this time. It's gotta look like a burglary. In and out. Anyway, she's not helpless, she'd put up one hell of a fight."

The conversation faded, as they moved into another room. Was this the Praetorian Alida mentioned? It didn't fit. The Praetorian would have a definite idea of why I was supposed to die. These guys were clueless. And if

Alida had friends like vampires, Sasquatch and goblins, I didn't think she'd be scared of these idiots. So who were they? What had I seen or heard? The one thing I had been a witness to was the horror at Faraday's lab and that was all over the news. Nothing to hide there. Unless... Two people got away. Maybe one or both of them thought I knew who they were and didn't want to be exposed. The problem was I didn't know who they were or what they were planning. First things, first. What should I do about Tweedle-dee and Tweedle-dum?

Having a brawl with two assassins in my apartment was iffy. Killing one or both of them would bring in the police, exciting the press and my employers even more. It was a remote possibility that I might be hurt or die and that was unacceptable. Childhood memories gave me an idea. *Heh, heh, this was going to be fun.*

Glass tinkled as it fell to the floor. Throwing the fire alarm, I darted down the hall to the storage room. Doors opened, as the residents responded to the emergency. With all my strength, I reached out to Mitch and Dave, funneling fear and confusion into their minds. Hoping that my ploy worked, I peeked out to watch. Startled people hurried to the stairs. The assassins didn't make an appearance right away, so I opened the gates wider. Emotions bordering on abject terror, they broke and flung my door open. Shoving my neighbors aside, Mitch and Dave ran for the exit as if their pants were on fire. *Bastards.*

As I entered my apartment, the phone rang. Having a good idea who it was I answered right away. "Yes?"

"Ms. Singer, is that you?"

"Yeah, it's me. What can I do for you Frank?"

"Well, I don't know if you heard but there's a fire.

You need to evacuate."

"I know all about it. Can I trust you, Frank?"

"Absolutely, with anything, Ms. Singer."

"I know it wasn't nice but I tripped the fire alarm. I needed to get rid of my brother and couldn't think of any other way. I'm sorry. I know this made your day more difficult but I didn't have another choice. Do you forgive me?"

"Sure, I understand. I'll let everyone know that it was an accident or some kids playing around. You're brother's that bad, huh?"

"Yeah, so could you maybe wait until he and his friend leave before you tell anyone?"

"Oh, there they go now. Damn! Excuse my French but they tore out of here like the devil was on their heels."

"He has arsonphobia."

"He's got what?"

"He's terrified of fire."

"Wow, he sure is. Anyway, it won't be a problem. They're gone. They just jumped in a van."

"Great. Thanks a lot Frank."

"Any time, Ms. Singer. I'm real sorry that I let him in. I didn't know."

"It's all right. No more relatives though, okay?"

"No ma'am. I'll just get everyone settled again."

"Thanks. Bye."

"Bye-bye."

Positive that the duo wouldn't be back any time soon, I still put the chain on the door and tucked a chair under the knob. On my way to check the windows, I clicked on the television. *Holy shit!* The twenty-four hour news station was playing a clip of Sasquatch's escape.

How had they managed to get it on film? Taken after I left, the next video was of the extraction of the cat-man at the lab. Writhing on the gurney, he changed into a full-blown Siberian tiger and back into a man for the entire world to see. The doctor rushed to inject a sedative into his arm and the picture cut to one of me leaving the Faraday estate with Sawyer.

"And here is the woman responsible for these amazing discoveries. Cheveyo Oneida Singer is an operative for the National Clandestine Service and reported the crime when her partner Anthony Vincent Romano was abducted. The question on everyone's mind today is 'what are these creatures and are they dangerous?' Dr. Herbert Anderson is with us to give his expert opinion. Doctor..."

"In answer to your question, they are legendary beings of different species. They have existed alongside man for millennia; staying hidden for the most part. The first film you showed was of an ogre."

"An ogre? What are they? Where do they live?"

Nauseous, I turned off the set. What was I going to do? Someone wanted me dead. My best friend was in the hospital and might not recover. I found out that fairy tale creatures do exist and exposed them to the world. According to Alida, they wouldn't be very happy with me and would try to kill me. Who could blame them? They stayed hidden for thousands of years and in one night, I ruined it all. My picture was splashed all over the television, which meant my career was over before it began. My apartment was trashed and I stunk! What the hell was I going to do? Flopping down on the sofa, I chewed my nail with that mantra running circles in my head. I wanted to cry; this was awful. I wanted Tony.

When I was upset, he always pulled me into his lap and rubbed my back until I felt better. He was my dad, brother and best friend all rolled into one. He would know what to do. He would... What would Tony do? He'd say, 'One problem at a time, brat. Panicking never helped anything.' Taking a deep breath, I cleared my head. I needed to prioritize. What was the most urgent problem? My nose wrinkled. Shower and try to come up with a plan.

Running off Mitch and Dave was a temporary solution. They'd be back. The Praetorian hadn't made an appearance, so I couldn't deal with them. Nothing could be done about the media; therefore, it was best to ignore that one. Tony was in the hospital but he wasn't in danger. He would wake up or he wouldn't. Either way, I couldn't do a thing to help him. My heart gave a twinge at the thought but I squelched it ruthlessly. As the CO, Tony would have to wake up before I heard where my job stood. Depending on how long he was unconscious, the Agency might contact me but they hadn't yet. As I saw it, the immediate threat was whoever had hired Mitch and Dave. I needed to know who they were and I needed to know now.

Fresh and clean, I had an objective and course of action. Propping the security bar against the sliding door to the balcony, I closed it behind me and watched it fall into place. The apartment secured, I climbed down the tree near the deck and crept around the side of the building. The press was still camped out on my doorstep but with my hair down and different clothes, I hoped they wouldn't notice me. Shielding my face with loose hair, I searched for an imaginary lost item in my bag. Parked next to a news truck, I was careful getting into the car.

Inside, I found my sunglasses and put them on before sitting up straight. Pausing, I checked to make sure that no one was watching. Phase 1 complete. Starting the Shelby, I pulled out of the lot slow and easy.

Phase 2 was to get into Faraday's house and find information on his partners. The cops should be done in there by now. The focus would be on the lab, so getting inside shouldn't be too tough. Driving north of the estate this time, I found a place to stash my car and trekked through the forest again.

Bright and sunny, birds chirped cheerful songs, while I walked the quarter mile to the house. It was much more pleasant this time. Creeping up to the wall, I didn't make a sound as I stepped onto the log and peeked over the top. I couldn't see the lab but there wasn't much activity up front. Guards stood at the entrance to the property and a crime scene technician walked toward the backyard.

Spotting a side door, I dropped to the ground and ran crouched to the front porch. Hidden behind a bush, I searched the house with my ability. One man worked upstairs but that was it. Jumping the rail, I was across the porch and in the door before anyone noticed.

Good luck and fortune shined in my direction. I was in the study, which was the most probable place for information. Traipsing around the house wouldn't be necessary, if I found what I was looking for in here. The room smelled sweet, like flowers and I saw a vase of Daffodils on the coffee table. Faraday must be partial to them. Starting with the desk, I went through the drawers finding nothing except office supplies and a bottle of whiskey. A computer sat on the desktop ready for a login and password. The police must have started with the lab or they would have taken it. On the chance that Faraday was the trusting sort, I clicked login without success. Examining the good doctor's collection of books, I found a journal stashed between two human physiology tomes. Flipping through the pages, I skimmed dozens of notes and sketches. One was titled Tweentown and depicted a medieval village surrounded by a wall. Some of the buildings had names above them.

"Cheveyo! What are you doing here?"

With my heart in my throat, I swung around to face Alida. Whispering, I said, "Damn it, Alida, you scared the living shit out of me! Why did you come back?"

"I was curious."

"That is no reason to risk getting caught. Go home."

"No, I want to help."

"There's nothing for you to help with."

"What about the laptop?"

"What about it?"

"Maybe I can hack into it."

Doubt riddled my voice. "You're a computer hacker."

"Why can I be a pixie but not a programmer?"

She had me there. Waving her toward the desk, I stepped back.

"Could you keep an eye out?"

Landing on the keyboard, she danced across the keys and the screen went blue. Shaking my head, I turned to the window. A big man wearing jeans and tank top strode across the grass toward the lab. He didn't look like a cop but maybe he was off duty. Dirty blond hair, tan skin and built like a professional wrestler, he stood well over six feet tall. In a word, he was yummy. As he passed another officer, I revised my estimate closer to seven feet.

The cop didn't acknowledge him or even look in his direction. *Odd.*

"I'm in."

Heading over to the desk, I saw Alida was logged into the computer. Now we were getting somewhere. "Let's see what files he has."

The documents folder held two hundred and thirty-three files. It was too many to read here but I might get lucky again. Alida made a strange squeak and I watched her disappear. Brows knitted, I said, "What the..."

"Ah, Ms. Singer, what an unexpected surprise."

Busted. Head turning horror movie slow, I pasted on my most endearing smile and faced the music. Grin drooping, I tried to figure out who they were. Obviously not the police, a man and woman both dressed in black leather, stood inside the door. About twenty, she was stern but pretty, five feet nine with dark hair and eyes. The man was about thirty, six feet three inches, two hundred forty pounds with brown hair and twinkling green eyes that were accustomed to getting their way.

Thinking these were my escapees, I straightened. This was great! No mysteries to solve, I had the culprits right here. Confident, I opted for a bold approach. "I don't think we've been introduced."

"Nay, lass we haven't but we know who ye are."

Scottish, that was different. "You have my name. I think it's only fair that I have yours."

Nodding, he said, "Aye, that would be fair." Bowing from the waist and never taking his sparkling eyes from mine, he said, "Kegan McIntyre, at yer service."

Bent over as he was, I was able to see a broadsword strapped to his back. Neither of them were what I expected from Faraday's cohorts. Extending mental fingers, I probed her first. Unlike the cold psyche I felt last night, she was angry and had been for a long time. Switching to Kegan I read arrogance, smug superiority and calculation on the surface but underneath was curiosity and attraction. That could be useful. Concentrating on him, I said, "Nice to meet you Kegan."

"Thank ye, lass. Likewise. May I call ye Chevy?"

"Yes, that would be fine."

Mirth glittered in his eyes and a radiant smile spread across his features. Pulled in by his infectious good humor, my lips curved in response. "Yer a breath of fresh air, lass."

Glancing to his mouth as he spoke chilled my blood. *Uh-oh.* Pearl white fangs said these two weren't the ones I was trying to find. Somehow, I doubted Faraday would team up with a vampire. Attempting to regain my former confidence, I said, "Since you didn't come here for me and we are getting along so well, how about you let me go about my business and I let you get on with yours?"

"Yer correct, I didn't come fer ye but I wouldn't be verra good at my job, if I passed up such a prime opportunity. I hope we can stay friends but my employer would like to speak to ye. Would ye do me the honor of accompanying me?"

Relaxed and pleasant, he seemed to be off guard but inside his brain was whirring. Oh and he was lying his ass off. Unwilling to take any chances, I drew my weapon, pointed it at him and said, "Can I ask you a question?"

Un-fazed, he answered, "Aye."

"How can a vampire be out on a sunny day?"

"Ah, tis a long tale indeed."

Anticipating her attack, I was ready when the woman flew across the room, knocking the gun from my hands. I had no idea what she was but human didn't enter into it. She moved so fast that I had a hard time countering her, even with my empathic talent. Her strength was unbelievable. If I let even one strike land, I was dead meat. The longer I was able to evade her blows the more incensed she became and a low growl emanated from her chest. Focusing all of my attention on the woman, I forgot the other threat. Kegan must have stepped in because something took the legs out from under me and the next thing I knew, the angry woman had my face shoved into the floor. Arms pinned behind my back, I was helpless. Hearing Kegan approach, I thought they would kill me right there. How could anything move that fast? Launching an emotional attack, I threw everything I had at them. They didn't react. *Great, now what?* The woman hogtied my wrists and ankles. My hair covered my face, blinding me to my fate. She got up and left the room. Still struggling with my hair, I attempted to flip it out of the way but couldn't. When she took me down, I must have landed on top of it. This is why I never wore it loose when I worked. Wriggling, as if I were a fish on a line, I tried to roll over. *Fuck!* Creaking leather reminded me that Kegan was watching. Humiliation bloomed and I was glad he couldn't see my face.

"Hold still." With gentle hands, he shifted my weight from side to side, gathering my hair at the nape of my neck and knotted it. "Better?"

Why was he being nice to me? He had me trussed up like a turkey, what else did he want? "Yeah, thanks. I need to cut it off."

"Bite yer tongue. Tis glorious, lass. Ye should treasure it."

Uncomfortable with the turn the conversation was taking, I averted my eyes and said, "Thank you."

"Yer welcome." Stroking a finger across my wrist, Kegan asked, "What's this?"

Accustomed to its presence, it took me a few seconds to figure out that he was referring to my tattoo. It was called the Eye of the Phoenix and had been on my wrist since I was a baby. Two opposing arcs were joined in the middle and surrounded a reversed S-shape with a swirl in the center. The symbol represented balance, rebirth, immortality and the cycle of life, among other things. My parents had never explained why they did it, other than to say it was my special destiny. My voice heavy with sarcasm, I said, "A tattoo, what does it look like?"

"Aye, I can see that. It's unusual. What do ye know of the symbol?"

"It's a Phoenix Eye."

Focusing his laughing eyes on mine, he said, "The Phoenix is said to be the keeper of the fires of creation and the soul of Osiris. Are ye a child of the gods? "

"What on earth? Are you always this superstitious? Just because I have an Eye of the Phoenix tattoo doesn't mean anything."

Studying my face for a moment, he said, "All right lass, I'll be direct. How were ye able to defend against Sophia?"

Puzzled, I frowned and said, "Training; I don't understand. She's fast and unnaturally strong but what are you really asking?"

"Nay, her strength is natural and yers is exceptional fer a human but ye predicted her moves. Ye compensated fer yer lack of speed. How?"

Damn it. I did not need to lose my ace in the hole. It might work later—I hoped. "Good genes?"

Deliberately misunderstanding me, he ogled my ass and said, "Aye, they are that."

Ugh, what an asshole. "Come on Kegan, let me go. No one needs to know you even saw me."

"And Sophia?"

"Can't you do some vampire mojo on her?"

I must have said something funny because he had a good long laugh. "Nay, lass. If I could, I would have used it on ye instead."

Oh, right. Scrambling for some other way to get out of my predicament, I came up with bupkis.

"Ye don't need to be afraid. My employer just wants to speak with ye."

He was lying but I wanted to believe him so much. "Butter wouldn't melt in your mouth, Kegan."

"I'm not familiar with the phrase."

"It means you're a charming liar."

For once, his face matched his emotions and it wasn't as satisfying as I imagined. Genuine hurt flashed in his eyes and I couldn't let it alone. "Look, I was trying to help your people. I'm sorry about the press but how could I have known? I'm not a threat to the Zephyri. If you let me go, I swear you'll never hear from me again."

Caressing my cheek, he answered, "Aye, I believe ye, Chevy. Some days I don't like my job verra much. Ye didn't mean any harm but I cannot let ye go." He got to his feet and walked away.

Could we go back to the pretty lies? "What good does killing me do? The damage is done and I don't know much more than the general public. I saved them from that man. You didn't know where they were but I found them and got them out. How can you kill me for that?"

"I have done nothing yet. We are taking ye to speak with our employer. He will decide what to do with ye."

Irritated with the whole situation, I said, "You can drop the employer crap. You're talking about the Tsái. Use the name; I'm too tired for all the tap dancing."

Tense silence stretched on for two full minutes. "And where did ye get this information?"

This time it was my turn to keep quiet. *Why couldn't I just shut my yap?*

"Verra well."

Sophia returned and it looked as if we were almost ready to go. Screaming like a banshee, I yelled, "HELP!"

She was on me before I took another breath, shoving a cloth into my mouth. As the bitch got up, she kicked me in the ribs.

Kegan said, "Enough Sophia. Take care of the evidence and I will handle our guest."

Spewing venom, she said, "She is a filthy human, how can you coddle her this way?"

"Chevy is fighting fer her life, she does what she must. She does not deserve cruelty but respect."

Growling, Sophia stomped over to the desk. As she picked up the laptop, it disappeared. Wow, that was handy. Did it cease to exist or did it go somewhere? Could she retrieve it the same way? Somehow, I didn't think she would tell me—if I could ask.

Stooped over me, Kegan loosened the tie that held my hands and feet together and I was able to lie down flat. Feeling like a pretzel, I rolled over onto my side, working out the kinks. If they let me walk, maybe I could get away. Sophia was fast but I might have a chance, if I did it right.

Shoving me over onto my back, Kegan picked me up and threw me over his shoulder. *So much for that idea.* Refusing to go without a fight, I squirmed and thrashed, trying to make him put me down.

Swatting me on the butt, he said "Behave."

Resigned for the moment, I held still and waited for my opportunity. Opening the door, they stopped and Kegan said, "I'll meet ye in the clearing. Go."

Peering under Kegan's arm, I watched her body melt down into a huge white wolf. None of the grotesque, bone popping seen in movies, accompanied the change. It was—beautiful, magical. Eyeing me for a second, Sophia turned and loped across the yard. Not slowing for an instant, she bounded over the wall in a single leap. *Cool.*

"Now lass, ye be still or I might drop ye."

Drop me? Why would he... Oh boy. In my position, I had a bird's eye view of his feet leaving the ground as he floated up and over the porch railing and the wall. With his shoulder in my stomach and the ground zooming by, getting sick was a real possibility. Flying upside down sucked, I don't recommend it at all. Upchucking all over the vampire's back did have its appeal but I'd choke with the gag in my mouth. Closing my eyes made my head spin and the nausea worse. I needed a fixed object to concentrate on, however, the only thing within view was Kegan's rear-end. Nice, as asses went, something was wrong with leering at the butt of the man that was going to execute you. Pride took a back seat to survival and I riveted my eyes to the vampire's derriere.

I was afraid to look but it felt as if we were descending. A bump and step confirmed my suspicion. Looking ahead under my captor's arm, I saw the human

Sophia waiting for us. As we approached, she turned her back and said, "*Anoigo.*" It sounded as if she said, "A knee go," but that didn't make any sense. The air in front of her shimmered and she vanished. Kegan's pace steady, he walked into the shimmering air and everything went black.

CHAPTER 4

Rapid-fire, I blinked and was able to restore my vision. We weren't in Kansas anymore or Charleston, for that matter. An open wooden gate made of twenty-five feet long wooden planks, bound by metal straps stood behind us. Beyond the gate was a void so black that you could cut it with a knife. To either side of the gate was a stone wall of the same height, which encompassed a medieval town. Swinging and twisting my dangling torso I was able to see cobblestone streets, shops and creatures of every size and shape, hurrying about their evening. Lampposts with glowing two-foot globes hanging from them, added to the full moon's scant illumination.

Regardless of my position and uncertain fate, I had a million questions. Grunting and muffled pleas were ignored and I resolved to wait until Kegan took the rag out of my mouth. I had no doubt that Sophia would leave the damn thing in place until hell froze over. Left to my own speculation, I concluded that this must be the Tweentown that Faraday drew in his journal. Had he been here himself? No wonder there weren't more sightings of these creatures. I couldn't begin to guess at some of the species but others were easy. Elves, fairies, swarms of pixies, zombies and dwarves all roamed the village without fear.

"Hello Kegan, Sophia. Who have you got there?"

Kegan stopped and Sophia answered, "A prisoner, Magnus. None of your concern."

Peering around the vampire's waist, I saw a handsome, pleasant looking man of about twenty-five with dark hair and eyes. He wore jeans and a T-shirt that read, *Grr, I'm a scary monster*. Nice. At least he warned you.

Magnus said, "Just curious. Relax Sophia, no need to get your hackles up."

Between the T-shirt and his comment, I couldn't help giggling and the bitch in question noticed the noise. She made a move to grab my hair and the vampire stepped out of reach so fast that it made me dizzy.

Kegan said, "Now, now, Sophia. None of that."

"What does it matter? She is going to die anyway."

"Aye, why does it matter? And nothing in this world is certain."

Magnus asked, "Is the other end as attractive as this one?"

Just when I was starting to like this guy, he had to go and turn into a jerk.

Sophia muttered, "Typical."

"Aye, she is, Magnus."

I was not hanging here while these two discussed my butt like a roast. Shaking my whole body, I umphed at them, "Pigs."

"Ooh and feisty too. Can I have her?"

"Nay. This is Chevy Singer."

"That's a shame."

"Aye. Excuse us, Magnus. We have to go."

Leaving the street, Kegan strode up a walk to the largest mansion I had ever seen. Three stories high, it was horseshoe shaped with chimneys at every corner. Gargoyles lined the edge of the roof and I could have sworn I saw one move. Recalling the journal map, Faraday had named this building the Council Chambers.

As we approached the huge front door, it swung open automatically. "Thank ye, Barmek."

Huh? Craning my neck, I saw a creature closing the door behind us. Two and a half feet tall, he had a potbelly and skinny legs. His almost bald, squat head sported long pointy ears, large eyes and almost no nose. Racing ahead of us, Barmek opened another door. The fifteen-foot door and twenty feet tall ceilings couldn't be meant for him. Who lived here? Goliath?

Kegan never broke stride and descended a winding stone staircase. Damp, cool and dark, it looked like a dungeon. More of the light globes dotted the walls all the way down. Over the side of the stairs was a lightless pit that echoed every step. Deep within the earth, or wherever we were, it took five minutes to reach a circular cut stone platform. A human-size cage hung over the abyss and I prayed they wouldn't lock me inside it. Torture devices lined the walls and a rack took center stage. Heavy iron clacking drew my attention forward. Kegan unlocked a heavy metal door and took me inside the room.

Setting me down, I wobbled until he steadied me and released my feet. Untying my hands made my shoulders ache and I moaned.

"I apologize, lass; I know tis uncomfortable." Reaching out with his big hands, he massaged my shoulders and upper arms until they felt better.

Pulling the gag out of my dry mouth, I said, "Thank you."

"Yer welcome. I only wish I could do more."

"Here's what you can do. Let me go!" Making a dash for the open door was cut short, as Kegan's arm thrust out, catching me around the waist.

Standing outside the cell, Sophia said, "Stop playing around Kegan."

Eyes filled with pity and remorse, he set me on my feet, stepping back. "Ye will remain here until we come back to get ye."

"For how long?"

"I don't know. Whenever the Tsái calls fer ye."

"This is wrong, you know it is. I helped them. How can you do this to me? Don't you people have any sense of justice—honor?"

"Aye, we do." With that, he closed the cell door and locked it.

Yelling at their backs through the barred porthole, I said, "Not from where I'm standing, buddy!"

Ignoring my retort, Sophia said, "Aren't you going to spell the door?"

"Nay, she's only human. She cannot escape."

Wanna bet? I was getting out of this shit hole come hell or high water, starting now. Listening to the receding footsteps, I waited for the door at the top to close. Once it did, I examined my temporary quarters. The light from the globes in the main room wasn't enough to see by, so I retrieved the phone from my pocket. Turning on the flashlight application, I studied the prison.

A ten foot cube, with no windows, one door and a drain in the floor, it was sparse, to say the least. They left me a bucket that I did not want to speculate about and a straw stuffed pallet in the corner. *Lovely.*

Okay, there didn't seem to be a way out. I had my cell phone though. Whom should I call? Tony was no help; he was still in the hospital. I didn't have contact information for the Agency. The police? How would I tell them to get here? They did have GPS but it was crappy on cells. It didn't matter. Maybe they could get a fix on my general location and we could figure it out from there.

Dialing 911, the phone responded 'no service'. Checking all my settings offered no solution. Didn't Tweentown have a single cell tower? Conserving power on the phone was my next priority and I set it to airplane mode. I was on my own.

Examining the door, I saw the hinges were on the outside with no handle or knob. The bars weren't loose, not that my hips would fit through the tiny hole. There was a two-inch gap under it but that didn't help either. The door was a bust.

Checking each stone slab for loose or broken mortar, I started with the sidewall, hoping to find a way into a neighboring room. With my own scraping and grunting, I failed to notice the noise right away. The hiss of something sharp being dragged across stone, snapped my head around. *What was that?* Straining my ears, I heard a swish and whispers. Someone else was down here. Running to the door, I yelled, "Hello! Can you hear me?" No one answered. "Hello! Please help me."

Voices speaking soft gibberish echoed in the dark. Pressing my face to the bars, I tried to see who was outside. Distorted shadows moved along the wall. "Please let me out. I'll do whatever you want, just unlock the door."

Knives scraped against the wall and I began to regret my offer. Bare feet padded along the floor. Craning my neck to the side, I watched for whoever was approaching. A black shape darted past my peripheral vision and I squinted to catch a glimpse of the shape.

Snarling, dagger-like teeth thrust into the window making me jump back two feet. Exposed gray muscles worked the grotesque creature's mouth, its jaws snapping at me through the opening. Saliva dripped from its chin and it rammed a hand with six-inch claws between the bars. Hissing, the monster stretched its long arm toward me. I backed across the cell, tripping over the bucket. The beast's grotesque limb retreated and the door shook, as it rattled the handle. Screams and scrabbling sounded like a fight. How many were there? Did it make any difference? If even one got in, I was fertilizer. Claws screeched against the metal and I covered my ears. Trembling, I looked around the room for something to defend myself. *Empty.*

Sibilant voices argued. "Open door."

"Wait."

"Open it."

"Fear makes meat sweet. Wait."

Whimpering, I attempted to swallow the lump in my throat. *They were going to eat me?*

The door at the top of the stairs opened. Snarls, hisses and scurrying feet fled. *Thank you, God.* Collapsing on the pallet, I waited for my visitor, trying to calm the tremors.

Had the Tsái called for me already? Kegan left me with the impression that it would be a long time. At this point, I didn't care. I just wanted out of here. The footsteps sounded soft like cloth. Moving fast, soon they were outside the door. Hands shaking and scared out of my wits, I jumped when a metal tray slid through the wall. I looked for a slot but couldn't see one; it appeared to have come through solid stone. On the tray was bread, cheese, fruit and a large cup of water.

Rushing over to the door, I said, "Who's there?"

No answer. Feeling for their mind, I found timid fear. "What's your name? Please talk to me."

Debating whether to answer, he paused for a minute before speaking. "Barmek."

"Oh, the one that opened the door for us."

"Yes, miss."

"Thank you for the food, Barmek. I haven't eaten since yesterday."

"You are welcome, miss."

He turned to go but I stopped him. "Please, please, don't leave me down here. They might come back."

"They, miss?"

"Horrible monsters. They were going to eat me."

"Ghouls, miss."

"That's what they were?"

"Yes. I will speak to Straton. They will not bother you again."

Desperate to keep him talking, I scrambled for something to say. "Can I ask you a question?"

"All right, miss."

"I hope this doesn't offend you but what are you?"

A slight snort and he answered, "A brownie, miss."

Remembering a little about myths and movies, I asked, "Is that like a house elf?"

"Yes, it is."

"So you take care of the Council Chambers?"

"Yes miss, I do."

"Could you stay and talk to me for a while?"

"Brownies are not good conversationalists."

"I don't mind. Please?"

"It is not a good idea."

"Why not?"

"My master might not approve."

"Master? Who's your master?"

"The Tsái, miss."

"He makes you call him master? Are you a slave?"

"No, miss. Not at all."

"Why would you call him master, if you aren't a slave?"

"We are an ancient society, miss. It is customary to refer to the head of the house as master."

"Oh, well, I suppose that's different but does he dictate who you can or can't talk to?"

"No miss, not usually."

"What's the problem then?"

"You are a prisoner, miss. You are awaiting judgment and my master is the judge. It feels— improper."

"Do you think I did something wrong?"

"No, I... I have other duties to attend to. I must go, miss."

"Please, Barmek. Don't leave. I'm sorry. I didn't mean to upset you."

"I am not angry, miss. The connection brownies have to their house and family is difficult to explain and I have other duties. I will be back in a few hours with your dinner."

"Do you have any idea how long they will keep me down here?"

"No, miss. That is up to the Tsái."

Padding steps retreated up the stairs and he was gone. Distractions removed, my ears strained for the ghouls return. Thirty minutes and not a sound. Maybe Barmek kept his word. My stomach growled and I let out a little 'eek'. *Get a grip, girl.* Taking the tray, I moved over to the pallet. Ravenous, I tore into the food, gulping it down as fast as I could.

***

Enormous, perfect hands descended from above me. Peace, warmth and love enveloped me as they took me from the cradle. Their image is clear, when everything else is shadow and light. On his pinky, he wears a silver ring with blue and green stones. Taking my wrist, he says "Sou gia panta," and the skin warms under his touch. Love, pure and complete overwhelms me.

Drifting up toward wakefulness, I considered the dream for the thousandth time. This was the love I had always sought and never found. It was unconditional and perfect. It was also a fantasy.

Metal scraped over stone, making me jerk awake. How could I have fallen asleep? Rubbing my eyes, I tried to see in the dim light. Two food trays sat in front of the wall, beside the door. "Barmek?"

"Yes, miss?"

"How long was I asleep?"

"It is morning in Charleston, miss."

"What's going on?"

"Going on?"

"Yeah, what happened with Tony and the Zephyri at the hospital?"

"They are gone, miss."

Horrified, I squeaked, "They died?"

"I do not know, miss. They are gone."

"Wait a minute. What do you mean they're gone?"

"They are no longer at the hospital. They are gone."

"Where did they go? Did someone kidnap them?"

"I presume that your government took them."

"What? Why? They wouldn't..."

Leaving that particular statement unfinished, I realized that they would. They had done it before—to me. Who knows what they would do to them? My childhood was a nightmare thanks to them, until John saved me. Yeah, they would.

Barmek said, "The Federal Bureau of Investigation has taken over the 'Butcher's' plantation."

"Butcher?"

"I believe his name is Michael Faraday."

"What about Tony? Is he okay?"

"I do not know who Tony is."

"He's the human that was at Faraday's lab. He went to the hospital with Malachai."

"Ah, he is gone with the rest."

Alarmed, I said, "No, no. I have to get out of here. I have to find him. Barmek, you have to let me out."

"I cannot, miss. Even if I were willing to ignore my master's wishes, I do not have the key."

"Can you get it?"

"I will not, miss. I am sorry."

Gritting my teeth in resentment, I said, "You *are* a slave."

"I am a servant, not a slave."

"Are you afraid of getting fired?"

"What is fired?"

"When your employer dismisses you."

"I cannot be dismissed, miss."

"Do you have a contract or something?"

"No miss. I am bound to the Tsái."

"That sounds like slavery to me."

"It is not."

"Does he pay you?"

"No, payment is not required."

"You are bound to the Tsái and you don't get any wages but you have to do everything he says. That is a textbook definition of slavery, Barmek."

"You are human and do not understand. Brownies are bound to a single family and live as long as the line survives. We care for and serve them gladly. We bring peace and tranquility to the home and the ones that live within it. We raise the children, care for the sick, prepare the meals and comfort those in need."

"Nice speech but without pay, you are a slave."

"Is your mother a slave? Have you paid her for all the sacrifices and care?"

Squirming, I said, "No."

"No. We are the soul of the household to which we belong. We hold the family together, make the building a home, serve as confidants, friends and companions. We are loved and taken care of in return. We are not slaves."

"All right. You made your point. So the Tsái's family are your masters?"

"The Tsái is yes, miss."

"He doesn't have a family?"

"Not any longer, miss."

"They died?"

Sounding sad, Barmek said, "Yes. All except the Tsái."

"I'm sorry, Barmek."

"Thank you, miss but it was a long time ago."

"So when he dies, you will too?"

"Yes, miss."

"That's terrible. Isn't there anything you can do?"

"I do not know. No one has ever tried. When the last of a line dies, the brownies bound to that family do not want to live."

"Is the Tsái good to you?"

"Of course."

"Why of course?"

"It is self-defeating to mistreat your brownie. If any family member were to abuse a brownie bound to the household, everyone would get sick, children would become rebellious, chores would go undone, any matter of chance would go against them, accidents would happen and financial ruin."

"I suppose that does make things more equitable."

"Yes miss, it does. I must return to my duties."

"Thanks for the company, Barmek."

"Yes, miss."

Checking the wall by the trays for an opening, I still couldn't find one. Returning to the pallet with both trays, I noticed that the empty one from the day before was gone. How had he done that? There must be a way in that I hadn't found yet. I wolfed down the food and determined to resume my search for a way out. My hunt for loose stones had only progressed half way down one wall. Imminent death was motivation enough but Tony's predicament made the situation more urgent.

With my concentration fixed on the wall, I didn't notice when it began but bit by bit, I became aware of a buzz coming from outside the door. *Oh crap. Were the ghouls back?* The sound wasn't the same though. Curious, I went over to investigate. Peering through the bars, I couldn't see the source of the sound. Tilting my head, I tried to look down at the floor. The angle was too sharp. Sending out mental feelers, I felt a familiar mind on the other side. "Alida?"

"Yeah. It's me."

"Can you get me out?"

"That's the idea."

"Oh, thank goodness!"

Grunting, she said, "Hold your thanks until we're out of here."

Metal clicked and I pulled on the bars. It wouldn't move. "What's the matter? It won't open."

"That was the first tumbler. Jeez, be patient."

"I'm in kind of a hurry."

"You wouldn't know it. I thought you two would never stop yapping."

"I didn't know you were out there."

"I hope no one else does either."

Guilt tugged at my conscience. "You could get into real trouble. Why are you doing this?"

"You let me out of my prison. I'm returning the favor."

Another tumbler fell into place. "Do you know where they took Tony?"

"Nope. I just heard that the Centers for Disease Control and Prevention took all of them and put them in quarantine."

"Quarantine? What for?"

Snick. Another tumbler moved.

"The official line is that they want to make sure they aren't contagious. As if you can catch a coma, forty inch incisions and staples up the wazoo."

"I don't think that's what they were talking about."

"I know. It's stupid. We're not diseased. We have been living here as long as humans and never infected anyone."

"Are you almost done?"

"Hold you're horses. This last one is a bitch to reach."

Click. "Got it!"

Yanking open the door, I slung Alida across the room. Thankfully, she put on the brakes before she hit the wall. "Thanks, Alida. I owe you."

Annoyed, the pixie lectured me. "I swear you don't listen to a word I say. I said the Praetorian was coming for you but you didn't listen. 'You can take care of yourself.' Nice job, by the way. Now I have to break you out of jail and face the Tsái, if we are caught. You had better listen from here on out. I told you to save your thanks until we are out of the mansion. We have a long way to go."

Racing up the spiral stairs made my head spin and I had to lean against the outer wall to keep from falling into the pit. Breathless, we reached the door at the top. Careful and quiet, I turned the knob slowly, easing it open far enough for Alida to get out.

Flitting out of view, she checked if anyone was around. She was gone for a few seconds. When she flew back into sight, she waved me ahead. A full sprint to the door and we were on the dark street.

Whispering, Alida said, "We need to stay off the road. Follow me and stay alert."

"No problem."

Keeping up with the pixie turned out to be harder

than I thought. She was fast. Leading me from bush to tree to alley, we made our way to the relative safety of a deserted building.

Leaning against the wall, I bent over and tried to catch my breath. "Why is it still dark out?"

"It's always night in Tweentown."

"Why? How is that even possible?"

"There are several species that can't take the light of the sun. Gargoyles and trolls turn to stone, vampires burn up. There are others too but you get the gist."

"But how?"

"Magic, how else? Tweentown is always moving with the earth to stay in the dark. That's why we don't have things like electricity."

"Or cell towers."

"Ha-ha. You tried your phone in the dungeon and it didn't work, huh?"

"No it didn't. What about all the lights on the street and in the mansion? They need electricity, don't they?"

"Those are *fanós*. They're magic and don't need power."

"How were you able to learn about computers, if you can't run one here?"

"At home, I siphon off electricity to run mine."

Frowning, I said, "Where's home? I thought you all lived here."

"Nah, Tweentown is a haven. Think of it like going to town, if you lived out in the sticks. There's the bank, the library, pubs, shops and all kinds of stuff."

"How come it's called Tweentown?"

"A couple of reasons. You can call the door from anywhere that is between two things. For example, between two parked cars, store aisles, walls, even the sky and ground, so it amounts to anywhere. The other reason is because it exists between dimensions."

Shaking my head in amazement, I said, "I've recovered; we can go if you want."

"It's not far to the Colony. We should be there in a few minutes."

"What's the Colony?"

"The Pixie Colony. Don't worry; no one will turn you in. They think you're the bomb. The Praetorian won't ever look for you here."

"Hold on. I have to go back to Charleston. I can't stay here. I have to find Tony."

"If you go back, the Praetorian will find you again and this time I won't be able to get you out."

Dismissing her concerns, I said, "I'll be careful. They won't find me. They got lucky this time."

"The timing might have been luck but they don't need it. They will find you, no matter where you go. It's what they do."

"It doesn't matter, Alida. I have to get Tony out of wherever the CDC stashed him. They probably took everybody to headquarters in Atlanta."

The pixie's attitude grew more serious and she said, "They're not there. The Tsái already had it searched. Cheveyo—Chevy, the shit is going to hit the fan. I didn't tell you before but there's a press conference this morning. The human public is screaming about what Faraday did and has forced the local government to put his trial on the fast track."

"That's great."

"Not really. The Council is going to make an appearance and demand the release of our people and custody of Faraday."

"Who are the Council?"

"Our leaders."

"I thought the Tsái was your leader."

"He is. It's complicated. The Tsái is over the Council. They are the kings and queen that represent each group of species. Whatever. The point is that the Council is going to show themselves to the world and demand Faraday and our people."

"Okay, that's reasonable. What aren't you telling me?"

Huffing, she said, "Do you think the United States government will let them go?"

"No, probably not."

"Right, so it may mean war. You will be safe here, from both threats. We can hide you from the Praetorian and you won't be in the middle of what happens next."

"Do you think there might be a war?"

"I don't know. Maybe but regardless, bad stuff is going down."

"I appreciate your help and concern but I have to do this. Tony is all I have."

"This is dumb. You don't know what you're dealing with."

"Are you saying you won't get me out of here?"

"No." Sighing, she said, "All right, I'll take you to the Antechamber."

"What's that?"

"The way out."

Backtracking three buildings, the Antechamber was red brick with two doors and windows. It was boring and small; I wasn't impressed. Alida led the way up to the left door and I opened it for her. Pulling it closed behind me, I looked up and did a double take.

Inside, it went on forever. Red doors lined two walls thirty feet apart to infinity. On each door was a dial, a brass plaque and a clock. In front of every door were a turnstile and a pair of handrails extending about eight feet toward the center aisle. Hanging from the ceiling above each aisle was a numbered sign with evens on the right and odds on the left. The little building held hundreds of Zephyri.

What could only be a gargoyle, appeared at my side, startling me. He was black with leathery skin and about three feet tall. A single horn protruded from the top of his head. Three inch pointed ears stuck out from the side and a large brow ridge loomed over round, glowing green eyes and a snout. Fangs extended from the upper jaw over his bottom lip. He hunched over and the ridges of his spine were evident through the green tunic he wore. Lanky arms extended to the floor and ended in long fingers with sharp talons tipping each one. Speaking in a nervous lisp, he said, "Welcome to the Antechamber, my name ith Doyle and I am the Greeter. Do you have a dethtination in mind?"

The pixie asked me, "Did you leave your transportation at Faraday's?"

"Yeah, my car."

Turning back to Doyle, Alida said, "We want to go to the Butcher's house, Doyle."

Giving me a good look, he said, "How did a human get into Tweentown?"

Flushing red, Alida hissed and bared a mouth full of pointed teeth. I couldn't believe I had never seen them.

Shaking and backing away, Doyle said, "Door one-thixteen." Turning tail, he scurried away, disappearing in the crowd.

I asked Alida, "What number did he say?"

"One-sixteen. Doyle has a lisp."

Snickering, I said, "Doyle the gargoyle is a greeter and has a lisp?"

"I know. It's hysterical. He's also a scaredy-cat."

Walking down to the sign that read one hundred sixteen, we turned between the rails. The dial on the door was an arc that showed a sun in the approximate position it would be in Charleston. When the sun reached the end of the arc's window, I presumed there would be a moon to take its place on the opposite side. Above the dial was a brass plaque that stated the address. Next to the sundial a clock read, nine-thirty. Alida flew over the turnstile and I followed. Opening the door, I gulped.

Alida held out her arm in a gallant gesture. "You first."

The same inky black void that surrounded Tweentown filled the portal and I hesitated before stepping through. "What is that stuff?"

She said, "It's called the *Rígma*. It won't hurt you."

Grow a pair, chickenshit! There's nothing to it.
Squaring my shoulders, I marched forward into nothing.

CHAPTER 5

Brilliant sunlight blinded me and I shaded my eyes, while watching for Alida. I wasn't big on trust and half expected her to ditch me. I wouldn't blame her if she did. Not the fierce little pixie, she was a trooper and appeared a moment later. The woods surrounding us were the same as the ones around Faraday's estate but I didn't know which way to go. "Where are we, Alida?"

"East of the estate."

"In that case, my car is this way."

Blazing a trail through the brush, I made it to the Shelby in fewer than fifteen minutes. When I opened the door, the pixie flew inside and made herself at home on the dash.

"Hey, you aren't coming with me. All I need is a place and time for the press conference and you can go home."

"I don't think so, Chevy. It's obvious that you need all the help you can get. I'm going with you; don't bother arguing."

"Come on, Alida. Tell me where it is. You're already in enough trouble. I'll be okay."

"Nope. That's final. Get in and drive, human."

"You're a bossy little shit. Do you know that?"

"I hear that a lot."

"I'll bet."

With the engine rumbling, I gave the pixie a pointed look and she said, "It's at the courthouse at ten. We better get moving if we want to make it."

The clock in the dash read nine-forty. I hoped traffic was light. Whipping a U-turn, I headed back for Charleston.

Right on time, I didn't bother trying to find another parking spot and pulled into the first handicapped slot I came to. I know. I know. I'm a horrible person.

Snatching my sunglasses off the visor clip, it occurred to me to wonder how I was going to get the pixie inside without being seen. Grabbing my boogie bag off the back seat, I said, "Get in."

"What? What's this?"

"It's the bag I keep in the car in case I need to get away fast. There are clothes and other stuff in it. Just get in."

Eyeing the bag with contempt, she said, "Okay but don't jostle me too much. I don't want to break a wing."

"You're the one who insisted on coming along."

Carefully lifting the bag to my shoulder, I pulled my hair around to cover my face and went inside. I didn't know if the sunglasses indoors would draw more attention than my exposed face but I decided to leave them in place.

The signs posted, told us which room the conference was in and we entered with the last of the media. Taking a seat in the back, I set the bag on my lap and tried to look inconspicuous.

Four men stood in front of the crowd. The one with a full head of white hair and a slight paunch was the mayor. Our Chief of Police was in his mid-fifties with a receding hairline and broad face. I didn't recognize the other two men. Mystery man number one was a large African-American male with medium brown skin and the other was a thin man in a gray suit, gray hair with a gray trim mustache and wire rim glasses.

The mayor began with introductions. "Welcome. I am Steve Johnson, Mayor of Charleston and this is Gene Carver, our Chief of Police. Here you have the Solicitor for the Ninth Judicial Circuit, Gary Swanson and last William Green the Director of the Federal Bureau of Investigation. As I'm sure most of you have heard, the FBI has taken over the situation at the Faraday plantation, however, Charleston will still be prosecuting Michael Faraday for his crimes. We will take questions after a brief statement from the Director."

The gray man said, "As the Mayor indicated, we have assumed control of the Faraday estate and the investigation is ongoing. Developments there have nation-wide implications and therefore, the Federal Bureau of Investigation has jurisdiction in this matter. The Centers for Disease Control and Prevention have taken the survivors to an undisclosed location and quarantined them until they are sure the victims pose no health risk to the public. We will now take questions, one at a time please."

The first reporter asked, "Was Faraday experimenting with contagious diseases?"

Green answered, "Not that we know of but contagion is a matter for the CDC to determine."

"If there isn't a specific disease, why did the CDC

quarantine them?"

"It is a precautionary measure. They will only be held until all the tests have been done."

The door opening drew my eye and I gaped in shock. Four fantastic creatures entered the room. Leading the party was a golden fairy about a foot tall that radiated power and grace. A double set of iridescent gold wings fluttered as she moved up the aisle. Hair, dress and crown all in gold, she seemed to glow.

Following in her wake was an Arabic looking man. Ebony hair brushed back from his high forehead, formed a cloud around his shoulders with long black lashes framing dark arrogant eyes. Standing six feet four inches, he wore a long electric blue tunic with large open sleeves. A goatee framed his pouty lips that twitched in disdain at the gawkers.

Next in the procession was another male who was clearly not human. Tall, willowy and elegant, he was pale skinned with slanted vivid green eyes and pointed ears peeked out of his light brown hair. He was aloof and aristocratic, his cloak making him look as though he floated through the room.

Bending almost in half to get under the doorframe, the last in line was a giant. I mean that in the literal sense. Gasps of awe sounded from everyone, including me. Standing almost fourteen feet tall, he was the definition of Aryan standards, with pale skin, blond hair and blue eyes. His roman nose complimented his long face and high cheekbones. Stooping in a T-shirt and jean jacket with a popped collar, he looked uncomfortable with the low ceiling. Taking a knee, he turned his attention to his royal peers. Launching her voice over the murmuring reporters, the fairy said, "That is unacceptable."

The director asked, "Exactly who are you?"

"I am Ellarian, queen of the fairies." With a graceful sweep of her arm, she indicated the elf. "This is Fenion, king of the elves." Pointing to the Arabic man she said, "This is Aadí, rajah of the shifters." Last, she indicated the blonde giant and said, "And this is Baldr, regent of the vampires." The last introduction induced several more gasps. As if being a giant wasn't bad enough, he had to be a vampire too. How much blood did he drink? That was a terrifying thought. Whispering to my bag, I asked, "Where is the Tsái?"

"They won't let anyone know he exists. We have to protect him at all cost."

"If he's so powerful, why do you have to protect him? Shouldn't he be protecting you?"

"Humans."

Continuing, Ellarian said, "We make up the ruling council of the Zephyri."

Green, the gray FBI man asked, "And the others with you?"

What others? Turning around, I noticed an entourage that I hadn't seen, at the back of the room. The Council had six guards for each royal personage. Six fairies of assorted colors; red, green, blue, purple, silver and gold hovered ahead of the other eighteen sentries. At one end, I found a familiar face and ducked back behind my hair.

Alida asked, "What's wrong?"

"One of the guards is someone that Kegan stopped to talk to in Tweentown."

"Which one?"

"On the end, Magnus."

"He's Aadí's right hand. The rajah doesn't go

anywhere without him."

The queen answered, "They are our escort."

Green said, "Well, it's nice to meet you but what did you find unacceptable?"

"Your imprisonment of our subjects. We want them returned to us immediately."

"I'm sorry, miss but that isn't feasible. We have to determine the health risks before we can discuss any release."

Indignant, the Fairy Queen said, "Are you implying that we are diseased?"

"No miss. I..."

One of the cameramen zoomed in on the queen and I was spellbound. Exotic gold eyes glittered with an elongated pupil like a cat. As she spoke, I could not look away.

"We further demand that you give us custody of the human, Michael Faraday."

Charleston's Solicitor, Gary Swanson, said, "I'm afraid that won't be possible. I assure you that Mr. Faraday will be prosecuted to the fullest extent of the law. We have even moved up his court date. If any of your people want to attend, it will be tomorrow at nine a.m."

"Is that so? Please, Mr. Swanson, tell me what he is charged with for butchering our people."

Swanson's face went from condescending to worry in a heartbeat. Mumbling, he said, "Animal cruelty, ma'am."

The crowd echoed his statement, incredulous and Ellarian stared at him for a moment. "Animal cruelty? I see. What is the penalty for this crime?"

"Five years in prison and a five thousand dollar fine,

ma'am but..."

"While that may be adequate for animals, it is unacceptable for our people. We are not beasts."

"I was not insinuating that you are but the law is written for humans, which is defined as homo sapiens. If we charged him with what he deserves, his defense attorney would get a dismissal before we went to trial."

Ellarian said, "Human laws are not our concern; they are wholly deficient. Turn Faraday over to us and the problem is solved."

"I'm sorry ma'am but we can't do that. The constitution guarantees a trial by a jury of your peers. We cannot violate his rights. You may petition the court to speak at his sentencing."

A tinkling, musical titter bubbled from the queen and she said, "We are rulers of the Zephyri Nation. We have not come to make requests or petitions."

Waving a dismissive hand at Swanson, Ellarian faced the FBI director and said, "You have thirty-six hours to return our people and give us Faraday. We will be back outside this building tomorrow evening at ten."

Shaking his head, the director said, "Miss, we don't know who or what you are. When the victims of these crimes are deemed safe, they will be released but not before. If what you have said is true, you are not even citizens of this country and therefore, illegal aliens."

Empty laughter filled the room as the air became cooler. Goosebumps prickled my bare arms. Had someone turned up the air conditioning? The temperature dropped further and my breath became visible. Reporters shivered, bouncing in their seats. A water glass on the podium froze solid as I watched. Realization drew all eyes to the queen and I dropped my shield to confirm our suspicions. Colder than the glacial chill of the room, the golden fairy's mind froze my heart. She was incensed but well past the hot irrational anger most people feel. Her mind was clear, anticipating every turn the situation might make and she looked placid, pleasant. This was a dangerous woman. I never wanted to get on this creature's bad side and I hoped the director would quit while he was ahead.

She said, "You are a child. You have no authority of your own. Relay this message to your masters. We, the other members of the Council and I, have lived in this country since before it was established. The United States exists on Zephyri soil and you reside here at *our* suffrage. We are not the aliens, you are. Nevertheless, the Zephyri are not greedy; we only require your respect now that we have revealed ourselves."

Cutting her off, the director said, "That's preposterous. You can't be more than twenty-five years old."

"Oh but I can. I am five hundred and sixty-three years old." The air became so cold that I coughed, unable to breathe. "I was here when your ancestors arrived, pillaging everything in sight. I was here when they fought war after war to claim land that was not theirs. I was here when the Spanish flu killed millions of humans and I will be here when this country is *dust*."

Looking over the city leaders and the FBI man, Ellarian said, "Gentlemen, you have our demands. I suggest you acquiesce. You will not enjoy the consequences."

Turning her back on the slack-jawed government officials, the fairy faced the press beaming a radiant smile and the air warmed. "Ladies and gentlemen, we would be happy to answer some questions."

Rising to their feet, the media hounds jabbed hands in the air. Recognizing one man, Ellarian pointed to him and said, "You sir."

"What do we call you? Your majesty?"

"Ellarian will be fine."

"Did you cause the room to freeze like that, Ellarian?"

"A small demonstration, nothing more. I apologize if you were uncomfortable."

"Ellarian, who are the creatures the CDC has quarantined?"

"They are not creatures; they are Zephyri of different species. My own subject, Gus, is a goblin. When my son was young, Gus was his constant companion and became a member of the family. The Regent, Baldr can tell you about Malachai."

Baldr, the giant, spoke with an unfamiliar accent. "Malachai Romanus is my personal aide and invaluable to me. The things that were done to him are reprehensible. The longer the US government keeps him, only prolongs his suffering. He needs to be taken home, so he can be healed properly."

"Regent, do you live on human blood? Is that what Malachai needs to heal?"

Arching an eyebrow, Baldr answered. "Yes, vampires live on human and some types of Zephyri blood, however, we do not steal it or kill our donors as your stories suggest. We have strict laws governing how our food is procured. Anything less would be suicide. As far as Malachai is concerned, he needs to be taken care of by his own kind. The CDC trying to treat him would be akin to a witch doctor treating an AIDS patient."

Still running the show, Ellarian nodded at another reporter. "Was the man that turned into a tiger one of your citizens, Rajah?"

"No, he is not. He is my nephew. His name is Cain Vanderpoole and he is my sister's eldest boy. You can imagine how distraught we have all been. His mother is very distressed about what the CDC is putting him through in the interest of science."

"Are you saying that the health concern is a lie?"

"Absolutely. There is no possibility of contagion. The Zephyri are disease free and our people are the ones at risk. Scientific study is the sole motivation for keeping our citizens imprisoned."

The Director, Bill Green started to protest but another question was shouted from the back of the room. "What happened to the ogre?"

Fenion, the elf stepped forward. "His name is Tagokk and he is a troll. After he escaped the lab, he made it home and is in good health."

"Was he able to tell you anything about his time in Faraday's lab?"

"Unfortunately, he was not. He has no memory beyond walking in the forest and waking up in the cell. Considering the damage that was done to our people, I can only hope the same is true for all of them."

"What's the difference between an ogre and a troll?"

"Ogres as a rule are larger with less hair and at the risk of offending some dear friends, not as intelligent. Trolls also do not tolerate the sun well, which is why Tagokk was in a hurry to leave."

Chuckling erupted and another member of the press asked, "What are you going to do if the CDC doesn't turn them over to you?"

Smiling, Ellarian said, "You would not want to spoil the surprise, would you? Thank you for your courtesy ladies and gentlemen. We must be going."

With that, the royal party left the room. The courteous ladies and gentlemen turned on the government representatives. No longer waiting to be called on, they shouted questions and accusations at the men.

Slipping out the door, we didn't stick around to watch the show. Listening to the Council made me more desperate to find Tony. It also gave me an idea. If I found the Zephyri and rescued them or gave their location to the Council, they would call off the Praetorian. They would have to call them off. Wouldn't they?

Without thinking, I threw the bag across the seat and heard Alida squeal. Sliding into the seat, I pulled the boogie bag into my lap and eased it open. "Are you all right? I'm sorry; I forgot."

Testing her wings, the pixie flew the short distance to the passenger seat. "I'm okay. Where are we going now?"

"That's all you have to say? You don't have any comment about the Council?"

Shrugging, she said, "I'm more worried about what happens tomorrow night."

She had a point. "We're going to see a friend of mine."

"Who?"

"John Murphy."

Turning onto highway 17, I drove out to the ferry for Dewees Island.

"Who's John Murphy? How do you know him?"

"That is a long story. I should start by telling you that I'm an empath."

"You mean you feel how everyone around you feels? That must be miserable."

"It would if I couldn't shield. My father taught me how, from the time I was small. Empathy isn't all of it though. I feel every living thing, even if it doesn't have emotions and I can use the earth to amplify my power. Normally, I can project an emotion to someone else but when I tried it on Kegan, it didn't work. That makes me think that it won't work on Zephyri."

"That's not surprising. The Praetorian are trained to avoid mind control."

"Oh? I don't know if I'm relieved or worried. Why would they need to guard against mind control?"

"Some of the Zephyri have the ability."

"Like who?"

"Some vampires, fairies and elves using magic."

"That is just..."

"Chevy, what about John?"

"Oh. Anyway, after my parents died, I was in an orphanage for a while before they discovered what I could do. Phone calls were made and the government came and took me to a lab. I was what you might call a difficult patient. I stayed there for about nine months and the people in charge must have decided to take a different approach because John came to see me one day. He had me transferred to another facility but it wasn't like a lab. It was a huge house with horses and a pool. My living quarters were my own and no one came in without my permission. The doctors treated me like a person and John became my friend. He protected me, cared about me and even paired me with Tony."

"You trust him?"

"Yes, I do."

"Why are we going to see him?"

"He may have an idea where they are holding the Zephyri and Tony. He's retired now but he still has a lot of influential friends and keeps up with what is going on."

Scowling, Alida said, "I don't know. I don't think this is a good idea."

"I've known him since I was ten and he's a good guy. You'll see."

"You're going to introduce me?"

"Why not? The cat is out of the bag. What's the harm? Besides, John will get a kick out of you."

Pulling in the lot, I loaded Alida back into the bag and we were in time to board the ferry. As the only passengers, I thought it was safe to let the pixie out and we enjoyed the trip over to Dewees Island. I called John to let him know we were on our way and arranged for him to pick us up. The island is private and undeveloped, other than the residents' homes. John moved there when he retired and when I finished my training, Tony and I decided to move to Charleston as well.

When we disembarked, John was waiting for us in his golf cart. Five feet ten, thin with straight, steel gray hair and glasses, he looked like an old professor. Hugging me, he said, "Where is this person you brought for me to meet?"

Opening the bag, I let the pixie out and she flew up to my shoulder. "John, meet Alida. Alida, this is John Murphy."

Wonder filled his face and he said, "Oh, my. I watched the press conference this morning but never thought to have the privilege in person. It's a pleasure to meet you, Alida."

Tilting her head, the pixie said, "Pleased to meet you too."

"If I may ask, could you educate an old man and tell me what species you are?"

"I'm a pixie."

"That is amazing. Let's go back to the house so that we can talk, hmm?"

Driving back to John's house, he pointed out all the sights and filled our ears with cheerful chatter. His palatial home was tucked in the shade of the trees and much cooler. Entering the living room, we had an excellent view of the beach and boats out on the water.

"Sit, Cheveyo, please."

Taking a seat on the couch, Alida landed on my shoulder.

"So what brings you here?"

"You said that you watched the press conference?"

"Yes."

"You know about Tony and the Zephyri."

"Yes, I do. It's terrible but not unexpected."

"John, do you have any idea where they would have taken them?"

"Hmm. Headquarters would be too public, they would need somewhere private. There are several places that I can think of right off the top of my head. Why are you asking? You aren't planning to do something rash are you, child?"

"Rash? No, not rash, just—proactive."

"Cheveyo, I know you are a capable girl, we made sure of that but this is big. So big that the government will stop at nothing. Am I making myself clear?"

"Yes, sir. I can't leave them there though. You know I can't. They don't deserve this, no one does. After what Faraday did to them, it's wrong. Haven't they suffered enough?"

"I feel awful about it but I can't help you commit suicide."

"You wouldn't be. The Zephyri will help. I won't be alone, John."

"I don't know."

"Please?"

Shaking his head, he said, "I'm not even sure where they are. I would be guessing."

"You know or think you know."

Sighing, John said, "Oh, I can't, Cheveyo. I just can't. I love Tony like a son but I won't lose you in his place. He is still alive and while that life might not be pleasant, it is much better than dead. I'm sorry but I..."

"John, this is a matter of life and death. Mine."

"Pardon me? What are you talking about?"

Alida squeaked, "Chevy, no."

"I'm sorry Alida but we need his help." Continuing with the story to John, I said, "Um, the Zephyri weren't very happy with me for calling the cops and exposing them. They're after me. They already caught me once. Alida helped me escape or I might be dead right now. If I could tell them the location of their people, I think they'll call off the dogs."

Grimacing, John said, "I see. Well, that does put a different spin on things. Thank you, Alida. I am in your debt."

The pixie said, "It was the least I could do."

Tapping a finger on his cheek, John said, "I believe the most probable place is in West Virginia. It's in the mountains and there isn't a way in except by helicopter."

Retrieving an atlas, he showed me the location. A

window shattered and I dove to the floor instinctively. Scanning the room, I saw that the window on the side of the house was broken. Another shot sunk into the wall behind me and we scrambled toward the couch. I think my assassins were back but how had they found me? "Do you have any weapons, John?"

"No, I don't usually have the need. Friends of yours?"

"You could say that."

Switching strategies, the hit men sprayed the living room with bullets and a few ricocheted off a bronze bust of Abraham Maslow. Teetering for a moment on the end table, it fell over onto John's head before I could stop it. "Shit! John, can you hear me?" No answer.

Peeking over the back of the couch, I saw Mitch and Dave's slow advance toward the house. I checked John's pulse and it was strong and even but he needed to get to a hospital. Blood ran down his temple. What could I do? *"Anoigo."*

The air shimmered, as if over hot pavement and I grabbed John under the arms, dragging him to the portal.

Alida asked, "What are you doing?"

"Getting out of here."

"You can't take him to Tweentown."

"Wanna bet? Watch me."

Buzzing over my head, the pixie flew through the door and disappeared. John in tow, I backed into the doorway and darkness.

John was gone.

CHAPTER 6

"Oh my God! Where is he?"

Glancing around, Alida said, "Keep it down. I told you. You can't bring a human into Tweentown. It's forbidden."

In a loud whisper, I asked, "What about me? I'm here; I'm human."

"The Praetorian brought you. When Kegan caught you, he or Sophia keyed the door to accept you. No human may enter without permission but you shouldn't have been able to open the portal in the first place."

"What do you mean?"

"All Zephyri are given access from the time they are born. The spell associated with the word *anoigo* only works for known Zephyri citizens; it doesn't work for anyone but Zephyri. Do you understand what I'm saying?"

"No, all I know is that John is helpless and we abandoned him. We have to go back."

"You'll never make it, Chevy. Doyle has told the Praetorian by now that we went through the Antechamber. They will be looking for you. Why don't we turn ourselves in?"

Incredulous, I shouted, "What! Are you nuts?"

"No, but you have the location that John gave you. Weren't you going to trade that for your life?"

"Yeah, but I don't know that they're there. I need to check first. If I show up and give them the information and the Zephyri aren't where I said, I'm done. I don't have anything and they might execute me anyway."

"True."

"What are we going to do?"

Her skin brightened to vivid pink and she said, "Let's go to the Colony. We can wait there and maybe find a way out later."

"But what about John?"

"Someone at the Colony could go and check on him for you."

Biting my thumbnail, I said, "You think they would?"

"Yeah, no problem."

"All right. Let's go."

Skirting the main streets, we made it to Alida's home in about ten minutes. Made of gray stone, it resembled a sixty-foot silo with a ring of windows around the top. The entrance was an arch with no door. Inside, it was similar to a huge chicken coop, with thousands of nests laid out in a grid, covering every inch of the walls. The cubicles were about one foot square at the bottom and half way to the top the size increased to two feet. A large ring in the center of the room served as a fire pit. When I walked in, hundreds of pixies in every shade of the rainbow mobbed us, shouting questions. Two magenta colored pixies hugged Alida with abandon.

"Oh, we were so worried. Are you okay?"

"Yes, mama, I'm fine. Lay off, will ya?"

"Don't sass your mother, Alida. When you disappeared again, she was beside herself. Then the Praetorian came here looking for you... Your poor mother nearly had apoplexy."

Alida said, "I know I made you worry but I'm fine and I brought company."

Extracting herself from the pink pixies, Alida came to hover in front of me and said, "Mama, Papa this is Chevy. Chevy, this is my mother, Shayle and my father, Jan."

The difference between them was slight. Jan was a touch bigger and Shayle's head was more round but that was all. I would never be able to tell one from the other without help. "It's nice to meet you. Alida has been an enormous help to me."

Jan responded, "As well she should be but she could have told us where she was going. You are welcome here, Chevy."

Shayle said, "Oh, where are my manners? We have a guest room for you. Come with me girls."

Girls? Keeping my comments to myself, I followed Shayle to the other side of the room. Another arch led to a beautiful human size room with a bed, dresser and bathroom.

"You will be comfortable here. We'll have to start the fire pit and make a special dinner."

Alida interrupted her mother and said, "Mama, we need to send someone to Charleston to check on a friend of Chevy's."

"Why? What happened?"

"Men shot at Chevy and her friend got knocked unconscious. She's afraid they might have done something to him and he needs healing."

"That's dreadful! Where is your friend?"

I said, "His name is John Murphy and he lives on Dewees Island."

"We'll take care of it. Cinny!"

Another pixie came in the room and Shayle said, "Cinny, take some of your brothers and sisters and check on Chevy's friend for her. His name is John Murphy and he's on Dewees Island. He's been hurt, so take some elixir but be careful; men with guns may still be around. Oh, Chevy dear, did you come in from there?"

"Yes ma'am."

"Well, that will make it much simpler; there will be a door in the Antechamber. On the double, Cinny. Go!"

Cinny flew out of the room like a shot and the commotion in the main chamber made me nervous. "Aren't you afraid they will be hurt?"

Laughing, she said, "Hurt? By humans? That's ridiculous! They can't hurt my babies."

Recalling Faraday's lab, I said, "If you say so, ma'am. I, uh, I'm grateful for your hospitality."

"It's nothing. You freed Alida. Anything we can do for you, just ask."

"Aren't you afraid the Praetorian will find out that you helped me?"

"Don't fret about it, dear. Everything will turn out fine. Now, you get settled, I'm going to get dinner started."

Shayle began shouting orders the moment she was out of the room. In an effort to distract myself from thoughts of my own mother, I concentrated on more immediate problems. I needed to find out who was behind the attempts to kill me and locate Tony. The

Praetorian would have to let bygones be bygones, if I found the other victims. The problem was I couldn't do anything while I was stuck in Tweentown. That thought reminded me of another question. "Alida?"

"Yeah."

"What did you mean that only Zephyri can call the door to Tweentown?"

"The Tsái created the spell to include all Zephyri. From the time they are born all of the species have access but no human is able to enter, unless they are escorted by a Zephyri and granted permission."

"What about loopholes? Could there be a mistake or something he overlooked?"

"There are no loopholes. The system has been in place for thousands of years and the Tsái doesn't make mistakes."

"You make him sound like a god."

"No, he isn't a god but he's been around forever and has literally thought of everything."

Frowning, I said, "Wait. Are you saying the current Tsái is the one that set up the spell, that he is thousands of years old?"

"There is no *current* Tsái. He's it. He not only set up the spell for the door but created Tweentown."

Scoffing, I said, "No one can live that long. It's impossible."

Tilting her head, Alida asked, "Chevy, how old do you think I am?"

"I don't know, maybe fifteen."

"Tack a zero on the end and you'd be close."

"Oh, come on."

Staring at me unblinking, Alida remained mute.

"You can't be."

Nodding, she said, "I'm one hundred and fifty-two years old. My parents are six hundred and some change. All Zephyri live at least five hundred years but some longer. Pixies live about a thousand years."

Dropping my boogie bag to the floor, I collapsed on the bed. How could this be? I couldn't process it. What would anyone do with a life that long? Wouldn't you get bored? What about everybody else? For the Zephyri that question was moot. Their family and friends lived just as long. "How old is the Tsái? What species is he?"

"Nobody knows."

"You have to have an idea."

"Uh-uh. He's been around longer than any story the old ones tell and no one knows what he is. His title means 'maker' in Greek."

"Maker of what?"

"Tweentown for one, beyond that, I don't know."

"I suppose that's enough to earn the title. So which species lives the longest?"

"Overall, I think it's the vampires. Barring power struggles, they live forever."

"Power struggles?"

"Sure. Fights for succession are constant."

"Haven't you guys ever heard of voting?"

"We aren't human, Chevy. No one is sent to prison for crimes they commit."

"What about the dungeon?"

"That's a holding area. Prisoners stay there until their leader has time to deal with them but it isn't considered a punishment."

"What's the penalty for, let's say—stealing?"

"It depends on the Council member's mood. They're very creative. It could be anything from losing everything to death."

Her attitude baffled me. "You seem so blasé about it. Don't you think death is a bit severe?"

Shrugging she repeated, "We aren't human. It's how things are done here."

One of the pixies came to the door and said, "Your friend is all right."

"Oh, you're back already? Were the gunmen gone?"

"Yeah, no sign of them. John was still unconscious but we gave him some elixir and he healed fine."

"Did you talk to him?"

Snickering, he said, "You could say that. He interrogated us like suspects until we convinced him that we were friends of yours. He didn't appreciate it when we refused to tell him where you were."

"No, he wouldn't but you told him I was okay?"

"Yes. He said not to worry about him and to take care of yourself."

Making a huge guess, I said, "Thank you, Cinny."

"You're welcome, Chevy." Winking at me, he said, "By the way, good guess."

Flaming red, I gave him a weak grin before he left. I was never going to be able to tell them apart.

Determined to make progress, I tried to get our conversation back on track. "How do we figure out why I was able to open the portal to Tweentown?"

"I don't know. We could look up your parents..."

"I've tried that. There are no records of them in any of the databases."

Scowling at me, she said, "As I was saying, we could look them up in the Library after dinner. We have a complete genealogy record for all species, including humans."

"How is that possible? No one can keep track of every family tree on the planet."

"Everything is possible with magic."

Unconvinced, I said, "Okay, we'll check but even if we find my parents in the records, it won't answer the question of how I was able to call the door. I'm human, not Zephyri. What about library staff? Won't we be seen?"

"There's no librarian and it's in a secluded section of town. Not many people go down there; we'll be fine if we're careful."

Shayle called from the other room. "Girls! Dinner's done."

A fire burned in the pit with a roast pig on a spit and the pixies had set up a table nearby. Shayle, I assumed, was perched on the back of the chair smiling. "Have a seat, Chevy. You're the guest of honor."

Taking flight as I sat, she waved in a group of four pixies bearing a loaded plate. Roast pork, bread, green beans, potatoes and a salad were on the menu. Two more pixies brought in a glass of wine and I said, "Thank you ma'am. It looks delicious."

"Oh, stop the ma'am business. Call me mama or Shayle."

"Yes—Shayle."

"That's better. Eat up."

Glancing around at all the pixies staring at me, I said, "What about the rest of you?"

Shayle said, "We've eaten."

"Alida hasn't."

Intervening, Alida said, "Chevy, how and what we eat wouldn't be very appetizing to you. I'll grab something later."

"What do you mean?"

"We prefer our food still kicking."

Uncomfortable and trying to ward off the mental images, I said, "Oh." Picking up the fork, I dug in. For creatures that didn't cook their food, the cuisine was delicious.

Alida said, "Mama, after Chevy eats, we're going to the Library to look up her ancestors."

"Why?"

"When the humans were shooting at us, Chevy opened the door to Tweentown."

A chorus of gasps hissed through the tower. Shocked, Jan and Shayle said, "What? That's impossible! How?"

"That's what we were wondering. She might have some Zephyri blood in her family."

One of the throng came forward sniffing my armpit. Surprised and insulted, I pulled away and shrieked, "Hey!"

Shayle said, "Bangle, that's rude!"

Bangle said, "Why? Anyway, she smells human."

Answering, Jan said, "Human's do not scent each other. It's considered rude in their society."

"That's dumb."

Jan said, "Enough. Apologize to Chevy."

Sulking, Bangle mumbled, "Sorry."

"It's okay. I didn't understand either."

Mollified, she landed on the table and watched with rapt interest, while I ate. Ignoring Bangle, I listened to the others speculate on my predecessors. It was ridiculous but I did want to see the records. My search for ancestors or extended family had been a dismal failure. If the Zephyri did have a list of my relatives, I wanted to see it.

Being alone sucked.

Finished with the meal, I thanked Shayle and offered to help clean up. True to form, the pixie matriarch refused. An odd mix of June Cleaver and General Patton, I liked Shayle a lot. When she asked me to call her mama, I almost did but couldn't out of respect for my own mother.

Bangle insisted on coming along and Shayle didn't object, so the three of us slipped around the Colony, into the shadows. Encountering no one, we made good time until voices caused us to dive for cover.

"Hit her again, Mel!"

Duck walking, we moved to a gap in the bushes and peered through the branches. Four boys ringed an angel, pelting her with stones. She stood, head held high and took the abuse stoically. How could these little delinquents hurt a beautiful angel? Intent on stopping the bullies, I started to stand, when Alida stopped me.

"You can't Chevy. If they see you, we're toast."

"But this is despicable."

"I know it's not the best behavior but it's not worth your life—or mine."

The angel's white hair, wings and dress made her the picture of purity and goodness. What had their parents taught these hooligans? It wasn't all right to do this to anyone, let alone a divine entity like this. Dropping my shield, I connected with the angel and fell into a deep well of sorrow. Unable to handle the anguish, I pulled away. Considering the ramifications, I thought that saving the creature might be worth my life but not Alida's and Bangle's. They didn't deserve death for helping me but... Taking a measure of the sadness that I had received, I channeled it into the boys. Trembling, they dropped the rocks and ran away sobbing. That should take care of them for a while.

Confused, the angel looked after the boys for a moment, before continuing. Grinning from ear to ear, I looked at Alida, proud of my accomplishment.

With a sour look, she said, "You shouldn't have done that."

"Why? Someone had to do something. This way, no one knows about me and I taught them a lesson. How could they pick on an angel? She didn't even defend herself."

Bangle giggled, while Alida frowned and explained. "First of all, she isn't an angel. Second, her name's Leukosia and she's evil. Those children were probably getting her back for something she did to them."

I shook my head and said, "I read her; the only feeling she had was grief. Whatever she is, it isn't evil; I'd bet my life on it. If she's not an angel, what is she?"

"Pure poison. The story is that the Tsái made her mute as punishment."

"Why?"

"We don't know but his justice is good enough for me."

"Is that right? So I deserve to die? That's why you're helping me? I haven't been real impressed by the Tsái's judgment."

"That's different. If you met her, you'd know."

"The sole difference between us is that he hasn't caught me. I read her emotions; they weren't evil, she's suffering. In this instance, I know her better than you do."

"It doesn't matter. We should get going."

The rest of our journey was silent. Alida may say the Tsái wasn't a god but she acted as if he was. No one was infallible and I counted two monstrous errors thus far. Taking away Leukosia's voice might be cleaner than cutting out her tongue but it was cruel, nonetheless. She hadn't protected herself because she couldn't—ever. No one would take the time to find out what had happened. They would assume the benevolent Tsái was just and she couldn't argue. If she did anything to those children, they had driven her to it.

Alida said, "We're here."

Jarred out of my thoughts, I noticed we were standing in front of a Tudor style house. This was the Library? Gables and diamond shaped glass panes appeared to be straight from old England. Who knew, maybe they were. Opening the door for Alida and her sister, we walked into the foyer. Wood paneling as far as the eye could see, a grand staircase curved up to the second level and doors led to the parlor and dining hall. I wasn't optimistic about finding anything in this mausoleum. "Which way?"

"Upstairs."

Art from every period blanketed the stair well and I thought some of it looked familiar. The entire second floor was the library and the high vaulted ceiling included another tier. A central cozy reading area was open to both levels. Wrought iron railing ran the length of the third floor and thousands of tomes lined hundreds of shelves. What were the chances they used the Dewey Decimal System? "Please tell me there's some form of organization."

Alida said, "From what I remember, it's in sections; genealogy, history, fiction, reference, religion, philosophy, science and magic. I think the genealogy section is over here."

Leading the way, Alida and Bangle took off down an aisle, with me bringing up the rear. Alida stopped at the back corner of the maze and said, "The records are split into species and surnames. We'll start with the human books and go from there."

The books weren't labeled on the spine but they were in alphabetical order. I had to pull each one off the shelf and read the first page to determine which letter it was. Written in long hand, that was more difficult than it sounded. I kept expecting the next book to begin the human section but was disappointed, as every book named another species and subspecies. What in the world is a huma? Four books later, I found humans. Stacking them on the floor as I went, I counted seventy-eight books before reaching humbaba, the next species. "I didn't ask what an abada was or an ettin or any of the others but what is a humbaba?"

"It's a lion faced giant. An abada is a kind of unicorn and an ettin is a three-headed giant. Do you want to know any more?"

"We don't have time for all my questions."

Alida shrugged and said, "Why not? We can't go anywhere until it cools off or the Praetorian are distracted."

Pointing to the stacks of books on the floor, I said, "Look at that pile. It will take forever to go through."

"Nah, it'll just feel like it. Let's get started."

It took ten trips to move the books to the reading area. Sorting through them, they were also alphabetical and only three were for the letter S. Maybe this wouldn't be as difficult as I thought. Flipping through them, I was able to locate the name Singer and within five minutes, my own name.

"I thought you said they had complete family trees. There's nothing here but my name."

Landing on the desk, Alida touched the name and it opened as if it were a program drop-down menu, replacing the text on every page. My name was gone. Catching on, I turned to the last page and discovered that it hadn't disappeared but had moved.

Pointing to my parents' listing I said, "See, Chaytan and Tokori Singer. I'm not Zephyri."

"I wasn't suggesting one or both of your parents were one of us. I meant that someone in your family may have been."

Next to my name was an image of my tattoo. Where did they get it? As I ran my finger over the names of my parents, it opened, showing the reason I was unable to find any information on them. The names I knew were aliases. I'm sure they were legitimate. Native Americans don't usually go by their Indian names but their legal Anglo names. At the time, I didn't think anything of it but now it made perfect sense. My father was Joseph and my mother was Nada Honanie. Following the names back, I discovered both sets of grandparents, great-grandparents and great-great-grandparents. What I had hoped to see wasn't there, no cousins, aunts or uncles. I came from an obscenely long line of only children. How does that happen? The farther I went, the more I discovered. Was it deliberate? "How can you tell if someone in the line is Zephyri?"

"There should be a notation for which species they are like the nationality."

"You mean I have to open every name on the tree?"

"Yup."

"Great."

Cross-eyed, hours later, I slammed the book closed. "Not a single Zephyri. It was interesting though. From North America to Asia to Africa; they traveled a long way."

"Haven't we all?"

"I've been thinking."

"Uh-oh."

"I'm serious Alida; my father told me stories about magical creatures like ogres, fairies and gnomes but he said they were real. When I was little, I believed him, of course but after I grew up, I knew they were just stories. I thought he was teasing me. Now, I don't know. What if my dad knew some of these creatures, was friends with them. What if that's how I was able to open a portal to Tweentown?"

"That might be the case. Gnomes, brownies and several other species are known to aid humans. If they do befriend one, they take care of the family as well but how would they arrange for you to be capable of calling a door?"

"I don't know. Something else is bothering me too. Why did my parents use their Indian names? It's almost as if they were hiding but from what?"

Bangle had knocked over a stack of the record books and was leafing through one of them. She said, "Chevy, isn't this your friend?"

"Who?"

"The one in the hospital."

Kneeling on the floor, I looked where she pointed and it was Tony. "Yes, that's him." Touching the name, it opened and I turned to the back of the book. Joined by a line indicating marriage, Tony was linked to a Layla Costa. Tony had been married? Why hadn't he said anything? Touching her name, two dates were listed 1976-1995. She died at the age of nineteen and had a child but not from Tony. The name of the baby was marked out but not the father. His name was Bram Ulfer and according to the information, he was a wolf shifter. Birth and death dates were given as 1801-1994.

Stunned, I wondered if Tony had known about the Zephyri all along. Is that why he was taken? Did he know his wife had an affair or a child by another man? How had she died? Had Tony killed the shifter?

Retrieving the records for wolf shifters, I poured over the tomes looking for answers to my questions.

CHAPTER 7

A piercing whistle, like a dentist's drill, made me jerk my head off the desk. Clapping my hands over my ears didn't help. Alida and Bangle looked around confused. We must have fallen asleep. Shouting over the horrible noise, I said, "What is that? Turn it off!"

"It's the general alarm. You can hear it?"

"I'd have to be deaf to miss that. What's it for?"

Alida said, "It means that all Zephyri are supposed to return to Tweentown. It means that something awful has happened but you shouldn't be able to hear it."

Still yelling, I said, "It's louder than an air raid siren. You could hear it for miles."

"You can stop shouting, Chevy. It's not an actual sound; it's in your head. The Tsái is sending it to all the Zephyri across the globe. It will stop in a minute."

"So only Zephyri can hear it?"

Nodding, she said, "The question is..."

"...Why can I? We spent hours proving that I'm not Zephyri; I guess others besides you *can* hear it."

"Regardless, we need to get back to the Colony and find out what's going on."

Pointing to the books strewn all over the reading area, I asked, "What about all this? We can't leave it a mess."

"The Library will take care of it when we go."

"Magic again?"

"Cool, huh?"

I shivered and said, "In a creepy sort of way."

Maybe it was because I wasn't paying attention on the trip over but once we stepped outside, nothing looked familiar. Landmarks that I did remember appeared farther away and the streets were choked with Zephyri. "Where did they all come from?"

"Everywhere. The Zephyri live all over the world."

"There are too many; how are we going to make it back without being recognized?"

"With a little luck, everyone will be too distracted to notice you. The crowd will help obliterate your smell. The good news is that we don't have to sneak around; keep your head down and follow us."

Doing as I was told, I tried to keep up but constant jostling made it difficult. Angry faces turned toward me every time I bumped into someone. I apologized to the first few but dropped the courtesy soon after. It was pointless and I kept exposing my face. Besides, the last person I said 'sorry, excuse me' to slimed me with some putrid smelling goo. "Alida!"

"What's wrong?"

"Other than the stench of unwashed bodies?"

"Yes, other than that."

"Shouldn't we be there by now? I know the people are slowing us down but this is taking too long. Are we lost?"

"That's insulting. Of course we aren't lost. It's

taking longer because Tweentown has grown to accommodate all the extra people."

"It can do that?"

"Sure. Any time we have a major gathering this happens. Tweentown wouldn't be able to handle millions of us otherwise."

"Millions! There are millions of Zephyri?"

"We don't take a census but yes."

"I had no idea. It will take hours to get back to the Colony."

"Nah, the majority of the growth occurs around the outer rim of the city. We should be there in about thirty minutes."

"I don't want to be out here any longer than we have to, so let's get going. I need a bath."

Taking me at my word, the pixies forged ahead and I soon fell behind. Periodic glimpses of the pair dwindled to nothing and I began to panic. Claustrophobia tightened my chest and I whirled around scanning for a quick way out of the moving mass of bodies. Fingers, elbows, legs and parts I wasn't familiar with, touched me and I am ashamed to say that I freaked out. I couldn't breathe. Throwing my body in the direction of the buildings, my hand pushed against a squishy substance and sank into it. My fingers had penetrated the rotting flesh of what must be a zombie. Repulsed, I backed away, running into a wall. Was it contagious? Is that how zombies were made? Wiping the filth on my pants, I did my best to clean off the goop.

A fist the size of my head clenched my hair and lifted me off my feet. Grabbing the arm of the creature that held me, I swung around to face him. Snorting, he blew foul breath in my face, making me wretch. Ten feet of grime covered muscle filled my vision. The monster had heavy brow ridges, a wide flat nose and tusks protruded from his lower jaw over his upper lip. My hand slipped from his greasy skin, my legs flailing. Murderous rage made my skin crawl and it was focused on me alone. What had I done? Blood pumping, I broke out in a cold sweat. Getting a better hold on his arm, I looked for an escape but it was futile. Nothing I did to him would make a dent. I was trapped.

He rumbled, "Crow hair."

A two-foot meat cleaver appeared in my peripheral vision and I reacted instinctively. Striking out with both feet, I nailed the bastard in the nuts as hard as I could. Roaring, he dropped the cleaver and me at the same time. A large clearing developed around us and I ran blind into the crowd, sheer terror finding a path.

"Aaarrrggh! Crow hair!"

Screaming bystanders sounded close behind me. Desperate, I scanned the horizon and saw my salvation. The Colony glowed in the silver moonlight like a beacon. Shoving people out of my way with callous disregard, I cut through the horde.

"Chevy!"

With my attention locked on my goal, it took a few seconds for the voice to register. "Chevy, this way."

Alida hovered ahead, waving her arms. Hope bloomed and I ran faster. With a final thrust, I stumbled out of the crush onto the grass surrounding the Colony.

Alida said, "Inside, he's coming!"

Glancing back, I saw she was right. Slow, unsuspecting Zephyri flew through the air or were trampled as the monster plowed through the masses.

"Crow hair!"

"Chevy, inside. Climb the wall!"

I ran. Climbing the wall as fast as I could, I peered over my shoulder to see the giant body squeeze through the open doorway. Twenty feet up, I stopped and looked down. Thousands of blood red pixies swarmed the creature, while he swung his cleaver to no effect.

"Aaahhh! No bite, no bite, nooooo!"

His gargantuan body rose off the floor, floating toward the door and into the night. My heart beating out of my chest, I closed my eyes, pressing my forehead against the solid stone. Knees shaking, I reached into the cool dry earth with my mind and concentrated on breathing. *Inhale, exhale...* I was still trembling from adrenaline overload but was calmer and opened my eyes. As I climbed down, I couldn't help noticing the nests that I passed were crammed with Christmas ornaments, chains, jewelry, nuts, bolts, mirrors, rocks and beads. All of it had one thing in common; it sparkled.

As my feet touched the ground, my knees buckled and I fell on my ass. Deciding to wait right there, I braced my back against the wall and tried not to cry. I could not afford to break down now. I had to keep it together, for Tony, for Alida. I would...

"Chevy! Are you all right?"

Perfect timing. "Yeah, I'm fine, Alida. What the hell was that thing?"

"The ogre?"

"Yeah, the ogre. What did you guys do with him?"

"We threw him in the lake. He was overdue for his yearly bath."

Glancing toward the door, I said, "Won't he come back?"

"Nah, ogres hate the water more than anything. He's

forgotten all about you by now."

"What was his problem? Why was he trying to kill me?"

Her brow wrinkled and she said, "I don't know. They don't go crazy like that. What did you do to him?"

"Me! What did *I* do to him? He's ten feet tall and built like a tank!"

"Chill out, Chevy. I didn't mean that you deserved it. I was just asking what happened."

"He picked me up by the hair and was going to cut off my head!"

"Why?"

"How the hell should I know?"

"He just picked you up for no reason?"

Irritated with her doubt and lack of concern, I snapped, "That's what I said, isn't it?"

"You don't have to get snippy. I'm trying to figure out why he went after you."

"And I'm telling you, I didn't do anything except bump into him. That's it."

"It doesn't make sense. He shouldn't have even noticed you. This isn't normal."

"What around here is?"

Pursing her lips, she said, "How did you get away from him?"

"I kicked him in the 'nads. When he dropped me, I ran."

"Well that explains the clackers."

"Huh?"

"He said something about throbbing clackers."

"Where is everyone else?" The hum of thousands of wings answered my question. A swarm of pixies flew through the entrance like colorful locusts. Acting as though they had scored the winning touchdown, they laughed and gave each other high-fives. *Unbelievable.*

Jan said, "Are you all right, Chevy?"

"I'm fine, thanks to you. Are you all okay?"

"Yes but I need a toothbrush. Ogres are foul tasting beasts."

They ate him? Eww. "Alida said you dropped him in the lake."

"We did but our hands aren't big enough to get a hold of something that large, so..." He chomped down with his bared teeth. "Don't worry, we only nibbled."

"I wasn't worried." *Just disgusted.* "Why did the alarm go off?"

"You heard it?"

"Yes."

Jan said, "Curious. Did you discover any Zephyri blood in your family?"

"Nope, I'm one hundred percent human."

"How is that possible?"

"I don't know. Why did the Tsái set off the alarm?"

"Oh, yes. The Butcher was killed last night and public sentiment has shifted against the Zephyri. The Tsái doesn't want anyone hurt."

"I don't know why he would care, since he allows creatures like the ogre to run free."

Shayle gasped and said, "Chevy! I'm shocked. How can you say that?"

Jan asked, "Who would you have him lock up? Vampires? Trolls? Shifters?"

Unashamed, I said, "No, just the dangerous ones."

"We are all dangerous. Did you know that pixies are one of the most feared Zephyri species?"

"That's ridiculous."

"Is it? Why, because we are small?"

"Well, yeah."

"We are able to strip a carcass the size of the ogre in less than a minute. Does that mean we should be locked up?"

"No. I meant..."

"I know what you meant, child. You are human and in your world, every threat is supposed to be removed from people's lives. You think the Tsái should remove all danger from our world but he cannot and we wouldn't want him to in any event."

"If he's capable of all this great stuff, why doesn't he protect you? Instead, you protect him."

"We are not children. We take care of ourselves. The Tsái is our leader, as the president is yours. Don't you protect your leaders?"

"Yes but according to you, he is capable of doing much more."

"He is and does. There is a lot you don't know or understand."

Nodding, I let it drop. I wasn't convinced but didn't want to argue with him. They were nice enough to let me stay here and it would be rude.

Jan said, "The Council is meeting with some United States representatives in an hour. It's a private conference but they are showing it at the Arena. We need to go now if we want a good spot."

"Hold it. What about Faraday? Who killed him?"

Jan answered, "We don't know yet."

"Do I have time for a bath before we go?"

"I'm sorry child but you can't come with us."

"Why?"

"The Praetorian and Troll guard will be all over the

Arena. We can't risk it."

"Sophia and Kegan are..."

"Those two would be bad enough but all the Praetorian have been recalled to duty, twenty-four in all. Add the Troll guard to them and it is too dangerous. You must stay here."

I shrugged and said, "Okay. I'll have a shower and see you afterwards."

Skeptical, Alida asked, "You're not going to argue?"

"No. I don't want to be caught again, so I'll stay here. I'm going to get cleaned up. See you guys later."

Alida followed me to the bedroom and into the bathroom. You'd think she didn't believe me. After shedding my repulsive clothing, I climbed into the bathtub, ignoring Alida. After some fiddling around with the controls, I figured out how the water worked.

Still suspicious, she said, "You have to stay here, Chevy."

"Does it look as if I'm going somewhere? Oh, this shampoo smells wonderful. What is it?"

"Lavender. You're really staying here?"

"Of course."

Silent, she hung in the air a minute more before leaving. I finished my shower and got dressed in fresh clothes from my boogie bag. Puttering around the bedroom, I braided my hair, inventoried my bag and smelled the cologne on the dresser. Thirty minutes had passed since Alida left the bedroom; they had a big enough head start.

Picturing Faraday's map in my mind, I used the Council Chambers as a reference point and made an educated guess as to the new location of the Arena. The streets weren't as congested as they were earlier. Walking with my head high, I tried to behave as if I belonged and the people ignored me. Trolls stood at every street corner like grotesque statues, watching the passers-by. Turning down a side street, I faced a round building that stood four stories tall with arches around the entire circumference. It resembled one of the coliseums from Greece. Every arch was lit with a *fanós* and I could hear the conference already in progress.

Tempted to hurry, I circled the outside of the structure instead. Troll guards stood at every entrance but I wasn't concerned about them. They were the equivalent of crowd control police officers and weren't looking for me in particular. Deciding to dive in head first, I entered the Arena and took the stairs to the top level. A support post offered an inconspicuous place for me to watch the show.

It was like a live 3-D movie, only better. Aadí, the shifter rajah was thirty feet tall, in a full color three-dimensional holographic image. The grainy, pixilated problem with enlarged pictures wasn't present. The meeting appeared to be taking place right here in Tweentown. *Wow*.

The attendees included the four members of the Zephyri Council, the FBI director, Bill Green, South Carolina's governor, Glenn Moyet and three others I did not recognize. Eight men sat around a table with the fairy queen standing on the top.

Red faced, Green said, "We know one of your people was responsible for killing Faraday. Turn him over to us."

The queen said, "And why do you assume that it was a male?"

"Women aren't capable of doing *that* to a man. He was skinned, eviscerated and his cell decorated with the entrails for God's sake. You know who it was. Turn him over or..."

"Or what? As I said before, once we know who killed Faraday, we will deal with it. If, however, the culprit turns out to be human we expect a formal apology given to the media and broadcast worldwide."

Livid, Green screamed, "That is unacceptable!"

A sly smile on her face, the queen said, "Which part?"

Laughter erupted from the spectators in the stands.

His red face turned purple and Green growled, "All of it." Taking a deep breath, the director tried to reign in his temper and continued. "We further demand the names and residences of the entire Zephyri nation and that all of you as leaders of these creatures sign this agreement, duly authorized by the president."

Staring at the document Green slid across the table, the queen didn't move.

Jeering, Green said, "I can read it to you if you would prefer."

The picture of sweetness, Ellarian said, "No, thank you. May I borrow your pen, Mr. Green?"

Leery, he walked the pen over, set it down and returned to his chair. Ellarian glanced at Aadí and he pulled the papers closer while the queen picked up the pen with both hands. Leaning on it like a crutch, she tapped her foot as she read. Tsking, she marked out a passage, then another and another as Aadí flipped the pages for her. Done, she asked the rest of the Council, "Is this agreeable to you, gentlemen?"

Fenion and Baldr skimmed through the papers and

nodded. Each man pulled out a pen from his pocket, signing the document. Using Green's pen, Ellarian was the last to autograph the agreement and the rajah slid it back across the table, stone-faced.

Annoyed, Green stomped back over to the Council and thrust out his hand. "My pen."

The fairy gave it to the man, smiled and said, "Yes, thank you. It writes so smoothly."

Reseated, Green and the man to his right looked through the changes the fairy had made. The director started to respond, when the man next to him touched his arm, cutting him off. "Was there a problem with the size or location of the reserve?"

The fairy responded, "No. Twelve thousand acres in the mountains of Wyoming is sufficient—for a goat herder."

"Do you have a place in mind more to your liking?"

"As a matter of fact, I do. Our present accommodations are adequate."

"And those are?"

"Everywhere and nowhere."

"Madam, that isn't an answer. Perhaps you are not familiar with the art of negotiation..."

Ellarian's eyes flashed and she said, "It is all the answer you will get. I will not be tutored in diplomacy by a representative from the Parks and Recreation Department."

Cheers burst from the crowd in the stadium.

"I beg your pardon. I am the Secretary of the Interior and a member of the president's cabinet. You have crossed out every item on the agreement except returning your people. It is customary in any discussion that both sides compromise. Our demands are not outrageous but we are willing to work with you to come to a resolution."

"Chevy! What are you doing here?"

Swallowing my heart, I realized that I hadn't been paying attention to my surroundings. I was so engrossed in the debate, I hadn't noticed Alida or anything else. Guilty, I scanned the area to see if anyone else had recognized me. The swarm of pixies was half way down the section, faced off with an ogre. I was sure it was the same creature that chased me. "You scared the hell out of me, Alida!"

Grabbing me by the shirt, she pulled me toward the exit. "Let's go."

"I'm already here. What's the hurry? I'll leave when the meeting is over."

"Later, move now!"

Her urgent voice got me moving. Once we reached the street, I asked, "What's wrong?"

"We'll talk at home. This way."

Leading me on a winding path through the city, I got the impression she was trying to get rid of someone following us. Nevertheless, every time I looked, no one was there. Could they be invisible? Maybe they turned into a lamppost or piece of garbage. I knew jack about magic; the possibilities were infinite. Turning a corner, the Colony came into view but instead of proceeding inside, Alida stopped and waited. We stood there for five minutes before the pixie declared it safe. "Come on."

She didn't stop in the main room but flew straight to the guest chamber and I followed. "What happened? No one saw me; I was careful."

"Someone almost saw you. Sophia was headed your way when I spotted you. My father picked a fight with that ogre to distract her."

Knitting my brow, I looked at the floor. "Oh."

"Yeah, oh is right. What were you thinking? You put everyone in danger!"

"I'm sorry Alida. I thought..."

"No you didn't. The only thing you thought about was what *you* wanted."

"You're right, it was selfish. I'm sorry."

Surprised by my admission, she looked at me with suspicion. "Really?"

"Yeah. Can you forgive me?"

"Maybe. You need to start listening to me though."

"I promise. What was all the cloak and dagger about, if your dad diverted Sophia?"

Alida opened her mouth to answer but someone else spoke. "She was concerned that Jan's pitiful ruse wouldn't work. She was right."

Alida turned a putrid shade of yellow and my head whipped around to the source of the comment. Sophia stood in the doorway with her hands on her hips. Strolling into the room, she sneered and said, "I have been waiting for quite a while. What kept you?"

I said, "Alida, you really need to have doors installed. It keeps out the riffraff."

Alida asked, "Where's your keeper, Sophia?"

Resentment burned in her eyes. "Kegan is *not* my keeper; he's my trainer and he is otherwise occupied."

Incredulous, I said, "You're a rookie?"

"Yes and already much more advanced than you, human."

"As I recall, I wasn't doing half bad. If Kegan hadn't knocked me down with that leg sweep, who knows how it would have ended?" Knowing the attack was imminent; I dropped my shields and focused all of my attention on the shifter.

She said, "I didn't need his help. Humans are soft, weak, pathetic creatures. I will enjoy taking your head."

"You're getting a little ahead of yourself, aren't you, newbie? First you have to catch me."

Three strides and she was on me. Sensing the muscle tension before she struck, I was able to avoid or block, punch after punch. Sophia dropped her guard, preparing for a kick and I took full advantage of it. Rotating my hips, I put every ounce of power I could muster into a right cross. Stumbling back into the wall, her hand flew to her eye and she stared aghast.

"How was that for weak, you mangy bitch?"

The last comment could have been a mistake. Her hands blurred and I couldn't keep up. Pure instinct guided my movements and I managed to land a kidney punch but left myself wide open for an instant. Sophia spun and I couldn't recover in time. Unable to block or get out of the way, I watched as both her palms came toward my ribs. This was going to hurt. Air rushed from my lungs in an explosion and I felt a crunch. Staring up at the ceiling, I concentrated on trying to breathe. Nothing else mattered until a huge white wolf lunged for my throat. Snapping jaws, filled with sharp teeth, strained against my weakening hold. Over one hundred pounds, the weight was too much and my arms began to drop. As I abandoned all hope of surviving, Sophia was ripped from my clutched fingers.

Kegan wrestled the white wolf across the room and said, "That will be enough, Sophia. Go outside and wait fer me."

Ears pinned back, the wolf whined in response.

"Now."

Slinking out of the room, she did as she was told. I wanted to leave too but I couldn't move. My ribs ground together every time I tried to take a breath.

The vampire said, "Alida, fetch a long bandage."

The pixie said, "Why don't I get some elixir?"

"Nay, the bandage will do. Get it."

Standing silent, Kegan studied me. The laughing eyes were gone. Alida returned with the bandage and the vampire took it, approaching me slowly.

"Alida, keep an eye on Sophia fer me, please." Once the pixie left, he said, "Remove yer shirt."

Having trouble putting the force behind the word I wanted to, I still managed to convey the intent. "No."

"If I take it off, ye will not be able to wear it again. Is that how ye want to meet the Tsái?"

"I don't want to meet the Tsái at all."

"It is inevitable, lass. Do it."

Struggling, I rolled onto my side and cried out.

Sighing, Kegan squatted next to me and helped me sit up. Working my top up to my armpits was as far as I was willing or able to go. Quick hands wrapped my ribs tight.

I said, "You've done this before."

"Aye, a few times. Is it better?"

"Yes, thank you. What are you doing here?"

"I came to find out what Sophia was doing. We heard that ye had a—bad day."

"What are you talking about?"

"Tales of a woman attacking Bob and running riot through the streets."

"Who's Bob?"

"The unfortunate ogre that ye abused."

"I abused *him*? He was trying to cut off my head! Why does everyone keep assuming I picked on him?"

"He said ye kicked him in the jewels with both feet. One foot would have been enough, lass."

"Bob, was it? Who the hell names a ten foot ogre Bob?"

"I doubt that he was that large when his mother had him."

"Whatever. The point is..." Kegan's eyes sparkled with mischief. "You're teasing me."

"Aye, just a bit."

"So what was the ogre's real name?"

"Oh, that part was true. His name is Bob."

"Why did he come after me?"

"He doesn't remember. Ogres tend to get distracted."

"You're going to take me to the Tsái, aren't you?"

"Aye. Will ye walk or do I have to carry ye?"

Batting my lashes, I asked, "Any chance that I can change your mind?"

Challenging me with his eyes, he dared me to do what I was considering. "There is always a chance."

I couldn't do it. Seduction was not something I had used before, in any capacity. I would make an ass of myself if I tried it now. "I'll walk."

CHAPTER 8

A vampire, a werewolf, a pixie and a human go to the Council Chambers... It sounded like a bad joke. I wasn't laughing. Kegan marched me through the open door of the mansion, followed by Alida and Sophia. The shifter's eye was puffing up nicely. I couldn't help gloating. She might have done more actual damage but hers was more visible. Noticing the brownie by the door, I said, "Hey, Barmek."

"Hello, miss. It is nice to see you again."

"Not really."

Kegan glanced between us and said, "The two of ye know each other?"

"The last time I was a—guest, we spoke."

Taking my arm, Kegan said, "Come. The Tsái is waiting."

Racing ahead, Barmek opened the doors to an incredible room. At about forty feet square, it was beautiful and opulent. Our footsteps echoed as we moved across the marble floor. The coffered ceiling featured more of the *fanós* dangling from golden chains in the center of each ceiling tray. White walls were embellished with a gold filigree pattern and the windows were covered with ivory drapes with gold accents, flowing from the crown molding to the white marble floor. A long mahogany table with three empty thrones was centered on one side. Based on the size alone, I guessed the farthest chair belonged to the Vampire Regent. The fourth throne, which was closest to the door, was occupied by someone I recognized from the Faraday estate. It was the sexy guy I saw crossing Faraday's yard; the one all the cops ignored. At this distance, I got a much better view and wasn't disappointed. He was about thirty with medium length, straight, dark blond hair, deep blue eyes and tan skin. Slouching in the undersized chair, he still wore jeans, tank top and cowboy boots and didn't seem to notice us.

A petite dark haired woman knelt in front of the table with escorts at either side. She said, "I don't care. I would do it again."

Sitting forward, the man braced his bulging arms on the table and said, "Mercedes, you jeopardized all the Zephyri. I cannot let this go."

"That animal slaughtered Dante like a pig! Was I supposed to let *that* go?"

"You were supposed to trust me. We would have taken care of it."

"You have grown soft, Tsái. In your bargaining with the humans, Dante would have been forgotten."

This was the all-powerful Tsái?

Rage so fierce that it penetrated my shields, flared in him. "You have left me no choice, Mercedes."

"I don't want to live. Kill me and I will join Dante."

"As you wish." He nodded to one of the sentries. Drawing a broadsword, the guard sliced through the air and her exposed neck. Head rolling across the pristine floor, it left a bloody trail in its wake. Unable to look away, I watched as blood pooled under the body. I was going to die.

The Tsái said, "Bury her next to Dante."

The guards carried the corpse out and when I looked back, the blood was gone. How convenient, self-cleaning floors. In the center of the white marble was a black seal surrounded by a gold ring. At five feet across, it took a minute to recognize. No wonder Kegan had been interested in my tattoo. The seal was an exact match.

A slight squeeze from Kegan and I got the message. We were next. All decorum fled my mind and I dug in my heels. This cold bastard was going to execute me and the last thing I would do was help. Confused by the sudden change in my demeanor, the vampire frowned and pulled me forward. Bucking against his grip, I made a futile effort to free myself. Sophia took my other arm with a smirk and together they drug me to the seal. Feet sliding across the symbol, my tattoo burned as if I were being branded. The shifter jerked her hand away, yelping in pain and my shields came crashing down. Every person present cowered, as I flooded the room with terror. I felt them all and could not stop. Dim minds, shadows of my own, surrounded me, adding to the emotion in a self-perpetuating loop.

Gradually, I became aware of warmth, as if I were standing in the sun. It penetrated my bones, encased my body, forcing me to withdraw the plague I had let loose. Peace and comfort covered me like a warm blanket. Eyes the color of a stormy sea held me in their grip. Pure power radiated from him but it was tranquil, calm and I reveled in the sensation. My gaze traced over his sandy hair, long nose and thin lips. Laugh lines bracketed his mouth and two days of whiskers marred his tan skin. His individual features were not handsome but the overall affect was stunning. A jerky, halting breath filled my lungs and I winced, breaking the connection.

What was going on? I assumed the similarity between my tattoo and the seal was coincidence but why the reaction? I had never lost control like that in my life. How had the Tsái pushed me back? What was he? The answer to all of my questions was simple, magic. Nothing was simple where magic was concerned and I hoped to live long enough to get a more detailed explanation.

Kegan said, "Tsái, this is Chevy Singer."

The Zephyri leader exuded expectation, anticipation, as if he was waiting for me to do something. Sophia didn't give me a chance to ponder over it and said, "Kneel human!"

Uh-uh, not happening. "I don't think so, bitch."

Kicking the backs of my knees, she forced the issue and I knelt anyway. Alida landed on my shoulder in silent support and glared at the shifter.

Anger boiled in the Tsái and I thought it was directed at me. Rumbling a warning, he said, "Do not touch her again."

Huh?

"What happened to your eye, Sophia?"

Humiliation reddened her cheeks and I tried to keep a straight face. "The human got in a lucky punch, sir."

Pride welled in the Tsái, confusing me even more. Probing deep into his consciousness, I tried to find the reason for his reactions. The door to his mind slammed shut, creating a void in the room. How had he done that?

He said, "Perhaps we should send you back to

combat class."

Sophia said, "That will not be necessary. I won't let it happen again." The last was said with a growl and meant as a threat to me.

The Tsái said, "As for you, Alida..."

I blurted out, "It wasn't her fault, it was mine."

Without looking my direction, he thundered, "Do NOT interrupt me." Eyes wide and my skin crawling with electricity, I gulped as he continued. "As I was saying... Alida, you and your entire family should have your wings clipped for thwarting the Praetorian. Why did you do it?"

Her voice shook as she said, "It wasn't fair."

"Fair? What are you talking about?"

"Chevy shouldn't have to die for saving us. She was trying to help. She didn't understand."

"You could have come to me, explained."

The pixie remained mute and dropped her head.

"It is easier to beg for forgiveness than ask permission. It does not matter that she didn't understand; the effect was the same. The damage is done."

Steel rang as Sophia drew a sword from thin air. It made an audible whoosh as it descended. Frozen, I couldn't warn Alida in time. I imagined the shifter's face, a mask of glee. I ached for Tony, imprisoned in a lab. I rejoiced that I would see my parents again.

Fury exploded from the Tsái and the blade never landed. A loud thud and clang snapped my head to the side. Sophia slid down the wall next to the door, slumping on the marble. Whimpering, she got to her hands and knees.

He said, "I said, do not touch her."

"I—apologize Tsái. I only wished to..."

"Do not make things worse by lying. Perhaps it was

a mistake to train one so young in the Praetorian."

Stricken, Sophia begged, "No! Please Tsái. I will do better. Please don't take this from me. It is all I have."

"I will discuss it with Aadí."

"Thank you, Tsái."

Turning back to me, he dismissed the shifter without a word. Puzzled, he tilted his head and stared at me. Uncomfortable under the scrutiny, I squirmed until I couldn't stand it anymore. Defiance brought me to my feet. Leaning back in his chair, the Tsái stroked his jaw in contemplation. What was he deliberating? "What?"

Cocking his brow, he said, "I am wondering what to do with you."

Emboldened by the calm response, I said, "I have a suggestion."

"Oh?"

"You can start by releasing me. You have no right to hold me prisoner."

"Don't I?"

"No. I am an American citizen and an agent of the National Clandestine Service. Bringing me here against my will constitutes kidnapping, which is a federal crime. Further, neither Alida nor I did anything wrong. If I hadn't stumbled into Faraday's lab, they could have been killed or worse. If anything, you should be grateful."

His face never showed any emotion as he listened. Folding his hands across his waist, he said, "I suppose I should be grateful that our world, which has remained hidden from humans for ten thousand years is now on every cable station in the world. I should be grateful that my subjects are even now being drugged and studied by every scientific method available to humans. I should be grateful that with one phone call you could have doomed your entire race. Do you have any idea what you have wrought?"

Put like that, I may have pushed it with the last statement. "Most people are good; if you give them a chance..."

"Good? What in all of history leads you to that conclusion? Humans will not stop until they possess all of our secrets and have killed every Zephyri on the planet. I will not allow that to happen. If I have to destroy every last man, woman and child to prevent it, I will."

"What! No, you can't!"

"Silence!" My chest quivered with the force of his command. "The future of your race depends on how willing your leaders are to accept my terms. It occurs to me that you might be of some use in that capacity."

Suspicious, I asked, "How?"

"Help me convince the human governments to sign our treaty."

"You drew up a treaty?"

"Yes."

"What does it say?"

"Essentially, that the Zephyri are completely autonomous, worldwide, with no human interference whatsoever."

It would never fly. I said, "That will take a shitload of convincing."

Lips twitching, he said, "Exactly."

"What if they don't agree?"

"I will have to resort to more—persuasive tactics."

"That sounds like a fantastic deal. 'Give me what I want or die.' I thought the purpose of a treaty was peace. It sounds as if you're more interested in a dictatorship."

Alida yanked on my hair but I wasn't going to be bullied.

"Why don't you just stage a coup? It would be easier than a treaty."

Raising an eyebrow at my attitude, he said, "I don't know. Do you think I should?"

"I realize that you're not from around here but I thought sarcasm was a universal language. I'll keep it simple. No, I don't think you should overthrow my government."

Resting his chin in his hand, he said, "I think perhaps it is you that missed the irony."

That hadn't gone as planned. "You're dodging the issue."

"Am I?"

"Yes, you are. Threats are not the way to negotiate a peace treaty."

"Is that right? Have you participated in many negotiations?"

The asshole was making fun of me. "Normally..."

He interrupted me. *"Normally*, the parties involved in a treaty are already at war. Threats are moot because they have done their worst and it isn't worth it any more. I would like to avoid the fields of corpses, burnt homes and rubble. Skipping the death and destruction of a war benefits everyone."

"That depends on what they have to give up in return."

"This treaty doesn't alter anything that didn't exist a week ago. It maintains the status quo."

Narrowing my eyes, I said, "Why don't I believe you?"

"I don't know."

"You're telling me that all you want is everything back to the way it was?"

"Nothing will ever be as it was but it is possible to coexist with mutual respect."

"What happens if I *don't* help you?"

Pausing for a moment, he said, "I will think of something suitable."

Recalling what Alida said about the punishments here and the Tsái's own statement about persuasive tactics, I would do almost anything to avoid Zephyri creativity and that damn dungeon. If he wasn't telling the truth, I would find out and blow the whistle. If he was then it was all good. Still reluctant, I said, "Okay, I'm in."

"Not so fast. There are conditions. You may find them unacceptable."

There's always a catch. I should have asked first. *Idiot.*

"You will work for me as a liaison to the human governments. You will never reveal anything you learn about the Zephyri or me to anyone without my express permission. Neither will you tell any human about the existence of Tweentown or any Zephyri home. You will not contact another human or leave Tweentown until the treaty is signed, unless I deem otherwise. You will do as I say in every situation without argument and of course, you will be compensated for your time. Do you understand and accept my terms?"

"What's behind door number three?"

The corner of his mouth quirked as he said, "Choose."

"There are a few problems with this arrangement."

"Please illuminate us."

Pursing my lips in annoyance, I said, "First of all, I work for the NCS."

"So you said."

"Won't there be a conflict of interest?"

"Not if you keep the alternative in mind."

"No. I mean that I have no idea what your real intentions are. I can't, I won't, reassure my government or any other that you mean them no harm if I don't know it's true. I will not lie for you."

"You are referring to your—ability."

"Yes."

Thoughtful for a minute, he said, "I will allow a certain amount of transparency to my mind when the situation calls for it. Will that soothe your conscience?"

"May I ask you something?"

"You don't seem to have a problem expressing yourself."

Rolling my eyes, I said, "How did you do that?"

"What?"

"Shut me out. You knew I was probing your mind and cut me off."

"In time, I may teach you."

"Are you telepathic?"

Eyes sparkling, he said, "Among other things, yes."

Replaying my thoughts since entering the room, my face warmed. *Oh, shit.*

"Oh shit is right."

Floundering, I tried to regain my footing. "Your conditions imply that you want me to parrot what you say, which brings me to my second point. I will give my own opinions along with whatever you want me to say and submit them as such. I will not be your puppet. Third, I will not harm another human, unless I deem it necessary. No order will supersede my free will. Fourth, I won't reveal anything about the Zephyri as long as they have done nothing wrong. I will not aid criminals. Fifth, I won't accept any money for this. It could be construed as treason. Last, I don't want any of the pixies punished for helping me."

Grim-faced, he said, "Your fourth point is unacceptable. If any of my people are responsible for a crime, you will inform the Praetorian or me. We will deal with it. You will not under any circumstance inform another human."

Thinking for a moment, I nodded. They weren't subject to human laws, so his *request* was reasonable.

He said, "I also do not accede to your demand for the pixies. Alida alone will bear the full responsibility for her family's actions. There must always be discipline or chaos rules."

I started to protest but he raised his hand and said, "Alida, since you seem to be so concerned with Ms. Singer's welfare, she is now your ward. You will keep her out of trouble, be her guide and protector. If she breaks our agreement, you will be in the pot alongside her. Understood?"

"Yes, sir but there are men trying to kill Chevy. What am I supposed to do about them with the no harm to humans order in effect?"

Sitting forward, he demanded, "Who are they?"

Answering for Alida, I said, "I don't know. I think it might be one of the people that were helping Faraday."

"When did this begin?"

"Right after I got home from the plantation. They said I saw something I shouldn't have. The second time was when I was visiting my friend John, yesterday after the press conference."

"Kegan, have it looked into."

"Aye."

"As she will be our guest in Tweentown for the immediate future, it won't be an issue but we will get to the bottom of it. Do we have an agreement?"

"One more thing."

Sighing, he said, "You are pushing my good will."

"Not this time. I think I can help with finding your people."

"How?"

"I think I know where they are."

"How did you come by this information?"

"A friend."

Suspicious, he asked, "What aren't you telling me?"

"I will give you the location, if I can go with the rescue team."

Glowering, he said, "Or I could pull it out of your head and leave you here."

"Yes, you could but I'm betting you won't."

Eyes narrowing, he asked, "Why?"

"Because you want my help with the humans and my trust."

Scowling, he knew I had him. "All right. You may go. Where is it?"

The door burst open admitting the rest of the Council.

Ellarian said, "Ugh! What is *that* doing here? Kill it. I have had enough of humans for today."

The Tsái growled, "Ellarian."

"Oh, relax Eryx. It was a joke. Well, mostly."

The fairy flew down to the center of the table and sat in a smaller throne I hadn't noticed before. It was almost cute. Almost.

Fenion, the elf king took in the room at a glance and sat next to the Tsái. The vampire regent ignored everyone and took his seat at the end of the table. Last in the procession was the rajah, who stopped to lift Sophia's chin, examining her. Aadí dropped his hand and circled me as if I were a used car. Patience at an all-time low, I said, "Are you going to kick the tires too?"

Completing his circuit, he stood in front of me and I had to look up. Meeting his gaze, I raised one brow. His eyes flared and he said, "No but I may take it for a test drive."

The Tsái said, "Enough, Aadí. What happened?"

Fenion answered, "Exactly what we expected."

Lowering his voice, Aadí said, "I will see you later, kitten."

A sour look on my face, I said, "When hell freezes over."

Laughing, he took his seat as well. Rejoining the more serious conversation, he said, "Yes, we reiterated that we expect our people back tonight and they refused again. What has been going on here?"

The Tsái said, "Mercedes is dead."

Ellarian asked, "She killed him because of Dante?"

Grimacing, the Tsái said, "Yes."

Confused, I worked up the nerve and said, "Can I ask a question?"

Fenion said, "You may ask."

"Who is Dante?"

"He was one of the Butcher's victims."

"But I don't remember a Dante. There was Gus, Malachai, Tagokk, Alida, Cain and Tony. Where was Dante?"

Sad eyes met mine, as the elf answered. "In the freezer, child."

"Oh no."

"Yes."

"How many?"

"Two dozen."

I hadn't saved anyone except Alida. I hadn't stopped anything. The ones that made it out alive were still in the same situation. They had just changed locations. "Do you have a map?"

"Of what, child?"

"West Virginia."

"Why do you need it?"

Answering for me, the Tsái said, "She may know where they are."

Holding out his hand, an atlas appeared in the elf's palm. Opening it to the great state of West Virginia, he said, "Please, show me."

Stepping up to the table, I pointed to the location on the map. "It's here on the border, on top of this mountain. There are no roads leading to it. The only access is by helicopter."

Fenion said, "A dwarf enclave is nearby; there will be a door in the Antechamber. We will send a party after dark. Thank you, Miss Singer."

I said, "Add me to the list."

"Pardon?"

"I'm going too."

"That would not be advisable."

Turning to the man in charge, I waited for him to say something. He sighed and said, "We made a deal."

"See?"

"But Eryx..."

"I know Fenion but she and Alida are going. Send Magnus, Kegan, Aspen and Nissa as well."

"Why Alida?"

"The pixie is responsible for her. They're a set."

I didn't want to interrupt but... "Excuse me, Tsái?"

"Call me Eryx, Miss Singer."

"Um, okay and my name is Cheveyo."

"Yes, I know."

Uncomfortable, I asked, "Eryx, I know you said that I couldn't leave Tweentown but I need to make a trip back to my apartment."

"I'm sure we can provide whatever it is you want."

"Weapons."

"What?"

"I need weapons. You know, guns, knives— weapons. Preferably my own."

"I see. I think we can come up with something to suit you. Come with me."

He stood and my jaw dropped. I knew he was big but—*damn*. I had never been this close to someone that much bigger than I was. Six feet eight and weighing about three twenty-five, he was huge. It was nothing compared to Baldr but something about him...

"Size isn't everything kitten."

Clapping my mouth shut, I looked at the rajah. "Huh?"

"Let her alone, Aadí."

"Is that an order, Tsái?"

Eryx said, "Shut up. That's an order." Laughter followed us into the foyer until the door closed. "Barmek, take Alida to the guest room. She and Miss Singer will be staying with us for a while."

"Yes, master. I have already had their things brought over."

"Excellent. Thank you."

"My pleasure, sir."

Leading me down a long hall, Eryx opened the door to a mercenary's wet dream. The room was separated into sections: artillery, blades and hand-to-hand weapons.

"Did you have something particular in mind?"

"Wow. This is amazing. A hand gun and knife would be fine."

Pulling a bowie knife from the wall, he said, "Here, try this."

It was a good fit. Shopping for a pistol was more difficult but I chose a 9mm CZ. It wasn't my Beretta but it would do in a pinch. I could have browsed all day but said, "I should take a nap if I'm going tonight. I didn't get much sleep."

"Why?"

"Alida took me to the Library to research my family tree."

"Oh?"

"Yeah. She had the ridiculous notion that I had some Zephyri in my background."

"I take it that you didn't find any."

"No."

"Why did she think you would?"

"Because I was able to open the door to Tweentown and I heard the alarm this morning."

Unruffled, he said, "I can see why she would draw that conclusion."

"We went through the whole thing and not a one. Then that ogre tried to kill me."

"Excuse me?"

"He picked me up by the hair and had this huge cleaver..." Electric slugs oozed over my skin and I stopped to look at Eryx. Muscles worked in his jaw and his eyes had gone dark.

"It's okay. I'm fine. He doesn't even remember me."

"What happened?"

"I uh, kicked him and he let me go."

"You kicked him."

"Yeah."

"That must have been one hell of a kick."

Grinning, I nodded and said, "Both feet."

Smirking, he said, "And that was the end of it?"

"Well, no. He chased me but the pixies threw him in the lake."

Roaring laughter rolled out of the Tsái and I couldn't help giggling too. Picturing it, I had to admit it was funny. If I hadn't been scared out of my wits, I would have seen the humor at the time.

Standing at the top of a grand staircase, Eryx opened another door; I realized we had been walking the whole time we talked. The room was breathtaking. A domed ceiling made of glass gave an underwater view of an aquarium. Ambient light showed colorful fish darting through the blue water. At the end was a king size bed with an electric blue comforter.

"Hey Chevy, isn't this great?" Above my head, Alida peered down from a cubby tucked into the wall.

"It's beautiful."

Arm held out toward one of the two doors, Eryx said, "That is the bathroom. I trust you will be comfortable here. Get some sleep. Kegan will let you know when it's time to go."

The door closed behind him and I took a deep breath. Controlling every single thought was damn near impossible and a strain. I couldn't be certain how much he could see, so it was better to do my thinking in private.

Swooping down to my shoulder, Alida asked, "What was that about?"

"What?"

"The Tsái laughing."

"I was telling him about Bob."

"Who is Bob?"

"The ogre."

"Bob?"

"I know."

"So what do you think of him?"

"Bob?"

"No the Tsái."

"I don't know. He's one big contradiction, wrapped in an enigma and he scares the crap out of me."

CHAPTER 9

Anxious to see Tony, I was dressed and ready when Kegan came to the door. "Are ye sure about this, lass?"

"I'm going. I have to get Tony out of there and I can take care of myself."

"Aye, I noticed. We're meeting at the Antechamber."

Tweentown had calmed down and the congested streets were passable again. As Alida zoomed ahead, I took the opportunity to say, "Kegan, I wanted to thank you for pulling Sophia off me. If you hadn't... Well, thank you."

"My pleasure, lass." Rubbing the back of his neck, he looked up through his lashes and said, "About earlier, I apologize for the rajah. I hope ye were not offended."

"It's okay. I've been around. Men just do that sort of thing."

"Not all men. Some of us are able to control ourselves in the company of a beautiful woman."

"The rajah would flirt with Mother Theresa, so the flattery isn't necessary. I'm not upset about it."

With a puzzled expression on his face, Kegan said,

"Twas not flattery but fact, lass."

When it came to sex, men were all the same. They were willing to say or do anything, if it increased the likelihood of getting laid. It was pointless to argue about it. "May I ask you a question?"

"Aye."

"Alida said that vampires burned in the sunlight. How can you stand it?"

"Long ago, only six vampires existed, the Empusae. They all had the same basic capabilities but each of the Six also had special talents. Every vampire inherits the powers that his or her maker possessed. Flight and the ability to walk in the sun were my maker, Kleítus' gifts and he passed them on to me. Quid pro quo?"

Uneasy about what he might want to know, I said, "All right."

"Is Tony yer lover?"

Coming to a dead stop, I stared at Kegan. "First of all, eww. Second, I can't believe you asked me that! Third, eww, eww, eww. I've known him since I was ten and I love him but Tony is like my big brother. That's just wrong."

Smiling, he said, "I'm sorry, lass. I was curious why ye were going to all this trouble for a coworker."

"Tony is much more than a coworker. He is my best friend and the only family I have left."

"I know yer parents died but don't ye have anyone else?"

"Well, there's John but he's more like a favorite uncle. We care about each other but we aren't as close as Tony and I."

Neither of us spoke for a minute and I said, "Kegan?"

"Aye?"

"Where did the symbol in the Council Chambers come from?"

"I thought ye might notice that. The Tsái laid it when he created Tweentown."

"Is it magic?"

"Everything here is magic."

"Okay, but does it have a purpose?"

"I don't know, lass. Ye would have to ask the Tsái."

The Antechamber was busy. Scurrying from creature to creature, Doyle looked frazzled. Eyes wandering, I saw a door at the front of the room that was new. Different from all the others, it was black with the Eye of the Phoenix set in the center. The location and night-day dial were missing. It must be for the Council's personal use.

Kegan scanned the room, pointed and said, "There they are."

Dressed all in black, three people waited in a group. One of them I recognized as Magnus. He stood about six-three with black hair and eyes. From our previous meeting, I got the impression he was a smart-ass. That and his T-shirt read, 'Paddle faster, I hear banjos'. Cute.

Next to him was the oddest looking and most beautiful woman I had ever seen. Five feet four, she had mahogany skin and silver hair, which was shaped into a latticework, designed to hold it out of her eyes. The pattern extended down to a level with her leaf shaped ears. Eyes the same color as her hair, tilted up but her thin brows were brown like her skin, which combined with high cheekbones, and rose-colored lips made her an exotic beauty. I didn't know what she was but it must be a type of elf.

The third in the group was a gold fairy like Ellarian but male. Twelve inches tall with gold wings and hair, he seemed to be trying to compensate for his size. Displaying his rippling physique for everyone to see, all he wore was a pair of black leather pants. He hadn't even bothered putting on shoes. How was a foot tall fairy going to carry an unconscious Zephyri down a mountain?

Handling the introductions, Kegan said, "Chevy, this is Magnus, Nissa and Aspen."

Holding out my hand to Nissa, the elf, I said, "Hi, nice to meet you." Looking me up and down, she said, "You are late."

What was it with female Zephyri? Was there a rule that said you had to be a bitch?

Without missing a beat, Magnus took my extended hand and said, "We already kinda met. I'm glad you're not dead."

"Uh, thanks, me too."

Catching one of my fingers, the fairy brought my hand to his mouth and kissed my knuckle. His penetrating gold gaze locked on mine and a deep voice said, "I'm enchanted."

Oh, Lord. What a piece of work. He must have cut a swath through the female fairy population. Although, he wasn't as attractive as Magnus or Kegan, he did have a magnetic presence. His cat eyes held you captive until he chose to release you. He might be dangerous if he was a few feet taller but what did he think he would do with a woman six times his height? "I thought Kegan said your name was Aspen."

A slow devilish smile spread across his face, making my eyes round in shock. Fangs on a fairy? Was he a vampire too? Would it be rude to ask? I never got into trouble keeping my mouth shut, so that's what I did.

Apparently, the elf was in charge because Nissa began briefing us. "I have already checked with Doyle; we will be using door eighteen. I was able to find blueprints for the building and have an idea where they are being held, so follow me once we get inside. Staffing will be the main obstacle for entrance. We will have to determine the best method on site." Shifting her attention to me she said, "In regard to you, Ms. Singer, I do not want you here but have been left no alternative. It is not personal; I do not know you and have nothing specific against humans. At best you will be a hindrance; worst case, we will all die. If you still insist on accompanying us, please remain quiet and out of the way." Turning her back to me, she walked toward our door without another word.

It wasn't personal? Ooh! Kegan tried to soothe my ego. "Lass, she..."

Cutting him off, I raised my hand and said, "Don't."

Following in the little Nazi's path, I tried to work it out myself. I needed to calm down but his excuses were just going to make it worse. *Unfrickenbelievable! Who the hell did she think she was? Remain quiet and out of the way? What was I, ten? Hell, I'd been doing this since I was ten.* Absorbed in my inner tirade, I didn't notice crossing the door's threshold onto the mountain.

Away from the crowd, I was able to open my shields and dump some of the hostility. Funneling it into the earth, I breathed in the night air and felt better. Mental fingers extended in every direction, as I stretched my mind to its maximum. We were alone.

Using hand signals, Nissa let us know to follow her. Putting aside all emotion, I moved through the forest,

silent as a ghost. At least I thought I was until I saw
Kegan. The vampire floated six inches off the ground,
which made me even more determined to prove myself.
Distracted by my own thoughts, I put my foot down on a
stick. As loud as a gunshot, I froze, wincing at the noise.
Unwilling to look at the elf, I refocused my attention on
the task at hand.

The forest thinned as we approached our goal. Glass
and steel glinted in the moonlight. Concentrating my
talent on the dark building, I tried to find Tony and the
others. Tendrils of power wove their way through each
room, working up to the third floor. I couldn't find a
single living thing. Confused, I pulled back and drove
into the earth looking for a basement. There wasn't one.

Nissa was directing Kegan to circle the structure,
when I whispered, "Something's wrong. Nobody's
home."

She either didn't hear me or was ignoring me.
Keeping to the tree line, the vampire came full circle and
reported to Nissa. The longer I remained *quiet and out of
the way*, the more convinced I was that we were in
danger. It didn't make sense. No one was here but
something was very wrong. My stomach felt as if I
swallowed a brick and I couldn't sit still any longer.
Making my way over to Nissa, I said, "Something's not
right. The building is empty."

"Regardless, we need to go inside. They may have
been here but moved elsewhere."

"No. It doesn't feel right."

Annoyance clear on her face, she said, "Since your
friend is not here, there is no need for you to come with
us. Remain outside."

"Please, I don't know what it is but don't go in

there."

Signaling Aspen and Kegan to advance, they moved out of the trees onto the grass. Duty bound, Alida stayed with me. Watching the sky, the trees and the building, I couldn't locate the source of the threat. Pushing hard, I stretched my ability further than ever before but found nothing. My mind bordered on hysteria; I couldn't stay put. I darted out behind the four. Nissa looked back long enough to roll her eyes but I didn't care. They were walking blind into something horrible. Half way across the yard, my skin crawled and nerves screamed. I had to make them listen. "Stop!"

Tiny shards of glass exploded from the building. Kegan whirled and hugged me to him, blocking my view. Blasting heat blew us off our feet, with the vampire landing on top of me. The impact drove all the air from my lungs and searing pain made me swoon. My ribs shrieked as I tried to breathe. Debris pelted the ground and my protector. Unable to do more than whisper, I said, "Kegan, get off me."

Shoving on the dead weight covering me, I realized he was unconscious. I *hoped* he was unconscious. Uncertain if vampires had a pulse, I touched his carotid and felt the reassuring thump. He was out cold. Reaching around, I tried to shift his bulk, so that I could move. Sharp bits of glass cut into my palms. By the light of the fire, I saw my hands were coated in his blood. Shameful thoughts flickered through my mind. How were vampires made? Was his blood mixing with mine enough? I did NOT want to be a blood-sucking monster. Disregarding the pain, I pushed, shoved and strained at his body.

Evil blue eyes laughed at me as I fought. He was too

big. Wrists pinned over my head, I felt him pull up my skirts. Fumbling fingers tore at my undergarments. A sadistic grin split his face, as he reached his goal. Foul corruption seeped into my soul and I was defenseless against it. Turning away in a futile attempt at escape, I fixed my gaze on the trees.

Struggling, the dark haired woman screamed as I watched from a distance. Splayed legs kicked as he pummeled her. Desperate for aid, her eyes met mine and she said, "Help me."

A second explosion shattered the illusion. Helpless, I closed my eyes and threw my hands up, trying to ward off rubble from the building. One second, two, I remained frozen. Nothing landed. Peering around Kegan's head, I saw twisted steel girders, chunks of cement and tree trunks suspended three feet over our heads. *What the hell?* In the dim light, I saw my arms were still outstretched. This wasn't possible. Wreckage settled and I reacted; fear strengthening my resolve. Rotating my head, I located Nissa and Magnus a few feet away. Where were Alida and Aspen? Kegan took a deep breath at my neck and stirred. Good, I could use the help. His respirations sped, as I'm sure he became aware of the pain in his back.

Nuzzling my throat, he moaned, "Mmm."

Nervous, I asked, "Kegan, are you okay?"

"Mmm, thirsty, so thirsty."

Oh, fuck! Slag and wood dropped a few inches. *Focus damn it! He won't hurt you. He won't—bite you.* Hot and wet, a tongue darted against my skin. "Kegan! Don't you dare."

Moving up to my ear he said, "Ye smell wonderful,

lass. Were ye hurt?"

Trying to ignore the feelings he was stirring in me, I kept my eyes riveted to a piece of glass dangling over my face. "No, I wasn't but you were."

"Aye, I know." Caressing my face with his own, his lips brushed across mine, as he raised his head to look at me. Blood surged as his intent became clear and my eyes went wide. In a hoarse whisper he said, "I'm glad yer all right." Slow and steady, he descended for a kiss and I froze in panic. The refuse creaked. Following the line of my aching arms, he saw our dilemma. "Och! Shite lass, why didn't ye say somethin'?"

Rolling off me, his movement was painful but it allowed me to breathe again. "Thank you."

Staring up at the ceiling, he asked, "Are ye holding it up?"

"I think so. Every time I get distracted, it starts to fall."

"How did ye manage it?"

"I don't know. It just happened. How do we get out?"

Screeching metal and rumbling answered my question. Silhouetted in the firelight was a bulky figure that had to be the Tsái. Our bubble exposed, he stomped over the debris toward me. Arms flopping to the ground, I closed my eyes and tears threatened. I didn't care how he knew to come, I was just happy he had. Expecting Kegan to brief his ruler, I took the opportunity to look for Alida and Aspen. A few moments and I found their mental signatures. Both were unconscious and had been blown back into the woods but seemed unharmed. Noticing the silence, I blinked and found Eryx squatting over me, his face furious.

"What? Why are you mad?"

"Someone trying to kill my—people tends to irritate me." His eyes skimmed down my body and he said, "You were hurt."

"Not as much as Kegan. He's covered in glass."

"No. You were injured before. Your ribs are broken."

"Oh, that."

Snarling, he said, "Yes, that. Why didn't you tell me?"

Frowning, I said, "I didn't know I was supposed to."

"How did it happen?"

"Sophia."

"She broke your ribs during the fight?"

What was his problem? "Uh-huh."

Livid, he turned on the vampire. "Why didn't you heal her? I should..."

What the hell? "Hey! Chill out. It was an object lesson. I'm fine. He saved me from looking like a pin cushion."

Sneering, Eryx said, "A lesson?"

"Yeah. Unless I totally missed the point, it was to teach me not to pick fights with shapeshifters. That was the goal wasn't it Kegan?"

"Aye, it was. I didn't think ye understood."

"I'm not as dumb as I look."

Smirking, he said, "Nay, yer not."

Frowning at the vampire, I didn't know how to take the last remark but Eryx didn't give me a chance to consider it. Glaring at Kegan, he said, "You had no right." Speaking to me, he said, "Hold still."

"I don't have much choice. What are you going to do?"

"Heal you. I will have to speak with Kegan about his tutoring methods."

"Let him be. He's saved me twice and I think I can stand a little discomfort."

"Twice?"

"Never mind."

Glancing from the vampire to me, he said, "Drop your shields."

"Why? Can I keep you out?"

"No but I do not want to cause you more pain."

Damn, for a second I had hope. As I opened my defenses, the sensation of a feather stroking the insides of my fingers, palms, and arms made me jump.

"You restored your shield. Please, trust me; I won't harm you. If you fight me, I might."

"Sorry, it was reflex." Straining against my natural inclination, I opened wide. The tickle began again, moving through my body like an itch I couldn't scratch. After the initial shock subsided, I enjoyed it. Tendrils of power radiated through my limbs. At my palms, it stopped and they became warm. Trailing goose bumps in his wake, my midsection grew hot. Energy filled me, as he finished the examination. His withdrawal left a hollow, bereft feeling but I could have run a marathon. "Thank you."

"You are welcome, *mikroula*."

"What does that mean?"

"Little one."

"I'm six feet tall, hardly small."

Lifting a brow, he stood and offered a hand up. A zing went up my arm as I touched him. Standing in front of him, I admitted to myself that he might think of me as small. "What was that?"

"Residual power. Was it unpleasant?"

"No. I'm good. In fact, I'm better than good, I'm great."

While the big guy healed the others, Kegan helped me out of the bandage around my middle. The site looked like a demolition zone, small fires burning amid the rubbish. Who had done this? Explosives smacked of human involvement but how had they known we were coming? Who could have leaked the information? John and I were the only humans that knew where we were going. If I *was* human. I didn't want to admit it but I was beginning to have serious doubts about my heritage. How was I able to stop the building from crushing us? I had never shown an aptitude for telekinesis before. Empathy and dreams were bad enough. Now I had to deal with visions, clairvoyance and moving things with my mind. Why couldn't I be normal? My skin was still creeping from the images of the woman being raped. It had seemed so real. I could even smell the bastard's sweat. Recalling the face of the woman, I had a new understanding of my favorite bitch.

"Lass? Are ye all right?"

Drawn back to the current situation, I said, "Hmm? Yeah, I'm okay. Thanks again, Kegan."

Without my realizing it, the vampire had moved. Standing behind me, he rested his hands on my waist and I could feel the heat from his body against my back. Rumbling in my ear, he said, "Twas my pleasure."

Fortunately, Eryx chose that moment to return with Alida, Aspen, Nissa and Magnus. Eryx's face had gone from angry to ferocious. What had happened? Waving his hand, the shards protruding from the vampire's back shot out in a violent evacuation. A spasm racked Kegan's body and he grunted in pain.

In a hoarse whisper, he said, "I apologize Tsái."

Eryx growled, "Quiet."

Horrified by his cruelty, I said, "Stop it! You're hurting him."

His voice dripping with contempt, he said, "Didn't you want him healed?"

"Yes but this is vicious."

Kegan said, "Tis all right, lass."

"No it's not. It's..."

The Tsái interrupted, "An object lesson." Heat and light erupted from Kegan's back and his spine arched as he screamed in agony. Dropping to a heap on the ground, the *healing* ended as did my patience.

Two strides and I punched the fucker in the chin. Hands clutched my arms, dragging me back. "Let me go! You fucking son-of-a-bitch! How can you be so cruel?"

Unfazed by the blow, he said, "Let her go and leave."

Nissa said, "But Tsái..."

Booming, Eryx shouted, "NOW!"

Too pissed to be smart, I was pleased when they released me. Taking a running start, I drove my feet into his stomach. I expected him to fall but it felt as if I hit a brick wall. Dragging my ass up off the ground, I tried to hit him again. He caught my fist in his huge hand and I followed it with the left, to the same result. Trapped, he jerked my arms behind my back, pulling me into his chest. Screaming in frustration, I kneed the asshole in the nuts. Lightning flashed across the sky and electricity prickled through me, as he roared. Startled, I looked up and saw his eyes glow an icy blue. Fury still clouding my judgment, I wrapped a leg around his and shoved, hard. I must have caught him off guard because we both hit the ground with a grunt but he never let go of my arms.

"Are you finished?"

"Not by half! You mother-fucking prick. You cruel, sadistic, monster, how could you?"

"Stop before you hurt yourself."

"I'm not the one that's going to be hurting." Biting down, I tried to take a chunk out of his chest. A satisfying hiss sounded above my head.

Holding both wrists in one paw, he raised my chin away from his skin. "Look at me. Look at me damn it!"

Irresistibly, my eyes slid to his. The light had died and they were just eyes again. He didn't say anything, he didn't move, staring into my eyes, waiting.

"How could you? He stopped Sophia from ripping out my throat. He took the shrapnel from the building and could have died. He was kind to me, even when you were going to kill me. He..." Scalding tears rolled down my cheeks.

"I was never going to kill you, *mikroula*. I told the vampire to bring you to me, nothing more. I punished him for keeping information from me. He should have told me what happened with the shifter."

Sniffling, I said, "Bullshit."

"Which part?"

"All of it."

"It's true."

"You're a bully and enjoyed hurting him."

"Did you sense this with your power?"

"No. You have me blocked but I could see it."

Fog lifted and his emotions became clear. A tempest swirled in his stormy mind as he said, "I never had any intention of killing you. Do you believe me?"

I did. "You tell me."

"I don't want to invade your mind without permission."

"Why not?"

"You were correct earlier. I want your trust but I do not like to eavesdrop needlessly on anyone."

"What about Kegan? Why were you mean to him?"

Hesitating, he said, "I already explained that."

"But you had me shut out. Tell me again."

Face blank, he said, "The vampire kept the details of the story from me to protect Sophia. That is why I punished him."

It was the truth, at least some of it. He was holding something back though. "I don't blame him. Look at what you did to her. Listen, don't hurt Sophia any more. She's paid enough."

"Sympathy for our angry young shifter?"

"Just a different perspective."

Frowning at me, he said, "Why? What happened?"

"I had a vision."

"Show me."

Surprised by his unquestioning acceptance, I replayed the scene in my head. A faraway look in his eyes transformed to confusion and he clouded his mind again. Releasing my arms, he got up and set me on my feet like a doll.

"What? What did you see?"

"That wasn't Sophia. It was her mother."

"But..."

"We need to get back." Palm up, he reached out and said, "Trust me?"

Scoffing, I said, "Not on your life. What about the vision and telekinesis?"

"Telekinesis? What do you mean?"

"When you cleared the debris off us, I was the one holding it up."

He murmured, "Interesting."

"That's all you have to say?"

"What?"

"It's not normal, that's what."

"It is for the Zephyri."

"But that's just it, I'm not Zephyri. What's happening to me?"

"I'm not altogether sure. I will have to run some tests."

Leery, I asked, "Tests? In a lab?"

"Yes, my lab. Is there a problem?"

"I don't like tests or labs."

Furrowing his brow, he said, "I see."

I wanted answers but what was I willing to endure to get them? "Let me think about it."

"All right. It can wait. Are you ready to go home?"

Home. Where was home? Long ago, it was a cabin in the mountains of Wyoming but that was gone. The moment I touched his hand, we appeared in the Council Chambers Receiving Room. Disoriented, I glanced around to get my bearings. The rest of the rescue team was already present including Kegan, who looked much better. Rounding the table, Eryx took his seat with the Council.

Baldr said, "Report."

Nissa explained, "We approached the structure and I sent Kegan to identify any guards or personnel outside. Finding no one, we advanced. Ms. Singer claimed something was amiss, that the building was vacant and attempted to stop us. The structure exploded, knocking me unconscious until the Tsái healed me. Someone else will have to give the other pertinent details."

The regent said, "Kegan?"

"I was out cold, sire."

"Magnus?"

"Me too, sir."

"Was anyone awake during the interim?"

Clearing my throat, I said, "I was."

Continuing as if I hadn't spoken, he said, "Our most powerful warriors and the only one to remain conscious was a weak little human female? Someone please explain how this is possible."

I said, "It wasn't their fault. The only reason I wasn't killed in the blast was that Kegan protected me."

Acknowledging me for the first time, he said, "I don't recall giving you permission to speak."

Clenching my jaw, I said, "I don't recall you specifying that the weak human wasn't allowed to answer."

His mammoth throne tipped over, as he jumped to his feet. The clatter reverberated through the room. Terrified, I almost cowered but managed to stand my ground.

Aadí, the rajah, sneered at the giant, "Sit down, vampire. She is correct and I would like to hear the rest of the tale. Proceed, girl."

Annoyed with both of them, I grumbled, "Thank you, Rajah. When the building exploded, Kegan took the force of the detonation. He landed on me when we fell and a few moments later there was another explosion. I saw Nissa and Magnus but not Aspen or Alida. The Tsái arrived soon after that and healed us all."

Baldr set his throne to rights and sat, pouting.

Fenion, the elf, asked, "Why did you try to stop the team from entering?"

"I don't know. I had a bad feeling. I knew no one was inside but I felt danger."

"You had a premonition?"

"I guess you could call it that."

"Have you had other similar episodes?"

"No."

"Was Kegan knocked out by the first or second discharge?"

"The first, sir."

"Were you able to escape his unfortunate position?"

"Uh, no, I was stuck."

"Covered in rubble, no doubt."

"Not exactly, sir."

Eryx intervened. "What Ms. Singer is trying to avoid saying is that she has developed another new ability. In addition to the clairvoyance, she was able to stop and hold the debris off Nissa, Magnus, Kegan and herself. When I arrived, she and the others were buried under a mountain of wreckage."

Fenion asked, "Some kind of latent telekinesis brought on by the stress of the situation?"

Flaming red, I didn't care for the direction the conversation had taken. I didn't understand what had happened and the candid speculation made me uncomfortable. Nissa and Baldr's attitudes made me realize how the Zephyri viewed humans. They saw us as useless and feeble. Compared to them, I suppose we were. Regardless, I hadn't done anything worthy of praise. The mental tricks just made me even weirder.

Eryx said, "Latent for sure but I don't think its telekinesis."

Fenion asked, "What then?"

"I will have to do some testing but I believe it is air manipulation."

Ellarian, the Fairy Queen, scoffed at the Tsái. "Impossible. She's human, it must be telekinesis."

"If it was she would have been able to move the pile. She couldn't. They were in a small envelope until I cleared the area."

Sniffing, the fairy said, "The fact remains that she is human and incapable of using magic. There must be another explanation."

His lip curling in derision, Baldr said, "I'm sure this is all very interesting but we have more important issues to discuss. How did the humans know we were coming if the woman has been in Tweentown?"

All eyes locked on me. "What? I don't know. I want Tony out as much as you want your friends back. I couldn't and wouldn't say anything to anyone."

Kegan said, "Perhaps the information was planted as a diversion."

The implication clear, I said, "John is a friend. He would never send me somewhere to die."

"I did not say that he was aware of the ruse, lass."

"You think he was duped?"

"Aye, it happens."

"He's not that stupid. Anyway, why does it have to be John? What about the Zephyri? Can you honestly tell me everyone is happy about the 'new world order'? Maybe you have a traitor here."

Shouts erupted from everyone except Alida, Eryx and I. Accusations flew and I cringed in the face of the hostility. This isn't what I had in mind. I just wanted to defend my friend. At this rate, I would be lucky if they didn't lynch me.

Eryx's bellow sounded above the clamor, "Enough!" Waiting for everyone's undivided attention, he said, "All possibilities will be investigated but the speculation will have to be postponed; we have more pressing matters."

The queen said, "Yes. We will deal with this problem later. You are all dismissed."

Eryx added, "Except for you, Ms. Singer."

What was going on? Watching the team file out, I noticed they looked as if they had come off a battlefield. Clothes torn and dirty grim faces made me dread looking in a mirror. Nissa gave me a hard stare as she passed. I don't think I impressed her. Hell, I hadn't impressed myself.

CHAPTER 10

Barmek closed the door and I turned back to the Council. "What's this about?"

Eryx answered, "You are going to start earning your keep tonight."

"How?"

"We each have a meeting with members of the Presidential Cabinet and you will be accompanying me to see this president of yours."

"In the middle of the night."

Eryx asked, "Do you think he keeps banker's hours?"

"No but it must be two in the morning."

"Yes, it is. You will help me persuade him to sign the treaty."

"How did you get a conference so fast? Doesn't it usually take longer than this?"

"I'm sure it does, however, this particular engagement is not on his agenda."

Perplexed, I asked, "So it's a secret?"

"No, it's a surprise."

"Wait, what?"

"I said, it's a surprise."

My hands went to my hips and I said, "Let me see if I have this straight. You are going to sneak into the White House at two in the morning and ask the President of the United States to sign a treaty with the Zephyri."

Eryx leaned back in his chair and said, "In essence, yes."

"You're insane. You can't do that."

"Why?"

Sputtering, I said, "He's the president, you just can't."

Four vampires entered the receiving room, carrying a large bowl of water. "Who are these guys?"

Aadi's mouth quirked on one side and he said, "They are our ride, kitten."

I mumbled, "We're all going to die."

Eryx said, "You have fifteen minutes to change. Alida, you can stay here."

The pixie said, "But Tsái, you said I was to protect Chevy wherever she went."

"Aren't I enough?"

Deflated, she said, "Yes, sir."

Was I the only one that saw how ridiculous this was? Eryx was still wearing his jeans and muscle shirt and I was filthy. There was so much wrong with this scenario that I didn't know where to start. "Not to sound like a girl but I have nothing to wear."

"Your closet is fully stocked. Find something."

"Please tell me you aren't going to wear that."

He didn't even glance down. "Yes, I am."

The queen snickered. At least she understood, even if she didn't care. This mission was doomed if I didn't get him to make some adjustments. Where did I begin?

"Okay, let's say we get in without being shot, don't you think that it might be a little intimidating for him?"

"I want to intimidate him."

"Scaring people is not the way to get what you want. Fear makes people unpredictable."

"It works for me."

Jeez, what was I supposed to say? What was the answer? Looking to Alida for help, I watched as she tilted her head in confusion. She was so cute when she did that but she didn't understand either. A light bulb flickered to life. "Alida needs to come with us."

"Are you trying to make me crazy? I can't meet with the president. I can't go in my clothes. I can't scare the humans. Now we have to take the pixie. Make up your mind, girl."

"It's made up. Will you let Alida go?"

"It makes no difference if she comes but I will allow it."

"Great. I'll be down in fifteen minutes."

"You have ten."

Racing up the stairs, I didn't waste time worrying about my outfit. Clean would have to do. Grabbing the first top and pants my hands touched, I threw them on the bed and ran for the bathroom. I didn't have time for a shower but the mirror showed my face was every bit as dirty as the others. Shedding the grimy clothes, I scrubbed my face and then noticed my hair. I looked like a wild woman. Twigs, leaves and a single white feather stuck out here and there. *Shit*. Pulling out the braid, I drug a brush through it and called it good. Throwing on the jeans and blue jewel-tone T-shirt, I sat and pulled on a pair of cowboy boots.

Sprinting back down the stairs eleven minutes later, I slid to a stop outside the doors. Squaring my shoulders, I lifted my chin and entered with a little dignity. The

Council was huddled around the bowl the vampires had brought and didn't see me.

Fenion said, "Now."

Ellarian, the Fairy Queen, landed on a burly vampire's shoulder and they both disappeared. Swirling his finger in the water, Fenion whispered something unintelligible and they all bent over the dish again.

Alida joined me and I asked, "What are they doing?"

"Scrying."

"Huh?"

"They are using the water to see the cabinet members. It's like magical surveillance."

"Oh."

Eryx said, "Are you ready?"

"I can't believe I'm going to meet the leader of the most powerful nation in the world wearing jeans and a T-shirt."

"You're not."

I brightened and asked, "I'm not? Did you reconsider?"

"No, he is not the leader of the most powerful nation. I am. As I recall, you were wearing jeans and a T-shirt when you met me."

"Yeah but you were wearing the same thing."

"True. Relax, we may catch him in his pajamas. Will that make you feel better?"

"You can't be serious." He was. My idea better work.

The Tsái said, "You will introduce me as one of the Council members. You will not reveal what I really am. He needs to understand that we mean business. I will be asking him to call an emergency session at the United Nations to present our treaty on behalf of the Zephyri. Every nation must sign it, however, the release of our people is more important. If sacrifices must be made, it will not be at their expense."

"What if they don't sign or release the captives?"

"As I said, we will have to proceed with more persuasive tactics."

"Right." Persuasive was bad.

Alida landed on my shoulder and Eryx offered his hand. A deep breath and I was ready. Drawing me into his side, he wrapped an arm around my waist and the gold and white chamber transformed into a large beige bedroom.

We had indeed caught the president in his PJ's. Preparing for a restless night's sleep, he stooped over his bed, turning back the covers. His mind worried at something like a dog with a bone and he was exhausted. Eryx cleared his throat.

Whirling to face us, he said, "Who are you? How did you get in here? Simons!" Thank goodness, no one opened the door. "Simons! Security breach, get in here!"

Eryx said, "They can't hear you."

Backing to the door, he tried the knob without success. Turning toward the exit, he twisted, pulled and pounded on the wood. "Help! Help me!" Terrified, he swung around and said, "It will do you no good. My death will accomplish nothing."

My mouth was as dry as a desert. I said, "Mr. President, we are not here to hurt you. I would like to introduce two friends of mine."

The president's eyes narrowed and he said, "I know you. You're the one that started all this. Everyone has been looking for you for days. We thought you were dead."

"Dead? No, sir. I'm fine. Why would you think I was

dead?"

"You disappeared, your apartment was wrecked and with everything else, we assumed..."

"Well, as you can see, I'm very much alive. I want to introduce, the Tsái, Eryx of the Zephyri Council."

Stiffening his spine and tugging at the hem of his shirt, he stepped away from the door. Forehead sweaty with fear, he tried to put up a good front. He studied the Tsái for a moment and noticed the pixie. Taking advantage of my icebreaker, he asked, "And who is this?"

"This is Alida. She's a pixie. Can she come shake your hand, sir?"

"Uh, well... I suppose that would be all right."

Alida gave me a quick wink and approached the nervous man slowly. She understood what I wanted and was doing her best. She shifted from her normal blue to bright green. Hovering in the air, she extended her hand and said, "Pleased to meet you sir."

Still unsure of the situation, the president watched her for a minute. Turning gray, she said in her most pitiful voice, "He won't shake my hand, Chevy."

"Why does she do that?"

I said, "Do what, Mr. President?"

"Change color like that."

"Why don't you ask her?"

"Why did you change color?"

Alida said, "Pixies change color with their mood. Green indicates curiosity and I faded to gray because I was sad."

"What made you sad?"

"You don't like me."

"Well, I don't know you. This is all new to me."

"It's new to me too."

"I suppose it is. May I shake your hand, Alida?"

Flaring pink, she said, "Sure. Put 'er there, sir."

Chuckling, the president shook the pixie's hand gingerly. "It's nice to meet you, Alida. I'm Andrew Greshner."

"Back at ya, Andy."

A residual smile still in place, Greshner looked up at Eryx and I. "Ms. Singer, you were saying..."

"Yes sir. This is the Tsái, Eryx with the Zephyri Council."

The leaders shook and Eryx must have gotten the idea because he softened his approach. "I apologize for the door but we wanted to see you alone. I mean you no harm."

"That remains to be seen. What did you want to discuss?"

Eryx held out his hand and a thick ream of paper materialized. "This is a treaty we have prepared. I want you to call an emergency session at the UN to present it and I want my people returned."

Donning his most sympathetic demeanor, the president said, "I understand how you must feel but the CDC hasn't given the all clear yet. When they do, we will release them immediately. I assure you that their health and welfare is my highest priority and our best people are caring for them. As to the contents of your accord, I have convened a special advisory panel to review the situation and recommend viable options."

Eryx said, "There are only two viable options."

Greshner took on a fatherly attitude and said, "I know it seems that way to you now but there are always alternatives. As a matter of fact the panel has already made several promising recommendations, so as you can see, holding me hostage is unnecessary. We are taking your people and your proposal seriously."

"Apparently, you misunderstood my purpose here tonight. I came to meet you and present our demands personally. The treaty is nonnegotiable. Every nation will sign it as it is written."

"Look son, you're young and ambitious. I understand but it isn't going to happen. We are prepared to work with you on this. I heard that the location of the reserve wasn't to your liking. The government owns land all over the country, perhaps..."

"No."

"Excuse me?"

"I said, no. I am not here to bargain and I am not your son."

Uh-oh. I was about to interrupt when Alida said, "Hold it. Can I ask a question?"

Greshner asked, "What is it, Alida?"

"If I understand what's in the treaty, why won't you sign it? We have always been here. You just know about us now. There wouldn't be any difference from before, except we would be friends."

"Well, I uh... You see... It's not that simple."

"What's so complicated?"

Greshner said, "There's the land issue. A nation must have land with borders."

"Why?"

"Law enforcement, government regulations and natural resources all depend on national borders. We cannot allow another country to take from our own citizens."

Shaking her head, Alida said, "The Zephyri have always lived among you and never taken anything from humans. We take care of ourselves."

The president's face lit up. "I have an idea. In fact, it's the perfect solution. I am reasonably sure that we can grant the Zephyri citizenship in the United States. I can't guarantee the other countries will do the same but I am willing to speak with them on your behalf to that end. The United States might even be able to take all of you. Exactly how many Zephyri are there and which species?" Congratulating himself for his genius, a huge grin stretched across his face. I wasn't sure Eryx would agree but it could work.

Eryx said, "You would have me give you control over my people? You know nothing of their needs, customs or beliefs. You don't even know what they are. How do you propose to rule people that you know nothing about?"

Undaunted, the president said, "The same way I do with the rest of the country. They will have all the same rights as every other US citizen. They will be able to vote, work and live the same as the rest of us. This is a melting pot, we have citizens from every country in the world. We will all learn together." Pleased with himself, he nodded and said, "Yes, it's the perfect compromise."

Eryx's face darkened and he said, "And how much will you pay in compensation, when you take them?"

I was as confused as Greshner. What was he talking about? "Pay? For what?"

Eryx was angry but why? This would accomplish everything he wanted. Wouldn't it?

"It is customary for the government to pay compensation when it takes what it wants from its people. Eminent domain isn't it? Ah, but it wouldn't apply in this situation. Citizens aren't considered property. Perhaps you will just abscond with them in the middle of the night and keep them as lab rats the way Faraday did. Just think of all you could learn, the advances that could be made. Who would be able to stop you?"

As the Tsái speculated, the president became more and more furious. In part, it was that he was insulted but some of what Eryx said struck a chord in Greshner. He either planned to do what he was being accused of or he knew it could happen. Either way, he wasn't about to admit it.

"Now, none of that is true. We would never allow those things to happen. We protect our own, we don't imprison them without reason."

"Yes, there is always a reason. There was good reason to imprison the Japanese, Italian and German US citizens during the second world war."

Greshner said, "It wasn't all of them and that was a long time ago. We would never do that now."

"A long time ago? No, it was only yesterday. That is too far back for you? Perhaps something more recent? You publicly acknowledged the government's right to assassinate its own citizens on unverified accusations of terrorism. What else are you willing to do? Any excuse would suffice to take them. Although, the public health hazard claim was a bit thin, even for monsters. Your own people didn't believe it any more than I do. Thank you for your *generous* offer but the answer is no."

Andrew was pissed as hell. He stood mute, glaring at Eryx. Trying to get his raging emotions under control, he attempted a smile three times before he managed it. "That only applied to known terrorist collaborators. This is a completely different situation." Throwing the papers at Eryx's feet he said, "I will not sign that. I will not present your ludicrous treaty to the UN and I will not return your people until I'm good and ready. You have my offer.

Take it or leave it. You certainly won't get better from another country."

"I will get the same from every country on earth. One way or another you will all agree to the treaty. Copies have been given to your contemporaries and four members of your cabinet. Schedule the presentation for 9 a.m.." Opening his hands, the scattered papers reordered themselves, landing neatly in Eryx's grasp. Setting the treaty on the president's night stand, he straightened and looked back at the scowling man. "You have two days to comply with our demands or we will be forced to use more compelling measures. We will be watching."

Returning to my side, he took my hand and Greshner said, "Watch all you like, Tsái. It won't change a thing. Ms. Singer, how can you betray your country and your species this way?"

Stunned at his conclusion, I said, "I haven't betrayed anyone, sir. They asked me to facilitate talks with you. That's all. I'm doing this to help my country. I'm still a member of the NCS and a loyal American."

"Facilitate? More like manipulate. I've heard about what you can do. Well, it didn't work on me. I'm too strong willed to succumb to emotional control."

"No! Sir, I would never do that to you. Please believe me. I didn't alter your emotions, I didn't even attempt it."

Eryx must have felt the conversation was over because we materialized in my bedroom at the mansion. Alida flew up to her nest without a word. "That could have gone better. Why did you leave? I wasn't finished talking to him."

"Nothing you said would convince him and it went as expected."

"You didn't expect for him to release your people or

agree to present the treaty?"

"No, I didn't. Realistically, they have no reason to see us as more than powerless peasants with no resources of our own. We need to convince them otherwise."

"Powerless? What about appearing in his room, the door and the papers? He has to know you have power."

Waving a hand in dismissal, Eryx said, "Parlor tricks. That isn't real power and he knows it. They were meant as a demonstration to convince the weak willed and foreshadow the main event. In his place I would refuse as he did."

"Then what did it accomplish?"

"Exactly what you said, an introduction. We both have a better feel for who we are dealing with."

"So what now?"

"A small attitude adjustment. In 48 hours we will proceed."

"I don't know, Eryx. Maybe you should have taken his offer. I understand your issues with it but you might be underestimating them."

"Where is the fighter I encountered on the mountain?"

"Oh, she's still here. I just don't like the odds. I know you're powerful but you can't even find your own people. Why is that?"

"Silver."

"Excuse me?"

"Silver disrupts Zephyri magic. I can't see them because they are either dead or the humans have surrounded them with silver. Faraday had silver coated beams in the walls of his lab as well."

"How did they figure that out?"

"The government got the information from Faraday before I was able to clean out his files."

"And Faraday?"

"I don't know."

"Sounds like you have a leak."

"Yes it does."

"Do you have any idea who it is?"

"None."

"Wonderful. Since they have your Achilles heel, doesn't it seem prudent to take his offer?"

"That is NOT an option. Don't suggest it again."

With my hands up, I said, "Okay, sorry."

His frown smoothed and he said, "I appreciated what you and Alida tried to do. If Greshner was any normal person he might have been swayed."

"What do you mean 'any normal person'?"

"He's a politician."

"And?"

"Politicians are impervious to rhetoric and ploys for sympathy. They don't actually listen. They analyze arguments for ways to get what they want or to manipulate their opponent. They look for weaknesses to exploit and turn in their favor."

"That's pretty cynical."

"Perhaps but it is true nonetheless."

"Why expose yourself then? Your absence from the first two conferences was deliberate wasn't it?"

"Yes."

"Why come out of the shadows then? I told him your name and he can assume that you are the true Zephyri ruler."

"Can he?"

"Yes. You haven't been seen before and you met with the president. I would assume the other Council members were stalking horses."

"Are you worried about me?"

The question was unexpected and left me floundering for a moment. Composing myself, I said, "Of course not. I'm just trying to understand the situation."

"You will be relieved to know that while Greshner will remember our discussion word for word, he'll be incapable of recalling my name or face until we meet again."

"I wasn't concerned. You're a big boy and can take care of yourself."

Opening the door, he said, "You must be tired. I'll let you get some sleep. If you need anything, call Barmek."

"Just say his name?"

"Yes. Good night, *mikroula.*"

"Night."

The door latch echoed in the sudden stillness. Unwilling to disturb my first peaceful moment in days, I closed my eyes and drank in the silence. I let go of everything and just breathed, allowing the solitude to wash over me. Gradually, whistling edged its way into my consciousness. Frowning, I searched the room for the source of the noise. It was Alida; she was snoring.

Too tired to consider a shower, I turned out the light and climbed between the sheets. Staring up at the colorful fish swimming through the soft glow of blue water, I drifted off to sleep.

CHAPTER 11

Choking black smoke scorched my eyes and throat,
as I crawled along the hall to my parents' room.
Engulfed in flame, the walls, curtains and doorframe
burned out of control. Shielding my face, I could see
daddy's blank eyes stare at me through the inferno.
"Daddy, hurry! We have to get out!"
He didn't move. He didn't blink. Desperate, I raced
through the fiery ring to the bed. Tugging at his arm, I
tried to get him up. "Daddy, daddy, you have to wake
up!" His head rolled to the side and I saw blood. Fear
made me drop his arm and look to my mother.
"Mommy?" She seemed to be sleeping but wasn't. Dark
liquid dripped from the gash in her throat and I backed
away. Staring wide-eyed, I shook my head and
whispered, "No—no." A crack vibrated through the air,
drawing my attention to the ceiling. Sparks showered the
bed as a support beam crashed to the floor.

Sitting bolt upright, I screamed, "NO!"
Strong arms enveloped me, stroking my hair as I
cried. They hadn't died like that, they couldn't have. I

remembered, I dreamed about their death for years. It wasn't true, it was an accident. Soft crooning, whispered in the dark, slowly soothed my tears. Sniffling, I dried my eyes on his shirt and pulled back. Worried, stormy blue eyes peered down at me and I gasped in surprise. I had assumed it was Tony comforting me. "Eryx?"

"Are you all right, *mikroula*?"

"Yes, I'll be fine. What are you doing here?"

"Your dream woke me."

Embarrassed, I mumbled, "I'm sorry."

"Don't be. I don't sleep much anyway."

"Do you have nightmares too?"

"Sometimes. I'm sorry about your parents; they loved you more than anything in this world."

Scowling with suspicion, I asked, "How do you know that?"

"From your memories."

"Oh."

"I was under the impression your parents died in the fire."

Nodding, I said, "They did."

"Not according to your dream."

Shuddering, I said, "I don't know where that came from; the reality of their deaths was horrible enough."

"And you remember what happened?"

"Of course."

"May I look?"

"You want me to dredge that up, so you can sneak a peek? After the nightmare I had? Uh-uh."

"No, no. Replaying the memories isn't necessary."

Cautious, I asked, "Why do you want to see them?"

"Don't you want to know what has changed? Why you had this altered dream?"

"I guess. I just don't like the idea of you poking around in my head."

A benevolent smile on his face, Eryx said, "I promise not to pry anywhere that isn't relevant."

Reluctantly, I nodded. "What do you want me to do?"

"Drop your shields and try to relax. You will be aware of me but there won't be any discomfort."

Warm reassurance flooded my senses as I tore down my own defenses. Hot dry palms cupped my cheeks and I flinched. Chagrined, my eyes darted to his patient ones and were caught. Careful, gentle affection, laced with possessive protection brushed my perception. Turning inward, I followed the sensation through my psyche. Examining layer upon layer of memories, his progress faltered the deeper he went but I still fell behind. Feeling as if I were moving through gelatin, I slowed to a stop. It was too hard and I was so tired. Lulled by the Tsái's soothing mind, I drifted into a semi-conscious state. Comfortable and safe, I curled up and floated on the familiar currents of my memories. Doubt niggled at me but I swatted it away, wrapping myself in a blanket of serenity.

Peace and tranquility shattered, as ruthless malevolence shook the room. A rush of hostility blew by, leaving me struggling to catch my breath. Alarmed, I snapped back to reality to find that I was nose to nose with wrath incarnate. Scrambling back to the headboard, I trembled. His eyes flashed like lightning again but I didn't have my own fury to rely on this time. Stuttering, I said, "Wh-what did I do?"

Face contorted with rage, he didn't appear to hear me. "How could I have been such a fool? They will pay.

They will all pay!"

"Who? Who are you angry with? What happened?"

His blazing eyes returned to normal, as he saw my fear. "I don't know but I will find out."

"What are you talking about? I don't understand."

"I apologize, *mikroula*. I found the memory you dreamt of."

"But it wasn't a memory. I was there. My parents died in the fire."

Silent sympathy etched lines of grief into his face as he shook his head.

"That isn't possible. I heard them scream. I can still hear them screaming. I stood outside safe while they burned alive."

"No you didn't. The true memory was your dream. It was buried and replaced with the one you recall."

"You're saying that I made up that horrible scene to substitute for what really happened?"

"No, I'm saying that the one responsible for your parents' death did."

"That's ridiculous. No one has been in my head except you."

"Someone has. Why were you unable to follow me? Why did you become lethargic and complacent? I was going through your most private memories and you wanted to go to sleep. Why?"

Setting my jaw, I said, "It was you. You made me feel cozy and safe."

"I didn't make you feel anything. It was a barrier to keep you away from the source and the answers."

"Okay, let's say you're right. I must have a memory of someone messing with my mind, so who was it?"

"I don't know. It is too deep. I didn't want to hurt

you. We will have to wait for it to surface on its own as this one did."

"Convenient." He started to respond but I held my hand up to silence him. "No one has screwed around in my head. I don't know what you're up to but it won't work. If you don't mind, I'd like to get back to sleep now."

Annoyance permeated the air. He stared down at me for a moment and left without another word. When the door closed, Alida asked, "Is everything all right, Chevy?"

"Yeah, sorry for waking you. Go back to sleep."

"Are you sure?"

"Yes, I'm fine."

"Okay. Night."

"Night."

Rolling over, I punched the pillow and grumbled to myself. *Was I an idiot? Oh, your memories have been altered. Of course, you can't remember because your memories were altered and we can't tell who did it or why because they booby-trapped your mind. What a crock! No one could get through my shields.* Well, except for Eryx or at least that's what he claimed. Maybe that was a load of crap too. Tossing and turning for an hour, my mind kept replaying the image of my parents with their throats cut. Frustrated, I got up and dressed. A walk might help clear my head.

Watching the ground in front of my feet, I wandered Tweentown without noticing where I was or where I was headed. Why had I dreamed about this now? It could be stress but my life was always crazy. What had happened when I crossed the seal? Was it the cause of all the changes? What had it done to me? I didn't have the answer. I didn't have *any* answers. How could I find out? The obvious solution was to ask Eryx but I refused to even consider it. There must be another way; someone I could trust that had some idea of what was going on in my head. John was a possibility. He had always been able to sort out my problems. Why had I agreed to stay? Oh yeah, the genocide of mankind. I didn't see how I was helping but if it kept everyone talking instead of killing, I would stick to the deal.

A door slammed and a man ran by, almost knocking me down. *What the hell?* The building he ran from was the Antechamber. Curious, I opened the door to absolute pandemonium.

Wall to wall zombies ambled about bumping into everything. They upended turnstiles, stanchion posts and people alike. Why would they assemble this many zombies if they couldn't control them? Doyle scampered from corpse to corpse shouting into deaf ears, "Be thtill! Thtop! Halt!"

Working my way through the putrid horde, careful not to touch them, I approached the gargoyle and asked, "Need some help?"

"I have already thent for help, thank you. I didn't know what elthe to do. It doesn't make any thense. They were fine a few minuteth ago."

"So this isn't normal behavior for zombies?"

"They wouldn't make an effective army if it were. It ith odd though. The Thái worked the spell himself."

Chuckling, I said, "This is an army?"

"Don't laugh. Controlled, they are unthtoppable and thith ith jutht the firtht batch."

"The first batch?"

"Yeth. The humanth don't have a chanth."

The door opened and we both turned to see one of the undead escaping. "Exthcuth me." Doyle ran for the fugitive and I stared out across the throng. An army. The Zephyri were going to attack. Flashes of living dead movies ran through my mind and my horror grew. Oh my God! They weren't going to talk, they were going to attack. I had been a fool; tricked, deceived. How could I have been that stupid? I hadn't trusted Eryx from the beginning; why had I believed him? The reason for the farce in my bedroom became clear. He wanted me distracted, doubting my own mind. Everything that had happened was engineered to manipulate me into trusting him. Everything. I had to do something but what? I could warn the president. No, that wouldn't work. I couldn't get within a mile of him and no one that I could call would take me seriously. What should I do? John! He had the contacts and would believe my fantastic story. How could I get to him? A door to his house was here somewhere but I had no idea which one. My car was still in the ferry parking lot for Dewees Island and my cycle was at home. I knew the door number for the Faraday estate but it was in the sticks and I had no guarantee the phones still worked. Shit! Another thought occurred to me. What about Alida? She would be punished if I left, maybe even killed. The whole human race compared to one pixie. The answer seemed obvious but I hesitated to make the choice. She was my friend and didn't deserve what would happen. Fenion's voice spurred me to action.

"Yes, I see the problem Doyle."

Weaving between the rotting zombies, I didn't wait to hear the king's solution. I tried to avoid touching rotting flesh but it was impossible. Would I turn into a walking corpse? Did they have to bite you first? How long would the transformation take? The movies said that it was a matter of hours but had they guessed right? Examining my clothes and skin, I resigned myself to find out the hard way. It would either happen or it wouldn't. The important thing was to warn people of what was coming.

Unsure where I was headed, I kept a close eye on the addresses posted, hoping to get lucky. Sooner or later I had to find a door to Charleston. Barring that, anywhere on the eastern seaboard would work as a last resort. Budapest, Cairo, Sacramento; wasn't there any kind of organization to this? With magic, it should be possible to at least group them according to continent. Listen to the expert on magic. *Ooh, Charleston.* Nope, that one was the capital of West Virginia. Coated in filth, I soon resembled the zombies I was shoving aside. They didn't seem to mind, thank goodness. Twenty minutes later, they continued to roam the chamber unchecked; evidently, Fenion didn't know what to do with them either. Good, if they couldn't be controlled, they couldn't fight. Cheered by the thought, I relaxed a little.

Ahead, I thought I saw 'Charleston' on one of the doors and hurried forward. It appeared my luck was changing for the better. *Almost there.* A subtle hot breeze blew through the milling crowd and the zombies straightened, turning in unison toward the entrance. Peering between the ranks, I saw they all stood at attention, shoulder-to-shoulder, eyes fixed on their master. Eryx, the lying bastard, towered over the tallest soldiers in full command of his army.

Damn it to hell. Keeping my head down, I tried for the door again. They wouldn't move. The most I could manage was forcing the zombies to lean, which allowed me to squeeze between them. Breathless, I reached the door and read the plaque. It was my apartment, not my building but my specific address. Who had been to my house? Maybe Alida had followed me or the Praetorian had been there. Shaking my head, I put the worry aside for now. What mattered was telling the president. A quick glance at Eryx confirmed that his attention was elsewhere. I opened the door far enough to slide through and was gone.

Appearing in the middle of my bedroom, my jaw dropped. Who the fuck had been in my room? It was trashed. Clothes, nick-knacks and broken glass littered the floor. Mitch and Dave had done some damage but this was much worse. Had they come back to finish the job? Had Kegan done this? It didn't seem in keeping with his character. I knew it wasn't Alida. It could have been Sophia. She had no reason to do it but her anger made her more than capable. Were the door to Tweentown and the destruction even connected? Doing a slow sweep of the wreckage, I found the telephone tangled in a curtain on the chair. Refocused on my objective, I made a B-line for it.

"Hello? Cheveyo, is that you?"

"Yeah, it's me, John. Are you okay?"

"Of course, I'm fine. Didn't Cinny give you my message? Where have you been?"

That was a question I had not decided how to answer. Should I reveal the existence of Tweentown? I was under no obligation to keep it secret. Eryx had violated our agreement, so the whole thing was invalid but what would happen to the pixies? They weren't responsible for what the Council was doing. Not all the Zephyri were bad. On the other hand, not all humans were good. "I'm sorry John, I can't tell you that."

"I see. Have you talked to Tony?"

"Tony? He's out? He's okay?"

"Yes, he is. He's worried sick about you."

"Where is he?"

"Searching for you."

"I'll call him right after I hang up. Listen John, I have to get a message to the president."

"That is a tall order. What has happened?"

"The Zephyri are building an army of zombies; they are going to attack. The peace talks are a sham."

Silence. "John, did you hear me?"

"You saw this army with your own eyes?"

Looking down at my clothes, I said, "Oh yeah, up close and real personal."

"I don't doubt you Cheveyo but are you sure of their intentions?"

"Absolutely. I'm sure. Eryx said they were still negotiating and then I found the army. Doyle said it was just the first batch and we didn't have a chance."

Another long pause and he said, "Did you say Eric?"

"No, Eryx with an X."

"Who was he negotiating with?"

"The president. He brought me along to help convince him. It didn't go well but when we got back, he said it was all right because it was expected. He said that they needed a small attitude adjustment to show that the Zephyri had real power. Thousands of zombies are not a small attitude adjustment."

"I suppose that depends on your frame of reference. So this Eryx is the real leader of the Zephyri?"

"Yes. Well, sort of. The other Council members are

the rulers of their people but Eryx rules the rulers. I know you don't rattle easily but I thought you would be more..."

"Upset? I might be if I believed that they were a threat."

"Um, maybe I'm not explaining the situation adequately."

"I think I have a grasp of the essentials. I am not suggesting we ignore the potential danger but in my opinion, Eryx is following through with what he told you of his plan. Call Tony, meet with him, so he can see for himself that you are all right and then I think you should go back."

"Go back! Are you nuts?"

"Settle down, young lady."

"Sorry.""

"It is understandable, given the circumstances. Now, has he hurt you? Abused you in any way?"

"No, it has been all manipulation and lies, which is funny because he tortured a vampire for hiding the truth from him."

"Perfectly reasonable behavior, considering his age and position. Is something else bothering you?"

This was the most surreal conversation of my life. Why would he want me to go back? Why would he defend Eryx? *Perfectly reasonable behavior*? To who? I did have another topic I wanted to discuss though.

"Yeah. Something strange happened when I was brought before Eryx."

"Go on."

"Well, it wasn't that, as much as the stuff that happened afterward. I need to know what's going on."

"I'll do my best to help."

"In the Council Chambers there's a seal in the floor that is an exact replica of my tattoo. When I crossed it, my arm burned."

"Interesting."

"Wait, it gets better. Since then I have had a pronounced expansion in my abilities."

"Oh? In what way?"

"In a high stress situation, I experienced precognition and telekinesis."

"Was this a single event?"

"Yes. I have also been able to hear and do things that only the Zephyri are able to."

"Hmm. I wonder if interbreeding is a possibility."

"It's not. I looked into that. I'm one hundred percent human."

"Have you discussed this with Eryx?"

"No."

"Why not? He would be..."

"I don't trust him."

"Nor should you, however, you don't have to trust someone to learn from them."

"But I thought..."

"You assumed I was siding with him. Nothing is farther from the truth. In the future, try to remember where and when he was born. Man's own past was brutal and the Zephyri being what they are can only be more so. That said, I also want you to be smart. Trust must be earned but there is no reason you can't pick his brain. As far as your new abilities, I think it's wonderful! I will try to find an answer for you but use all the resources at your disposal. Be smart."

"All right. Thanks, John."

"You're welcome. Call if you need anything."

"I will. Bye."

"Goodbye."

Weird didn't begin to describe that conversation. Staring at the phone, I tried to decide what to do. Was John right? Was I overreacting? Maybe but maybe not. I'd let Tony make the call. He answered on the first ring.

"Where the hell have you been, brat?"

"Simmer down Tony. I'm fine. I'm at home but I can't stay here. Do you want to meet me at your cabin?"

"What's going on? Why can't you stay at your apartment?"

I did not want to get into long explanations now. "I'll explain when I see you."

"Call me back on your cell and explain on the way."

Sighing, I said, "I don't have my cell and I'll be taking the bike."

"That's a long ride on the cycle. Where's your phone?"

"Never mind; I'll see you there."

"Damn it, Chevy!"

"It's nice to hear you bellow again, Tony. Bye." I hung up. A shower would be nice but I didn't have time. Throwing a change of clothes in a bag from the floor, I checked the closet for a gun. They were gone. *Shit!*

The sun was coming over the horizon as I pulled out of the lot. Two and a half hours later, I rode into the driveway at Tony's cabin. He hadn't arrived yet, so I let myself in with my key. Musty, stagnant air greeted me.

Taking care of business first, I opened the windows and went outside to turn the water main back on. Old and corroded, it was difficult to turn. Straightening to catch my breath, plastic covered my face. Panic set in and I clawed at the bag. Strong hands caught my wrists and shoved me into the side of the house. I couldn't breathe, couldn't move. No! Think, damn it. Slack from the plastic drew into my mouth with each attempted breath. Gathering my wits, I stomped down on the man's foot, missing the instep. Steel toes prevented any damage I might have done. Dropping my shield, I flung my emotions at him like a spear. A satisfying shriek and he dropped my twisted arms. Sinking to my knees, I tore at the bag and was able to open a hole over my mouth. Sucking in fresh air, it took a few breaths to recover. My hands trembled as I ripped the remaining plastic from my face. Searching for my attacker, I staggered to my feet and whirled around. He was gone.

Making my way to the stairs, I collapsed on the second step and was still there when Tony arrived a few minutes later. My face must have said something was wrong because Tony looked concerned when he got out of his SUV. Approaching slowly, he asked, "Chevy? Are you all right? What happened?"

It was too much. I couldn't say a word. Tears filled my eyes and he sat, pulling me into his lap. Burying my face in his neck, I said, "I'm so happy to see you. I was so worried."

"You were worried? They finally let me out of that lab and I couldn't find you anywhere. The cops thought you were dead and almost had me convinced as well. John said you were fine but didn't have any idea where you were either."

Leaning back, I looked at him and sniffled. "I'm sorry. I couldn't tell anybody."

Wincing, he said, "Christ, you stink! What the hell have you been into?"

I picked at a chunk on my pants and said, "It's

zombie goo."

"Zombies! Are you hurt?"

"No, I'm fine, I think. They didn't do anything to me."

Tony pulled at the plastic necklace I wore. "What's with the grocery bag?"

"I think the assassins found me. I don't know how they could have but it must have been them."

"The ones from John's place?"

Nodding, I said, "I was trying to turn on the water and someone got me from behind. I scared him off by flooding him with my fear but never got a look at him."

"Who are they? What do they want with you?"

"The only thing I can think of is that they were hired by Faraday's partners. They must think I saw them."

"Are you sure it isn't these Zephyri things?"

"Yeah. If the Zephyri were trying to kill me, I'd be dead and not by suffocation."

"John said they were after you but that some pixie was helping you."

"It turns out they wanted my help or maybe not. I don't know anymore."

"You lost me, brat."

Climbing out of his lap, I said, "Let's get this water back on, so I can get cleaned up and I'll try to explain."

After a hot shower and clean clothes, I felt more like myself than I had in days. Still fastening my belt, I walked out of the bedroom saying, "Okay, I'm ready for explanations now."

"I'm glad to hear that, lass."

Startled, I jerked my head up. Kegan stood behind Tony's chair, sword drawn, ready to run him through. "Uh, hi Kegan."

"Hello, lass."

"What are you doing here?"

"The Tsái sent me to retrieve ye."

"How did you find me?"

Cocking his eyebrow, he said, "I'm a Praetorian guard, tis my job."

Glancing at my friend, I asked, "You're not going to hurt Tony, are you?"

"Not if ye both behave yerselves."

The threat was loud and clear. "Where's Sophia?"

"She had other duties to attend to. Come to me, lass."

Tony said, "Don't do it, Chevy. Don't worry about me, just run."

Kegan pricked Tony's back with his sword. "I would expect better advice from her mentor. Come to me, lass."

Staring into Tony's eyes, I couldn't let Kegan kill him, even if it meant the lives of every other human on the planet. I walked to the vampire's side and Tony got to his feet.

Wrapping an arm around my waist, Kegan said, "She will not be harmed, ye have my word."

"Where are you taking her?"

"Somewhere ye cannot follow. I'll protect her with me own life, man. Trust me."

Whispering, *anoigo*, he walked me through the door. My last look at freedom was Tony's worried face as he tried to follow us. Shrugging off the vampire's hold, I stomped through town toward the Council Chambers.

Grabbing my arm, he swung me around and asked, "Why did ye run, lass?"

"He's going to attack the humans and I won't be a

part of it."

"Who?"

"Oh, please. Who else?"

"Ye mean the Tsái?"

"You can drop the act."

"That's news to me, lass. Where did ye get such a farfetched notion?"

"Come on, Kegan. I saw them. I know."

"Saw who?"

"The army."

Comprehension widened his eyes and I said, "I won't let him get away with it. I'll find a way to stop him. Do you understand me?"

"Oh, aye."

Jerking my arm free again, I marched through the front door and straight to my room.

CHAPTER 12

Where was Alida? What had they done to her? It had been over an hour since Kegan locked me in my room. Lying on the bed, I stared at the water, an occasional fish swimming by and worried. She wasn't here and he refused to say a word, if he was even out there. If anything happened to her, it would be all my fault.

A key slid into the lock and I sat up. It was Kegan. "Where is Alida?"

"She will be back soon."

Relieved, I dropped back on the bed and said, "Don't you knock?"

"I apologize, lass but the Tsái would like to speak to ye."

"If he wants to talk to me, he can come to me. I'm busy."

"Is that so? And what would ye be doing?"

"Inventory."

"Of what exactly?"

"Fish."

"Aye, we have been meaning to do that fer years. I

appreciate the help. There is another task that needs doing if ye've a mind to lend me a hand."

"I'm not going to see the Tsái."

"Aye, ye said that. I'll relay the message but could ye do me this favor first?"

"What's that?"

"There is an old tabby cat running around the mansion with a wounded paw but no one can get close enough to heal him. Would ye mind soothing the beast, so that we can catch him?"

"A cat?"

"Aye. He is a favorite of the queen's daughter, Zanna. She is worried sick about him."

Suspicious I tuned into Kegan and asked, "What's his name?"

"Xyre."

"Is this a trick?"

"To what end, lass?"

"I don't know. Answer the question."

"Nay."

He seemed sincere but it was hard to tell with Kegan. "Okay, I'll help."

Escorting me down the hall, he said, "Thank ye, lass. I only thought to ask because I saw him go into the room next to yers."

"No problem." Kegan smiled and opened the door to the other bedroom. I thought my room was spectacular but this was incredible. In addition to the curved glass ceiling, like mine, the bed was on a platform, surrounded by water. An arched bridge connected it to the rest of the room, which was cavernous. A desk piled high with papers occupied one corner and a sitting area ringed a fireplace in another. Kegan closed the door behind us and a huge man rose from an oversized chair by the hearth. I should have known better.

Scowling at the vampire, I said, "You lying bastard."

"Wrong on both counts, lass. I did not lie and me mum and da were married well before I came to be."

"Well, that is the biggest damn tabby cat I've ever seen and his paws look fine."

"I was speaking figuratively, lass."

Mimicking his accent, I said, "Is that so?"

The kitty in question interrupted. "What are you two babbling about?"

"Kegan was explaining to me, how to manipulate and lie to an empath but you don't need any instruction in that area. The two of you should teach a class."

Incredulous, he asked, "You think I lied to you?"

Bracing my hands on my hips, I said, "I know you did."

"Is that why you ran?"

"I wasn't running away; I was warning them."

Eryx rubbed his forehead and glared at Kegan. Something passed between them because the Tsái's face relaxed. He said, "You have broken our agreement."

"I don't keep promises made under false pretenses. I told you that I wouldn't betray my people. Did you think I would stand by and let you slaughter them to keep my word? No, you thought I was stupid enough to swallow all your bullshit. I was supposed to be a good little girl, stay in my cell until it was all over or you needed me to reassure nervous diplomats. Well, I've ruined all your plans. They'll be ready for you now."

He stared at me for a minute before he started to snicker. Pressing his lips tight, he turned red and tears rolled down his cheeks as his composure slipped. Holding his stomach, he roared with laughter.

"You son-of-a-bitch! Don't you dare laugh at me!"

My protest only made it worse. Clenching my fists, I stamped my foot and yelled, "Stop it. Stop it this instant."

He fell to his knees, gasping for air. Grabbing a vase off a side table, I threw it at his head. One hand flew up, catching it before it struck. *Ooh!* Reaching for another missile, I cocked my arm, ready to launch it at him, when all good humor left his face. "Do not throw that. It's six thousand years old."

Acting before the thought had time to form, I flung it straight down at the floor. Pottery shattered across the flagstones. Cocking my eyebrow, I gave him a snotty smile and said, "Oops."

"That was childish and pointless." Waving his hand, the clay shards fit back together and floated to the mantle, out of my reach.

"Childish? I am a grown woman!"

"Behaving as a spoiled *koutsoúvelo* in need of a spanking."

"What does that mean?"

"Brat."

"I'm a brat? Why? Because I won't kiss your ass? I won't meekly follow your orders? I think you have enough people doing that already. That's the real reason you won't accept the president's offer. You talk about concern for what will happen to the Zephyri but that isn't it. Deep down you're just pissed that he dared to say 'no'. A puny human had the gall to defy the great Tsái." The longer I went on the darker his face became. His eyes began flashing but I couldn't stop; I was on a roll. "This attack you're planning is your version of a tantrum. What happens to your beloved people being held by the CDC? You don't care. You just want your way come hell or high water. I'm a spoiled child? You're a hypocrite."

His fists clenched, Eryx said, "I have excused your arrogant, myopic view of me and our world, time and again. I have made allowances for your age but I will not tolerate this presumptuous, self-righteous, insolence."

"And what are you going to do? Kill me? Torture me? Nothing you do to me will change the fact that you are a tyrant with a god complex. I'm the only one able to see it or the guts to say it. What's the matter? Didn't daddy love you? Weren't you good enough? Did he think you were a failure? And now, look at you. He'd be so proud but he's not here to see it, no one is. No family, no friends, no one that loves or even likes you. They only fear you."

His lips had disappeared and he was breathing heavy, nostrils flaring like a bull. Never taking his eyes from me, he snarled, "Get her out of here." When we didn't move he shouted, "NOW!"

Kegan grabbed me by the arm and dragged me from the room. As soon as I was clear of the door, he slammed it shut.

"What the hell did you do that for? I wasn't finished."

"Oh aye, ye were. Ye've done it..."

The distinct sound of cracking glass could be heard an instant before a boom, as if a tidal wave crashed against a rock. Water leaked under the door to Eryx's bedroom. Gulping, I asked, "Did he just..."

Shoving me toward my room, Kegan said, "Move, lass."

Hustling me through my own door, he locked it behind me. *Holy shit.* The room shuddered and I watched the glass nervously.

Startled, Alida flew to my shoulder and asked, "What's going on?"

A queasy look on my face, I said, "I made Eryx lose his temper."

"Uh-oh. Not smart, Chevy."

John's parting words to me echoed in my head. "Yeah, maybe I went a little too far."

"What did you do?"

As I recounted every word, the pixie turned a putrid shade of yellow and developed crinkles over her eyes. "Oh my God, Chevy. What were you thinking?"

"Mostly about hurting him."

"Why?"

"Because I believed him and he lied to me. Because he's going to kill a lot of people and there is nothing I can do."

"At least you warned them. That's something."

"No, I didn't. I told John but he wasn't worried, so I don't think he'll spread the word. I never got a chance to tell Tony."

"Well, we can't just sit here then."

"What? Another escape?"

"Hell yeah. There must be a way out of here you haven't tried."

"Are you sure you want to do that?"

"Definitely."

Grinning, I said, "Thanks, Alida."

"No problem. Now, what do you need?"

"The door is locked but I could pick it if I had something to work with."

"Leave it to me. I'm an expert with locks."

A few minutes later, the last tumbler clicked. I turned the knob but it wouldn't open.

Alida said, "Damn! They spelled the door."

Unwilling to give up, I marched to the window but it wouldn't budge either. There had to be a way. Spotting my bag on the floor, I picked it up to see what I had that might help. I didn't find a screwdriver but I did have my bowie knife.

Looking skeptical, Alida asked, "What are you going to do with that?"

"If we can't use the door, we'll make our own."

"Huh?"

Knocking on the wall to find the studs, I slid the knife through the plaster and lath. The serrated edge got stuck a few times but over all, it worked well. Dropping the panel to the floor raised a cloud of white dust. The beams were far enough apart that I should be able to squeeze through without too much trouble. Tackling the other side of the wall went even better. As the blade reached the final corner, I pushed on the cutout and hoped it didn't make too much noise. Grinning like an idiot, I wiggled into the opening. As my head poked into the hall, I noticed a pair of leather boots at eye-level. Following them up, I found Kegan's amused face.

"I like ye, lass. Ye've got spirit."

"Hi Kegan. Been out here long?"

"Oh, aye. Thank ye fer keeping it interesting. Guard duty tends to get dull."

"We wouldn't want that. Excuse me, please."

"Take yer time, lass. I have eternity."

Squirming back into the bedroom, I scowled and said, "Kegan's out there."

"I know, I heard."

"What are we going to do?"

"I don't know."

Motioning her to follow me, I went over to the window and whispered, "We could break the glass."

Shouting through the door, Kegan said, "It won't work, lass. Too much noise. I'd hear it fer sure."

"Fuck off, Kegan!"

A deep belly laugh was his response. How were we going to get out? We had tried everything possible. If we weren't already in Tweentown, I would call a door but... It couldn't be that simple. Could it? I almost asked Alida if it would work but stopped myself in time. Would thinking the word open a portal? There was one way to find out.

Anoigo. Nothing. Maybe if I concentrated harder. Focusing my entire mind on the word and what I wanted, I thought *anoigo*. Nope, no door. You had to say it but how loud? Mouthing the word, I was careful to allow only a bare breath to escape. The air shimmered. It worked! Holding a finger to my lips, I pointed out the air to Alida. She turned a vibrant purple and clapped her hands. Wasting no time, we hurried through the portal, landing at the gate.

Concerned more with speed than stealth, we walked down the middle of the street and no one noticed us. Hoping Doyle was busy with the zombies, I cracked open the door to the Antechamber. The way station had tripled in size and held hundreds of thousands of walking dead. Huge alcoves had been added to house the waiting hordes. This was bad. Was there a limit to how many they could make?

I couldn't remember the number for my apartment

but I knew about where it was, so I led the way. Keeping my head down, I wove my way through the overflow of bodies. Almost to my destination, I heard a woman say, "You! Stop!"

Glancing over my shoulder, I saw Sophia and she was yelling at *us*. Sidling, sliding and shuffling, I tried to move faster. The shifter's strength gave her an edge, as she shoved anything in her way aside. She was gaining ground. Forging ahead, I moved faster. A squeal made me look back. Standing atop three downed zombies, the bitch had caught Alida by one leg.

Alida shouted, "Go, Chevy. Run! Stop this before it's too late."

Staring at her for a long second, I dropped to the floor and crawled to the nearest door. I found myself on my knees inside a bathroom stall. Music pulsed through the walls.

"Did you see the titties on that blonde?"

"Fuckin' A, man. Gonna get me some of that."

"She wouldn't touch you with a ten foot cattle-prod."

"She will, if I pay her enough."

Nice. Where was I? Sophia was right behind me. I couldn't afford to hang around waiting for them to leave. Straightening my shirt, I dusted off my pants and took a deep breath. Pushing open the stall door drew the attention of the men standing at the urinals. *Lovely.* They zipped up quick and turned leering smiles my way.

"Well, well, what have we here? See something you like, darlin'?"

Balding, middle-aged men with paunches were not my idea of prime dating material. The assholes didn't even notice how dirty I was; female was enough for them. Be still my heart... "Excuse me gentlemen, I must have made a mistake."

"Hey, honey. When do you go on? I'd like to see the show."

Show? Ignoring the question, I ducked out. *Oh, fuck!* Pink and blue neon ran the length of a runway stage where a naked woman danced around a pole. I had seen enough. Where was the door? A red exit sign glowed to my right and I had a hard time keeping my pace to a walk. Thankfully, the lobby was empty except for the doorman and a bank of pay phones. Picking up one of the receivers, I started to dial Tony but realized I had no idea where I was. My face warmed as I asked the attendant, "Where am I?"

"The Body Shop, ma'am."

Hesitating for a second, I said, "What city are we in?"

"That must have been one hell of a party."

"Could you just tell me what city and state I'm in?"

"Are you all right, sugar? Somethin' happen to you?"

"I'm fine, thank you."

"Okay, if you say so. This is Charleston, South Carolina and you're in a club named The Body Shop. I can give you the address if you want."

"That's okay. Thanks."

Dialing Tony's number, it rang three times and I didn't think he would answer.

"Romano."

"Tony, it's me."

"Chevy! Where are you? Are you okay?"

Glancing at the doorman, I asked, "Can you come pick me up?"

"Yeah. Where?"

Keeping my voice low, I said, "It's a club called The Body Shop. It's a..."

"I know what it is. What the hell are you doing there?"

"Don't ask. When can you get here?"

"About twenty minutes."

"Fantastic."

"Did that vampire hurt you?"

"Kegan? Of course not."

"Good. I'm on my way. Wait outside for me, around the side of the building."

"Okay."

The parking lot was well lit but the side where Tony told me to wait was almost pitch black. Why did he want me over here? Maybe he didn't want the guys coming out of the club hitting on me. Typical. If I ever had a date, he would be impossible. It had been about ten minutes when something bit me in the leg. Slapping a hand over the spot, I felt a dart protruding from my pants. Woozy already, I pulled it out and concentrated on remaining conscious. Holding onto the wall, I walked back toward the front of the building but didn't make it more than five steps.

***

"Cheeevyyyy. Cheeevyyyy. It's time to wake up."

My head felt as if it was floating in water. When I opened my eyes, I couldn't focus. Rolling my head back and forth, it looked as if I was in a dim hall but everything was a hazy blur. Letting my head fall forward, I realized I was sitting on the floor and my hands were free. *Yay.*

"Cheeevyyyy. Can you hear me?"

The distorted, demonic voice was coming from my left. My muscles didn't want to cooperate but I managed to turn my head. A man's silhouette stood at the end of the hall surrounded by a white halo. I had to get away. He did this to me. I had to move.

"Whooo are you, Cheeevyyyy? Why does he waaant you?"

Sliding down the wall, I lay on my side for a few moments letting the dizziness fade. Rolling onto my stomach was the hardest thing I had ever done but I had to get up.

"Why are yoouu sssoo important? What are you?"

"I don't know what you're talking about."

"The Tssssái. What are you?"

Leaning heavily on the wall, I made it to my feet. "I'm human."

"Nooo. You caaalled a dooor."

The walls flowed like water and I had to close my eyes before I fell. "I'm not important. Who are you?"

My head jerked back and a wavy misshapen face came into view. "Whooo are you? Why does he waaant you? Are you a looover or maybe a pet?"

"I'm nobody. I don't know what you're talking about." The face clarified for an instant. *No! It couldn't be. He would never hurt me. My mind was playing tricks on me; it was the drug.* I clawed at his eyes, forcing him to release my hair. Hurling myself down the hall, I tried to run.

"Cheeevyyyy. You can't get away. Yoouurr mine. Tell me what I waaant to know. Whooo are you?"

Tears streamed down my face, as I stumbled toward the light at the end of the hall. "Please, someone help me."

"Nooo one can help you. Yooouu're alll alone. I'm coming Cheeevyyyy, coming to geeet you."

"No! I don't know anything. Leave me alone."

Shadowy arms grabbed me and I screamed, lashing out from the depths of my being. Hands shook me and I screamed again. The face, his face; it was Tony and then it was Eryx. Screeching like a banshee, I struck again and again. I wanted to hurt him—them. Thrashing, kicking, scratching, I fought with every fiber of strength I had.

The warped voice said, "*Mikroula,* stop! It's me. Stop! You are in no danger."

No, I would not stop. Bright light blinded me. "I don't know. I don't know anything. Leave me alone."

Searing heat raced up my arms and legs to my chest. I looked down and saw the fire. It scorched my skin, leaving it charred and black. Shrieking from the pain, I lashed out again. Blood. My father's bloody open wound. "No! Daddy, no!" Flames consumed us; I wasn't standing outside anymore. I lay beside him, in my mother's place. Holding him close, I let the blaze take us both. Cauterized nerves felt cooler and the agony receded. Strong arms held me, as we went to meet my mother. Peace washed over me, filling my heart with serene acceptance. Everything would be all right now. I was where I was supposed to be, where I should have been all along. Filled with comfortable satisfaction, my eyes drifted open.

Horrified to have been cuddled up with my tormentor, I scuttled into the corner. Open wounds covered his arms, chest and face but he didn't seem to notice them. With the lights on and drugs out of my system, I could see we were in an abandoned building. Peeling paint, plaster and garbage littered the floor. Pipes and loose wiring hung from holes in the walls and missing ceiling tiles. Eryx beamed down at me. I wanted to wipe the gratified smile off his face. What did he have to be happy about? I was a captive again, at the mercy of a sadistic asshole, bent on world domination. What was next? Bamboo under my fingernails? No, he enjoyed fucking with my mind more than anything else.

He said, "I am happy that you are alive and well."

"Sure. No more fun and games if your toy breaks."

Mission accomplished. The smile faded and he said, "I am not responsible for this. I came to rescue you."

"Oh really? How did you find me? How do you always find me?"

He hesitated. "We are connected. I am always aware of you. I know when you are in trouble."

"So you have a metaphysical LoJack on me? You have me tagged like an animal?"

"In a manner of speaking but not in the way you think. Can't you sense it?"

"The only thing I sense is lies. Why are you doing this to me? Life must get boring after thousands of years but can't you find another way to get your kicks? Or is this punishment for the things I said to you?"

He sighed in frustration and said, "Every evil in the world cannot be laid at my feet. IF I wanted to punish you, I would never resort to drugs."

"I saw you."

"You were given a powerful hallucinogen. You saw your father also, was he here as well?"

Pouting, I looked at the floor. "No."

"Who else did you see?"

"It doesn't matter. It wasn't real."

"Did they say anything to you?"

Still suspicious, I said, "He kept asking me who I was. What did you want with me? Why was I important."

His face became an unreadable mask and he said nothing. "Why am I important, Eryx? What *do* you want with me?"

"I told you. I want your help negotiating with the humans."

Flimsy. "He also asked what I was. Can you answer that because I can't."

"No but now I know what power you developed on the mountain."

"I wasn't aware that it was still in question. I'm human, so it's precognition and telekinesis."

"The precognition is a forgone conclusion but not the telekinesis. What you have is called air manipulation."

"I've never heard of it."

"That is because it's a Zephyri talent."

"We've already established that I'm human."

"Yes, you are."

"So you must be wrong."

"Not in this case. There is one power that combines the capabilities you have shown thus far."

"Air manipulation."

"Yes."

"It's not as if I started a tornado or something."

"Power over the air is not that limited. Holding the air still, forms a shield like you created on the mountain. Thrusting a concentrated burst of air can cut or bludgeon, as well as many other things."

Eyeing his injuries, I asked, "Is that what happened to you?"

"Yes."

The lacerations and bruises covering his body elated me. If I could do that to *him*, maybe there was still hope.

Eryx said, "I would like you to work with someone, so that you can learn to control it."

"And who might that be? You?"

"No, I'm far too busy at the moment."

"Oh, right. Taking over the planet does tend to keep your schedule full. Who did you have in mind?"

"Aspen."

"The fairy?"

"Yes. It's one of his many talents."

"I don't think so."

"You're bound to get bored."

Scrutinizing him, I asked, "Why?"

With an amused look, he said, "Because you won't be leaving your room for a few days. You're grounded."

Getting up off the floor, I put my hands on my hips and yelled, "Grounded? I'm not a child!"

Leaning his shoulder against the wall, he examined a cut on his hand and said, "So you keep saying. Regardless, you aren't going anywhere. Every possible escape route has been eliminated. I do want to commend you on your last ingenious getaway. No one has ever even considered what you did, however, if you persist in trying to leave, I will be forced to put you back in the dungeon."

Folding my arms, I said, "So I'm a prisoner."

"Only if you choose to be."

Kegan appeared in the doorway. Looking me over, he said, "I'm glad yer all right, lass. Ye scared the hell out of me."

Eryx asked, "Did you find him?"

"Nay, sir but I will be bringing Sophia back to get

the scent. We'll track him down."

Nodding, he said, "Good."

I asked, "Speaking of Sophia... She didn't hurt Alida, did she?"

"Nay, lass. Alida is fine. No more field trips though. Yer runnin' me ragged."

Straightening, Eryx said, "I have to get back. There is another problem with the zombies. After you return her to her room, find Aspen and send him to me. I'm going to have him train Miss Singer."

My skin prickled with jealousy and resentment. Stiff as a board, Kegan clenched his jaw and stared at the wall while he responded. "It is the lady's choice but I'm sure she needs no training in that area, Tsái. If she decides guidance is necessary, there are much more suitable instructors available."

Why would Kegan object to Aspen training me?

Eryx's eyes flared for a moment and he said, "He is to tutor her in air manipulation and *nothing* else. Have I made myself clear?"

Beneath the five o'clock shadow, the vampire's cheeks flushed. "Aye. Sorry, sir."

Scowling at his guard, Eryx vanished.

CHAPTER 13

"Jeez! I thought he'd never leave."

Swallowing my heart, I said, "Alida, you scared me half to death! Where did you come from?"

"Kegan was kind enough to give me a ride."

The vampire said, "I thought ye were confined to yer room."

"Confined? No. Besides, I was worried about Chevy."

"Why? You told me to run."

"When the Tsái said you were in trouble, I knew it had to be bad. I've never seen him that anxious. Hey, where are we anyway?"

Looking to Kegan for the answer, he said, "An abandoned naval shipyard."

Of all the places he could have staged this, why here? Mistrust was driving me insane. I had to look at it from every angle. I had to figure this out. My life depended on it. If I assumed Eryx was responsible for this latest episode, it was the most convoluted, elaborate scheme ever devised. The Tsái was capable of anything but what was the purpose? There must be some logic to

it. A human government building and human drugs
would lead anyone to believe it was a human culprit,
which could be the point. He could be going through all
of this to convince me how evil my fellow humans were
and that he was my only refuge. On the other hand, if
Eryx wasn't responsible, it had to be a human. Again, the
question was why? What did they hope to gain? The
assassins and their employers wanted me dead, so it
couldn't be them. Who else would be interested in me?
Or what I might know? A government building and high-
grade drugs could mean the president wasn't as clueless
as I thought. Ugh, I needed more information but that
wasn't going to happen sitting in my luxurious cell in
Tweentown.

Kegan asked, "Lass, did ye hear me?"

"I'm sorry, no. What did you say?"

"I said it's time to be goin'."

"Hang on a minute. I want to have a look around
first."

"Ye don't have to worry; I'll do a thorough
investigation."

"I need to look for myself."

Frowning, he said, "Be quick."

Retracing my steps, I walked the hall to where I
awoke. Kicking over rubble and trash, I looked for
anything to give me a clue. Shifting a piece of newspaper,
I found a flower. A yellow daffodil in this rat infested
heap? Faraday liked daffodils but he was dead. Wasn't
he? What was the significance? Was it a gift? Was I
wrong about everything? Did I have a run of the mill,
psycho stalker after me?

Kegan came up behind me and asked, "Find
something, lass?"

Moving the paper back into place, I said, "No, nothing."

"Don't ye worry, we'll find him. We need to return, lass."

"Hey, Kegan. Since we're in Charleston, can we stop by my apartment? If I'm going to be stuck in my room for a while, I'd like to get some things to keep me busy."

"I'd like to oblige ye, lass but the Tsái wouldn't..."

"He didn't say we had to be back right away. He just said when you get back. Pleeease?"

Charmed but suspicious, he said, "Nay. Yer up to somethin'. I'll not lose ye again. The Tsái would have my head."

Pouting and looking through my lashes, I said, "All right. You caught me but all I wanted to do was use my computer. Someone knows too much about what's going on. I thought we could check the FBI database for a lead. I won't try to escape. Honest."

"Never trust anyone who ends a sentence with 'honest'. Ye had me until then."

"I'm telling the truth. Come on, Kegan."

"Ye can't get into the FBI computers, so nay."

"I can't but Alida can. Can't you, Alida?"

The pixie gave a thumbs up sign and said, "Piece of cake. I've got a way into every major government database in the country."

Doubtful, Kegan said, "Is that so?"

Nodding with pride, I said, "You should see her. It's amazing what she can do."

We stared at the vampire expectantly. Rubbing the back of his neck, he considered his answer. I knew what he would say, so I remained quiet. Given the Tsái's instructions, he wouldn't pass up the opportunity to gain more intelligence.

"Okay, lass. We'll go to yer apartment but if ye so much as take one step out of line, I'll put ye over my knee. Understand?"

Grinning like a twit, I said, "I'll behave, I promise. Thanks, Kegan."

"Don't thank me yet. We may all be whipped for this." Taking my hand, he said, "Come on."

When we got to the door, he scooped me up and I squealed. "What are you doing?"

"It's this way or over my shoulder. I thought ye would be more comfortable in this position."

"You're not carrying me anywhere. Put me down!"

Insulted, he said, "Unless yer hiding a pair of wings under that T-shirt, ye'll have to suffer my touch."

"Oh, no Kegan. I didn't mean... I just don't like feeling dependent."

Somewhat mollified, he nodded and said, "Wrap yer arms round my neck."

Doing as he instructed, I couldn't help feeling self-conscious. "I'm sorry I'm so heavy."

"I hope yer not fishing' fer a compliment, lass. I didn't think ye were the type."

A blaze of heat rushed up my neck and I said, "No, I wasn't. I didn't mean that I'm fat. I'm not. Actually, I'm on the skinny side. It's just that I'm too tall and that makes me heavier than most women."

Without warning, he jumped into the air. Startled, I held him tighter, my cheek against his. Speaking into my ear, he said, "Yer not too tall, nor too thin, nor do ye weigh too much. Yer perfect the way ye are, lass. A man that does not possess the strength, patience and intelligence to provide fer and protect a woman is no man at all."

I froze. I had no idea how to react. My heart raced and I couldn't catch my breath. He was a Neanderthal from a different time and I was an independent, capable woman that didn't need coddling. I should be angry but my insides felt like hot caramel. Flustered, I decided to ignore his statement and put it out of my mind but his body pressed against mine made it impossible.

"Chevy?"

Reluctantly, I turned toward him. Lifting my gaze, I met his laughing eyes. He knew. He couldn't read my mind but he knew how I felt, what I was thinking.

"Relax. Ye'll be stiff by the time we get there. Look at the bridge."

Relieved to have something else to focus on, I scanned the horizon. Spanning the Cooper River, the Arthur Ravenel Jr. Bridge was beautiful at night. The lighting made the cables look like a fountain. Alida flew beside us and I was astounded that she was able to keep up. As Kegan intended, once my attention was elsewhere, my muscles unwound and I enjoyed the flight. Passing a seagull, out after his bedtime, I laughed and pointed it out to him.

Breathless with excitement, we set down outside my building. "That was wonderful! Thank you, Kegan."

"My pleasure, lass."

Leading the way, I made my way upstairs and opened the door to my apartment. "The computer is in my room. I hope it wasn't damaged."

Kegan and Alida followed me in and the vampire said, "I may have to rethink a few things. Do ye always live like this?"

"Huh?" Scanning the room, I realized what he was referring to. "No! The hit men did some of it but the mess was much worse when I came back. I thought that maybe you and Sophia had done it."

"Nay. I've never been here. Why would ye assume we did this?"

"There's a door from the Antechamber in my bedroom. Whoever finished trashing the place probably left that way. Unless you made the door, Alida."

She said, "It wasn't me."

"Could it have been Eryx?"

"I doubt it, lass but we can ask him."

"If it wasn't him, why would another Zephyri have been in my apartment?"

They both shook their heads.

Finding my laptop on the bathroom floor, I set it up, crossed my fingers and turned it on. The login screen came up. *Yay!* Now for the hard part. Entering my password, I chewed my nail until the last start-up application loaded. We were good to go. Bringing up the browser, I glanced over my shoulder to make sure my watchdog hadn't snuck up on me.

Alida asked, "What are you doing? I thought you wanted me to break into the FBI system."

"I do but I want to look up something else first. Would you mind keeping Kegan busy for a while?"

"Okay but what are you looking for?"

"I'll let you know when I find it."

She took off without another word and I closed the door behind her. Clicking in the search window, I typed 'daffodil symbolism'. *Daffodil or narcissus symbolize rebirth and new beginnings*. The rest of the passage was interesting but not what I was looking for. Maybe it was the specific breed. Searching for a picture of the flowers, I kept seeing, turned out to be easier than I anticipated. Called a Carlton daffodil, it didn't appear to have any particular meaning other than the general daffodil. Checking over my shoulder again, I looked up Narcissus. Reading through the familiar story of the man who fell in love with his own reflection, I almost clicked on another site. At the bottom, a reference to Persephone, queen of the underworld, was mentioned.

According to a linked article, the goddess played in a field with her friends, the nymphs, while her mother, Demeter, went to check her crops. Zeus, at the behest of Hades, had the flower narcissus created to lure Persephone into a trap laid by the god of the Underworld. When she was taken to Hades' realm, Demeter was angry with the nymphs for not protecting her daughter. Turning them into sirens, she banished them to a flowery island.

Staring at the picture next to the story, I began to piece some things together. A quick search on sirens showed the names of the three creatures were Parthenope, Ligeia and Leukosia. *Shit, shit, shit!* No wonder Eryx had a leak. The angel was a siren and Eryx had taken her voice. She had plenty of reason to hate him. The Zephyri had been cruel to her as well. Was she evil though? Was she my enemy or just the Zephyri? Was the enemy of my enemy, my friend? I hadn't been hurt tonight. Could she be an ally? Wait, I was jumping to conclusions again. Just because she was at the shipyard, did not mean she was working with the man that terrorized me. *Think it through.* She could be the woman from Faraday's. If that was the case, she had taken Tony and the Zephyri. She had been a part of torturing them, killing them but Eryx had made her mute. According to the Zephyri, his magic was infallible. What about the trouble with the zombies? Had she found a way to break the spell? Who was the second man working with Faraday? Was he human or Zephyri? He could be either. The use of human assassins no longer meant that it had to be a human. I was right back where I started. I didn't know anything or at least not much. Leukosia was involved but I had no idea with what or how much. If I assumed she was the woman from Faraday's and she was up to her neck in his schemes, how did I feel about that? Could I call someone capable of those actions an ally, if it meant the survival of the human race?

Alida whispered, "Hurry, change your clothes!"

Almost jumping out of my skin, I said, "What? Why?"

"One, you really need it and two, that's the reason I gave Kegan to keep him out."

"Oh." Grabbing the first thing my hand touched, I dressed as fast as I could.

She said, "Let down your hair."

"What on earth for?"

"You're not very smart are you?"

Scowling at the pixie, I said, "Hey! I am too."

"He likes you. You have nice hair. It will distract him. Get it?"

Pursing my lips, I said, "I guess but why do you think he likes me?"

"For real? Are we going to play that game? Come on! It's as plain as the fangs in his mouth."

"Well, I didn't think it was obvious."

"...Because you're not very smart."

Glaring at the pixie, I finished taking out the braid and had a thought. "Won't he think I'm doing this for his benefit?"

"Probably."

"That's the last thing I need."

"I think you could use a little of *that*. So what did you find?"

Confused by the situation, I said, "I don't know yet. I'll tell you when I work it out." It wasn't a lie—exactly.

Kegan knocked on the door. "Lass, are ye finished?"

"Yeah, come in."

Alida was already dancing away on the keyboard. As the pixie predicted, Kegan fixated on my hair. Encouraging him was wrong. I wasn't interested at all. Not really. Well, even if I were curious, it was superficial. Mild attraction and curiosity were not good reasons to get involved with a man, especially a vampire.

Alida said, "Okay, I'm in. What do you want me to look for?"

Dismissing Kegan's stare, I said, "Look for any entries that refer to Faraday's name, address, date or the Zephyri."

In a husky voice, the vampire asked, "What are ye searching fer?"

I refused to look at him. "I want to know what they found."

"Nothing. We cleaned the place out."

"Maybe you missed something."

"Nay, we did not."

Alida paused in her inquiry. "There are no reference files."

I asked, "What do you mean?"

"The files don't exist."

Kegan said, "See, lass, we didn't miss anything."

"No, that isn't what she's saying. Alida, why?"

"I don't know. They're just gone."

"Check Homeland Security."

As Alida switched systems, Kegan moved into my line of sight. Given no choice, I glanced at him and the floor. He said, "What's wrong?"

Biting my nail, I said, "There should be a case file of some kind but there isn't. It's either been erased or moved."

He didn't answer but his palpable gaze heated a trail across my skin. Squirming, I had to ask. "Is something wrong?"

"Nay. Ye took out the braid."

"Uh, yeah."

The pixie said, "They're not here either, Chevy. Who's next?"

Taking advantage of the distraction, I riveted my eyes to Alida. "I don't know, it doesn't make sense. There has to be a record somewhere. Try the NSA." Giving me a pointed, 'I told you so' look, she smiled and went back to the computer.

Kegan said, "It's pretty."

Baffled, I couldn't help looking at him. "Huh?"

He stepped forward. "Yer hair down around yer shoulders. It brings out yer eyes."

Retreating to keep the distance between us, I gulped and said, "My eyes?"

"Aye. The black makes them appear even greener."

Advancing again, he backed me into the wall. Babbling, I said, "You have green eyes too." *Lame.*

"Aye but they're not the lovely mossy color of yers. It reminds me of the hills of home." Reaching out, he leaned one hand against the wall and touched my hair with the other. "Black silk."

So addled that I couldn't form a coherent thought, I blurted, "I can't cook."

A broad smile covered his face, flashing full fang. "That's not a weakness in my book, lass."

Alida said, "Sorry for interrupting the mating ritual but I found something."

Thank God! I ducked under his arm and hurried to sit in front of the computer. Noticing a pair of panties on the desk, I snatched them up and threw them toward the bathroom. Chuckling, the vampire braced his hands on the back of my chair and leaned over my shoulder.

Closing my eyes, I tried to compose myself, to think. *Damn it. What was wrong with me? A man flirted with me and I fell apart?* It wasn't something I was accustomed to but I had to get a grip. Stretching my awareness, I touched the earth and centered my mind. A deep breath and I was ready. Focusing on the monitor, I saw a list of files.

Alida said, "They've all been moved here, into a USAP."

"Everybody knows about the Zephyri and what happened at the lab. What are they hiding?"

Frowning, Kegan said, "I understand that they moved the files but perhaps the NSA took over. Why do ye believe they are hiding anything?"

"The USAP. There is no other reason to put that kind of security in place."

"What's a USAP?"

"It's an Unacknowledged Special Access Program. They are used to safeguard information."

"Doesn't top secret clearance accomplish the same thing?"

"This is higher than that. It restricts access to

authorized personnel only, despite clearance. No one with knowledge of the program will even admit to its existence."

"What about funding? Somewhere, someone holds the purse strings."

"They could give basic information or lie about the purpose of the program. There is also a waived status, called Deep Black, which says they don't have to brief anyone in Congress. No matter how you look at it, they are hiding something huge. The only people that can initiate a program like this are the top six members of the cabinet and their deputies or the president himself."

"Would those six people be the ones the Council visited?"

"Yep."

Reading down the list of files, I didn't know where to begin. They included Faraday's journal, autopsy reports, Zephyri species notes, a Tweentown map, a medical report on the captive victims and an inventory of evidence taken from Faraday's house and lab. "Are you sure they don't know we're in here? It could be a while."

The pixie said, "No way. We have all night."

"I don't want to take that long. Let's get the boring stuff out of the way. Start with the inventory."

Opening the file, showed an itemized description with pictures. Surgical tools, specimen jars, books, keys, flasks, beakers and test tubes. "Stop, go back."

Amidst all the chemistry paraphernalia was a necklace. A disc shaped charm that reminded me of a spiral lollipop hanging from a silver chain. Six concentric circles alternating silver and inlaid blue opal were transected by two silver lines at the bottom. It was the strangest piece of jewelry I had ever seen. Where had it come from? Cool but not informative. "Open the medical reports, Alida."

Scanning through all the medical jargon gave me a headache and the news wasn't encouraging. Malachai, the vampire was kept on an intravenous drug cocktail night and day to prevent him from waking. The doctors were fixated on trying to cure him of his disease and their treatment did not include giving him blood, as that would just feed the addiction. His physical condition had deteriorated to the point that they didn't know if he would survive. The shifter was described as combative and no one was allowed inside his cell under any circumstance. He had attacked a nurse and she required more than one hundred stitches. Gus refused to eat and was kept strapped to a bed, being fed intravenously. He lay in bed, staring at the ceiling, unresponsive. According to his file, there was considerable debate as to his exact species. For some reason, the staff did not believe the Zephyri Council's claim that he was a goblin. A folklore specialist was flown in to help with species classification. A shiver ran up my spine, as I read between the lines, my mind filling in the all too real details of what their lives had become. Tiny sniffles caught my attention and I reached for the mouse to close the file.

Alida asked, "What's in Lyme, Connecticut?"

"Not much. It's where Lyme Disease got its name but that's about all I know. Why?"

"There's a file with the name of a motel in that town."

Examining the list, I saw the file. Opening the folder, I found an expense report for several rooms charged to a single account. Had someone included it accidentally? "It doesn't make sense. Alida, bring up a map of Lyme."

Flaring red, the pixie said, "Yes *ma'am*. You know, I am sick of you giving me orders. I'm not your personal gopher."

Shocked, I leaned back and said, "I know. I apologize; I didn't mean to be rude." I realized what was bothering her and added, "I'm sorry about Gus too. He's your friend and I'm trying to find him. Would you please show me a map of Lyme?"

Hanging her head, Alida said, "I shouldn't have snapped at you. You're right, I'm worried about Gus."

"I understand and I do have a tendency to be bossy."

Keys clicked and the map appeared. I couldn't see anything that would interest the government in the area. "Can you zoom out?" Five miles from Long Island Sound, forests, parks, rivers and lakes surrounded it. Thinking aloud, I said, "Why are they there? What does it have to do with the Zephyri?"

Kegan said, "I don't know, lass but it is time to be going."

"No. We can't go yet. We haven't looked at all the files. Don't you want to find them?"

"Aye but I don't see how."

Alida said, "Chevy, what's this? Why do I know the name?"

Turning back to the screen, Alida had zoomed in on an island off the tip of Long Island. I said, "Plum Island. I don't recognize it. You do?"

"Yes, I just can't remember why."

Typing in another search, we found out why she knew the name. It was an animal research center.

Alida said, "Oh yeah! They had several scandals over releasing diseases on the mainland, they had a biological weapons program during the Cold War, two deformed animals washed up on shore in Montauk and a dead man was found on the Plum Island Beach. Conspiracy theorists went wild."

Alida and I stared at each other for a minute. "Do you think..."

"Yeah, I do. We found them."

On full alert, Kegan said, "Time to go, lass. We need to get this information to the Tsái immediately."

"But what about the journal?"

"We can look into that later."

"There might not be a later. We have to do it now."

"I have no interest in the personal thoughts of the Butcher."

Desperate to get his attention, I said, "What if the name of the leak is in there?"

"Ye know about that?"

"Yes."

"Perhaps we have more than one leak."

"Settle down, Kegan. Eryx told me about it."

Skeptical, he asked, "Is that right?"

"Yes it is. So do you want to tell him that you passed up an opportunity like this or shall I?"

"There's probably nothing important in the man's diary. It would be a waste of time. We need to get them out of that *pit,* now."

Understanding made my eyes widen. "Malachai is your friend."

"Aye."

"I'm sorry, I didn't know."

"Nay, yer right. I have let my emotions rule me. The Tsái needs to know everything."

"We'll hurry. I promise."

CHAPTER 14

"Okay Alida, let's see the journal."

Old school, the diary was written in a composition notebook and someone had taken the time to scan every page into the computer. Beginning a mere six months before, it wasn't long.

Wednesday, January 18, 2012

After our discovery, Bruce tells me that I must keep a journal, as an historical reference. My response? Gladly! I want to shout the news to the world but I need to be careful. My enemies, past, present and future would destroy me if they knew what I've uncovered.

***

11:13am –

He was yelling again. "Here! Turn here, you

idiot!"

"I heard you, Bruce. You don't have to shout."

"You don't seem to understand how important this is. We have to find it."

"I know. You explained it to me but anyone firing a gun in a game management area will be long gone by now. It's been an hour already." The clouds looked like rain again. We needed to get home. "We can come back tomorrow, Bruce. We'll get wet, if we don't leave soon."

"It'll be too late tomorrow. Don't be a whiny, mama's boy! How I got stuck with such a faggoty bitch is beyond me."

Movement caught my eye and I asked, "What is that?"

It was the wrong shape to be an alligator. Bruce said, "That's it; we found it. Get over there!"

Barely distinguishable from the muck, it appeared to be a person, buried up to their waist in pluff mud. The sulfurous paste covered every square inch of skin and I couldn't tell if it was a male or female but they obviously needed assistance. With the tide coming in, they would drown if left out here alone. Maneuvering the boat alongside them, I worked at setting the mud monster free.

***

2:10pm –

We managed to get back to the landing without rain adding to my miseries. Our refugee drifted in and out of consciousness. As I loaded her into the Jeep, I found out, by accident, that she was indeed a female with a careless hand placement. The drive home was excruciating. I was wet, dirty and smelled to high heaven. Bruce's constant prattle grated on my last nerve. I was as anxious as he was to discover her identity and purpose in the marsh but he wouldn't shut up. I was worried about her too. It was impossible to be certain but I thought she was injured. She never made a sound as I pulled her from the bog or lifted her from the boat but she did flinch. If she had been hit by one of the shots we heard…

We stopped at the outdoor shower and I was grateful she was still asleep, as I pulled off her filthy dress. Bruce's crass comments made my face flush. Doing my best to ignore him, I scrubbed the drying sludge from her body. Layer upon layer was swept away, revealing the most incredible beauty ever created. Bruce was right, this is my destiny; she is the reason I was born.

Three appendages were marred with bullet holes,

which bled profusely. Given no alternative, I whisked
her into the kitchen. As an operating theatre, crude
was an understatement but I wasn't going to allow
her to bleed to death. Four hours later, I had all the
bullets removed and the wounds closed. I hoped that
her physiology was similar enough to ours that I
didn't unknowingly cause more damage to her already
frail body.

Carefully, I bathed and dressed her, laying her in
my parents' bed. After a quick shower, I sat sketching
her face while I waited.

Bruce said, "When will she wake up?"

"I don't know, when she's ready, I suppose."

"You suppose? What the fuck is that? Fucking
pansy. Can't you give her something to speed it up?"

"No, I can't. She's not human. Anything I give
her might do more harm."

"Ugh! This is taking forever. How can you just sit
there doodling?"

"It's relaxing and she is so beautiful, I can't
resist."

Bruce said, "You will have to burn that."

"Pardon me?"

"The picture."

"Why?"

"They might find it. We can't run the risk."

I tried to reason with him. "They don't know where I am. We're hidden from their instruments, how could they find it?"

"If I found you, so can they, dumbass."

"I really don't appreciate the name-calling, Bruce."

"Get over it, douche bag."

***

Thursday, January 19,2012
2:24pm -

I burned the drawing as Bruce instructed. It was my best work to date and it pained me to do it but he was right. Bruce was always right. With the smell of smoke still fresh, I noticed my patient stirring.

Her eyes fluttered open and she looked around the room, confused. Simply stunning. She was a goddess come to life. Noticing me, she tried to sit up and recoiled in pain.

"It's all right. I'm not going to hurt you. My name is Michael, what's yours?"

A suspicious frown creased her brow and she said nothing. Keeping me in her sight, she touched her bandages gingerly.

"You were shot. I was able to remove the bullets but I was afraid to give you any pain medication. I'm

not sure how to put this delicately, so I'll just ask.
What kind of creature are you? Are you allergic to
human drugs? I have Ibuprofen, Acetaminophen,
Tramadol, Oxycodone and Morphine."

No reaction. She stared at me with the same
expression and remained silent.

Bruce said, "Maybe she doesn't speak English. Try
something else."

Fluent in Spanish and French, I tried those first,
to no affect. Making a mangled attempt at German
and Italian garnered the same result. I was at an
impasse. Everything hinged on being able to
communicate with her. How could I do that if she
didn't understand me?

Bruce said, "I hand you the opportunity of a
lifetime and you fuck it up. What a loser."

***

5:31pm –

She refused all medication but didn't seem to
object to my cooking, which was a relief. Hoping to
soothe her fears, I spoke incessantly, chattering on like
a monkey, as she ate. I took heart, as slowly she
became more comfortable with my presence.

"Since you can't tell me your name, I hope you
don't mind if I give you one until I learn yours. I've

been toying with a few and I fancy Danica. It means morning star. What do you think?"

Bruce said, "I think only a woman would come up with such a pretty name. Was that the one you were going to use after the sex change operation?"

"Shut up, Bruce."

Glancing around the room, she frowned at me and went back to her supper. "Do you like it?" I moved to the bed, sitting on the edge. "Danica?"

She looked up at me and I pointed to her. "Danica?"

The corners of her mouth turned up slightly and I beamed with satisfaction. She liked it. "Of course, it can't compare to you but it is a lovely name, don't you think? I've always been partial to it. As soon as you're ready, I'll take you on a tour of the grounds. The daffodils will be blooming in a week or so. You should be up and around by then, I'd say."

Skimming through the pages, it was more of the same. Faraday was not what I expected, if this was an accurate picture. I almost felt sorry for the man's horrible death. I couldn't be sure but it appeared that Danica was Leukosia. Nothing in the text suggested her identity, thanks to Faraday's paranoia, which meant my discovery was safe for the moment. The most important clue thus far was Bruce. Was he the other man at the estate the night everything went to hell? Hoping to find another hint to his identity, I read more.

Saturday, January 28, 2012
2:22pm -

Today was the day. I had been so patient and now I was being rewarded. The weather was perfect; Danica was healing well and best of all, the spring flowers were in full bloom a month early. It was a sign. This week with my morning star was unparalleled and now I would make her mine. It was time to meet my destiny, our destiny. Beaming with satisfaction, I entered my ladylove's room.

"I thought we would have lunch in the garden today. Do you feel up to it, darling?"

She said nothing but took my offered hand when I approached. Throwing the coverlet aside, she stood easily.

Escorting my morning star along the winding brick path, she gazed at the cheerful blooms wistfully. Red camellias, pink saucer magnolias, yellow daffodils and white lady banks filled the air with perfume. Lunch waited for us under an old oak, draped with Spanish moss. It was perfect, if I did say so myself.

Seating her at the wrought iron patio table, I said, "I hope you like the meal. It's crab cakes, creamy corn, baby corn muffins, iced tea and for dessert, lemon pie."

Bruce said, "What a pussy."

"Shut up, Bruce. Go away. As I was saying, Danica, I also took the liberty of bringing some champagne. We can celebrate your speedy recovery."

Silently, she picked up her fork and ate. Too nervous to eat, I remarked on the weather, the flowers, the history of the estate and anything else I could think of to pass the time.

When she set her fork down at long last, I nearly burst. "Danica, I have a present for you." Reaching in my pocket, I retrieved the box and said, "I found this in a shop on my trip to Greece. It's ancient and purported to have magical properties. It is my most precious possession; I want you to wear it as a token of my love."

A crease appeared in her brow as she took the box. Unable to contain myself, I jumped up and put it around her dainty neck. "Do you like it? Will you wear it?"

Radiant with joy, a lovely smile slid across her face. "Oh, yes I love it, Michael but I have one question that has been bothering me. Who is Bruce?"

Her voice sounded as if a chorus of angels serenaded me. I didn't even mind the uncomfortable question. Nothing mattered except that she was mine.

"Don't worry about him. He's my personal cross to bear. I'm so happy to hear your voice. Why didn't you speak before? You have a good grasp of the English language."

"That is a long story. One best left alone for now."

"You're right, it's not important. I can't tell you how happy you've made me, Danica. Oh, but that's not your name."

"It is a beautiful name, much more so than my own. Please, continue using it."

"All right. Can you at least tell me what you are or how you got stuck in the marsh?"

"I was shot by a trigger-happy hunter, as I am sure you've already surmised. As to your other question, I am a %$*@+ and a fringe member of the Zephyri nation."

What do you mean by 'fringe'?"

"An outcast, existing on the outer edge of my society."

"But why? You're perfect. Why wouldn't they accept you?"

"Thank you, Michael but as I said, it is a long story. Perhaps, when we know each other better, I will tell you the tale and maybe you will share the story of Bruce."

I was as confused as Danica. Who was Bruce? If

Danica was there, why didn't she know? Weeks went by with no answer to those questions. Danica related the basic facts of Zephyri life, races and powers, a kernel at a time but Faraday didn't reciprocate; he was obsessed with learning all he could about the magical creatures.

***

Sunday, February 26, 2012
11:16pm —

Screaming woke me and I hurried to Danica's room to find her still sleeping and in the throes of a terrible nightmare. Shaking her, I said, "Danica, precious, wake up. It's a dream. Wake up, sweetheart."

She sat up, clinging to me, covered in perspiration. Stroking her hair, I rocked her saying, "It was only a dream, just a dream."

Her voice was choked with tears and she said, "It was real, not a dream. It was real."

"No, darling. It was your imagination. You're safe, I'm here. No one will harm you."

"You don't understand. It was a memory, not a dream."

"Sometimes, if I talk about a nightmare, it helps. Do you want to tell me about it?"

She whispered, "You will hate me."

"Nonsense. I could never hate you. I love you. You

know that."

"I know but for this, you would send me away, as they did."

Hugging her tightly, I said, "Never! No matter what, I will never send you away. I can't live without my morning star."

Reluctantly, she said, "It... It was when I killed my sisters."

Horrified, I froze. "You killed your sisters?"

"I didn't want to, they forced me to do it."

"Who made you?"

"The Council."

"They made you kill your own family?"

Nodding, she said, "It was part of the sentence for my crime."

"Oh, my God! What crime could be that awful?"

"Betrayal. My people are not as forgiving as humans. We are barbaric, bloodthirsty creatures. Long ago, I was betrothed. It was arranged, I had no love for the man but due to his position, I was given no choice in the decision. Of all the Zephyri, he chose me and you cannot say no to the Tsái. After the date was set, I was inconsolable for months. My sisters did their best to comfort me but nothing helped. He is a cruel, heartless man and I felt doomed to a miserable existence. A week before the wedding, I packed a bag and stole out of our home, intending to run away. I didn't have anywhere to go but I couldn't wed that monster.

My sisters met me at the gate, insisting on fleeing with me. I tried to talk them out of it but they would not hear of it. Therefore, we left, planning to live on some deserted island or other. Eryx discovered our treachery and sent his Praetorian in pursuit. No one escapes the Tsái's personal guard.

We were captured soon after and brought before the Council, in the Arena. Thousands of Zephyri watched, as we were led inside. The Council and the Tsái sat at a table in the center of the floor. Eryx made a grand speech about his love for me and how I had betrayed that love. Abdicating his right to punish me, he allowed the Council judgment. He claimed that it was too personal an issue for him to decide but they were not to kill me.

The lead Council member at the time, Orrek, asked if Eryx would still have me. He said, 'The faithless slut was running away to meet her lover. I will not take a whore to wife.' I tried to tell them that there was no one else but they would not listen. Orrek pronounced sentence. 'You and your sisters were given the highest honor ever bestowed on any Zephyri. You are all guilty of treason, for which the penalty is

death. However, since we cannot carry out this
sentence on the primary offender, we have come up
with an alternative.' Speaking directly to me, he said,
'Your sisters will die today for their crimes. Your
punishment is exile and to determine the manner of
their death. They will either be thrown to the crowd
and torn apart...' The spectators cheered. '...or you will
kill them yourself. Choose.'

I could barely see my sisters through the tears
and I kept repeating no, no, no. They both pleaded
with me to kill them but I could not. Time ran out
and the Praetorian came forward to take my beloved
sisters into the throng. I said, 'No, stop! I will do it.'
Someone put a dagger in my hand. It shook so badly
that I almost dropped it. Helpful as always, the eldest
stepped forward. She grasped my wrist lovingly and
smiled before she pulled it into her breast."

Breaking down into fitful sobs, she couldn't
continue. Those vile, evil demons! Hatred unlike
anything I had ever felt, boiled in my chest. They
must pay. My morning star would have justice.

Bruce said, "It's about time you grew some
cajones. Now we're getting somewhere. If I had known
getting you laid would do the trick, I would have done
it ages ago."

Danica still wept on my chest and I didn't want

to disturb her but I couldn't let him disparage her reputation. Speaking to Bruce internally was uncomfortable, so I rarely addressed him in that way, however... "You will not insult her! She is pure and innocent; I will not tolerate it. Do I make myself clear?"

"Sure, man. I got it. I was just sayin'."

"Well, don't. We have done nothing untoward."

"Aww, come on! I thought we were making progress. Now you go and ruin it with more pantywaist shit. You're hopeless. How are you ever going to save the human race, talking like that?"

"What do you mean? Is that the destiny you're here to help me fulfill?"

"Fuck! It wasn't time yet."

"You already spilled the beans. Tell me the rest."

"I can't give you all of it but I guess it won't alter history, if I just tell you some of it. In my time, you and Danica are responsible for the destruction of the Zephyri. You save the whole world from their evil domination. Imagine my surprise when I get here and you're a total fucking pussy. Historical figures are never what they're cracked up to be but no one will ever believe what a bitch you were."

"How?"

"Jesus Christ! Do I have to tell you everything?"

"No."

"Apparently I do. Let's count the ways... First, it took three years to get you off those damn meds. 'Oh no Bruce, I won't listen to you. The doctors say I'm sick. You're a manifestation of my illness.' Then you fought me the entire time you were in medical school. 'Oh no Bruce, it's too hard. I can't concentrate. I don't like touching the icky bodies. I've got blood on my clothes. Eww!' After that..."

"Stop. You made your point. You're right. You're always right."

"You're damn right, I'm always right. Burn it into your brain, fucker."

Kegan chuckled and said, "He's totally doolally."

"He's what?"

"He's cracked, lass, mental."

"Oh, crazy."

"Aye."

"So you don't think this Bruce could be real?"

Staring at me as if I had lost my mind as well, he said, "A time traveler? And an invisible one at that? Nay."

"How was I supposed to know? With all the magic creatures, powers and spells, how can you not at least wonder?"

"He's dead and the Zephyri are still here. If Bruce was a time traveler, he got his wires crossed somewhere along the time line. Faraday isn't my concern, the woman is. Her story doesn't ring a bell, if it is true."

"So you have no idea who it could be?"

"None. The bastard was careful to give no descriptions, species, or abilities, nothing that would allow me to identify her. There is nothing here I can use. Let's go."

"But what about the rest of it? He's about to tell..."

"What? How he tortured and killed dozens of Zephyri all in the name of love? If ye want to satisfy yer morbid curiosity, ye can come back later. I've let ye waste enough time. We are leaving, now. Alida, turn that off."

The pixie backed out of the program and shut down the computer. I had a feeling that we were missing something important but Kegan was not in the mood to listen. Calling a door, he wrapped his arm around my waist and pulled me through after him.

"Where the hell have you been?"

Eryx towered over us, fists clenched. Jeez, everybody was crabby tonight.

Kegan answered, "We found them, Tsái."

"What? Found who?"

"Malachai and the others. Well, Alida and Chevy found them or we think they did."

"Where?"

"Plum Island."

"Get a team together. We leave in an hour."

I said, "I just need my weapons..."

"Nay, lass. Not this time."

"Hey, you wouldn't even know where to look if it weren't for us. I'm going."

Gritting his teeth, Eryx said, "No, you're not. Go to your room."

"We're back to that again? I'm not a child. You can't ground me."

"I do not have time for this." He shooed me away with his hand and just like that, I was standing in my bedroom. *Ooh!*

CHAPTER 15

Padding on bare feet, I made my way to the edge of the first doorway. Something waited for me. It seethed with want, with need. Terror swamped me but I had to move. Dim light revealed shadowed portals to utter blackness lining the walls. Creatures of unknown race and motivation lurked in every one. Bracing myself, I stepped in front of the first doorway. A hand, gray and shriveled, shot out, grabbing for my throat. Backing against the opposite wall, I watched as Malachai's tortured face appeared. His breath escaped in a whisper as he repeated the same words again and again. I couldn't understand him and I didn't care, I just wanted out. Straining across the gap, the vampire almost reached me but was unwilling or unable to move past the doorframe. Sliding down the wall, I eased to the next opening.

"Chevy. You came back."

Spinning back the way I had come, a large shadow stood at the end of the hall.

"Leave me alone! I told you, I don't know anything."

Darting to the other side of the hall, I scooted sideways along the broken plaster. Bob, the ogre's face and huge hand thrust from the void. He shouted but no sound came out. Footsteps clicked behind me.

"Chevy. Where are you going? It's time to play."

He was getting closer. A warm golden light shone at the end of the gauntlet, my only escape.

A harsh whisper sounded next to my ear. "Chevy! What are you?"

With my heart in my throat, I raced toward the exit. Deformed, grotesque creatures announced my arrival with silent screams. Claws shredded my nightgown and tore at my skin, as I fought to get through.

"Chevy, who are you? Tell me!"

"I don't know."

"You do. You know. One way or another you're going to tell me."

"No!"

The door was closer; golden light filled the room beyond but didn't affect the shadows in the passage. A few steps more. My nightgown wrapped around my body like a cocoon, stopping me mid-stride.

"You know what you are and you will tell me. If I must slice your skin off one strip at a time, you will tell me."

"NO!" Striking out with venomous hatred, I slashed at the hand holding me. I fell to my knees, as he released me and scurried through the door, slamming it in my wake.

Searing heat scalded my skin. The room, my parent's room, was engulfed in flame. Getting to my feet, I watched as fire dripped from the ceiling like rain, onto my parents' lifeless bodies.

Movement caught my attention and I turned to see Leukosia, standing near the bed. Wings extended, she pointed at the window. In the firelight, I could see my reflection but it was that of a little girl with a soot-smudged face. Tears left tracks of clean skin that showed through the grime on my round cheeks.

A man appeared behind me and I whirled to defend myself. Taller than me by a few inches, he wore only black leather pants and muscles bulged everywhere. He must have weighed close to three hundred pounds. My foot flew out, in a kick to the groin. Swatting my leg aside like a gnat, he spun me away. Python arms wound around my upper body, ending the fight before it began. My feet flailed at his shins uselessly. Still struggling against the inevitable, I said, "I told you, I don't know what I am. Let me go!"

"Chevy, it's me, Aspen."

"I don't give a shit who you are. Let me go."

"Stop fighting and listen to me. I'm here to help. You remember me, don't you? The gold fairy at the Antechamber. Of course, you do. How could you forget?" As he spoke, the scene faded, morphing into a picturesque forest with a brook running through it. "We're going to sit by the stream and chat. Okay?"

"I can't tell you anything because I don't know."

"You said that but I don't know what you're talking about. Chevy, you're dreaming. This is a nightmare, it's not real."

My squirming body froze. A nightmare? It should have occurred to me before. "I'm dreaming?"

"Yes. Now will you walk with me?"

Setting me down, he slowly released me. Without the adrenaline surging through my veins, I realized that my *feet were burned. Clutching him for support, I gasped in pain. Without a word, he picked me back up and strode to the water's edge. Sitting on the bank, he held me in his lap and examined my feet.*

I asked, "How do I know this is a nightmare?"

"Are you always this suspicious?"

"Lately, yeah."

"Any particular reason for that?"

"Too many people playing too many games."

Easing my feet into the water, he said, "You must have stepped on hot coals back there. What was that about? Who were the people in the bed?"

The cool liquid felt so good that I sighed in relief. "My parents. They died in a fire but I keep having this altered dream where they were killed beforehand."

"Maybe it's a memory resurfacing."

"That's what Eryx said."

Intent on my blisters, Aspen murmured, "He's usually right. It doesn't sound as if you believe it though."

"I don't."

"Why not?"

"I remember what happened that night, so it can't be a memory. Besides, I don't trust him."

"How come?"

"He's one of the people playing games."

Chuckling, he said, "Sweetheart, everyone is playing, whether they know it or not."

"I'm not."

"Sure you are. You're one of the major competitors. The only way you can avoid it is to sit on the sidelines."

"Whatever. You're entitled to your opinion, I guess. Why are you here?"

"Like I said, to help. It seemed as if you needed it, so here I am."

Producing a cloth out of thin air, he dipped it into the water. Squeezing out the excess, he brushed aside my hair and began washing my face. Shivering at the feel of the cool water hitting my sweaty skin, I closed my eyes and reveled in the sensation. "Mmm, that feels good. "How are you going to help?"

"Pulling you out of the mouth of hell doesn't count? You're a harsh mistress."

"Oh, sorry. Thank you for that. This is much better but I meant why are you still here? Did I make you up?"

"Am I the man of your dreams?"

"Very funny. I'm serious."

"No, I'm the real Aspen. We're still here because you look like a ragamuffin."

"Okay, how are you here?"

His deep voice rumbled, "It's one of my many talents. Dream manipulation, sponge baths, the list goes on but I don't want to brag."

"But you're so big."

"Nice of you to notice. I work hard to keep this physique."

"No, I meant you aren't a fairy anymore. Where are your wings?"

"I can appear any way I desire in dreams."

Finishing my face, he moved on to my neck and shoulders. "How did you know I needed help?"

Aspen said, "Kegan and I came by; we couldn't wake you up. So I took a nap and ta-da. Here we are."

Alarmed, I asked, "You couldn't wake me? Are we stuck here?"

"As pleasant as that sounds, no we're not. We'll go

in a bit. I have a question for you."

"What's that?"

"What were you going on about? What don't you know?"

"When I was kidnapped and drugged, the man kept asking me who and what I was. I didn't know what he was talking about. I must have added him into my dream. Before I got to my parents' bedroom, he was chasing me down a hall of doors. He grabbed me just as I reached the room but I got away."

"Where did the scratches and tears in your nightie come from?"

"The creatures in the hall. They tried to catch me."

"Wow. You managed to get all the monsters in one shot didn't you? But why would you dream about Leukosia? It's not as if she doesn't fit in the whole nightmare theme..."

Dipping my head, I said, "I don't know."

Aspen lifted my chin, staring at me with those piercing, eerie, gold eyes. Suddenly, I realized how close we were and my heart pounded. Leaning forward, I thought he was going to kiss me and I tensed.

Revealing his fangs, he grinned and said, "Relax sweetness, I won't bite—unless you ask. I'm just rinsing the cloth."

My face warmed. "Oh. Right."

Going to work on my scuffed knees, he said, "In dreams, there is always a purpose. What do you suppose is the reason behind the images here?"

"My life hasn't been peaches and cream the last few days. What do you think?"

"I think under the circumstances, most people would have nightmares given your situation."

"See? Eryx's whole theory of my memory being altered is garbage."

"You didn't let me finish."

"Sorry."

"People dream for different reasons, one of them is a method to cope with stress. Nevertheless, on my way to you, I encountered a barrier that was very difficult to penetrate. Considering that and our inability to wake you, I think this is more than your mind dealing with a bad week."

"Of course, you would agree with Eryx, he's your Tsái."

"The Tsái doesn't tolerate sycophants and I don't kiss ass regardless. You need to face whatever this is for your own sake. I might not be there the next time."

Hackles rising, I said, "I don't need a babysitter; I'm a grown woman. I can take care of myself."

"Don't get your panties in a bunch. Everyone needs help now and then. I was just pointing out that if you wanted to maintain your, 'I am woman, hear me roar' persona, you might want to consider something other than denial. It's clearly not working for you."

Of all the arrogant, conceited, egotistical... Without conscious decision, I pinched his chest, twisting to make it more painful.

Giving me a slow grunt, I was satisfied, until he brought his face within an inch of my own. His eyes heated and bored into mine. "That's nice but I prefer nails."

Eyes the size of saucers, I stammered, "No, I uh... I mean, I didn't... That's not..."

Raising an eyebrow, he said, "...your cup of tea?"

I looked around and said, "Maybe we should get

back."

"Whenever you're ready."

The purr in his voice said that he meant the double entendre. I didn't respond. Climbing out of his lap without touching him was awkward but I managed. Staring at the forest, I didn't know what to do. "How do we get out of here?"

"I'll handle that but once I dissipate the dream, I don't want to lose you. Hold onto me until we wake up. If you let go, I might not be able to find you again."

"Why? You found me this time."

"We're deep in your subconscious; farther than I've ever had to go to invade another's dreams. If you were any deeper, I don't think I would make it to you, let alone out again."

"You sound serious."

"I am. It's important you understand the consequences."

"What would happen if I was trapped here?"

"Living in a dream world? That depends on your mind. It could be like the nightmare or it could be like this. In the real world, you would be a vegetable. If you were able to resolve the reason you're here to begin with, you might make it out. Maybe."

Gulping, I stepped closer to him.

"Ready?"

Nodding, I looked up at him and frowned.

"What's wrong?"

"Other than the fact you just scared the shit out of me?"

"Yeah."

"It's weird. You're taller than I am."

Smirking, he wrapped his arm around my waist and

said, "Remember, don't let go."

I clasped my hands behind his back. The trees and stream faded to a misty image and disappeared, leaving us floating in a lightless void. I could still see Aspen, even in the dark. He glowed with an inner light like the sun. Soaring straight up, we sped toward what resembled an asteroid belt. "What is that?"

"The barrier."

"It didn't look like that before."

"It's breaking up. Now do you grasp why this isn't stress related?"

Seeing it first-hand, I was starting to believe. I couldn't fathom how it had happened but I couldn't deny that it existed.

"When we go in, it will be difficult to stay awake but you have to hang on to me. No matter what. Do you understand?"

"I get it but you're holding me."

"Your choice to leave with me is what will determine if you escape. I can help with the mechanics but I can't make the decision for you."

Taking a deep breath, I nodded and said, "Okay, let's go."

Fatigue marked the edge of the barrier. Aspen slowed more with every body length we traveled. Weariness turned to exhaustion and the fairy's progress diminished to a crawl. It was as if we were swimming through jelly. My eyelids drifted shut and snapped open several times. Remembering his warning, I began to chant. "Have to get out. Stay with Aspen. Don't let go."

"That's good, Chevy. Keep it up."

The last time my eyes closed, I strained but couldn't pry them open again. Compensating, I ground the words *out, putting all my faith in them.*

The realization that I had drifted off startled me and my eyes flew open. Blinking in the bright light, it took a moment to focus. Kegan's smiling face greeted me.

"Yer back. I was worried about ye."

"Am I? This isn't another dream?"

Stroking my cheek, the vampire said, "Nay, I'm real."

A deep voice grumbled, "Don't mind me. I'll be fine."

Glancing down, I saw Aspen lying across my chest, glowering at Kegan.

"It took ye long enough, fairy. It's been over an hour. What were ye doing in there?"

Sneering, Aspen said, "What you couldn't, vampire. Gratitude isn't necessary. Chevy already took care of that."

Eyes darting back and forth between them, I felt uncomfortable and lost. "What's going on?"

"Nothing, lass, I was concerned, that's all."

He was lying but I didn't have the energy to deal with his shit right then. "I feel as if I was put through a knothole backwards."

Aspen said, "I know what you mean. I need another nap."

Curling up on his side, the fairy rested his head on my breast and closed his eyes. That did it. I was awake. Sliding back against the headboard, I sat up. Aspen tumbled down to my lap.

Testing his wings, he said, "Careful! You could have broken a vein."

Kegan curled his lip and said, "I think it's time for

you to go, fairy."

I agreed but didn't care for him giving the orders. This was my room and they both needed to leave.

Aspen said, "Uh-uh. No can do. We have lessons, besides she can't be left alone. We wouldn't want a repeat performance. Would we?"

What was I going to do? This could happen again? I couldn't go without any sleep. Kegan's brow furrowed in worry, as he looked at me.

"What does she need to do?"

"The barrier is most of what is preventing her from sleeping and dreaming in the usual way. If that was gone, I think she would be fine."

Kegan growled, "Then remove it."

"I can't. Dreams are my bag, not mental constructs. It might hurt her if it was removed. That's probably why the Tsái didn't take care of it himself."

Aspen said, "I'll stay here with her. Go get the Tsái."

"Uh, guys. I'm right here. Did it occur to either of you to ask me what I want?"

"Sorry, lass. Yer right but there seems to be only one option."

"There's always a choice. No one is tinkering around in my brain."

"But..."

"I said, no. I'm tired. Get out both of you."

Aspen said, "One of us is staying. Since I'm able to actually help, if you do go to sleep, it'll be me."

I hated that he was right. Sighing, I said, "Fine, whatever."

"Lass, may I speak to ye in private?"

"What now?"

"Please?"

Aggravated with everyone, I threw back the covers and stomped into the bathroom. Folding my arms across my chest, I said, "What?"

Closing the door behind him, Kegan said, "When ye were dreaming, did Aspen... Did he, eh..."

"Jeez, Kegan, just spit it out."

"Very well. Did the fairy molest ye?"

"Really? That's what was so important? Unfrickinbelievable! No, he didn't *molest* me. He was a perfect gentleman." *Mostly.* "You're not my father, boyfriend or brother. If anything had happened, it would be none of your business, unless I volunteered the information. Is that clear?"

Stiffening, he said, "Aye, crystal."

"Good. Were there any other burning questions you wanted to ask?"

"Nay."

He opened the door and left altogether. On a roll, I stormed back into the bedroom. Aspen was snickering.

"I guess you set him straight."

"Shut up, Aspen. You started this shit."

"I don't know what you mean."

"Oh, yes you do. Everything you did since waking up was a performance designed to get at him. You knew it would drive him crazy and that's what you wanted. What was the point?"

"I was bored."

"Bored, my ass. Why?"

Shrugging, he said, "It seemed like a good idea at the time."

"That's not an answer."

Shrugging, he drawled, "It's the only one you're

going to get."

"You're a real bastard."

A malicious grin spread across his face. "You have no idea."

"So what now? Do we sit around and play cards?"

"Nope. Time for school. Get dressed."

"Listen, Aspen, I appreciate everything you did but I don't need lessons."

"Wrong. You do need to be trained and we don't have a choice, in any event. The Tsái says teach you, I obey."

"You obey?"

"Yes, if it's the Tsái's order or if it suits me. In this case it's both."

Folding my arms across my chest, I said, "It doesn't suit me."

"Too bad. Get dressed."

"I don't have to do jack." Scoffing, I said, "What are you going to do? Make me? You're a quarter my size."

"Haven't you learned anything from us?"

"Oh, sure. I've learned that you're cruel, brutal and can't be trusted."

Frowning, he said, "Me or the Zephyri?"

"The Zephyri."

"That's pretty racist..."

Clenching my fists, I shouted, "I'm not a racist!"

"Racism is defined as a belief that races have cultural characteristics that make them superior to others. According to your statement, I presume you believe humans are kind, humane and honest."

"In general, yes."

"Okay, so why did I pull you out of that nightmare?

What was my ulterior motive?"

"I don't know."

"You and Alida are friends. What is her secret plan to betray you?"

"The pixies are different."

"If you think that the pixies aren't brutal, you haven't been invited to dinner yet."

"You admit it?"

"That we're brutal? Absolutely but humans are no less so."

"Oh, please."

"Have you ever seen a battlefield? Taken a tour of the morgue? Been to a crime scene?"

I didn't respond.

"No answer? How many courtrooms are filled with people suing for fraud? Prisons are overcrowded with criminals but you're right, it's not all humans. Nevertheless, I would argue that most humans are cruel, brutal and untrustworthy, at one time or another. The same goes for the Zephyri. People are the same everywhere, no matter the race."

"We don't slaughter people in the oval office."

"That is a difference in etiquette. Your government still executes criminals."

"By electrocution, gas or lethal injection and it's not done in public."

"None of which would work on a vampire or a majority of the Zephyri. You're upset that you had to see it. Mercedes' death wouldn't bother you at all if it was kept in a back room somewhere."

"That's not true."

"So you don't think she should have been put to death? Are you aware of what she did to Faraday? Do you know how many lives are at stake because of her actions?"

"I know and I didn't say she didn't deserve it."

"You accuse the entire Zephyri nation of being dishonest but in this we are better than humans. We don't dress up the facts of life in pleasant platitudes. We don't hide from the uglier parts of the world. We don't expect to be saved from ourselves. Truth isn't neat, pretty or nice, it's messy, offensive and nasty but you know where you stand."

Slack-jawed, I stared at the fairy playboy. He wasn't stupid, far from it but I hadn't expected—this.

Taking my silence as a forfeit, he said, "Philosophy 101 is over. Next up, Basic Air Manipulation. Get dressed, unless you don't care if I ogle you. I certainly don't mind."

Following up his comment with a lecherous look, I realized that I was still in my nightgown. Running for the closet, I decided to argue with him later.

CHAPTER 16

Wearing a comfortable pair of jeans and T-shirt, I went back into the bedroom. "Aspen, I still don't think this is necessary."

"You have a handle on your new power already? Wow, you're good."

Rolling my eyes, I said, "Well, no but since I won't be using it, this is a waste of time."

"Did you choose to use your empathic ability, when you were young?"

"No. This is different though. It's an active power, so I have a choice this time."

"If you lose your temper or encounter a stressful situation, you have a fifty-fifty chance of hurting someone nearby. Are you willing to risk that?"

I set my jaw and said, "I won't let that happen."

"How are you going to prevent it?"

"I'm an empath, I can control my emotions."

Scoffing, he said, "Like you did on the mountain or with the Tsái? You are the one that cut him up, aren't you?"

"Ahem, yes that was me."

"If you refuse to learn how to control this power, I would look for the deepest hole you can find and move in. No one will be safe in your presence."

"That's a little melodramatic."

Throwing his arms in the air, he said, "You have no clue, do you?"

Narrowing my eyes, I asked, "What are you talking about?"

"Forget the basic level, you don't know anything. We'll have to start with remedial lessons."

"I'm not stupid!"

"Chill, girlfriend. I didn't say you were but you don't even know what you have. Air manipulation, simply put, is control over the air."

Gritting my teeth, I said, "You're starting to piss me off, fairy."

"Join the club. Now, sit down, shut up and you might learn something."

Of all the... "I am not going to stand here..."

"You're right. I said, sit down."

The muscles in my legs gave out, dropping me into the chair behind me. "What the fuck?"

"I also said, shut up."

Opening my mouth, I tried to tell him where to stick it but nothing came out. Attempting it a few more times didn't help. I couldn't speak.

"Stop it. You look like a guppy."

Fuming, I braced my knees with my hands and struggled to stand but nothing worked.

Looking at the ceiling, he said, "Where was I? Oh, yes. Air manipulation is the power to control air in all its forms. A person with this ability can create anything from a small puff of air to a hurricane. Other uses are air blades, as you already know, air shields, you've done that one too, walking on air, gliding, levitating, flight, propulsion, vacuums or bubbles, controlling sound waves and thermal resistance. All of these effects are produced through manipulating the density and movement of the atmosphere. Do you have any questions so far?"

Glaring at him, I mouthed silently, "I can't speak."

Wagging his finger at me, he said, "I'll give it back but be a good girl or I'll do it again."

As soon as my vocal cords worked, I cleared my throat and yelled, "You son-of-a-bitch!" That was all I managed to get out before he cut me off.

"Since there are no questions, we'll proceed to practical applications. Lectures are so boring without visual aids. Don't you think?"

Slow and deliberate, I said, "Fuck you."

Pulling his outer ear forward, he said, "What was that? I couldn't hear you. No? Okay, we'll move on. I need a volunteer from the audience. You, miss? Thank you for your trust."

I flipped him the bird. Being unable to speak or move didn't mean I was without resources. He thought he was funny? Fine. Recalling the time Tony fell face down in the mud; I smiled at the fairy and sent out mental tentacles. He was still lecturing but I ignored it. There wouldn't be a test. Funneling emotion into his mind, he snorted once in the middle of a sentence. Furrowing his brow, he tried to regain his train of thought. A giggle escaped, as I increased the intensity, until he had broken into gales of laughter. Convulsing in giant braying guffaws, forced him to the floor, where he clutched at his stomach. Tears ran down his face as he tried to speak. Panting, he said, "You—bitch." The insane cackling took the sting out of his comment.

Anticipating the return of my voice and muscle control, I kept trying to speak but it wasn't working. What had he done to me? There was no way he could maintain concentration in his condition. His wheezing laughter, stopped so suddenly, it startled me. I didn't want to kill him, just teach him a lesson but he was still going. I just couldn't hear him. Had he halted the sound waves? What did he think that would accomplish? It was getting hot and I was dizzy. Reaching up to fan myself, I hit something solid. Confused, I felt around my head with both hands. Whatever it was covered me from the neck up but I couldn't see it. A bubble, he had said he could make a bubble. *Damn it*. If I passed out, I could be in a world of hurt. My chest tightened, as my air ran out. Left with no alternative, I let him go.

Aspen lay motionless for a moment, breathing but I still couldn't. Banging on the side table, I got his attention. He said something but I couldn't hear him. I slapped the tabletop and pointed at my face. Sound was restored. Leaning back in the chair, I gulped in the fresh air.

After regaining my breath, I lifted my head and looked at the fairy. He sat cross-legged on the floor, staring at me with a strange expression on his face. "What?"

"I'm trying to figure out what to do with you."

"You could start by not treating me like a baby."

"That's hard to do when you insist on acting like one."

"I am tired of everyone saying I'm childish. How does trying to protect my friends and species make me immature? Why does my anger at being deceived and manipulated make me a brat? Is the Zephyri definition of maturity quiet acceptance of being spoon-fed lies?"

"Do you want a real answer?"

What kind of a question was that? "No, lie to me. I like it."

The fairy mumbled, "You seem to."

"What's that supposed to mean?"

He leaned forward, resting his arms on his thighs. "You refuse to accept anything, if it isn't what you want to hear."

"That's not true."

Continuing as if I hadn't said anything, he said, "And you don't listen."

Fed up with being dismissed, I stood and said, "Not to people who just issue orders."

"You don't give them any other option."

"Oh, I get it. I have to follow orders first and then I will be treated like an adult."

"Sometimes but the point is that to listen, you must have respect. You don't respect anyone."

Folding my arms, I said, "Respect is earned."

"Yes, it is but there are certain things you respect before you understand them."

Snorting, I said, "Like you or the Tsái? Nice logic."

"For starters, yeah."

"Why would I do that? I can't respect liars."

"When have I lied to you?"

"You said that you were messing with Kegan out of boredom. That was a lie."

Aspen's arms extended, "Okay, you caught me. I apologize. When else?"

Furrowing my brow, I said, "I don't know."

"How do you know when someone is lying to you? I

presume you use your ability."

"Sometimes but mostly its reading body language."

"How do you choose between the two?"

"I drop my shields but I don't like to invade other people's privacy."

Aspen stood and flew up to face me. "From now on, I give you permission to read me whenever you like. In fact, I insist on it." Leaning forward, he looked at me expectantly.

"What? Now?"

"Would there be a more convenient time?"

"You're a smartass."

"Pot and kettle, baby."

Shields down, I felt calm arrogance permeating every layer of his mind. He didn't lack confidence in anything. It must be nice.

"Now that you can accurately gauge my sincerity, I'll answer your question from earlier. I can only speak for myself but I think there are several reasons people call you childish. One, I already mentioned. You don't respect others. This is an ancient society and we are slow to change because generations are much longer than humans. The Zephyri still adhere to the belief that you respect people, especially your elders and superiors, regardless of your personal opinions. The Tsái is due respect because he is our leader, older than anyone on the planet and he is a good man."

Giving him a wry look, I said, "In your opinion."

"Yes, the last was my personal belief. It is also obvious that you do not respect our people or way of life. You have known about us for less than a week and you judge us." With a faraway look in his eyes, he said, "I wonder if an alien race set down on this world for a few days, what they would see in human society. Would they consider you kind, honest and humane?" Shaking his head, the fairy saw me again. "Anyway, your attitude doesn't help. In addition, you're rash and rebellious. Those are adolescent traits; however, the biggest factor is that to us, you are a child."

"We already covered that. All of you think I'm nothing more than a bratty kid."

"I was speaking about your age, not your attitude or reactions. Everyone you meet here is going to be older than your grandparents are. You're about twenty, right?"

"Twenty-one."

"Fairies aren't considered adults until they are seventy-five. My sister, Zanna, had her ascension party a few months ago."

"How long do fairies live?"

"About a thousand years. The Zephyri try to take into account, the difference between the species but it still colors our actions. You can't help that but you can try not to make it harder for yourself."

Everything he said was the truth, as he saw it. I was torn between anger and self-pity. Why couldn't they see how wrong everything was?

"I listened to you. Now, you listen to me. I don't give a damn what you or the Zephyri think of me. You don't have to like me. I'm here against my will. It is ludicrous to expect someone to respect people that are keeping her prisoner. The Tsái is not just keeping me captive; he's amassing an army to attack my people, when they have done nothing to the Zephyri. He told me that he is willing to wipe my race off the face of the earth. He tortured Kegan and knocked Sophia across the room but allows creatures like Bob to run around loose. If *we* have someone that is dangerous to others, we lock him up. The Tsái is cruel, barbaric and has a god complex. I don't understand how you all think he's the greatest thing since sliced bread."

Aspen's forehead crinkled and he said, "I like you."

Confused, I shook my head and said, "What?"

"I said, I like you."

"But you..."

"I said, the reason we treat you like a child is that you act like one. I never said I didn't like you. Kegan *more* than likes you. Alida, Jan, Shayle, the Tsái, Aadí and Magnus, they all like you."

"Now I know you're lying. Eryx hates me."

"I thought I told you to keep your shields down."

"They are."

"Then why don't you believe me."

Waving his objections away, I said, "This is stupid. It doesn't matter who likes me and who doesn't. Out of everything I said, why is that the first thing out of your mouth?"

"Because it was the first thing *you* said and the most untrue. I can explain most of the other things but that was patently false."

Incredulous, I said, "You have a reasonable explanation for everything I mentioned? This I have to hear."

"You are being held in Tweentown because your relative discomfort is not as important as the damage you will do, if we let you leave."

"Right. Eryx is afraid I will ruin his plans for world domination."

"It is that assumption that could ruin any prospects for a peaceful resolution. You would run around screaming fire in a theater because you saw someone smoking. Details make a big difference."

Hands on my hips, I argued, "I saw the zombies, you can't deny it. Doyle said it was an army and they're unstoppable."

Unruffled, he asked, "Does the United States have an army?"

"Of course."

"Now, so do we."

I noticed he didn't elaborate on that.

Aspen continued, "Discipline within Zephyri society is harsh according to modern human standards but we stick with what works."

"That's your rational justification?"

"Sure. What do you think we should do?"

"It depends on the offense. Stealing is a jail term; murder varies from prison to death."

"And that works for humans? They don't re-offend?"

"You know it doesn't."

"Think about this. What would happen if the Zephyri were unruly? What would it mean to the world to have them behave as humans do?"

Considering their powers, that was a scary proposition. "I see your point but you shouldn't rule through terror."

"It is the *only* way to rule. Fear of the consequences is the sole reason that anyone acts contrary to their desires. Even the most devout Christian follows the teachings in the bible because of the consequences."

"What about Bob? You've explained everything else. I don't know if I agree with any of it but I may as well hear it all."

"Bob has been confined, until Fenion finds out what happened. The ogre has no memory of trying to kill you or running amok through the streets."

Deflated, I said something brilliant. "Oh."

"So... What do I do with you?"

"Are you asking me?"

Nodding, Aspen said, "Yes. Tell me how to train you."

"You don't."

"That's not an option. What's the problem? It's not as if you're busy. Why don't you want to learn?"

Refusing to look at him, I said, "I'm weird enough."

His voice softened, and he said, "Ignoring your power doesn't make it go away. It will escape. Wouldn't you rather have control over the where and when?"

"How do you know I'll lose control? I could go the rest of my life without using it."

"It's part of who you are. No one can suppress everything all the time. Why should you even try? Learn how to control it and it only happens when and how you allow it. Besides, you can do cool shit with it."

Laughing, I said, "Okay, I'll try."

"Were you listening earlier, when I explained the applications?"

"I heard most of it."

"All right. We need to start with how to identify air."

Confused, I asked, "What do you mean?"

"Every element has a sensation when you connect with it. You have to figure out how to find it."

"How do you do it?"

Deep in thought, Aspen stroked his jaw and said, "I don't know. It's been so long since I learned that I can't remember."

"Some teacher you are."

Waving away my remark, he said, "It doesn't matter how I do it. Everyone is different. When you have used air in the past how did it feel?"

"I don't know. I was kind of busy when it happened."

"What did you do?"

Shrugging, I said, "Basically, I threw everything I had in one direction."

"No finesse but we can work with that. Do it."

"Right here?"

Backing across the room, he moved his hands in a come gesture. "Yeah. Throw everything you have at me."

"I don't want to hurt you."

"I won't let you. Come on. Are you chicken?"

"That doesn't work outside of grammar school."

Clucking and flapping his wings, he taunted me anyway. He looked ridiculous. Trying not to smile, I said, "Cut it out. I can't concentrate with you doing that."

He stopped and I hurled a mental ball at him. I couldn't tell if I had done anything. "Well?"

"Nothing. Hmm. What were you feeling when you used air before?"

"I was terrified."

"Okay, try again but this time focus on how you felt when the building exploded."

"Are you ready?"

"Yep. Let me have it."

Closing my eyes, I pictured the scene. Kegan unconscious on top of me, the second explosion, I was helpless. The rubble flew toward me and I thrust out with my whole being. A thud made me open my eyes. Aspen lay at the base of the wall, in a heap.

Running over to him, I said, "Are you all right? I'm so sorry. I thought you weren't going to let me hurt you."

Righting himself, he said, "I wasn't ready."

"You said you were."

"I didn't anticipate that kind of power. I only had up a minimal shield. It won't happen again. Now, tell me how it felt."

"I don't know. I pushed out with everything I had."

"Did you feel what you were affecting?"

"No. I don't know what you mean."

"Damn. How do I get you to understand?"

We stared at each other for a moment. I could feel his frustration, determination and pleasure. He liked teaching. I smiled at the thought. He didn't look like any instructor I ever had.

He asked, "What are you grinning about?"

"You."

"Me hitting the wall was funny, huh?"

"No, not at all. I can feel how much you enjoy training."

A stunned look covered his face and he hit his forehead. "I'm a fucking moron. Of course!"

"What?"

He pointed at me and said, "You're an empath."

Duh. "And?"

"We use what you know. I'll demonstrate while you observe with your ability."

Shrugging, I said, "It makes sense."

Hovering in the middle of the room he said, "I'm going to keep it small, so the technique is more obvious. Ready?"

Bringing his emotions to the forefront, I nodded. He

began and I could see how it was done. It was similar to how I sent feelers through earth, plants and trees. The difference was that he wasn't just receiving impressions. He pulled the air into his aura and sent it out again. Everything I touched with empathy had a different texture to it, a signature. Air was different from all the others. It was softer, wispy, and ephemeral. I may have been sensing it my whole life but never knew it was there, it was that subtle.

Aspen asked, "Is it working?"

"Yeah. I get it. You can stop."

"How did it feel?"

"Similar to what I already do when I touch the earth. You are just more interactive."

"What do you mean by 'touch the earth'?"

"I use my empathy to get impressions from everything around me. That's how I can move through a forest in the dark or find someone hiding from me."

"Nifty."

"Nifty?"

"Yeah, neat, excellent, cool."

"Wrong century, Aspen."

Folding his arms across his chest, he said, "It's fifty years old, not a hundred."

That made me curious. "You said your sister was seventy-five years old. How old are you?"

"Four hundred and twenty-seven."

I was floored. "Holy crap! You're an old man."

Shaking his finger at me again, he said, "Not by a long shot. You had better watch it, little girl. I'm not even middle-aged."

Staring at him, I shook my head. "I can't get used to the age thing. It's weird. You look as if you're about twenty-five."

Pursing his lips, he mumbled, "I shouldn't have told you that."

"Why?"

"Never mind. Let's get busy. You have a lot to learn. We'll start with a breeze. Try it."

Attempting to grasp the intangible, I found I couldn't. This was harder than I thought. It kept slipping through my mental fingers.

"Don't try to *grab* the air. It's more like breathing. Draw it in and exhale."

The technique started working but I lost it within a few seconds and didn't know what went wrong. Concentrating, I tried again and again. "I don't get it. I had it, what happened?"

"You have to relax. As soon as the air moved, you tensed up. You are the master; have confidence in that. The air will respond to your command."

It hadn't thus far but I refocused, took a deep breath and closed my eyes. Picturing myself as the center of gravity, I pulled in the air. When it reached me, I sent it back out. *I did it!*

"That's good. Now, increase the intensity."

"How?"

"Condense the area of input and output."

"Huh?"

"Picture a vacuum hose. Suck it in on one end and shoot it out the other."

Giving the imagery a chance, I said, "That works much better. Thanks."

"No problem. Now, dial it back some."

The air responded as if a switch was thrown and I opened my eyes. Aspen's hair was plastered back against his skull and he held onto the table leg but beamed approval. Consciously cutting the power, I made the wind die and Aspen dropped to his feet.

"Perfect. You did great."

Smug, I said, "I did, didn't I?"

"Yes you did. I think you have the basics of movement. We'll fine-tune it later. Let's try shields. This one is different. You have to mold and compress the air into an impenetrable surface. Create a shield about one foot square in front of you. I don't care much about the shape; I just want you to hold it there."

Thinking hard, I tried to picture what I wanted and mentally make it happen. After a few minutes, I was red faced with the effort.

"You're trying to force it. Relax. Command. Remember how it felt to pull the air in the tube?"

"That was different. You said it yourself."

"What you are doing with it and the effects are different. The way you accomplish it is the same. Pull the air into your shield and suspend it there until you can't fit any more inside the defined space."

Using the same mental picture, I pumped air into the box and held it still until I thought it was full. "Okay, I think I'm ready."

Flying up to my invisible shield, he ran his fingers over the outside edge. It looked square. *Yay me!* Rapping his knuckles on it like a door, it seemed solid. He pulled out a small knife. Where had he hidden that? Using the hilt, he knocked on my shield. It sounded as if he was hitting glass. He tossed the blade in the air, flipping his grip and stabbed into the hardened air. It shattered.

"Damn it! Why did it break?"

"It wasn't compressed enough. You did well for a

first try though. This time, keep adding more air until you can't get any more inside it. The only way to know you have enough is overflow."

Repeating the same process, it went faster this time. "Done."

Skipping the preliminaries, Aspen thrust the knife at the shield. It scraped and bounced off with a horrendous screech.

Cringing, I said, "Don't do that again."

"That is the sound of success. When you hear that sound, it means you're still breathing. Learn to love it. Now, I want you to turn the square over horizontally and drop it to about one foot above the floor."

"Why?"

"Just do it."

Following orders, I positioned the block of air where he wanted and nodded.

"Stand up."

Knowing better, I didn't argue this time and stood.

"Now step on the shield and hold it in place underneath you."

Gingerly, I rested my foot on the invisible step. It was just twelve inches off the ground but it still made me nervous. Easing my weight up, I balanced on the shield.

"Good. Do it again, two feet in front of the other one."

Concerned, I said, "Won't the first one fall apart?"

Giving me an evil grin, he said, "Not if you're careful."

"Great."

"Aww. Are you afraid of falling?"

I murmured, "Asshole."

"You know it."

I stuck my tongue out at him and got down to business. Forming the next box was relatively easy except that I was worried about losing the first one. It trembled once but held as I built the next stepping-stone. I realized as I worked, that it was on a sort of psychic tether. I had to let go of it, for the air to revert to its normal behavior. Confident now, I stood on both blocks and put my hands on my hips.

Aspen chuckled and said, "You look like Peter Pan."

"I feel like him."

"So that's how you walk on air—the hard way."

"What do you mean 'the hard way'?"

"Normally, we just form the air to our feet and stop it where we want to step. You don't have to keep forming more shields. The air doesn't have to be impenetrable either. Your first try would have been sufficient."

"Then why did you have me do it this way?"

"It covers more of the fundamentals. Now that you have this worked out, cut down the brick to where your feet make contact. When you have that, keep it on the bottom of your shoes as you move. Stop the air where you want to step."

Awkward at first, I kept at it until it felt more natural. "This is so cool!"

"Told ya. Are you ready for the next lesson?"

"Yeah. What are we doing now?"

"Going outside."

"Why?"

"The Tsái probably wouldn't appreciate you destroying your room."

Grinning, I said, "Sounds like fun. I'll grab my bag."

CHAPTER 17

Bounding down the stairs, I was laughing when the door to the Council Chambers opened. Kegan stepped out and I almost ran into him. "Oh! Hi Kegan, sorry about that."

Stiffening at the sight of me, he said, "Ye seem to be in better spirits. Where might ye be headed?"

"We're going outside for more lessons."

"Has this been approved by the Tsái?"

Aspen drawled, "Oh, yes. The Tsái most definitely approves."

Jealousy filled the air like heavy perfume, wiping the smile from my face. "What's wrong, Kegan?"

"Nothing. As long as the Tsái allows it, yer activities are none of my concern." With that, he walked away.

At a loss, I stared after him. I knew my remarks earlier had made him mad but his reaction was over the top. Why was he acting like this? We weren't dating; we weren't anything. If we were, which was a BIG if, there was still nothing to be jealous over. Why did a twelve-inch fairy threaten him?

Aspen asked, "Ready?"

"Oh, yeah. Let's go."

Preoccupied, I walked the main street of Tweentown biting my thumbnail. A slight weight on my shoulder drew my attention back to the present. Aspen had landed on my shoulder and was making himself comfortable.

"You don't mind do you?"

I said, "I guess not."

Taking hold of my hair for balance, he said, "Are you all right?"

"Yeah. I just don't understand."

"He's jealous."

"No shit. What was your first clue?"

"You have a smart mouth."

"Really?"

"Really."

Returning to our original subject, I said, "What I don't understand is why. He has no reason to be jealous."

"Doesn't he?"

"No. We aren't dating."

"That has nothing to do with it. He cares about you and you shut him down pretty hard. On top of that, I'm spending time with you. His imagination must be running wild."

Giggling, I said, "What could he possibly be imagining?"

Stroking my ear he murmured, "The same things I am. You dismiss me because of my size. *Don't.*"

Clearing my throat, I turned to stare in the shop window. My face burned and my heart was in my throat, as I remembered the dream. Aspen, more than anyone else, had a way of putting me at ease. It made me forget the man from my dream. Yes, I had to admit, Aspen was a threat.

Back to his normal self, Aspen asked, "Do you want to go in?"

Focusing my eyes, I saw we were standing in front of a curiosity shop. At least that's what I thought it was. Not in a hurry to be alone with the fairy, I said, "Can we?"

"Sure. We have time."

Rows of glass shelves lined with dishes, dolls, toys, statues, shrunken heads, jewelry and boxes filled the building. Aspen took off to investigate and I meandered down the aisles trying to distract myself from my dilemma. Several items were marked with signs that read 'Don't Touch!' I wondered why but didn't dare experiment on my own. For all I knew they would take my arm off or pull me into an alternate universe. Turning down the next row, something tugged at my awareness. The feeling was subtle but steady.

Paying more attention, I examined every item carefully. Midway down the aisle, I noticed a statue buried at the back of the shelf. Mindful of the signs earlier, I didn't pick it up but cleared the area in front of it. Made of polished wood, the statue was incredibly lifelike. It was a woman wearing a peplos, the traditional dress of ancient Greece. Her hair blew in the wind as four children played at her feet. Every fold of fabric and strand of hair was carved in exquisite detail. Her eyes... As I studied her face, I realized it was me. It couldn't be me but it was. With gentle hands, I picked it up. The surface was as smooth as glass.

Old and gray, a woman lay on her deathbed straining to speak. "Do not fret child. I have one last prophecy to give you hope. One will come, both guardian and key, bringing life, balance—order."

The scene faded into mist and reformed. The statue became real, as the woman stood on a stone precipice looking out to sea. Her children amused themselves while she waited for something or someone.

A swarthy man approached saying, "Fýlax, you are needed at the forum."

"Chevy? Are you okay? Chevy?"

The illusion disintegrated. I shook my head to clear my mind. *What the heck was that?*

On the verge of panic, the fairy shouted, "Answer me!"

"I'm fine, Aspen."

"What happened?"

I murmured, "I wish I knew."

Irritated, he said, "Please elaborate."

"You're going to ruin your image using words like that."

Growling, he said, "Chevy..."

"I had a vision when I picked this up."

"Then put it down."

"It's gone. I barely got anything. Definitely not enough."

"What did you see?"

"Nothing that made sense. An old woman giving someone a prophecy and a live version of the statue."

Closely examining the carved woman, he said, "It looks just like you."

"Yeah, that's why I picked it up."

Chuckling, he asked, "Did you see the lucky father to be?"

"Uh, no."

Turning the statue over, I saw a sticker with 6g written on it. Wow, prices were cheap here. "I want to buy it."

Shaking his head, he said, "You can't, they don't take credit cards."

"I have cash."

"They don't take that either."

"What do you guys use?"

"Gold. I can get it for you though."

That would go over well with Kegan. "I don't think so. Isn't there somewhere to exchange money for your currency?"

"Not currency, bars. The bank can do that but you have to have an account."

"Well, let's go to the bank then."

Reluctant, he said in an apologetic tone, "I don't know if they'll let you, Chevy. I can just exchange the money for you if you insist on buying it yourself."

Sick of the restrictions and prejudice against humans, I set my jaw and said, "I insist."

Guiding me two blocks down, Aspen kept trying to talk me out of getting my own account. The more he pushed, the more determined I became. What were they going to do? Say no?

The building was wide, two stories and in the Tudor style, which was common in Tweentown. Twelve-foot doors opened into a large, almost empty marble room, with a single desk in the center of the chamber. A small man sat writing in a thick tome. Short and stocky, with a full beard, he had to be a dwarf.

He raised his broad face at our approach and grumped, "What can I do for you?"

I donned my most endearing smile and said, "I'd like to open an account."

"Name?"

"Cheveyo Singer."

He said, "Nope," and went back to his ledger.

That was fast. "What do you mean, no?"

Sighing, he didn't look up when he said, "You're that human girl. No human accounts."

Trying to remain reasonable, I asked, "Why not?"

Scribbling again, the dwarf said, "It's not done, that's why."

"Have you had any other humans ask for one?"

"Can't say that I have."

"Is there some rule saying I'm not allowed to have an account?"

His hand stopped moving. "Er, well, I don't know."

"Maybe you should check with your superiors. I wouldn't want you to get into trouble."

Insulted, he threw down his pen and said, "I don't have any superiors. This is my bank. What I say goes."

Gotcha. "It's settled then. I would like to open an account." Extending my hand, I said, "My name is Cheveyo Singer and you are?"

Hesitant, he shook my hand. "Ritgir Blackfist."

"Nice to meet you Ritgir."

Glancing at Aspen, the dwarf said, "She's a real piece of work, ain't she?"

The fairy grumbled, "You have no idea."

Chuckling, he said, "All right, you can have an account. What have you got to deposit?"

Digging through my bag, I extracted my wallet and handed him all the money inside it.

Counting the bills, he grumbled, "Two hundred

dollars? Hardly worth my time."

"But you said..."

"I didn't say I wouldn't take it." Pointing to the fairy, he asked, "Did he explain how things work?"

"No."

"Definitely not worth my time. I'll keep it simple. You being human and all, might not understand the intricacies of our banking system."

Annoyed, I said, "I'll do my best to follow along."

"No need for the sarcasm, girly. How it works is, you deposit gold, jewels, etcetera in my bank. Silver is NOT accepted under any circumstance. I issue you a signet piece. When you want to buy goods or services from a vendor, you stamp the receipt with the signet piece. The funds are transferred between the accounts automatically. I don't send out statements, notices or reports. It's not my job to keep you informed. If for any reason you lose track of how much you have in the account, you can come in and file a request for a nominal fee. The application will take thirty days to process. If you don't have the funds to pay for something, the signet won't work. I don't do overdrafts. If you need a vault larger than the standard size, I charge extra but you're in no danger with this measly bit. If you want to make a withdrawal or retrieve an item you have stored here, I will get it for you. No one is allowed in the vaults. Any questions?"

"What's a signet piece?"

"It's a unique symbol or pattern assigned to you alone. Most people have it in the form of a ring but some do pendants or a stamp. Anything else?"

"How large is a standard vault?"

"Roughly a ten foot cube."

"How much is the fee for account information?"

"It depends on my mood. I've charged as much as five pounds."

"Pounds?"

He huffed and said, "Of gold. Are you sure you're getting all this?"

"Positive. What does that convert to in dollars?"

Eyes drifting toward the ceiling, he calculated and said, "About ninety-four thousand American dollars."

Horrified, I said, "That's obscene!"

"Listen, missy, it's my bank and my rules. I'm not forcing you to open an account. What's it going to be?"

Scowling, I said, "I want the account."

"The next step is a signet piece. Is there something specific you want?"

Showing the dwarf my tattoo, I said, "What about this?"

A queasy expression pinched his face. "Excuse me." Ritgir disappeared through a door in the corner.

Puzzled, I asked, "What was that about? Where is he going?"

"I imagine he is going to tattle on you."

"For what? To who?"

"The Tsái. I have been meaning to ask you about the ink on your wrist. Where did you get it?"

"My parents did it when I was a baby. Is this because of the seal in the Council Chambers?"

"You could say that. The symbol is the Tsái's personal insignia."

Stunned, I stared for a moment and said, "You're kidding. Tell me you're joking."

"Sorry."

"Oh, for the love of... What do we do?"

"We wait, he'll be back. You didn't know it was his?"

"Eryx's? No, I didn't. Kegan told me that he laid the seal when he created Tweentown but that was all. I thought it was a strange coincidence but didn't give it much thought."

A contemplative frown was his response, so I leaned against the desk and waited.

Ten minutes later, Ritgir bustled through the door; a huge smile blanketed his face. "Miss Singer, Cheveyo. I'm sorry I kept you waiting. I have your signet ring ready. I hope it meets with your approval."

He set the ring on the desktop with an expectant look but I was more interested in the sudden attitude improvement. "Didn't you speak to Eryx?"

The dwarf asked, "Who?"

"The Tsái."

"Oh! Yes. I was concerned about confusion between your signets but the Tsái was very helpful with the design. He also mentioned something about a small stipend for services rendered. The funds have already been transferred to your account."

The bastard. "I don't want it. Give it back."

"I'm afraid I can't do that. If there is a problem, I'm sure the Tsái can come up with a reasonable solution."

Sighing, I asked, "How much was it?"

"The deposit was ten pounds bringing your balance to ten pounds and four grams."

"Good Lord. How much is that?"

"In American dollars... About two hundred and twenty-six thousand."

At least I knew why Ritgir changed his tune. Growling, I said, "Thank you. I'll take it up with the

Tsái."

"Excellent. And the ring? Is it acceptable?"

Snatching it off the desk, I was ready to complain about the slightest flaw. It just wasn't my day. Made of platinum, the teardrops shapes were set with inlaid blue opal and orange sapphire. The center spiral was onyx and the similarity to the ring from my dream couldn't be coincidence. Sliding it onto my ring finger, I grumbled under my breath.

Ritgir asked, "Is something wrong?"

I sighed and said, "No. It's perfect."

How had he done it? I hated gold; the ring was platinum. I preferred simple designs that didn't catch on everything. It rested flush against my hand, without prongs or raised edges. He even got the size right.

As I stared at the blue and orange stones, I could hear my mother say, *Balance, Cheveyo. Heart and mind must be an equal fusion of fire and ice or one will destroy the other.*

Walking us to the door, the dwarf said, "Wonderful. Then we're all set. If you need anything, let me know."

"Thank you, Ritgir."

We left the bank, heading back to the shop for my statue. I kept looking at the ring and shaking my head. The only way he could have known what I would choose is that he picked my brain. So much for trust.

"Don't you like it?"

I grumbled, "I love it."

"I'll never understand women."

Ignoring his comment, I asked, "What does *fýlax* mean?"

"Could you be more specific? What language?"

"I don't know but it might be Greek."

"It could be a name. I'm not familiar with Greek other than the few terms we use."

"What terms?"

"Tsái, *fanós* and *anoigo* are all Greek words."

"You're over four hundred years old and don't know one of the oldest languages on the planet?"

"It's on my to-do list. Why are you asking anyway?"

"I just heard it somewhere and was curious."

"The Tsái speaks Greek. You could ask him."

Why did everyone keep referring me to Eryx? Did they all go running to him for everything? "He's busy plotting his world takeover."

"Are you back on that?"

"I never got off it."

"I explained the business about the army."

"Yes, you did but I don't agree with your interpretation."

"You have to be the most stubborn female on earth."

Opening the door to the shop, I said, "It's a possibility."

"That wasn't a compliment."

With a bright smile, I said, "It was to me."

Aspen followed me to the aisle, where I found the statue. Leery, I hesitated before picking it up. When my fingers touched the cool surface, nothing happened.

"Anything?"

"No."

"Good. How much is it?"

"Cheap. It's only six dollars."

"That can't be right. Turn it over."

Showing him the sticker, I said, "See? It says six."

"It says six grams, as in grams of gold."

Oh. I frowned and asked, "How much is that?"

Exasperated, he sighed and said, "It fluctuates but a gram is equal to about fifty dollars. So the statue is..."

"Three hundred dollars. Shit. What am I going to do?"

"I thought you were going to buy it."

Groaning, I said, "I don't have enough."

"What are you talking about? There's more than two hundred grand in your account."

"That's not my money. I only have two hundred in there."

"Oh, for pity's sake. Buy the damn thing."

"I have to give that money back to Eryx."

"He's not going to take it."

"He'd better."

"Or what?"

Good question. How was I going to make him take the money back? "I wish Tweentown had an ATM. I have the money in Charleston."

"So buy it and replace the gold later."

Aspen was right. I wasn't really borrowing it since I already had the money. I was just moving things around. Soothed by my justification, I took the statue to the counter. A little old man waddled over. He was three feet tall, pot-bellied, with a wide, baldhead and huge ears. Smiling, his wrinkles folded like an accordion.

He asked, "How may I serve you?"

"I want to buy this statue."

"Ah. A magnificent piece."

I asked, "Do you know where it came from?"

"Indeed, I do. An elven seer named Aerandir carved it from a piece of Cyprus about twenty years ago. He named it 'Dawn of Hope'. It has no magical properties to speak of but the craftsmanship is splendid."

Hoping to find out more about my vision, I asked, "Yes, it is. Do you know where the artist is now?"

"Sadly, he was one of the Butcher's more unfortunate victims." Glancing between the statue and me, the shopkeeper said, "The resemblance is amazing."

"Odd coincidence, isn't it?"

"More along the lines of Providence, I'd say. Aerandir was a seer. He didn't pull your likeness out of his imagination, Miss Singer."

"You know who I am?"

Wrapping the carving in a soft cloth, he said, "Yes. My wife and I watch the news every morning. It's good to keep up with current events, even if they don't affect you personally. When I turned on the television the other morning, you could have tipped me over with a feather. I never would have thought the day would come... Well, that is neither here nor there. Will this be deducted from his Lordship's account?"

Aspen answered for me. "No, Hanlin. The lady has her own account."

"Ritgir allowed it? Oh my! Astonishing. Next you'll tell me the sun rose in the west this morning."

"Chevy can be quite persistent."

Nodding his head, Hanlin scratched out a receipt and turned it toward me. "That will be six grams, Miss Singer. Press your signet to the blank here at the bottom."

An exact replica of the ring's face appeared on the paper. Hanlin handed me the receipt. "Your copy, miss."

"I thought this was yours."

"No. Mine is in the ledger. It wouldn't do to have random scraps of paper lying all over the place."

Tucking the statue into my bag, I said, "Oh. Well,

thank you Hanlin. It was nice meeting you."

"Likewise, miss. Have a pleasant evening."

Outside the shop, I said, "He was nice but what was he?"

"A gnome."

"Why did he look that old? I thought all you guys lived more than five hundred years and never aged."

"We do but gnomes are born that way."

"You mean like a Shar-Pei?"

Shaking his head, he laughed and said, "Yeah, sort of."

"Where are we going?"

"The lake."

We walked in silence, apart from Aspen's occasional directions. The vision occupied my thoughts. I assumed the scenes were from the past but couldn't be sure. The woman that looked like me could have lived long ago. She could have been one of my ancestors. No, that didn't make sense. No one in my family tree had more than one child. I suppose they didn't have to be her children. They could belong to a neighbor or friend. And what about the old woman? Who was she talking to? Maybe that's how they were connected. The crone was speaking to my doppelganger. Later, the young woman was waiting for whoever the old woman foresaw. The forum could have been an important meeting that they needed this guardian's help with. It all fit, except that Aerandir created the statue twenty years ago, not two thousand years past. He could have been seeing an historical event. That would explain it.

"Chevy?"

"Hmm?"

"Have you considered the possibility that you might

be related to the Tsái?"

Thunderstruck, I stopped in my tracks. "Where the hell did you get that idea? It's the most ridiculous thing I've ever heard."

"Think about it. No one knows what he is or where he came from. You can open the door to Tweentown, you're faster and stronger than normal, you're an empath, you have visions, the power of air manipulation, precognition and you bear his mark. What else can explain all that?"

"I'm human. There is no doubt about it. No matter how much you all want it to be otherwise, it's a fact. The Zephyri would like nothing better than to attribute my abilities to some mixture of their blood. That would tie up the enigma of me in a nice little bow. It's sheer arrogance to insist that any power a human might have must have come from you. I am so tired of the constant prejudice. It permeates everything you all say and do. You preached about respect but what you really meant was respect for the Zephyri alone. You're a hypocrite!"

Hovering in front of me, he said nothing for a moment. "You're right."

Taken aback, I said, "I am?"

"About some of it, yes. We all took it for granted that your abilities must have come from us, which is arrogant. Looking at it from your perspective, we do view humans as inferior. If you are one hundred percent human, you are the only one in history to develop these powers. Do you see where that might cause us to jump to conclusions?"

"Yes but..."

Cutting me off, he continued, "I called you a racist and we are just as guilty. Our powers give us a convenient excuse to look down on humans. An adult doesn't look down on a child for his lack of skills. That said, my bias against the human race doesn't make the theory invalid. How do you know you're human?"

Frustrated, I began walking again. "Alida and I went to the Library. We researched my family tree back to the beginning and there were no Zephyri in the line anywhere. I can't be related to Eryx."

"No Zephyri in your bloodline doesn't mean you can't be related to the Tsái. He isn't Zephyri."

Waving my hands in the air, I said, "How can you say that? He's your leader."

"Yes but he isn't one of us. He doesn't belong to any kingdom or species. He's the 'maker'."

"The maker of what?"

"I don't know."

"Has anyone tried asking him?"

"I doubt it. He inspires fear, loyalty and devotion, not intimate conversation."

I didn't agree with the assessment but kept my mouth shut.

Aspen said, "We're here."

Raising my eyes, I saw we were outside the city, standing before medium sized lake. The moon reflected off the black water and no one else was around. "It's so quiet that it's eerie. Where is everyone?"

In a hushed voice, the fairy said, "Not many people frequent the lake. Tweentown is normally used for shopping, banking and a way station. I think they forget it's here."

"That's a shame. It's beautiful."

Aspen said, "I'm glad. I enjoy the peaceful solitude but that's not why we're here."

"Why are we here?"

"We needed the space and the lake makes a good safety net."

"Why would I need a safety net?"

"Flying."

Adamant, I shook my head and said, "Oh, no. I'm not flying. I can't."

"Are you afraid of heights?"

"No."

"Then you're flying."

"What if I had said yes?"

"I still would have made you. Relax, we'll start with what you already know and work up to it."

Throwing my bag on the beach, I said, "I thought we were going to break stuff."

"With any luck, you will. We won't get to all of it today but we need to cover tornadoes, blades, flight, propulsion, bubbles and vacuums. The water helps with all of them. What I want you to do is follow me and try to keep up."

Puzzled, I asked, "That's it?"

"Yep."

Aspen flew out over the water and paused, waiting for me. Taking a deep breath, I shook out my hands and concentrated. I formed air to my feet and stepped out over the water. The fairy flitted farther away, as I moved. Painstakingly slow to begin, I started to get the hang of it after the first circuit around the lake.

Aspen asked, "Do you run?"

"All the time. Why?"

"You look as if you could use some exercise."

He took off at a quicker pace and I had to jog to keep up. Freezing the air in place became second nature, as he flew faster and faster. I was sprinting by the time he went to the center of the water and stopped.

"Excellent job. Now, I want you to spin a tornado around us."

"How?"

"Use your head. You know how."

Ensuring I had a firm grip on the tether for my feet, I sucked in the air, swirling it at the last second.

"Make it bigger."

Enlarging my mental hose, I kicked up the power and the tornado swelled to fifteen feet tall. My hair rose straight up from my scalp, as we stood in the eye.

"More!"

Opening the floodgates, I drove up the intensity to the point that it sounded like a train circled us. I could no longer see outside the tempest and mist dampened my face.

Coming close to my ear, Aspen said, "Look down."

It took a minute for me to understand what I was seeing. In the dim light, I could just make out the muddy floor of the lake. Stunned, I looked back at Aspen. Small hands framed my mouth, as he kissed me softly. Tiny fangs scraped my lower lip and he said, "You're incredible."

Before I knew what happened, I was under water, straining to reach the surface. *Oh my God, he kissed me.* With my feet weighed down by my tennis shoes, it took longer to swim than usual. Either that or I was a lot deeper than I thought.

Surfacing, I found Aspen floating above my head laughing his ass off. "I'm sorry, Chevy. I didn't mean to make you fall."

"The apology would carry a lot more weight if you

weren't giggling through it."

"I know. It's sincere but you have to admit, this is funny."

"I'm all wet and I don't see the humor."

"Get out. I'll show you how to dry off."

I began swimming to shore and Aspen said, "Where are you going?"

"I'm getting out."

"Why not here?"

Learning magic wasn't just about the mechanics. I had to change the way I thought as well, which was the hard part. Compressed air sliced through the water and attached to my shoes, allowing me to climb out on invisible stairs. Wringing out my hair and shirt, I said, "I'm cold. How do I dry off?"

"Have you ever been to the car wash?"

"Yeah."

"Do you understand how the dryer at the end works?"

"It blows the water off."

"Right. You aren't going to evaporate the water by exciting the molecules but push it out."

"Theoretically, I should be able to warm the air around me, so that I'm not cold too. Right?"

"Yes but I don't want you to burn yourself. It's easy to get the air moving but hard to get the temperature right. The drying shouldn't take long."

Considering what I wanted to do, I began at the top of my head. Weaving the air molecules through my hair was a strange sensation. The steady runoff streamed back into the lake below us, as the air tugged at my hair and clothes. My shoes were the most difficult but I got them dry enough, so they didn't squish when I walked.

Aspen said, "We've been at this for hours. Let's take a break. Come on."

He flitted toward land and I followed him. We sat on the beach and stared out at the water for a long time. "Aspen?"

"Hmm?"

"Why did you kiss me?"

"I told you why."

"That doesn't answer my question."

"Yes it does. I have been pushing you hard and you keep coming back for more. You're learning so fast, it's amazing."

"So you kissed me because I'm a good student?"

Standing, he flew up to eye-level. "No. I kissed you because I wanted to. Because you're spirited, intelligent, funny, honest, adventurous and drop dead gorgeous. I couldn't help myself."

My heart raced and I couldn't seem to get enough air. I didn't know what to say, what to do.

Aspen said, "I'm glad you're sitting down."

"Huh?"

"You had that same look just before you went for a swim. What are you thinking?"

Thinking? I couldn't think. "Nothing."

"There must be something going on in your head."

"I have no idea what to say or do."

"What do you *want* to do?"

Considering his question, I said, "I don't know."

Aspen looked at me sideways and said, "I'm going to ask you something and I don't want you to get upset. I'm just trying to understand."

"Okay."

"Chevy—have you ever had a boyfriend?"

Why would that question upset me? "No."

Dumbfounded, he asked, "How is that possible?"

"I was raised in a government training facility from the age of ten. Socializing isn't real high on their priority list."

"There you are. You were starting to scare me."

"Why?"

"You were giving me one word answers and acting—weird. I thought you might be having a panic attack."

I was? "I don't know. I've never had one before. My heart was pounding and I couldn't breathe for a minute. Is that what happens?"

"I was wrong. It wasn't an anxiety attack."

"What was it?"

"Hormones and confusion."

Embarrassed, I dropped my head.

Aspen's hand pulled at my chin. "It's nothing to be ashamed of, Chevy. Everyone feels that way sometimes. The difference is that I know what I want."

CHAPTER 18

Aspen and I decided to stop for the day. As we approached the mansion, I hoped that Kegan wasn't waiting for us. I shouldn't feel guilty. I had done nothing wrong but I did. Pushing the front door open a crack, I found the foyer empty.

Aspen asked, "What are you doing?"

"Eh, nothing."

"Looking for Kegan?"

"Is it that obvious?"

He didn't answer and I started across the foyer when I heard the door to the Council Chambers close. My head snapped around and I felt for the identity of the person behind the door. It was the vampire. He heard us and was hurt. *Damn.* That was the last thing I wanted to do. Trudging up the stairs, I went to my room.

Flopping down in the chair, I stared at the floor.

Aspen said, "Are you hungry? I'm famished."

"I *was.*"

"Barmek?"

The brownie appeared carrying a tray filled with food. Setting it down on the table, he laid a hand on my arm. I met his sympathetic eyes and felt warm affection creep up my arm.

Giving him a tight-lipped smile, I said, "Thank you. I'll be fine."

"Yes, you will, miss, as will he."

"You're sure?"

Nodding, Barmek stepped back and disappeared. Aspen flew over and filled a fairy-sized plate. The brownie hadn't said or done much but I felt a little better. As I watched Aspen wolf down his food, I began to regain my appetite. Wow, the boy could eat. He went back for seconds and then thirds. "Are you going to leave me any?"

"Not if you don't move it."

"How can you eat that much? If you keep going, you'll burst."

"Fairies have a high metabolism. If I didn't eat like this, I'd be a bag of bones."

It looked good, so I picked at the tray. Flavor exploded on my tongue. Barmek had outdone himself. I didn't know what it was but it was delicious. I ate so fast that I didn't realize I was full until it was too late. Slumping in the chair, I moaned, "Stick a fork in me, I'm done."

"Yeah, I need a nap."

"I wish I could. No sleep for me. What am I going to do about that? I can't go forever without any sleep. I doubt I'll make it two days."

"I've been thinking."

"About what?"

"Your sleeping issue. If you really don't want the Tsái poking around in your head, there's only one other option I can see."

"What's that?"

"Sleeping with me."

"Aspen!"

Chagrined, he said, "That didn't come out right. What I meant was that we go to sleep and I keep watch over your dreams."

"Will it work?"

"It should. You go to sleep. I'll join you in dream and you go to sleep in the dream."

"I can't do that for very long. We have to come up with another solution."

"Dealing with the cause is the only way to make it stop."

"I know the barrier is real but I can't buy the altered memory theory. There must be another explanation."

Pursing his lips, he said, "The sole reason you don't believe it is because the Tsái came up with it."

"What can I say? I don't trust him."

"You mentioned that. What I don't understand is why. You're suspicion of him borders on compulsion. Do you see that?"

"No, I don't. I have good reasons for not trusting him." I would not become one of Eryx's devoted fans under any circumstance. He didn't deserve the adulation. He didn't deserve anything.

Aspen changed the subject. "When do you want to try my idea?"

I stood and said, "I'm tired now."

Kicking off my damp shoes, I climbed into bed. The sheets were cool and it felt good to lie down. Aspen settled on my chest and I said, "What do you think you're doing?"

"Going to sleep."

"Not on top of me, you're not."

"Contact makes the connection more stable. I don't want to lose you."

Skeptical, I shook my finger at him. "No monkey business."

Raising his hand, he said, "I swear."

Sighing, I got comfortable and closed my eyes. Aspen's slight weight on my chest was reassuring and I fell asleep in no time.

Why was I awake? I was standing in my room at the mansion and I didn't remember getting up. The bed was rumpled but Aspen was gone. "Aspen?"

"I'm here."

Startled, I whirled around. Thank goodness, I was dreaming. Larger than life, the six feet four inch fairy stood behind me smiling. "Oh, hi."

"Hi. Ready to get some rest?"

"Yes. I'm exhausted."

Taking my hand, he led me to the bed. My heart started pounding and I froze.

Looking back at me, Aspen smiled gently and said, "None of that now. We're just going to sleep."

My feet moved again as I spoke. "I know, I'm sorry. I don't know what's wrong with me."

Sitting me down on the bed, he said, "Don't worry about it. Just lie back and relax."

Turning on my side, I hugged the pillow and closed my eyes. As I took a couple of deep breaths, I began to calm down. A heavy weight at my back made me jump. Aspen's thick body moved against me from shoulders to hips. "What are you doing?"

Wrapping his arm around my waist, he said, "I

believe it's called spooning."

"That's not funny. Why are you in the bed?"

"You're not the only one that needs rest."

"But..."

"Relax, sweetheart. I won't let anything happen to you. Go to sleep."

Sliding his arm beneath the pillow, he tucked me under his chin. The solid warmth at my back made me feel safe and the rhythmic rise and fall of his chest lulled me to sleep.

***

Refreshed, I awoke still cocooned in Aspen's embrace. One arm circled my chest and the other below my waist. Careful not to wake him, I stretched like a cat and yawned.

Aspen asked, "Did you sleep well?"

"You're awake? Yes. I feel wonderful."

Easing up on his elbow, he leaned over me and said, "I've been up for hours."

"I'm sorry. Why didn't you get me up?"

"You needed the rest, besides, I didn't mind."

"Thanks."

"You're welcome."

Looking around at the dream room, I asked, "Why are we still here? Why didn't we wake up for real?"

"I didn't want anything disturbing you prematurely."

"I've had enough sleep. You can let us out now."

"Not yet."

Frowning up at him, I watched his eyes glaze. Grasping a lock of hair that had fallen across my neck, he brushed it against his cheek. My breathing came faster and my face flushed as his eyes bored into mine. Licking my dry lips, I said, "Why not?"

"I need to do something first."

I swallowed and asked, "What?"

Dropping my hair, he slid his hand under my waist and flipped me onto my back. Gasping at the sudden movement, my heart rate doubled.

He rumbled, "That's better."

"What's better?"

"The position. I also have your full attention."

Opening my mouth, I started to argue but he pressed his finger to my lips. "Shh. Don't say anything, don't think, just feel."

Bending closer, he nuzzled my cheek, working his way back. Lips nibbled on the shell of my ear, sending tingles down my arms. Unsure what to do, I grasped a fistful of the sheet as my back arched. Aspen's lazy laugh blew warm breath across my neck, as he came back into view. Dipping his head, his tongue darted against my lower lip and I opened instinctively. Soft and slow our tongues entwined. My fingers speared through his hair, as a hot spike pierced my chest. My shields crashed down and our emotions became one. Every sensation was a double image and amplified. I felt the tug of my hands in his hair, the soft skin of my back against his hand. The languorous kiss became desperate, fervent. Fingers kneaded my skin and I drew him closer, driving deeper. In my reckless fumbling, a sharp pain stung my lip but I didn't care. I wanted more. As he pulled away, I clung to him, not wanting it to end.

A chuckle vibrated from his chest, "We're getting carried away." His thumb stroked across my lips. "I've marked you."

"You didn't hear me complaining."

"No, I didn't but I just wanted a kiss. Then you—I don't know. What did you do to me?"

"What do you mean?"

"I could feel everything, not just my side."

Embarrassed, I mumbled, "Oh. I'm sorry. I must have been projecting. "

"Don't be. It was incredible."

"You liked it?"

"Didn't you?"

Self-conscious, I blushed and looked away. Kissing my forehead, Aspen said, "Are you ready to wake up Sleeping Beauty?"

"Yes but how?"

"Will yourself awake. There won't be any long trips this time."

He lay down next to me again and I closed my eyes.

"Aspen?"

"Hmm?"

"I liked it."

I heard Kegan say, "Are they all right?"

"Oh, they're fine but not for long."

Squinting, I saw Eryx, arms folded across his chest, scowling down at me. Now what had I done? "What's going on?"

Kegan said, "Chevy! Yer awake. Ye scared me half to death."

It looked like he was over his mad-on. Giggling, I said, "Good one, Kegan."

"I'm serious, lass. I thought ye were lost."

Stretching, I yawned and said, "No, I just needed some sleep."

Eryx growled, "You're going to need a soft cushion when I get done with you."

Frowning, I asked, "Why? I haven't done anything—lately."

Aspen moved to the bed, shaking his head at me. He mouthed, "He saw us."

Oh shit.

Turning his anger on the fairy, Eryx clenched his jaw and said, "Aspen, did Kegan relay my message concerning Cheveyo's training?"

Cowering, Aspen answered, "Yes, sir."

"Did he include the part where I said the *only* thing you were to instruct her in was air manipulation?"

"Yes, sir."

How dare he! I was an adult. I made my own choices. I stood with my hands on my hips, looking up into his surly face. "Wait just a damn minute! Aspen didn't force himself on me. You don't have the right to manage my personal life. You can't control my dreams. What the hell were you doing skulking around in my mind anyway?"

Leaning over, he yelled in my face so loud that my hair blew back with each syllable. "I was not SPEAKING to YOU!" Swinging back to the fairy, he said, "Aspen, go see Ellarian. She has a job for you or I would strip your powers this instant. Get out of my sight!"

The fairy saw his chance and darted for the door. *Chicken.*

Drowning me in possessive fury, Eryx gritted his teeth and said, "You wanted my undivided attention. NOW, you may have it." Dropping his clenched fists to his sides, he towered over me. "I was not in your dream. I was checking on the welfare of one of my subjects and a guest in my home. It doesn't matter that Aspen didn't force himself on you. He violated a direct order from his Tsái. And your personal life is *definitely* my business—while you are here."

"Who do you think you are? My father?"

"I have no desire to be your father. He would roll over in his grave, to see your behavior."

Throwing my arms up I screamed, "It was just a kiss for Pete's sake!"

The tension in the room dropped a notch and in the silence, I heard Kegan sigh.

Eryx said, "Kegan, get out."

The vampire rushed through the door, leaving me alone with three hundred pounds of pissed off Tsái.

When the door closed, Eryx stammered, "I didn't know. I saw... I just assumed..." Closing his eyes for a moment, he took a breath and said, "It doesn't make any difference what I thought. Your father wouldn't have wanted..."

He was calming down but I wasn't even warmed up yet. Poking his chest, I said, "You have no idea what my father wanted."

He gritted his teeth and he said, "I know exactly what your father wanted. He was my friend."

Astonished, I asked, "What did you say?"

It was obvious that Eryx hadn't intended to relay that information or maybe that's what he wanted me to think. Mumbling, he said, "Chaytan was my friend."

"That's not possible."

"It's true. I knew him his entire life. Your mother as well."

Searching for the holes in his assertion, I said, "You didn't. You couldn't have. I would remember you."

"After you were born, I—didn't come around."

How convenient. "You're lying."

"No, I'm not. When you were twelve, I went to visit your parents. The house was gone. All that was left was the overgrown foundation. I went into town to ask where they were. A woman there told me you all died in a fire. 'Tragic, so sorry,' she said. I was so upset that I never checked. I should have looked into it. Everything you went through when you were a child was my fault. I can never make up for what you suffered. I'm sorry. I should have had faith, I never should have..." Pausing, he took a shuddering breath and continued. "Then I heard your name on the news. I refused to believe it at first but it had to be you. Who else would name a child Cheveyo except Chaytan?"

He looked so sincere that I was almost convinced. "You know about my name?"

Nodding, he said, "A Hopi ogre that comes to get bad children. Chaytan had a warped sense of humor. I can't believe Tokori allowed it but she did. Anyway, when I saw you on television, I knew. Your eyes convinced me. When you were born, it was apparent even through the blue haze that they would be green. I sent out the Praetorian to find you."

"Why didn't you tell me before?"

"You hated me on sight. You wouldn't have accepted it."

"I don't believe you now." Eryx straightened and I said, "You get an A for effort though. I especially liked the part about my mother allowing my name. Nice touch. I notice you haven't let me see your emotions. All I'm getting is overflow."

Bewildered, he asked, "Where did all this blind

hatred come from?"

"I'm not blind, everyone else is. They can't see through your lies but I can."

"We have had this discussion before and I have no intention of repeating it." Turning his back to me, he announced, "Aspen will not be training you in air manipulation anymore."

"I thought it was important for me to learn to control it."

"It is. That is why I will be taking over your tutoring."

"That should be *fun*."

Rounding on me, he said, "I can be fun."

"Oh, yeah. You're a real hoot."

Donning a more dignified air, he said, "Well, it's been two days since Aspen began. How far did you get?"

"What do you mean, 'two days'? What day is it?"

"Tuesday."

"What time is it?"

"About two in the afternoon."

"Wow."

"What?"

"I slept for over twelve hours. I've never slept that long in my life. No wonder I felt good."

"No nightmares?"

"Uh-uh. That's why Aspen was with me. He was keeping me safe. Jeez, he must have been bored out of his skull. He said he was awake for hours but I had no clue."

Uncomfortable, he said, "I apologize for jumping to conclusions."

"So you'll let Aspen continue training me?"

His eyes flared for a moment and he said, "No. You won't be seeing *him* for a while."

"Why? You said you were wrong."

"The fairy is busy with other things."

Hands on my hips, I asked, "How am I going to sleep?"

"With the barrier breaking up, I think it's safe for me to remove it."

"No way, buddy. You've spent enough time digging around in my head."

"What are you talking about? The only time I spent 'digging around in your head' was with your permission."

"Really? Then how did you know about my name and how do you explain this?" I shoved my ring finger in his face.

As Eryx took hold of my hand, a zing of electricity ran up my arm and I said, "What was that?"

"I don't know. As upset as you are it was probably a reaction between our powers. And I don't see anything wrong with the ring. It's beautiful."

"Yes, it is. That's just it."

Dragging his hands through his hair, he exhaled through his nose and said, "What?!"

"How did you know that this is what I would have chosen, if you didn't pull it out of my head?"

"I did nothing of the sort but I'm glad to hear that you like it."

"Baloney. Why did you choose the stones, the setting?"

"You're unbelievable. You're angry because you like a ring. It must be a *huge* conspiracy." Glaring at me, he jammed his hand into his pocket, pulled out a ring and stuck it on his pinky. Holding it out for me to see, he said, "This is why I designed it that way."

It was a masculine version of my ring. His setting was a solid piece, where mine showed skin but the styles and stones were identical. It was an exact copy of the ring from my dream. He *had* been in my mind.

"Ah-hah! You just gave me proof that you have been in my head."

He looked up at the ceiling. "Aaaahhh! God, why me?" Looking back at me, he said, "What the hell are you talking about?"

"Your ring. It's the one from my dream. The only way you could have the same one is if you pulled it from my memories."

"You dreamed of my signet?"

"It's not yours! You stole it. You're trying to manipulate me again."

Wandering over to a chair, he dropped into it; the wood creaked under his weight. Slumping over, he rubbed his eyes and said, "You're exhausting. I feel like I haven't slept in a week. Nothing I say or do means anything. According to you, every word that comes out of my mouth is a lie and every action is a manipulation. Please explain why you have this unreasoning distrust of me."

"I know it. You have been lying to me from the first time I laid eyes on you."

Shaking his head, he said, "I'm at a loss. I have no idea what to do but I'm hungry, so let's eat."

"Pardon me?"

Seeming to shake off my allegations, he said, "No one thinks well on an empty stomach and you haven't eaten in over twelve hours, so we'll eat. Then we'll work on your skills with air. Barmek."

"I am here, master."

The brownie stood near the door with a huge platter.

Eryx said, "There you are." Waving his hand, a table and two chairs appeared.

Barmek slid the tray onto the table and said, "Will there be anything else, master?"

"No. Thank you."

He said, "My pleasure, sir," and was gone.

Eryx set the table. Placing the last utensil, he said, "Aren't you hungry?"

This was bizarre but I sat anyway. Suspicious, I watched as the big man draped a cloth napkin across his thigh and cut his steak. He was switching tactics but I couldn't figure out his strategy. With impeccable table manners, he began eating his lunch. What was he up to?

"Aren't you going to eat, *mikroula*?"

"Stop calling me that. I'm not a little girl."

He didn't respond. The food smelled good and my stomach rumbled in protest. Sighing, I picked up my fork and took a bite, darting furtive glances at him for cues on proper form. Table etiquette had never been my best subject. We ate in silence for a few minutes and I started to relax.

Stopping to take a sip of wine, Eryx asked, "What did Aspen cover with you?"

Making sure to swallow my food first, I said, "Wind, shields, walking on air and tornadoes."

His eyebrows rose, as he said, "In one day?"

Proud of myself, I boasted, "Yes. We also went shopping and I opened an account with Ritgir."

"I heard about the bank but didn't know why you wanted the account."

"Oh, that reminds me, you have to take the money back. I told you that I wouldn't accept it."

Ignoring my statement, he asked, "What did you buy?"

I didn't allow him to sidestep the issue. "A statue. What about the money? My government will think..."

"I don't want to argue, it gives me indigestion. What kind of statue was it?"

Bragging was a mistake. It gets you in trouble every time. "A wooden one."

Sighing, he said, "Who made it?"

"An elf named Aerandir."

His face lit with interest. "Is that right? May I see it?"

"Why?"

"His work is flawless; I would like to see which one you bought."

Unable to come up with a good excuse, I got up to retrieve the carving. Setting the wrapped figure on the table, I sat back down and became engrossed with my meal. Eryx removed the cloth with care. Leaning back in his chair, he didn't move for a long time.

Eryx asked, "What is it called?"

Tucking my food in my cheek, I said, "Dawn of Hope."

"When did he create it?"

"Twenty years ago."

My plate was empty; I had to look up. He wasn't staring at the figure but at me, with an expression I couldn't name. "Why were you trying to hide this from me?"

Shrugging, I didn't answer.

"What happened?"

I still refused to speak.

"I can ask Aspen."

Damn it. Mumbling, I said, "I had a vision."

"What did you see?"

"It was just flashes. Nothing made sense."

Enunciating every syllable, he said, "What did you see?"

Annoyed with his prying, I glowered and said, "A dying old woman and the live version of the statue."

"What did the old woman say?"

"Why do you think she said anything?"

"Because you don't want to tell me."

Taking a deep breath, I sighed. "She said, 'Do not fret child. I have one last prophecy to give you hope. One will come, both guardian and key, bringing life, balance and order.'"

Eyes riveted to my face, he asked, "Was that all?"

"No."

"What else did she say?"

"Nothing."

Chortling, he leaned his elbows on the table and put his face in his hands. "You would test the patience of a saint. Please, tell me what else you saw."

"Why do you want to know?"

Staring at me, he didn't answer.

"Fine. It wasn't a big deal. A man came to get the young woman in the carving. He said, '*Fýlax*, you are needed at the forum.'"

"What was the woman doing?"

"Waiting, looking out to sea."

"Was that so painful?"

Grumbling, I said, "Yes."

"Any discomfort was of your own making. What was your take on the visions?"

"Why?"

Shrugging, he said, "I wondered what you thought."

"I think the young woman was an ancestor of mine. The old woman was speaking to her before she died."

"You believe it was in the distant past."

"Yes."

"And the children?"

Why would he ask that, unless... "You know that my line only had one child per generation?"

"Yes, I do, so who are the children?"

"I don't know. Maybe she was babysitting."

"Who do you think she was waiting for?"

"The guardian."

Nodding, he said, "All very logical but there is one problem with your interpretation."

I had taken everything into consideration. There was no flaw. "What problem?"

"The young woman *is* the guardian."

Scoffing, I asked, "How do you know?"

"I speak Greek."

Oh. "The word *fýlax* is Greek?"

"Yes, it means guardian. The word for key in this instance is *lýsi.*"

Thinking aloud, I said, "If the old woman was talking about the girl, who was she giving hope to and why?"

"That is for you to deduce. While you're pondering those questions, ask yourself why it was shown to you."

Sneering at Eryx, I said, "It was shown to Aerandir, I just received an echo."

Picking up the statue, Eryx stood and walked it over to the mantle. Setting it down, he said, "When you find the answers to your questions, will you let me know?"

"Maybe. Why?"

"It is a mystery that I would like the answer to." Turning to face me, he clasped his hands behind his back and said, "Before I was distracted, you were telling me about creating a tornado. I assume you weren't in the house. Where were you?"

"The lake."

"How did it go?"

"Good. Aspen was impressed."

"How big was it?"

"I don't know but it went to the bottom of the lake."

"Were you tired afterward?"

"No."

"Are you confident in your ability to air-walk?"

Laughing, I said, "Oh, yeah."

"What's funny?"

"Aspen had me doing laps around the lake."

"Running?"

"Sprinting."

"What was next on his agenda?"

"I don't think he had a plan. He threw stuff at me at random. I was chasing him around the lake when he veered to the center and stopped. When I caught up, he said to make a tornado and wouldn't tell me how. Then he said to make it bigger, so I did. He taught me to dry off using air too."

"You're advancing much faster than I hoped. The lake is a good place to practice. Are you ready?"

"Now?"

"Did you have other plans?"

Giving him a sour look, I said, "No, I'm grounded. Remember?"

Holding out his hand, he smiled and said, "Yes, you are."

When we reappeared, we stood over the water. Clutching at Eryx, I balanced on his boots until I formed air to my feet.

Giving him a whack on the shoulder, I said, "That was a dirty trick."

"It wasn't intentional. I apologize."

"Wow. Twice in one day."

Cocking one eyebrow, he said, "Two to nothing, it's your turn next."

"Was that a joke?"

"Not a good one but yes."

"I didn't think you were capable."

Ignoring my comment, he said, "Form a shield around us."

"Won't that cut off our air supply?"

"You control the air. How might you form the bubble and allow us to continue breathing?"

Thinking it through, I said, "If I added to the thickness of the shield, we could use the added air to breathe."

"That would work but what would you do with the carbon dioxide?"

Frowning, I said, "I don't know."

"Our atmosphere is made up of nitrogen, oxygen and carbon dioxide. As long as those elements remain in gaseous form, they are under your control. If your shield must remain air tight and you need to be inside it for any length of time, you must convert the carbon dioxide to oxygen."

"Recycle it."

"Precisely. It isn't a long term solution but it will work for a while."

"Can I ask you something?"

"You may ask."

"Fair enough. Why did you tell me to call you Eryx and not Tsái, like everyone else?"

"Not everyone calls me Tsái. The Council calls me Eryx."

"Okay but why?"

"I'm not Tsái to you."

"It means 'maker', right?"

"Yes."

"Maker of what?"

"The term is a throw-back to well before my time. Now it is just a word. The translation doesn't mean anything." Changing the subject, he said, "Create the bubble but make it about an inch thick."

He was lying again. I couldn't feel it but I knew. Forming the shield, I asked, "What now?"

"Move us under water."

Nervous about the bubble holding, I descended, watching for any leaks. Once we were submerged, I began recycling our air. It was surprisingly simple, almost automatic. It was dark but I could see the plants and fish nearby. Very cool.

"How do you feel?"

"Fine. Why?"

"I'll explain later. Now, I want you to use the extra air in the shield to propel us forward."

"Okay."

Expelling the added air, the bubble just spun in place, going nowhere. I was glad we weren't standing on it. I should have thought it through. I needed a rudder, which meant I would have to use more of the air from the bubble's surface. Adding the rudder helped but now we were spinning in another direction. *Okay, I could do this.*

What do submarines have? Fins, I needed fins. Using more of my air, I added fins to the top and sides. We stopped spinning and moved forward. "Why are we doing it this way? It was much easier to move the bubble through the water. Propulsion sucks."

Apparently, Eryx thought that was amusing. He laughed so hard that tears streamed down his face. Wiping his eyes, he said, "You can take us up now."

Standing above the lake, I let the shield go and we breathed fresh air again.

"I had you do it that way because you needed to know how it is done. You needed to understand the mechanics of it. Power levels fluctuate from person to person, so not everyone would be able to do what you did."

Puzzled, I said, "I assumed strength differed but I don't understand. What did I do?"

"Have you ever held a ball under water?"

"Yes."

"The bigger the ball, the more difficult it is. Right?"

"Yeah."

"How big was your ball?"

"Pretty big but are you saying that not everyone could have held it under the water?"

"Yes. Normally, you should have created a second bubble around the first to help with the descent. If you allow water to fill the outer shell, it makes it much easier and uses a lot less power."

I didn't appreciate that he let me make a fool of myself. Scowling at him, I asked, "Why didn't you tell me?"

"I wanted to see what you would do; how you would handle it. You did well."

"That's why you asked how I felt."

"Yes. On top of the sheer strength that it took to hold us under, you were dealing with at least eight other tasks. I see why Aspen was impressed." Eryx's brow creased for no reason and he said, "I'm sorry, I have to cut this short. We can resume tomorrow."

"Another zombie emergency?"

"Yes. It's maddening. I can't understand it. Periodically, the spell just stops working and they go berserk."

"Yeah, that is weird."

CHAPTER 19

Alone. I was so tired of being tired and alone. No one had come to see me in three days and I hadn't slept at all. Where was everyone? Even Barmek had sent food instead of bringing it himself. I was so lonely that I even missed Eryx. Sitting on the bathroom floor, I had finished my latest training session and was contemplating what I should do next, in the quest for sleeplessness.

"What the hell happened in here?!"

Ooh, a person. Scrambling off the floor, I ran for the bedroom. Eryx and Kegan stood in the middle of the room with their mouths open.

Smiling cheerfully, I said, "Hi guys! What's up?"

Eryx asked, "Why does your room look like a war zone?"

"Oh, that."

"Yes, that. What happened?"

"I've been practicing."

"What? Demolition?"

"Hey! You made another joke."

"I'm not laughing. Why were you practicing on your own?"

"I was tired and I had to do something to stay awake. Besides, no one else was teaching me..."

"That is dangerous. You could have hurt yourself."

"I didn't, so it's all good."

"Look at your room. This is not good. I don't think there is a single thing in here that's salvageable."

"That's not true. The mattress is still comfy and my statue is in one piece. Oh and I left the books alone."

"You will have to be disciplined for this."

Giggling, I said, "What are you going to do? Ground me?"

A bark of laughter escaped Kegan, which he quickly squelched. "Sorry, sir."

"I will come up with something suitable later. Go take a shower, you're a mess."

"Why? Am I going somewhere?"

"The second deadline was two days ago. It's time..."

"You didn't! You son-of-a-bitch! You sent out the army."

"Yes but..."

"I'm not going anywhere with you. Did you think I would want to come watch you kill innocent people? You're sick."

"I need your help..."

"No way. I wasn't able to stop you but I'll be damned if I'm going to help you in any way."

Rubbing his forehead, he gritted his teeth and said, "Take a shower and dress."

"No."

"Shower now."

"No."

"If you do not do as you're told, I will force you. And you will not like it. You are going one way or another. Will it be easy or hard and humiliating?"

I shouted, "I'm NOT GOING!"

Eryx waved his hand and I felt a draft. Examining my new clothes, I was wearing super-short cutoffs, a halter-top and stilettos. The shorts let half my ass hang out and the top barely covered my nipples. I looked like a hillbilly whore! Folding my arms across my chest in an attempt at modesty, I said, "It doesn't matter what I'm wearing, no one is going to see me except for you, pervert."

"The clothes you wear are your choice but we are leaving. Change or come as you are."

I refused to move.

"All right. Remember, this was your decision."

Stepping forward, he tried to grab me around the waist but I put up a shield. I wasn't defenseless against him anymore. His hands bounced off the air in front of me and I gave him a smug grin. *Take that!* Cocking his eyebrow, I felt the tethers to my shield being torn from my grasp. With the shield gone, he bent and threw me over his shoulder. Realizing my cheeks were hanging out in the breeze, I turned seven shades of red and started pounding on the bastard's back. "Put me down! I'm not going. I told you. Put me down!"

Eryx opened the door and a familiar voice said, "I'd know that butt anywhere. Nice to see you again, Chevy."

"Fuck you, Magnus! Put me down, you asshole! You can't take me anywhere like this."

Kegan said, "Now, now, such language coming from a bonnie lass. Shame on ye."

"Fuck you, fuck you, fuck you!"

Panicked, I resorted to kicking and squealing like a girl. Images of me being paraded down the street with my backside in the air, kept flashing through my mind.

Kegan said, "She's in a bit of a snit. Give her a swat, she'll calm down."

Eryx said, "Really?"

Kegan answered, "It worked fer me."

My ass stung. Squealing louder, I bit Eryx on the back. He said, "Ow! It didn't work for me."

"Of course it didn't work, you jackasses! I'm not a child. Put me DOWN!"

Kegan said, "She looks so sweet."

Eryx grunted in response and said, "Is everything ready?"

"Aye. Is she really going to London like this?"

Eryx's shoulders lifted, jostling me and he said, "It was her choice."

I asked, "London? Why London?"

Eryx answered, "The Opening Ceremony for the Summer Olympics is today."

Oh my God! "No, you can't. Please don't do this. The city will be packed. You can't murder all those people. Eryx, please."

Kegan said, "*Anoigo*."

I couldn't do it. I couldn't go looking like this because I was obviously going. Maybe something could be done when I got there but it wouldn't help anyone with me dressed like Daisy Duke's slutty sister. "Wait, wait! I'll change, just let me down."

Everyone froze for a second. Eryx set me on my feet with a satisfied expression. Glaring at him, I darted into the closet to Magnus' disappointed moan. Taking my time, I tried to come up with a plan. The problem was I had no idea what was happening. It's hard to scheme when you don't know the details. I put on jeans, a T-shirt and boots without thinking. Maybe something would come up, a situation that I could use. Regardless, it felt good to be covered up again.

Eryx said, "No more dawdling. It's time to go."

Pouting and fully aware that I looked like a recalcitrant child, I stomped out and joined the men.

Magnus chuckled at me and said, "You're twins."

"Huh?"

I saw what he was talking about, as soon as I looked down. I was wearing the same clothes as Eryx, right down to the cowboy boots. Turning around, I started to go change again but the Tsái caught me by the arm and said, "This will do."

Dragging me behind him, he stepped through the door into chaos. We appeared in the center of the room but I noticed that the other members of the Council were at the four corners of the room. Each had their entourage of six guards with them. The rest of the room was filled with about two hundred men and women milling around talking or arguing. Chairs were moved off to the sides to clear floor space. A group of men was gathered in front of a large white board with what looked like a diagram of the stadium.

The Olympic Stadium was unique. Shaped like a bowl, it was built on the land where three rivers crossed, which limited public access to bridges.

I asked, "What's going on?"

Kegan said, "I think they're trying to find a way out."

"What do you mean?"

President Greshner stormed across the room, flanked by four men in suits that had to be Secret Service. Hair tousled, he wore no jacket and his sleeves were rolled up past his elbows with sweat rings under his arms. Pointing at Eryx and red faced, he said, "You! This was your doing!"

What was he talking about? Had the attack begun already? Was I too late? The Secret Service drew their guns, pointing them at the four of us.

Greshner said, "You call off those monsters this instant."

Eryx asked, "Have you signed the treaty yet?"

"Of course not. I won't be made to do anything at gunpoint."

"You are the one with the guns."

"You know what I mean. It's a figure of speech." To his guards he said, "Put those away; he can't hurt me." Turning back to Eryx, he said, "How can you expect us to take this seriously? You are holding us hostage in exchange for a treaty. That is terrorism and the United States does not negotiate with terrorists."

We were drawing a crowd. Leaders from most of the larger countries were present and coming closer to listen.

Eryx said, "I suppose you could classify our actions as terrorism. On the other hand, I could call what the US has done the same thing."

Sputtering, the president said, "What? How dare you. I offered you..."

"You offered me *skatá*." A gasp sounded from somewhere to my right. I don't know what the word meant but it had to be bad. "You held my people prisoner and offered citizenship. Why would the rest of us be safe? You offered slavery. You expected me to sacrifice the entire Zephyri population for the four that you held. So perhaps we should sit down and talk, terrorist to terrorist."

"I am *not* a terrorist. We have done nothing violent nor threatened anyone."

"Haven't you? The mobs in the streets haven't killed anyone? They haven't tortured anyone? All the while, you and the authorities stood by doing nothing. You haven't caused any of my people to have sleepless nights, in fear of what you were doing to their loved ones? If I had not found them, they would have died horrible deaths, which would have been an improvement. The only thing you were interested in was studying them. After they died, whom would you have replaced them with? No one. I will not allow it. You will never get your hands on another one of my people—ever."

Eryx scanned the silent room and said, "The same applies to the rest of you. In every country represented here, there has been violence that was intended for my people. Death squads, dragging people out of their homes in the middle of the night, state sanctioned executions, people burned at the stake, beheadings and all of it meant for the Zephyri. So I ask you, who are the terrorists?"

Holy shit! What had been going on? Was it true? The expressions on the faces of the humans in the room said, yes. He was using the zombies to hold the leaders of the world ransom. Would it work? I found myself hoping that it would.

Greshner, the self-appointed representative, asked, "What do you mean 'it was *meant* for the Zephyri'?"

An evil smile stretched Eryx's lips. "Not a single one of those people were Zephyri. They were all human. You were killing your own kind. We have remained hidden for thousands of years. Did you think it would be that easy?"

The room erupted in pandemonium. Greshner raised his arms, trying to quiet the crowd. When they were silent, he said, "Be that as it may, this is no way to go about it. There are more than eighty thousand people here. You can't hold us indefinitely. Now, if you would like to schedule some time to discuss options for the Zephyri, I'm sure something can be worked out."

Was he kidding? Every leader here was responsible for the deaths of their own people and all he was concerned with was winning. Be that as it may? He still wasn't listening. He didn't care. He didn't even try to deny it. It occurred to me that I had done the same thing. I hadn't listened to him either. Hell, most of the time I didn't let him finish a sentence. I was as guilty as Greshner. Eryx was a monster from the get-go and that was it. I didn't know if I believed everything he said but I was ashamed of myself. Maybe he wasn't the villain I thought he was. Looking at the big man, I wasn't sure this would work but mentally said, *"I'm sorry."*

Eryx didn't look at me but I heard him in my head. *"Thank you, mikroula."*

Sending a thought back to him, I said, *"Stop calling me that."*

Grinning, Eryx glanced down at me.

Greshner had continued while we had our private conversation. "...So call off your corpses and..."

I couldn't stand it anymore. "You don't get it, do you?"

"What I get is that this is a discussion for world leaders, not little girls."

I was sick of people calling me that. Snapping my head around, I caught Eryx smirking and glared at him.

Eryx asked me, "What doesn't he see, *mikroula*?"

Sighing, I turned to the president and tried to come up with something that would get his attention. "What you seem to be missing, sir, is that he *can* keep you here indefinitely. You seem to be missing the point of the zombies. You seem to be missing that he can do whatever he wants. He's *choosing* to deal with you, not violence. I came here hoping to stop him from killing everyone. I thought the army was for an attack, that he was going to slaughter every human in London. I was wrong. This is a demonstration. Do you understand?"

Anne Thomas, the British Prime Minister, stepped out of the group at Greshner's back and said, "I understand. I hesitate to compare you with Ghandi for obvious reasons but I, for one, can learn from history. I have no wish to repeat past mistakes."

Greshner was livid. "You're our ally how can you agree to this?"

She said, "I have consented to nothing more than listening with an open mind."

The bickering began and no one wanted to be left out. I gave up trying to sort out which suit belonged to what country.

Ellarian's voice sounded over the din. "Ladies and gentlemen, perhaps if we sit down and discuss this in an orderly manner, we might make more progress."

Where were they going to seat fifty... A long table with a ream of papers at each seat appeared behind the gathered politicians. A collective gasp echoed through the room. The Zephyri Council members directed people to chairs and the discussion began. Knowing they would all sign eventually, I had no interest and wandered off to wait in a corner.

A radiant smile on his face, Kegan joined me. I

smiled and said, "Hi."

"Hello, lass. Mind if I sit with ye?"

"Not at all. I thought you were mad at me."

"Aye, I was but... I'm sorry, lass. I had no right to stick my nose into yer personal business."

"I know you were just trying to protect me. I shouldn't have yelled at you."

"Nay, twas pure jealousy."

"Whoa. You admit it?"

"Aye. I'm old enough to know better."

"How old are you anyway?"

"Two thousand and eleven."

Shaking my head, I said, "Yeah. You should know better by now."

He said, "Speaking of..."

Dropping my eyes to the floor, I said, "Yeah, yeah. I was wrong. Bad wrong. Why didn't you tell me what he was doing?"

"Ye were so prone to jumping to conclusions and escaping, the Tsái forbid it. Ye wouldn't listen to anyone."

"I'm sorry. I had no idea what was going on out here. With everyone chasing me all over hell and back, I never had a chance to catch up on world events. Maybe after they work out the treaty, I'll be able to get back to a normal life."

"What is normal, lass?"

"I don't know anymore. Do you think they'll keep coming after me?"

"That I cannot say. Sophia and I went back to the shipyard to find yer kidnapper but the trail vanished. Sophia has the scent, so if she ever gets near him, she'll know."

Leukosia. Where did she fit in? I still didn't know. Eryx might not be a monster but that didn't automatically mean that she was. I was trying to stop Eryx, until a few minutes ago. What about the story she told to Faraday? Was it true? How could I find out? Did it even matter? She was responsible for the deaths of dozens of Zephyri and I was almost positive that she was the one messing with the zombies. What should I do? The same questions circled my brain, round and round.

***

"Greshner is finally starting to come around but no one can convince him that having zombies in an army without magic is useless."

Jerking awake, I squinted up at Magnus. I must have dozed off. I hadn't slept since my twelve hour nap with Aspen and I was surprised I had lasted this long. Rubbing my cheek, I looked over and realized that I had been sleeping on Kegan's shoulder. "Sorry, Kegan."

"Don't be. I didn't mind at all."

"How long was I out?"

"Six hours."

The president got up from the table, headed for the men's room. He must have gotten something he wanted because he was pleased with himself. The restroom sounded like a good idea to me, so I tried to get up but fell back into the chair. My legs were asleep and I started rubbing them to restore circulation.

Magnus said, "Need any help with that?"

"In your dreams, degenerate."

Waggling his eyebrows, he said, "I'd rather be in yours. I heard you have nice dreams. "

"Get bent, Magnus."

"That's what I'm trying to do, Chevy."

Ugh. Sparring with the shifter was futile. Greshner exited the bathroom and made a B-line for the table. His attitude had changed drastically. His mind boiled with fury that wasn't present a few moments ago. What had happened?

Someone at the table called out, "Are you ready to sign, Andy?"

The president snarled and said, "I will never sign that trash! They're monsters, animals." He reached into the jacket of a Secret Service agent and drew his weapon. Turning on his heel, he marched toward us, eyes fixed with blind hatred. I tried to stand but still couldn't.

Leveling the gun at me, he said, "This is your fault. You're a traitor to your race and country."

What was wrong with him? His mind was blank, except for murderous rage. Nothing else existed for him. Throwing myself to the floor, I tried to get out of the way. Staring into the black hole of the barrel, I saw the muzzle flash, heard the explosion and knew I was going to die. A heavy weight pressed me into the floor and Kegan's body jerked as the bullet hit him in the back.

"Oh! Kegan, are you okay?"

Growling in my ear, he said, "Aye, I'll be fine, lass. It's just a flesh wound."

"Doesn't it hurt?"

"It burns like a bitch."

He was getting heavy but I wasn't about to complain. "I'm sorry. It seems as if you're always saving me."

Snorting, he said, "Tis getting to be a full time job."

The vampire crawled off me and stood. Magnus gave me a hand up and I saw that the Secret Service

agents had Greshner pinned to the floor. He fought like a
wild man, mindless and savage. They tried to reason with
him, talk him down but he couldn't hear them. I hadn't
seen anything like it since I tried to carry Tony out of his
cell. Whipping my head toward the bathroom door, it
clicked. Searching for Eryx, I found him immediately.

Mentally, I called him. *"Eryx, can you hear me?"*

"Yes, what's wrong?"

"This was Leukosia's doing."

"No, she isn't capable of harming anyone."

"Yes, she is. Shit, there's too much." I threw all the
information I had at him and hoped he understood.

"Stop, mikroula. It's a jumble. Let me look."

Images flashed, as Eryx rifled through my
memories. His eyes narrowed and he disappeared.

A horrified expression on his face, one of the
president's security men asked, "What the hell is the
matter with him? He's lost his mind."

Opening my mouth, I closed it again. I didn't know
what to say. How could I explain?

Eryx said, "She has escaped."

He stepped toward the writhing president and the
agent shouted, "Don't come any closer!"

Eryx said, "I can help him."

"How do I know you didn't cause this?"

"I am responsible. It is my fault. One of my enemies
took control of his mind to hurt me. Let me help him,
please."

The man turned toward me, looking for verification.

Filling every word I said with certainty and
reassurance, I said, "It's true. Her name is Leukosia. She
is trying to sabotage the treaty. Let us help him."

"Can you fix him?"

"With Eryx's help, yes. Will you let us try?"

Eyes darting between us, he nodded. "What do you want me to do?"

"Just keep him there." I sent Eryx a message. *"Can you fix him?"*

"Yes but it would be easier if he were calm."

"I'll handle that."

Diving into the president's mind, I gathered the frayed threads of his emotions one by one. Weaving them together, I took them from his mind. His movements became less desperate and more restless. Pooling all the tranquility I could summon, I poured it into Greshner and he lay still.

Sighing with relief, the agent said, "Thank you."

"We're not done yet. I calmed him down. Eryx has to do the rest."

A woman's voice asked, "Who is Leukosia?"

Searching for the source of the question, I saw the entire table had gathered around us. Addressing the British Prime Minister, I said, "She's a siren, Ms. Thomas. Not the kind with a fish tail but wings. She is the creature that was helping Michael Faraday abduct the Zephyri and experiment on them."

"This Leukosia is Zephyri as well?"

"Yes, ma'am."

"Simons, what are you doing? Get off me!" The president was back to himself. The agent jumped up, helping Greshner to his feet. "What's going on? Why are you all gawking at me?"

Simons answered, "Sir, you went crazy. You tried to kill Ms. Singer."

"That's ludicrous; I did not. I want you in for drug screening and a psych test."

Ms. Thomas said, "It's true Andrew. You came out of the loo, took Mr. Simons gun and shot at Ms. Singer. If that man hadn't jumped in the way, she would be dead. The Tsái and Ms. Singer brought you out of it."

Greshner said, "Have you all gone insane?" He scanned the spectators for support and found everyone nodding in agreement. "It can't be. I'm not deranged. I wouldn't do something like that."

I said, "It wasn't you, sir. It was a siren named Leukosia. She took over your mind. She made you do it."

"Are you saying a mermaid made me attack you?"

"No, sir. She actually resembles an angel but she did force you to try to kill me."

"Why don't I remember?"

Eryx answered, "She has the power to control men's minds. When they are no longer under her spell, they don't remember anything, if she commands it."

"Why? Isn't she one of your people?"

"Yes. I knew she hated me but I thought she was— nullified. I am to blame for this situation but you have my word that I will find her and take appropriate action."

The president said, "I seem to recall Ms. Ellarian claimed that another traitor killed Faraday without your consent. We don't even know if you found the culprit or punished them accordingly. If this is an example of how your people behave, I think we should reconsider a few points of the treaty."

Eryx said, "The Zephyri population as a whole is peaceful. The vampire responsible for Faraday's death was executed a week ago."

"How do you know it was this vampire?"

"She gave a full confession."

Shaking his head, Greshner said, "I have no way to

verify this."

I said, "Yes, you do. I was there, sir. I heard her confess and witnessed her execution."

"A woman did that?"

"Yes, sir. Her lover was one of Faraday's victims. There was no doubt; it was her. Eryx didn't know about Leukosia. He thought she was helpless. Faraday is the one that restored her voice and power. I just don't understand why he didn't react as all the others did. His mind wasn't under her control. Why didn't she affect him?"

Eryx said, "He had a cochlear implant. He couldn't hear her voice in the normal sense."

Greshner spoke to Eryx. "You can't guarantee that your people won't break the law. There must be an extradition agreement in the treaty."

"Extradition will not work. You do not have the capability to handle the Zephyri in your penal system."

Throwing his hands up, he said, "Well, we have to do something. I won't agree unless there are provisions made to deal with these kinds of situations. If we can't manage the Zephyri criminals, you'll have to but I won't be left wondering."

Ms. Thomas said, "Perhaps a joint police force?"

Eryx said, "We police our own people."

Greshner nodded and said, "We do too. It seems to me that all we need is an agency to fill in the gap, a group to cover crimes that involve both nations."

Thomas said, "It should employ members of both species."

"Good, Anne. That would certainly help with public relations."

Mulling the idea over in my head I mumbled, "An

interspecies crime unit."

Greshner lit up and said, "That's perfect!"

"What?"

"The name. The Interspecies Crime Unit, it has a nice ring to it and covers the essentials. How many agents would we need?"

Thomas said, "We should test the idea first, Andrew. A trial run to work out all the bugs before doing anything on a large scale."

"You're right." Glancing at Eryx and the other Council members, he remembered he wasn't the only leader involved. "Don't you have any input, Eryx? Fenion?"

Fenion said, "The Zephyri encompasses four separate kingdoms, which should each be represented within an agency of this kind."

Greshner said, "Yes, it should be equal across the board. Eryx, do you have any comment?"

"I agree to whatever the Council decides, with one stipulation. This agency will remain under Zephyri rule."

"Now, hold on. I am not..."

"It is non-negotiable. I am not excluding humans from oversight but human law is inadequate. There is also the matter of our society. The majority of our citizens live separate from humans. I will not have humans I do not control, traipsing through our city exposing our secrets to the world."

Greshner drawled, "What do you have to hide?"

"Humans have shown their hostility toward us. It will not end overnight. When it does, we can revisit this issue." He turned around and left the circle, ending any further argument. Sitting in a chair against the wall, he looked tired.

Working my way over to him, I sat. "Are you okay?"

"Yes."

"Can I ask you a personal question?"

Giving his stock answer, he said, "You may ask."

"Will you drop your, whatever, so I can see if you're lying?"

"If I choose to answer the question, yes."

"I want you to let me in before I ask."

Frowning, he looked at me and said, "What's the matter?"

"Will you do it?"

"Is it important?"

"Yes."

"All right."

He was exhausted. Mild curiosity peppered the surface of his mind and he was listening to the discussion between the leaders. I felt his connection to the zombies outside and his guilt over Leukosia. His mind spun on so many fronts that it was staggering. Feeling a twinge of regret about my trivial question, I asked anyway. "Are you married?"

Puzzled and amused, he asked, "Are you proposing?"

"No. I'm serious."

"No, I'm not."

"Have you ever been married or engaged?"

I could feel his full attention center on me. Completely perplexed now, he said, "No. Why do you ask?"

"Never in your whole life?"

"I'm not likely to forget something like that."

I said, "Say it."

"What? This is..."

"Just make the statement."

Pursing his lips, he said, "I have never in my entire life been married, engaged or asked anyone to marry me."

"Or ordered?"

"What? No!"

He was telling the truth. "I had to be sure. I'm sorry that I didn't tell you about Leukosia. I could have ruined everything."

"I know you don't trust me but why didn't you tell me about her? She killed my people; she took your friend, Tony."

"Don't you know?"

"No. Why?"

"I thought you would have seen it when I let you look in my head."

"I must have missed it. Tell me."

"In Faraday's journal, he relayed a story that Danica told him. She said you wanted to marry her and forced her into it. She and her sisters ran away, so you sent the Praetorian to hunt her down. The Council made her kill her own sisters as punishment and exiled her."

Dragging his hands through his hair, he looked at the ceiling and said, "Leukosia killed her sisters all right. They had a competition to see who was more beautiful. The sisters left a trail of dead bodies across Europe, as they forced the men to demonstrate their love. When it was over, Leukosia came in last. In a jealous rage, she killed Parthenope and Ligeia. I sent an all-female Praetorian detail after her. When they brought her before me, I took her voice."

"After what she did, why didn't you execute her?"

Sneering in self-derision, he said, "It was during my rehabilitation phase. I thought without her voice she would learn, change but she only grew bitterer. I don't understand how she got back in. Did someone help her?"

"What do you mean?"

"If she left Tweentown, she wouldn't be able to return without her voice or help."

"I never thought of that. She got her voice back at the end of January. Was she missing for any length of time before that?"

"I don't know. I wasn't paying attention."

"Would Doyle know?"

The frown cleared and he said, "Probably. I'll ask him."

Magnus approached and said, "Chevy, you've been drafted."

"Huh?"

"Greshner is insisting that you be one of the human agents in ICU."

I was about to argue, when Eryx said, "No. I forbid it."

Bristling, I said, "You couldn't do it, could you?"

Eryx asked, "What?"

"You couldn't be decent for more than five minutes. You can't tell me what to do. I'm an adult, I make my own decisions."

"If the Zephyri control the agency, I can say who will be employed there."

Magnus said, "Uh, Tsái, that isn't exactly true."

"What are you talking about? Of course, it's true."

"Um, no, sir. The Council already agreed to allow the humans to choose their own people."

Ha! Nothing in the world could keep me from

accepting that job now. "Magnus, tell the president that I would be more than happy to accept."

"I don't think he was asking but I'll tell them." The shifter went to deliver the message.

Triumphant, I turned to gloat at Eryx. A satisfied smile had replaced the scowl. "What are you grinning at? I won."

"Oh, you're on the team but that makes me your boss. I guess I *can* tell you what to do after all, *mikroula*."

CHAPTER 20

Thirteen hours of bickering and I was ready for the loony bin but the treaty was signed. Eryx, Kegan and I took the express train back to the mansion. It was over. I looked around my room, hoping to see Alida but she must still be attending to Gus. I said, "Well, I guess it's time for me to go home now."

Clearing his throat, Eryx said in a gruff voice, "You could always stay here."

"Thanks but I don't think either of us would like that arrangement much."

"Leukosia is still out there and she wants you dead. I would feel better if you stayed close to me."

"I can take care of myself. I'll be fine. Besides, with the treaty signed she'll probably leave me alone."

"I don't like it. I'll send a guard with you."

"Oh, no you won't. I'm not having some stranger moving in with me."

"It could be someone you know."

"Oh, yeah? Like who? Kegan? Aspen? I don't think Sophia and I would get along. No, I want to go home, sleep in my own bed and eat my own food. Eww. The food in my refrigerator must be nasty. Maybe I'll watch some television. I never was a fan but not having it has made me miss it."

Kegan said, "What about sleeping, lass? Ye still have that problem to deal with."

"I forgot about it, with all the excitement. I've had a couple of naps in the last twelve hours and haven't had a problem. Maybe it's gone. I can't believe you guys left me alone for three days though. I could have been in a coma."

Eryx said, "You were in no danger. I removed the barrier."

My jaw dropped. "You did what?"

"You are under my protection. Did you think I would leave you alone without making sure you were safe?"

"You fiddled around in my mind after I specifically said no?"

"You already believe I have. What's the difference? If I had to pay for it, I might as well get something for the trouble. Now, you're safe."

"Fucking lying bastard! I'm supposed to trust you?"

His top lip disappeared and he moved so close our noses almost touched. "Trust this: I protect what is mine—always. I will not allow any harm to come to you no matter how much you beg for it. Kegan, escort her home." Turning on his heel, he left the room.

"Ahh! What's his?! Not in this lifetime. Who does he think he is? Monkeying around in my brain... Fucking son-of-a-bitch... What am I, some kind of pet? Sit *mikroula*, speak *mikroula*... He picked the wrong woman to fuck with..."

"Lass?"

"What?"

"Is there anything you needed to take with ye?"

Stomping around the room, I gathered my things, muttering under my breath. I was glad this happened. I was actually starting to believe his bullshit. I needed the reminder. He was a controlling, manipulative, egotistical, lying asshole.

Slinging the bag over my head, I said, "Get me out of here."

Grumbling the whole way, we walked to the Antechamber. I barely noticed crossing the threshold to my apartment. Ready to grump about the condition of my room, I looked around and it was clean. Everything was in its place and in one piece. "What happened? It was a mess."

"I uh, picked up a wee bit."

"You did this?"

"Aye. There's nothing worse than going away on a trip and returning to a messy house."

"Thank you, Kegan. This is wonderful but how did you fix the broken stuff?"

"An elven spell. Twas nothing."

"This was so thoughtful, thank you."

Leaning in, I hugged him and gave him a peck on the cheek. When I started to pull away, he held me to him for an extra beat. My heart fluttered, as I read the intent in his eyes. Turning my back to him, I went to open the sliding glass door. It was hot and stuffy in here.

Kegan asked, "Yer cycle, it's a Triumph?"

"Yep."

"She's a beauty. I'd like to go fer a ride sometime."

"Okay. Any time."

"What about now?"

"We can't, it's still up at Tony's cabin."

"Nay. Sophia brought her back. She's in the lot, so is the Shelby."

Surprised, I whirled around to face him. "Really? Wow. You thought of everything. Thank you again."

"Twas the least I could do. Would ye want to go fer a ride now?"

"It's five o'clock in the morning."

"Are ye tired?"

"No."

"Why not then? It'll be quiet. We'd have the road to ourselves."

There wasn't any reason we couldn't go. Shrugging, I said, "Okay, sure. Now is good."

As the elevator opened, I cringed for a moment at the thought of Frank being in the lobby. It wasn't light out yet, so he wasn't there. *Yay.*

Delilah was in her slot and looked fine. Throwing my leg over the bike, I sat and waited for Kegan to mount. He didn't move. Frowning, I asked, "Is something wrong?"

Rubbing the back of his neck he said, "I assumed that I would be in front. Yer slight and..."

"I wouldn't have said yes, if I couldn't handle it. You only have a few pounds on Tony and I've had him on the back. Get on."

As the cycle sank under his weight, I started the engine. Hands clasping my waist, he adjusted his seat before sliding his arms around my middle. His thighs gripped my hips and my heart jumped. Maybe this wasn't a good idea.

I didn't move for a few seconds and Kegan asked, "Are ye sure about this?"

No. "Yeah. You ready?"

"Aye."

We rode for half an hour and when I stopped at a light, Kegan said, "Would ye mind if I took the reins fer a bit?"

"Do you know what you're doing?"

"Aye. I've been on a bike or two."

"Okay."

Pulling into a gas station, we switched. When I got comfortable, he said, "Hang on, lass." Unsure what he was going to do, I wound my arms around his waist and held on tight. Once we were out on the street, he popped a wheelie and held it for a block. *Show off.* I couldn't help giggling though. It was fun. He took us on the expressway and broke every speed limit we came across. Taking us back downtown, he made too many turns for me to keep track. I was lost. Pulling into a lot on James Island, he parked the bike and waited for me to get off. "Where are we?"

"A park. I thought we could stretch our legs."

"All right, that sounds nice."

The salty breeze and sounds of surf in the dark unwound my muscles and I took a shuddering breath. The path made a sharp turn but Kegan took my hand and guided me to a bench overlooking the water. Sitting down, he pulled me onto his lap. My back was ramrod straight. I was uncomfortable and looked it but I didn't know how to react. Sitting quietly, he didn't seem to notice and stared out over the dark water. His fingers played with a zipper on my jacket. The sky was beginning to lighten. "We're going to get to see the sunrise."

"They're lovely from this spot."

"Do you come here much?"

"Aye, most mornings."

Our conversation faded into a companionable silence. Kegan's hand rubbed circles on the small of my back and I enjoyed the sensation. As the sun rose above the edge of the world, I gasped at the color. "It's beautiful."

"Aye."

Smiling, I looked down at him and realized he was staring at me. Our eyes locked and my breath hitched. Slipping his hand behind my neck, he drew me into him. Soft, firm lips explored my own, tugging and sucking until I was swept away in the torrent. Shields collapsing around me, sensation assaulted me from every quarter. The feel of the wind, water, sand and Kegan combined, thwarted my control. Probing the warm, moist depths of his mouth, I was overcome with desire. Breathless, Kegan pulled back, pressing his forehead to mine.

"Ye need to slow down, lass."

"You don't like it?"

"Aye. I do but look around us."

We sat in the eye of a small tornado. *Shit*. Closing my eyes, I tried to calm down and released the air. As the tornado dissipated, we were showered with sand and debris. Laughter cut through the remaining tension.

Kegan said, "I've never been on both sides of a kiss before. It was... I cannot explain it."

"I was projecting again. Sorry, I should have better control."

"I wasn't objecting, lass. On the contrary. Yer not what one would call—seasoned. Tis a normal reaction."

Embarrassed, I looked away. "Is it that obvious?"

Laughing, he tickled me and said, "Aye, tis a good

thing though." Kissing me lightly on the lips, he said, "Are ye ready to go?"

Teasing him a little, I said, "Aye."

"Verra funny. Let's get ye home." Getting up, he swatted my rear and we raced back to the bike. He let me win, so I gave him the front.

When we got back, I could see Frank busy in the lobby and I groaned.

Kegan asked, "What's wrong?"

"Frank is here. I was hoping to avoid him."

"Not a problem. Ye left the sliding glass door open."

"Right but..."

Scooping me up, he flew into the air and I clutched at him, giggling. Landing on the balcony, he didn't put me down right away.

"Now that we've had our first date, ye won't be nervous next time."

"This was a date?"

"Aye."

"How come you didn't tell me?"

"I thought it best to sneak it by ye and fill ye in later."

"You could get in trouble doing things like that."

He whispered, "Better to ask forgiveness..." Lips hovering above mine, he said, "Do ye forgive me?"

"Kiss me and I'll let you know."

Keeping it soft and slow, he nevertheless did a thorough job. My blood pumped and skin tingled, as he set me on my feet. Woozy, I tottered to the side and he caught me, helping me restore my balance.

"Am I forgiven?"

"For what?"

Chuckling he said, "Good day, Chevy."

"Bye."

Launching into the air, he flew over the eve of the building and was gone. Elated, I closed the door and curtains. A huge yawn convinced me that I could use a nap but first I needed a shower. Constant interaction with the Zephyri had screwed up my schedule.

I slid between the sheets with a smile still on my face and was asleep before I counted to five.

***

A hard hand across my mouth woke me up in a panic. With wild eyes, I found Tony's face above me and relaxed. Smiling under his fingers, I tried to speak but he wouldn't let go. I was glad he was there but the game was over, now that I had seen him. Reaching up to pull his hand away, I realized my arms were tied to the bed. *What the hell? Why would he do that?* Scrutinizing him, I noticed his eyes were glazed and he didn't look—right. His emotions weren't normal either. He was furious. *What had I done? Why was he angry with me?*

Pulling a cloth from his belt, he stuffed it into my mouth and held it in place with a bandanna. Still more confused than afraid, I tried to move my legs, to kick him away from me. They were secured to the bed as well. What was wrong with him?

A woman's melodic voice sounded from behind my friend. "Perhaps you are wondering what is happening?"

Leukosia in all her angelic splendor stepped into view. White wings, hair, skin and dress, she was the vision of purity, however, when she lifted her eyes to mine, I almost choked on the rag. No pupils, no irises, they were inky pits of blackness, pure evil. *Fuck, fuck,*

fuck. NOT good. Terrified, I looked around in a frenzy. I had to get out of there.

Leukosia said, "I am not very pleased with you. Every time I try to kill you, someone comes to the rescue. The ogre, the bomb, twice with Tony and the president all failed. Why? I pondered that question for a long time. I even had Tony ask but you would not say. Right dear?"

Tony said, "Yes, my love."

Pooling all my fear, I sent it to the siren. Laughing, she said, "Was that you? Are you trying your pitiful powers on me? Tsk, tsk, tsk." Standing next to the bed, she stroked my face softly, reeking of daffodils. "What is special about one weak human? It must be magic but I cannot identify it. You are not as beautiful as I am, yet every male you encounter is smitten and comes to your aid. What do you think, Tony? Who is the loveliest creature in the world?"

His voice filled with adoration, Tony breathed, "You are, my darling."

"See? I am." Climbing atop the bed, she straddled my chest, kneeling on my shoulders. Shifting her weight, I thought she would dislocate my arms. I refused to give her the satisfaction, by crying out. "Perhaps, it is pity. Do they feel sorry for you? Is that why they always save you? Not to worry, my duckling, no one will hear you today. They are far too busy to bother with you. I have made sure of it. Poor little human, all alone."

Grinding her knees into my arms, I felt a pop and screamed. Giggling, she said, "Oops! Was that painful?"

After the wave of nausea passed, I glared at her, fighting the ghosts of the past. "Hmm. Mayhap it is your eyes? They are a nice color, unusual for a human. Your only redeeming feature really. Maybe I will keep them as a remembrance of our time together or use them myself. I would be comely in green eyes. Would I not?"

Prying my lids open, she examined my eyes and I shook her hands off. "I am in the mood for a little entertainment. Tony, cut her."

Reaching behind his back, he pulled a bowie knife from its holster. Pressing it against my inner arm, he drew a trail of blood. Stifled shrieks hardly registered, as the pain fogged my mind. Tony raised the blade to where he had started.

"That is enough for the moment, dear, thank you." Leaning into my shoulders again, I felt the other one pop and choked on the cloth, as I drew a breath. Memories sucked me into the maelstrom and I strained against the pull. I was a small child, helpless against the power of others. No one would save me.

A whisper in my ear drew me back. "You murdered my love, Michael, just as surely as if you wielded the blade yourself. I will revel in every drop of blood you shed, every shriek of pain. You will suffer as he suffered, bleed as he bled, and squeal as he squealed. Tony, I don't think she is listening, cut her again."

Without hesitation, he inserted the tip and drew another six-inch slice down my arm. I tried not to scream but couldn't help it. Sweat ran into my eyes and I blinked at the burn, sending tears down my temples. I tried to call on the air but couldn't concentrate. It didn't come to me.

Tittering she said, "Oh, I love that sound. Do not cry dear. All your problems will be over soon. Tony, again."

Blood pooled on the white sheets and I screeched in agony. "Mmm, once more, Tony. It is music to my ears."

The fourth incision went deeper, cutting into the muscle. When he was done, tears flowed freely and I was whimpering. Her white hair slapped my face, as she turned to look at something. Hope flared to life. Had someone come to help me? Following her gaze, I didn't see anyone and my hope shattered.

Screaming in frustration, she said, "How?!" Moving off my chest, she said, "Quickly Tony, give me her heart."

Completely vulnerable, I screamed, "NO!" Time slowed as I saw the blade descend. A wave like the aftershock of an explosion, swept the air in front of me, sending Tony and Leukosia slamming into the wall. Climbing to her feet, the siren was livid. Screeching, she stamped toward me.

Kegan's voice said, "Fuck me!"

Whipping my head to the source of the shout, I sighed in profound relief. The cavalry had arrived after all. Kegan, Sophia and Eryx stood in the middle of the room wearing horrified expressions. Turning back to the siren, I caught a glimpse of her wing, as she flew from the balcony. The group congregated around the bed and Eryx didn't even look out the window. Sitting on the edge of the bed, he held his hand over my arm, while Sophia and Kegan removed my gag and bindings. By the time I was free, the cuts were healed and Eryx began on my shoulders. I don't know what he did but I felt no pain, as he reset the joints. Heat warmed my skin, while he repaired the muscles and tendons damaged by the siren. When he removed his hands, I tested my arms and found that everything worked. Concerned, Eryx held my hand and stared at me for a moment in silence.

Teary eyed, I smiled and said, "I don't know what to say except, thank you."

"You don't need to say anything, *mikroula*."

For once, I didn't gripe about the name. He still hadn't looked out the window. He didn't want to leave me. "Go get that bitch. I want her wings for my wall."

Smirking, he said, "Yes, *ma'am*," and disappeared.

Taking his place, Kegan pulled me into his arms and almost crushed my ribs. "Take it easy, Kegan, I'm all right."

Moaning came from the floor and we all turned to see Tony struggling to his feet. The vampire snarled and moved so fast that I couldn't see him. Picking Tony up by the hair, he looked as if he was going to break his neck. "Kegan, no! Don't hurt him. He didn't know what he was doing."

At the sound of my voice, Tony began to writhe, trying to get to me. Sophia stepped in his line of sight and he stopped dead.

"Layla? Oh my God! Layla!"

Chest vibrating with a low growl, Sophia said, "I am not Layla. Do not speak that human's name."

"Oh, Layla, what have they done to you? Why didn't you tell me you were alive? I've missed you."

Despite my recent trauma, the pieces clicked into place. Tony's wife, Layla, was Sophia's mother, which meant she was the one from my vision. Bram had raped Layla.

Tony said, "Please, honey. Don't you remember me?"

Tears choked his voice and I couldn't stand to listen anymore. I got up and went to him. "Tony?" He wouldn't look away from Sophia. Taking his face in my hands, I turned his eyes away from the shifter and he saw me. "Tony, this isn't your wife. It's Sophia, her daughter."

"No, you never met her. This is Layla."

"No it's not. Her name is Sophia. She's Zephyri, a shifter."

Confused, he stared at Sophia. "But... She has to be Layla."

The wolf in question said, "So help me, if he says that name once more..."

Shaking his head, Tony said, "No, you're wrong Chevy. That's Layla; they did something to her, made her forget."

Sophia screamed and knocked me aside to get at Tony. Kegan dropped the lovesick man and restrained the wolf. Launching her across the room, he shouted, "Go home, Sophia. Now!"

Landing in a crouch, Sophia snarled at Tony and stepped into a portal to Tweentown. Tony cried out and ran to where the shifter had been a moment before. "No! Where is she? Come back. Layla, please come back. I love you." Collapsing on the floor, Tony did something I had never seen him do. He sobbed like a child.

Pity overwhelmed me. Sitting next to him, I held his head in my lap. Stroking his hair, I tried to soothe him as he had done for me.

His convulsions quieted and he said, "She looks exactly like her."

"How did she die?"

"She killed herself. It was my fault. I didn't believe her. One day I came home and she was gone. No note, no sign of violence, she was just gone. We looked for her but couldn't find a trace. I refused to have a memorial because I knew she wasn't dead. I could feel it. Ten months later, she came back. She was a mess; so skinny that you could see her bones, hollow-eyed, and clinically depressed, the doctors said. She said a monster had raped her before she was abducted. They took her because they wanted the baby. She said that after she had it, they let her go. I took her in to the doctor and they confirmed she had borne a child. The psychiatrist told me she was delusional and put her on medication. Every day she sat and stared out the window. Every night she woke screaming. I tried to help her but she wouldn't talk to me. A few months later, I came home and she had swallowed a bunch of pills. She was nineteen. When I saw... What was the girl's name?"

"Sophia."

"When I saw Sophia, I thought it was all a mistake. That someone had taken her again, faked her death... It doesn't make sense, I know but..."

Stroking his hair, I said, "it's okay, Tony. I understand."

"Why did she leave? Why did she get angry?"

I answered, "Sophia is terminally angry."

Kegan said, "She hates both of her parents but especially her mother. That is the source of her rage."

Tony sat up and looked at Kegan, "Why? Layla was the sweetest, most loving person I have ever known. How could she hate her?"

"She didn't get a chance to find that out. Layla abandoned her. She was given the choice to stay or go and she left."

"That's cruel! You made her choose between her child and her husband, between living with her rapist and going home?"

"Nay, Bram, the one that did it, was executed for his crimes. Layla had the option to stay and she whole-heartedly refused to have anything to do with Sophia. She wouldn't even nurse her."

"She was raped by that monster! How was she supposed to feel? You put her through hell for months."

"Aye, she was raped and that was horrible but while she was with the shifters, she was treated like a princess. The deed could not be undone but the rajah did his best."

"Why take her child? No wonder she killed herself. It's your fault she's dead. She had to make an impossible choice."

"Sophia is a full-blooded wolf shifter. How do ye think she would have fared in the human world? Or her children, if they had been shifters instead of her. She would have wound up in a lab somewhere without anyone. The rajah adopted her, so she hasn't been alone but she grew up knowing the circumstances of her birth. Yer wife hated her babe and Sophia knows it."

"You don't know how she felt. She was probably trying to separate herself..."

"Nay, I know. She tried to abort Sophia several times using scissors, a hanger and when nothing else was available, she refused to eat. She starved herself to the point that the rajah had to feed her through a tube. After the babe came she would scream anytime she was near, calling her a demon."

Tony stared at the floor, looking lost. I felt a little like that myself. How awful must Sophia's life have been as a child, with the other children tormenting her about her mother's behavior, blaming herself? No wonder she was furious.

Leaning forward, Kegan said, "I did not care fer yer wife, while she was with us because of her treatment of Sophia. As for ye, the only reason I have not snapped yer neck is because Chevy asked me not to."

Jumping to his feet, Tony said, "Fuck you, vampire.

Chevy has been like a daughter for..."

Standing in between them, I tried to keep Tony from getting himself hurt. "Kegan this is cruel, stop it."

Ignoring my comment, he spoke to Tony. "I know twas not yer doing but I'd like to murder ye all the same."

"What do you mean?"

I said, "Kegan, let him alone. He doesn't know."

"Nay, lass. He almost killed ye. I will not harm him but he'll hear what I witnessed. The Tsái heard her call for help too late. When we arrived, she was tied down to the bed like a sacrifice and ye were driving a knife toward her heart. Ye had already sliced her up. Four, six-inch gashes down her arm. Before we could act, she knocked ye across the room."

Horror and dismay covered Tony's face. "No. I didn't. I couldn't—ever." He looked at me. "Tell him I didn't do that."

I couldn't meet his eyes. "I'm sorry, Tony."

"No. He's lying. I wouldn't do anything to hurt you."

"It wasn't your fault. The siren made you do it."

"Siren?"

"It's too complicated. She's a bad guy and she was controlling you. That's the reason you did those things." Showing him my arm, I said, "I'm all right now, see?"

Noticing my bloody nightshirt for the first time, his eyes widened and slid to the bed. He looked ill and ran for the bathroom.

Listening to Tony throw up, I said, "You sadist! He couldn't help himself. You didn't have to tell him about me or his wife."

"Aye, I did. Layla ruined Sophia's life and he thought she was a saint."

Sheet white and wiping his mouth, Tony came out of the bathroom.

"Tony? Are you okay?"

Refusing to look at me, he whispered hoarsely, "I'm sorry, Chevy, more than I can say." He opened the door and left. I started to follow him but Kegan stopped me.

"Give him time, lass."

Rounding on him, I yelled, "Why did you tell him? That was cruel."

"He needed to know."

"You did it because you were pissed."

"Aye, that too but he was going to come out of his stupor and ask what the hell happened. Yer bed looks like a slaughter house."

Working up the nerve, I glanced at the bed. He was right, it resembled a murder scene. I wondered if the smell bothered him but didn't ask. I didn't want the answer. Not today.

"Go take a shower, lass. I'll take care of this."

"A hot shower sounds good but I need to clean up out here first."

"The rules of almost dying are ye don't have to clean up the mess. Go on."

As I looked in the mirror, I thought it was a miracle Kegan hadn't killed Tony on sight. My hair was matted with sticky blood along with the entire right side of my shirt. My eyes were puffy from crying and raw, red rings circled my wrists and ankles. My lips were swollen too.

Setting the water as hot as I could stand, I climbed inside it. A pink river rushed down the drain. Reaching for the soap, my hand trembled violently. Clutching it to my breast, I tried to hold it still. A sob shook my chest. I was fine. Where had that come from? Lathering the soap, the suds ran over my wrist and burned.

Tony's snarling face leered down at me with hollow black eyes. The knife plunged into my chest and I gasped. It wasn't real. I washed quickly before I lost it completely. Throwing on a robe, I opened the door. Kegan was waiting for me.

Holding a hot cup of coffee and a plate of cookies, he said, "Sit down before ye fall down."

"I look that good, huh?" Sitting on the clean bed, I scooted back against the headboard.

"Ye look like a ghost. Eat."

Sighing, I ate the cookies and drank the coffee. The ache in my chest subsided and the shakes faded. "What did Leukosia do to distract you guys?"

"The same as before but much worse."

"The zombies?"

"Aye. She sent them tearing all over Tweentown, destroying everything in sight. We still hadn't caught them all when we left."

"What about..."

"Hush, lass. Lie down. There's nothing you need worry about today."

Kegan let me under the covers. "Are you leaving?"

"Nay. Wild ghouls couldn't make me leave ye alone."

"Good. Kegan?"

"Aye?"

"Thank you."

"Yer welcome, lass.

CHAPTER 21

Aspen shouted, "What the hell are you doing in Chevy's house?"

Kegan answered, "Taking care of her."

"Get out."

"Nay, *ye* need to leave. Keep yer voice down, ye'll wake her."

"You have no right to be here. She's mine."

"Wrong again, fairy. She is mine."

What in the world was going on? It sounded as if Aspen and Kegan were going to kill each other. Flying out of bed, I pulled on some sweats.

"She picked me. You're out, bloodsucker."

"She changed her mind. I've known her longer, I'm better looking and I was human. It makes more sense fer us to be together."

Ticking off his points on his fingers, the fairy said, "Better looking? Maybe but I can change that. You're a vampire, not human and you're too old for her. Besides, she kissed *me*."

"At least I *was* human. We went on a date this morning and I had the pleasure of kissing the lass—*twice*.

Yer kiss wasn't even real."

Kegan and Aspen were squared off, nose to face. Alida hovered to one side, her skin bright orange. All this male chest thumping was giving me a headache. Letting loose a piercing whistle, I got everyone's attention. "Will someone please tell me what's going on?"

Aspen zipped over to me and said, "Chevy, sweetheart, I'm glad you're okay. Tell that bloodsucker to leave. I'll take care of you."

Glaring at both of them, I said, "I'm going to say this once, so listen up. I don't belong to anyone. I never made a choice and both of you need to get the hell out of my house. I can take care of myself."

Both men said in unison, "I'm not going anywhere."

Kegan glanced at Aspen annoyed and said to me, "What about Leukosia? We must watch over ye."

Aspen followed up saying, "We can't leave you alone and helpless."

Helpless? Assholes. "Maybe you're not up on current events, Aspen but *I'm* the one that saved me. I'm far from helpless." Kegan was grinning. Narrowing my eyes on the vampire, I stuck my finger in his face and said, "As for you Kegan, don't gloat. You're no better. I should kick your ass for the way you treated Tony. He is my only family. You had no right to do what you did."

Kegan said, "But lass, he…"

"I don't give a shit what he did. It wasn't him. Get out both of you!"

Aspen said, "Chevy, we can't leave you alone. Leukosia…"

"Get out before I say something I'll regret. I don't want to see either of your faces for a while." Pointing at my bedroom door, I said, "Go."

Scowling at each other, they stalked through the door, leaving me alone with Alida. "Good riddance. I swear all men are two years old. Mine, mine, mine is all they can say."

"Just as all women say they don't need any help."

No, not another one. Eryx stood behind me. Spinning around, I asked, "What are you doing here?"

"I thought you might be curious about Leukosia. Evidently, I was wrong. I will see you in six weeks."

"Wait! I wasn't referring to you."

Lifting an eyebrow, he said, "This time."

"What happened? Did you catch her?"

"No, she escaped. Again. I was tracking her and she disappeared from my senses. No wings for your wall today, I'm afraid."

Biting my thumbnail, I mumbled, "She must have put the necklace back on."

He snarled, "What necklace?"

Sighing, I asked, "When I let you look through my brain, what *did* you see. I thought you were up to speed."

Glancing toward the ceiling, as if for patience, he said, "I was in a hurry, if you'll recall. What necklace?"

"The one Faraday gave her. It was round with concentric rings, alternating silver and blue opal. In the journal, she couldn't speak but when Faraday gave it to her, she could. I thought it was a good bet that it was responsible for returning her voice."

"The center was silver?"

"Yeah."

"Were there two spokes in a V-shape at the bottom?"

"Yeah. Why? Do you recognize it?"

His face clouded and he shouted, "Fuck!"

Wow, I had never heard him drop the F-bomb. "I'll take that as a yes. What is it?"

"An amulet that renders Zephyri magic null. It's called the *Damastís*. It was lost thousands of years ago."

"Uh-oh. Is that how she messed with the zombies?"

"No. She wouldn't be able to bring it into Tweentown. It would void the door. She did that just using her voice."

"Okay, so how do we find her?"

"We don't. I do. Stay away from her."

"Gladly. I'm more worried about keeping her away from me."

Distracted, he said, "I installed a spell around your apartment to keep her out."

"Um, what good is that going to do, if she has the necklace?"

A sour look pursed his lips. "Not much. I put it up before you relayed that little tidbit."

"So what you're saying is that I'm a sitting duck."

He didn't answer. Staring at me with blank eyes, I watched his mind work furiously. "You will move back to the mansion."

"Oh, no. No way, no how, buddy. I'm out and I'm staying out. Anyway, she doesn't have any problem getting into Tweentown."

"I have barred her from Tweentown; she can never return. Gather your things. You will be safe with me."

"I said no and I meant no. I will not hide like a scared rabbit."

His top lip disappeared and he said, "I can force you..."

Hands on my hips, I said, "You can't keep me prisoner for the rest of my life."

Both of us scowled in silence, glaring at each other for a few minutes. I was not going to back down. He flinched first. "You will have a guard."

"We already discussed this. No one is following me around twenty-four-seven. I'll be fine. I can take..."

"...Care of yourself. Yes, you've mentioned that once or twice." Staring at me for another minute, he said, "I will have an alarm system installed by the end of the day."

"See? You can be reasonable, when you try. Don't worry so much. You'll give yourself an ulcer."

Ignoring my comment, Eryx said, "Alida, stay with her."

"Yes, sir."

"Be careful, *mikroula*."

He didn't wait for a response and popped out. I wished I could do that. Giving Alida a big grin, I said, "Come on, let's sit down and catch up."

"That sounds like it will take a while."

"Probably. Do you have somewhere else to be? Is Gus all right?"

Landing on the couch, she said, "He's better. He's still not himself but he's through the worst of it. Uh, Chevy? You do realize that you have a guard, right?"

"What?"

"Think about what just happened."

Frowning at her, I didn't know what she meant.

Alida motioned with her hand and said, "Wait for it... Wait for it..."

It hit me. "That son-of-a-bitch! Well, you're not staying."

"Are you going to throw me out? I'll get in trouble."

"Ooh! He's such a... That... Ooh! You have better

things to do than babysit me."

Shrugging, she said, "I don't mind. It'll be fun."

"I can't believe he snuck that by me."

"I'm sure it was just the thing with Leukosia throwing you off. What happened anyway? I heard she paid you a visit."

She was patronizing me but I let it go. "Yeah. You were right, she's evil and my name is at the top of her hit list."

"Do the guys know?"

"They know she came after me but none of them asked what she said."

"Not smart, Chevy. Why didn't you say something?"

"Eryx would drag me back to Tweentown by my hair. He'd never let me out of my room again."

"Maybe for now, that's not a bad idea."

"Oh, come on. Put yourself in my place. You wouldn't like it any more than I do."

"True. What did she say?"

"She holds me responsible for Faraday's death and is the one that has been trying to kill me. The bomb in West Virginia was set specifically for me; everyone else was just gravy. I still can't figure out how she knew where we were going though. She sent Tony to kidnap and drug me. He was also the one that put the bag over my head at the cabin and she sent Bob too."

"No wonder he couldn't remember why he chased you."

"I know. Since she was one of Faraday's partners, she might also be in on the assassins but she didn't mention it."

"At least that narrows down the list. Humans, we

can handle and Leukosia..."

"We can handle her too."

"Like you did today? I told you before and I'm telling you again. Stay away from her. She is pure evil."

"I'm not stupid."

"That's debatable."

Sticking my tongue out at her, I said, "Here's something else you missed. When Aspen was training me, I found a statue. It was made by Aerandir."

"Wow. Really? How much was it?"

"Three hundred dollars."

"That's cheap."

"Focus, Alida."

Shrugging, she said, "Well, it is."

"Anyway, the statue was a woman that looked like me with children around her. When I picked it up, I had two visions. The first one said something about being a prophecy of hope. That someone would come bringing life, balance and order. The second one was the same as the statue. The name of the carving is 'Dawn of Hope'."

"So you're the hope?"

"No but I think she was one of my ancestors. I'm pretty sure this answers the question of why I can access Tweentown."

"You lost me."

"I had a talk with Eryx."

She murmured, "That must have gone well."

"No, it didn't but he told me that he knew my parents their whole lives, that they were his friends. I didn't believe him at the time but now..."

"Then that's your answer. He gave them and their descendant's access."

"It's more complicated than that."

Sighing, she said, "Of course it is."

"The woman, the guardian, was one of my ancestors and *she* and her descendants were given a pass to Tweentown for whatever she did. That is why Eryx knew my parents. You said that some families are protected through all the generations, for doing favors for the Zephyri. It makes sense, right?"

"So now you believe him?"

"I think he protected my parents but I doubt they were actually friends. I also think they had some sort of falling out."

"Why?"

"When I said that I didn't remember him, he told me that after I was born, he didn't come around. Why else would that have happened? This explains why my father knew about the Zephyri. He wasn't just telling me fairy tales. It also solves the tattoo mystery."

"Did your parents have them?"

"I didn't see one but they must have."

"Then why didn't they have the mark by their names?"

"I don't know, maybe because they died."

Shaking her head, she said, "I guess it sounds logical but something about it doesn't ring true."

"What?"

"I have no idea."

Grinning, I said, "I'm right, you'll see."

"Like with the *attack*."

"That's not funny. I really thought he was going to kill everyone."

"You had me convinced too. I should have known better. I felt like an ass. So what happened?"

"A lot of boring stuff but it sounds as if they're

forming a joint investigation team."

"Yeah, I already heard about it. You're on it."

Giggling, I said, "Eryx wasn't happy about that. I wonder who else they'll get."

"Magnus, Nissa, Kegan, Aspen, Sophia and I are the Zephyri members. I don't know who the humans will be."

"Oh, cool. Did they tell you what you'll be doing?"

"My specialty."

"Computers?"

"Yep. What about you?"

Rolling my eyes, I said, "If Eryx has his way, nothing but secretarial work. Ugh. I suck at that stuff."

"I'm sure you'll find a way to get into plenty of trouble."

"Hey, I don't go out and look for it; trouble just seems to find me."

"Uh-huh. What are you going to do about Aspen and Kegan? If you keep them hanging they're liable to tear each other apart."

Making a sour face, I said, "I don't know. At the moment, they're both on my shit list. You should have seen what Kegan did to Tony. It was cruel."

"He told me what happened before Aspen dropped by. I have to say, I agree with him, Chevy."

"But..."

Raising her hand, she warded off my argument. "I know Tony didn't know what he was doing but he needed to understand how close he came and so do you. Leukosia could come back for him. She knows he's close to you. I know you love him but you can't afford to trust him the way you did."

"That's ridiculous."

"How can either of you stop her? She took over his mind once; she can do it again. He tried to kill you at the cabin. He drugged and scared the crap out of you at the shipyard. Who knows how that would have ended, if the Tsái and Kegan hadn't come? He sliced up your arm and came within an inch of stabbing you through the heart. How many chances are you going to give him?"

I knew she was right but I wasn't giving up Tony. "This isn't fair. It's not his fault."

"I know but it doesn't change the facts."

"There is only one way to fix it."

"Chevy..."

"No. He's all I had for a long time. I'm not going to abandon him because of that bitch."

"I wasn't suggesting you do. I said you can't trust him like you used to. Don't go after her, Chevy."

I didn't want to argue. "So what should I do about the boys?"

"Chevy."

"Don't you have an opinion?"

Sighing, she said, "I always have an opinion but this is more important than your love life. She wants you dead. Don't fuck with her."

"The feeling's mutual." Putting on a happy face, I said, "Don't worry, Alida, I won't do anything stupid."

"Since when?"